PRAISE FOR TAHOE HIJACK

"BEGINNING TO READ TAHOE HIJACK IS LIKE FLOOR-BOARDING A RACE CAR... RATING: A+"
- *Cathy Cole, Kittling Books*

"A THRILLING READ... any reader will find the pages of his thrillers impossible to stop turning"
- *Caleb Cage, The Nevada Review*

"THE BOOK CLIMAXES WITH A TWIST THE READER DOESN'T SEE COMING, WORTHY OF MICHAEL CONNELLY"
- *Heather Gould, Tahoe Mountain News*

"I HAD TO HOLD MY BREATH DURING THE LAST PART OF THIS FAST-PACED THRILLER"
- *Harvee Lau, Book Dilettante*

PRAISE FOR TAHOE HEAT

"IN TAHOE HEAT, BORG MASTERFULLY WRITES A SEQUENCE OF EVENTS SO INTENSE THAT IT BELONGS IN AN EARLY TOM CLANCY NOVEL"
- *Caleb Cage, Nevada Review*

"TAHOE HEAT IS A RIVETING THRILLER"
- *John Burroughs, Midwest Book Review*

"WILL KEEP READERS TURNING THE PAGES AS OWEN RACES TO CATCH A VICIOUS KILLER"
- *Barbara Bibel, Booklist*

"THE READER CAN'T HELP BUT ROOT FOR McKENNA AS THE BIG, GENEROUS, IRISH-BLOODED, STREET-WISE-YET-BOOK-SMART FORMER COP"
- *Taylor Flynn, Tahoe Mountain News*

PRAISE FOR TAHOE NIGHT

"BORG HAS WRITTEN ANOTHER WHITE-KNUCKLE THRILLER... A sure bet for mystery buffs waiting for the next Robert B. Parker and Lee Child novels"
- *Jo Ann Vicarel, Library Journal*

"AN ACTION-PACKED THRILLER WITH A NICE-GUY HERO, AN EVEN NICER DOG..."   *- Kirkus Reviews*

"A KILLER PLOT... EVERY ONE OF ITS 350 PAGES WANTS TO GET TURNED... *FAST*"
- Taylor Flynn, Tahoe Mountain News

"A FASCINATING STORY OF FORGERY, MURDER..."
- Nancy Hayden, Tahoe Daily Tribune

PRAISE FOR TAHOE AVALANCHE

ONE OF THE TOP 5 MYSTERIES OF THE YEAR!
- Gayle Wedgwood, Mystery News

"BORG IS A SUPERB STORYTELLER...A MASTER OF THE GENRE"
- Midwest Book Review

"EXPLODES INTO A COMPLEX PLOT THAT LEADS TO MURDER AND INTRIGUE"
- Nancy Hayden, Tahoe Daily Tribune

PRAISE FOR TAHOE SILENCE

WINNER, BEN FRANKLIN AWARD, BEST MYSTERY OF THE YEAR!

"A HEART-WRENCHING MYSTERY THAT IS ALSO ONE OF THE BEST NOVELS WRITTEN ABOUT AUTISM"
STARRED REVIEW - Jo Ann Vicarel, Library Journal

CHOSEN BY LIBRARY JOURNAL AS ONE OF THE FIVE BEST MYSTERIES OF THE YEAR

"THIS IS ONE ENGROSSING NOVEL...IT IS SUPERB"
- Gayle Wedgwood, Mystery News

"ANOTHER EXCITING ENTRY INTO THIS TOO-LITTLE-KNOWN SERIES"   *- Mary Frances Wilkens, Booklist*

PRAISE FOR TAHOE KILLSHOT

"BORG BELONGS ON THE BESTSELLER LISTS with Parker, Paretsky and Coben" *- Merry Cutler, Annie's Book Stop, Sharon, Massachusetts*

"A GREAT READ!" -Shelley Glodowski, Midwest Book Review

"A WONDERFUL BOOK" - Gayle Wedgwood, Mystery News

PRAISE FOR TAHOE ICE GRAVE

"BAFFLING CLUES...CONSISTENTLY ENTERTAINS"
- Kirkus Reviews

"A CLEVER PLOT... RECOMMEND THIS MYSTERY"
- John Rowen, Booklist

"A BIG THUMBS UP... MR. BORG'S PLOTS ARE SUPER-TWISTERS"
- Shelley Glodowski, Midwest Book Review

"GREAT CHARACTERS, LOTS OF ACTION, AND SOME CLEVER
PLOT TWISTS...Readers have to figure they are in for a good ride, and
Todd Borg does not disappoint."
- John Orr, San Jose Mercury News

PRAISE FOR TAHOE BLOWUP

"A COMPELLING TALE OF ARSON ON THE MOUNTAIN"
- Barbara Peters, The Poisoned Pen Bookstore

"RIVETING... A MUST READ FOR MYSTERY FANS!"
- Karen Dini, Addison Public Library, Addison, Illinois

WINNER! BEST MYSTERY OF THE YEAR
- Bay Area Independent Publishers Association

PRAISE FOR TAHOE DEATHFALL

"THRILLING, EXTENDED RESCUE/CHASE" – Kirkus Reviews

"A TREMENDOUS READ FROM A GREAT WRITER"
- Shelley Glodowski, Midwest Book Review

WINNER! BEST THRILLER OF THE YEAR
- Bay Area Independent Publishers Association

"A TAUT MYSTERY... A SCREECHING CLIMAX"
- Karen Dini, Addison Public Library, Addison, Illinois

TAHOE
DEEP

by

Todd Borg

THRILLER PRESS

Thriller Press First Edition, August 2019

Library of Congress Control Number: 2019904066

ISBN: 978-1-931296-27-4

Cover design and map by Keith Carlson

Manufactured in the United States of America

For Kit

ACKNOWLEDGMENTS

I want to thank the New Millennium Dive Expedition, the group that made the first dive to the wreck of the SS Tahoe Steamer. The New Millennium divers were instrumental in getting the wreck designated as a historic site. The combination of great depths and high altitude makes for extremely hazardous diving. These divers figured it out, and we have all benefited from their efforts.

Several times in the past, I've participated in character-name auctions. As part of a charity fund raiser, people bid for the right to have their name used for a character in a novel. Last August, the Kids & Horses charity fund raiser auctioned off two names in the book that follows. The auction winners were Ed Filusch and Tanna Havlick. My hearty thanks to both for their generous support of Kids & Horses! (I should point out that nothing about the characters in the book is based on Mr. Filusch or Ms. Havlick.)

As for editing, each year I send off manuscripts to my editors convinced that this will finally be the year when I need no help and my pages will be returned with no red marks. I have, of course, achieved such mastery over English usage that there couldn't possibly any mistakes to correct or any phrasings to make less awkward, right? Ha, ha.

Liz Johnston, Eric Berglund, Christel Hall, and my wife Kit find enough mistakes and problems to sink any novel. I imagine that they are likely getting together to plan an intervention and convince me to find work as a dog walker

Any mistakes that remain are mine. The countless, invisible fixes are theirs. I can't thank them enough.

Have you ever thought about freediving? Searching the underwater depths with no air beyond what you can hold in a single breath? This book's cover, by Keith Carlson, may convince you to stay out of the water even as it entices you to dive into the book!

As always, thanks to Kit, more than I can say.

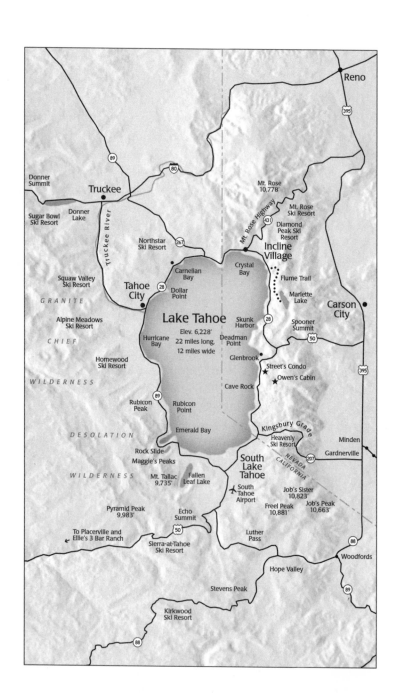

PROLOGUE

August 28, 1940

"How wrong could it be to murder a murderer?" the young man asked.

"You're not serious," the young woman said.

The young man spoke slowly, ignoring her comment, pondering his idea. "Jack Questman robbed and killed someone. He doesn't deserve to live. Not only would we be doing the world a favor, we could get rich in the process. I know right where to look in his bedroom for the take from his latest crime. He showed me his secret hiding place."

"Please tell me this is a hypothetical question," the woman said.

"But there are two problems with killing him," the man continued, lost in his thoughts, not hearing her.

The woman and her date walked along the narrow gravel road in Tahoe City, California, on the northwest side of Lake Tahoe. It was a brilliant morning, the high-altitude sun scouring the landscape and turning the lake's waves into a show of sparkling gemstones. In the far distance, the summer snowfields on the mountains above the South Shore still glistened white.

The woman decided to play along. "Let me guess," she said. "We'd have to entice him out of his mansion and lure him to a place where there'd be no witnesses."

"Yeah, that's the first problem," the man said.

"What's the second?" the woman asked.

The man stopped walking and stared out at the giant lake. His frown was severe.

The woman looked up at his face. At 26 years of age, he was older than she was by four years. He had a demeanor of wisdom. Ever since she'd first met him, when he came up to the lake the summer before, she'd been impressed with his intensity and focus. He traveled and camped alone, a real adult among the kids his age.

"The second problem is how we to dispose of the body," the man said. "When cops find a body, the higher-up detectives are very good at figuring out aspects of the victim and the crime that you would never think of. I learned about it in my criminal justice class. It's called forensic science. We'd have to hide the body in a great place."

The woman looked off toward the lake where the old Tahoe Steamer ship was floating. "I think I know how to dispose of the body," she said. "Maybe how to lure him out of his house, too."

The man raised his eyebrows. "You do?"

The woman smiled, a little mischief in her eyes. "You saw the way Questman looked at me. Up and down like I was a beauty contestant and he was a teenager. He flirted continuously. Even got a little fresh with me."

"Where are you going with this?" the man asked.

"I ask him to join me tonight. A rowboat date. He probably knows that the Tahoe Steamer has been taken out of dry dock. They're towing it across the lake to Glenbrook. Tomorrow or the next day."

"I saw that the ship was floated a few days ago," the man said. "But I didn't know they were going to tow it to Glenbrook. Why?"

"They're going to sink it there, where it was first launched forty-some years ago. So I'll invite our victim to come with me out to the steamer. For a last look at the boat before it's gone. I can tell him I have a bottle of wine. He'll think we're going on a little romantic adventure."

The woman's companion turned on his heel very slowly and began walking again. "And after you get him out there?"

"I remember some large lockers on the main level, just below the bridge. I can get him curious, let him peek inside, then you step out from around the corner and hit him on the head with something, maybe the bottle of wine. We'll shut his body inside the locker, and he'll go down with the ship when they scuttle it at Glenbrook. There's no better way to hide a body than at the bottom of Lake Tahoe. Both problems solved."

"Tell me more about the steamer," the man said.

"You've probably heard of the lumber bigshot D.L. Bliss. I don't know much, but my dad is a history buff, and he knows everything about Bliss. Anyway, Bliss had the steamer built back in the eighteen nineties, before the road was built around the lake. The steamer hauled summer tourists and workers and building things and groceries. Even the mail. I was still in my teens when they finished building the first decent road around the lake. That was about six years ago. The road made it so people no longer had to ride the steamer to get around the lake. So it went out of business. They pulled the steamer out of the water and put it in dry dock storage. Now that it's no longer used, Bliss's son William is going to sink it. It's the cheapest way to dispose of it."

"How do you know the boat's layout?" the young man asked. "The lockers and such."

The woman giggled. "It's a long story."

"I've got time," the man said.

"Ever since the steamer stopped being used, the boat's been nothing more than a late-night hangout for kids. Both when it was at anchor on the water and later when it was in dry dock."

The man paused. "You're saying that kids snuck onto the steamer even when it was up on blocks?"

"Kids will be kids," the woman said. "The boat is huge. It's something like one hundred seventy feet long. The grandest boat to ever cruise Tahoe, or so my father says." She pointed toward where the ship was moored. "Most of the ship is the main passenger lounge. It's surrounded by the promenade deck. The upper deck has the pilothouse and the lifeboats. And the lower level has the boiler room and engine room. So there are lots of places to, you know, have fun."

"Are you sure they're actually going to sink it? It seems a boat like that would still be useful for something. Your plan would fall apart if it wasn't sunk."

"Word is that the son, William Bliss, wants to create

something called an underwater museum."

"What's that?" the man asked. He still frowned, deep in thought.

"Bliss thinks that tourists will pay to ride glass-bottomed boats out to look down on the greatest boat to ever cruise Lake Tahoe."

They walked in silence for a long moment.

"You think you can use a bottle of wine to entice our target out onto the steamer?" the man asked. "What if he's not a drinker?"

The woman grinned and lightly slugged the man on the shoulder. "Don't be dense. I don't even like wine. That's just, you know... an accessory. It's my girly charms that'll get the job done."

"I don't know," the man said. "How would you and he get out to the steamer?"

"The Fullers keep a rowboat in the marina."

"Who are the Fullers?"

"They're the couple in the cabin just south of our family's cabin." The woman pointed down toward the docks. "It's the red rowboat at the second dock. It's locked with a chain and padlock. The Fullers let us use it, so I know where they hide the key. They keep the oars in the boat. I know they wouldn't mind if I borrowed it. Not that they'd ever know."

"Could you take me out to the steamer now and show me the layout?" the man asked.

The woman hesitated. She stared out toward the steamer. "I suppose I could," she eventually said.

The woman led the man onto a walkway that went from the street down to the water. From there, it was a short walk to the docks. In the middle of the second dock was the rowboat. The couple unlocked the boat, untied the mooring lines, got into the rowboat, and headed out of the marina. The man sat on the middle seat facing to the rear. He rowed. The woman sat on the rear seat, helping him steer to the steamer, which was moored just a quarter mile offshore. They tied the rowboat's line to the big ship's access ladder near the stern and climbed up and over the railing to the first level and went inside.

Danny Callahan had left the family cabin to go exploring. He was out with his binoculars, a present he'd received for his 13th birthday. Danny had joked with his parents about them giving binoculars to a blind boy. But the present was what he'd wanted, what he'd requested. The reality was that, while he was legally blind and couldn't see any detail sufficient to read or make out faces, he could see blurry shapes. Danny had compensated by developing many other skills.

Danny's hearing was exceptional, not in terms of what frequencies he could hear or the threshold of volume he could pick up. What was exceptional was what he noticed and observed. His sense of smell was also highly focused and not just for the scents that caught other people's attention - fresh-baked bread or cut flowers or wood smoke. Danny noticed the scents associated with every moment of his day. He could identify people and buildings and animals by their sounds and smells.

Even his foggy vision helped him make exceptional observations. He could see general shapes and movement, and he could recognize individuals by their gait, murky as their image was.

With binoculars, Danny could bring those vague shapes eight times closer.

As Danny sat in the bushes near the shore of Lake Tahoe, scanning with his binoculars to see the cloudy movements of passersby, he saw a couple who walked down the dock. He heard some murmurs, figured out some of their words.

It seemed from the blurred shapes that the couple got into a rowboat and rowed out to the big old steamship. Danny waited patiently while the couple climbed up onto the Tahoe Steamer.

They were gone for nearly a half hour.

Eventually, there was movement again, and the rowboat separated from the big ship and came back to the docks.

Quite soon, it became clear to Danny that the rowboat only held one person. And as that person tied the rowboat to the dock and walked back to the shore, coming closer to Danny than before, it was equally clear to Danny that the rowboat's single passenger was the woman.

Danny wondered why she'd come back from the steamer without the man. For a moment he had a wild thought about what might have happened. He tried to put the thought out of his head. The very idea was monstrous. Unthinkable.

But Danny couldn't unthink a thought once he'd had it. Just like the woman couldn't undo whatever had happened out on the ship. And the more Danny tried to resist the idea, the more he realized it was possible.

Because he knew the young woman. Knew the way she operated, knew how her mind worked.

She was his older sister Nora.

ONE

Present Day

I was at my office dealing with a coffee emergency, since the machine had suddenly clogged and wouldn't run the hot water up and over the grounds. Because I imagined myself a resourceful guy, I'd found the internal rubber tube and flushed it out, but the clip that held it in place fell to the floor where it apparently met its antimatter and was annihilated. No clip meant no repair. It reminded me it's the parts of life you most take for granted that always seem to go wrong.

The phone started jangling while I was on my hands and knees performing a clip search-and-rescue mission. I arced my arm up above my head to grope my desktop, knocked the old 20th-century phone handset off its cradle and onto the floor, where it made a clatter that would likely damage the eardrums of the caller. My Harlequin Great Dane Spot had been lying on his splotchy black-on-white Harlequin camo rug. He opened one eye at the noise.

"Sorry," I answered when I finally got the phone to my ear.

"Thank you for answering," the woman on the phone said, her voice so loud it was almost a shout. "I'm calling about something dangerous that has happened to my neighbor. Can you help me? Please tell me you're free and can come help me!"

Her vocal tones had a round, warm musical quality like those of a woodwind instrument. But she was shaky, tentative, afraid.

"What's wrong?" I asked.

"My neighbor's in trouble. The South Lake Tahoe cops came first thing this morning. But they said they couldn't do anything. I can't accept that. So I asked the lead cop what I could do. I think he's called a commander."

"Commander Mallory of the South Lake Tahoe Police Department?"

"Yes, that's him," the woman said. "He said maybe if I called a private investigator, I could learn something more."

"What do you want to learn more about?" I asked.

"What happened to my neighbor."

"What happened?"

"He was beat up." The woman's voice broke as if she were starting to cry. "The cops said it looked like a home invasion. But nothing obvious was stolen. Someone broke into his house and hit him repeatedly."

"Did they take him to the hospital?"

"No. He refused to go."

"How badly is your neighbor hurt?"

"Really bad. His face is banged up. Terrible bruises, all swollen. And there's a gash on one of his cheekbones. Who knows what kind of injuries could be hidden by his clothes."

"Is your neighbor conscious?"

"Yes. His brain seems okay. At least now, anyway. But he could have internal bleeding. Even his brain could be hemorrhaging!"

"Was he able to say anything about what happened?"

"He could. But he won't! He won't say a thing."

"But he told you he was beat up?" I said.

"No. He said he fell. Give me a break. His door was broken. It's hanging off one of its hinges. And his face looks like it was a punching bag."

"The cops called the paramedics, right?" I asked.

"Yes. They all came after my nine-one-one call. Two police cars, an ambulance, and a fire truck. They wanted to take my neighbor to the hospital. But he said no way. I told the cops they should take him against his wishes because he could have deadly injuries. But my neighbor said that if they took him by force against his will, that would be kidnapping, and that he knew the father of the district attorney and he'd use that influence to press charges. So the cops told me there was nothing they could do."

"Maybe your neighbor isn't hurt as bad as he looks?"

"No, I can tell, he's seriously hurt. Black and blue and brown.

The bones in his face could be broken."

"I wonder why he won't go to the hospital," I said.

"I don't know! I tried to reason with him. But he's as stubborn as they come."

"How do you think I can help?" I asked.

"Find out what happened! Find out why someone would break into his house and beat him up!"

"If that's what happened," I said.

"It IS what happened. I know it. The police know it, too!" The woman was gasping. It seemed she couldn't breathe.

"Okay, let's slow down. Let me ask some questions while you take a breath." I waited but didn't hear any breathing.

"What do you want to know?!" The tension in her voice was so dramatic, it seemed that she might pop a blood vessel worrying about her neighbor.

"Please take a deep breath."

I heard her make an audible breath, heavy with frustration. "Okay! I took a breath. Now help me!"

"Let's start with your name."

"Mae. With an E. M-A-E. Mae O'Sullivan."

"Where do you live, and what do you do?" Getting people to answer such prosaic questions often calms them.

"I live in the Bijou neighborhood, just a few blocks from the South Lake Tahoe Library. I'm a librarian there."

"And what is your neighbor's name?" I asked.

"Daniel Callahan."

"Do you have any idea why someone would break into Mr. Callahan's home and beat him up? Does he have enemies?" I was thinking about the usual reasons why men get beat up. Crime, sex, aggression.

"No! It makes no sense. He's just a sweet old guy. Keeps to himself. Never hurt anybody."

I asked, "How old is Mr. Callahan?"

"I don't know. Somewhere in his nineties."

Just to be sure I heard correctly, I said, "You're saying someone beat up a guy in his nineties?"

"Yes. It's an incredible crime. Unconscionable."

"How far from Mr. Callahan do you live?"

"Right next door. I check on him every day. He was fine last night. But when I went over today, his front door was broken and hanging crooked. So I called out and went in, and found him on the floor bleeding. I think he was lying on the floor all night. It's terrible! You have to do something!" The woman was shouting again. "I told the police commander that Mr. Callahan could have internal bleeding. The policeman agreed. But he said that if a victim is lucid and sober and won't allow a doctor to look at him, then there is nothing they can do."

"Is Mr. Callahan able to move?"

"Yes. He's sitting up. But I don't think he adequately knows the state of his injuries."

"But he's gauged his injuries and his bruises, right? He's looked in the mirror."

"He can feel them, but he can't see them," Mae said. "Daniel is blind."

TWO

"He's blind?" I asked.

Mae said, "He can tell if it's day or night. He can make out vague shapes and sense movement. But he can't see your face or read, no matter how big the letters. And he can't go outside the house without his cane."

"Blindness would complicate dealing with injuries," I said. "The best indicators for how serious some bruises are is how they look."

"And his look bad. Especially his face and left arm. Daniel won't say how he feels about anything. He's a real stoic, all held in. I tried to describe to him what his bruises looked like. But it made no difference. He refuses to go to the hospital."

"You said you found him lying on the floor."

"Lying, moaning, making little choking sounds like he was having trouble breathing. I had to lift him up off the floor and get him to his rocking chair. Luckily, he's light and I'm strong. I was worried I'd cause his death if he had a broken neck or some kind of internal rupture. But he insisted. He practically yelled at me to get him up. So I did as he wished. Maybe that was wrong."

"If he hasn't gotten worse, it was probably fine. With some injuries, it's better to get the patient sitting upright. You said Commander Mallory spoke to Daniel?" I asked.

"That's right. He asked Daniel how he ended up on the floor and how he got his bruises. Daniel said he slipped and fell and hit his face and arm."

"Mallory didn't believe him?"

"No, of course not."

"What about the break-in?" I asked. "That's a crime even if Daniel says he wasn't beaten."

"Daniel says there was no break-in. He says he stepped out

for some fresh air last night and the fall happened as he walked back to his door, and that's what broke the door."

"No doubt Mallory didn't believe that, either."

"No. It's obvious to everyone what happened. But Daniel is sticking to his story."

"What would you like me to do?"

"I'd like you to come over and talk to him. Mallory said you're a pretty good investigator. Maybe you would be able to figure out what really happened."

I paused for a moment on the 'pretty good' description. Mallory and I didn't have a flawless history, the result of a major mistaken-suspect incident I caused a couple of years before when searching for a kidnapped autistic girl. 'Pretty good' might be accurate from Mallory's point of view. Telling it to others might be payback for the trouble I caused.

I hadn't spoken when Mae added, "I have some money saved. I can pay your fee. At least, in the beginning."

I got the address and directions from Mae and told her I'd be there in fifteen minutes.

She didn't respond.

After several seconds, I said, "Mae? Are you there?"

"Hold on, I'm checking something."

I turned toward Spot, who was now lying on his back in a large arc, all four legs up in the air, jowls flopping open revealing large fangs. His eyes were closed, and air was rasping through his throat in a soft snore. His faux diamond ear stud sparkled. He was no longer on his camo rug, but off on the linoleum floor. Maybe the hard surface made for better back muscle massage.

I moved the phone away from my mouth so Mae wouldn't hear me. "Largeness?"

Spot stayed motionless except for opening his eyes. His lower eyelids, hanging upside down, drooped toward the top of his eyes and made him look demented.

"Duty calls," I said, pushing my chair back from my desk.

Spot straightened out the arc of his body and rolled to his side and then onto his chest and elbows. With gravity now going the normal direction, he looked less crazed but a bit confused. He shook his head as if to shake some alertness into his brain.

"Something's wrong," Mae suddenly said in my ear.

"What?"

"A maroon pickup drove by a minute ago. It drove by an hour ago, too. And I think I saw it yesterday afternoon. It's not right." Mae's shaky voice was back. But this time the fear was more pronounced.

"What's not right?"

"It says 'First Rate Dry Cleaning' on the side. One of those stick-on signs. Magnetic or something."

"Looking for an address to make a pickup or a delivery?" I said.

"No. This isn't a dry-cleaning neighborhood. This is a working-class neighborhood, teachers and librarians like me, not doctors or business types who wear professionally-cleaned suits. And why would a dry cleaning business have a pickup? They always have vans. I'm worried."

"Does it say anything else on the pickup?"

"Yes. Under the business name is a phone number."

"What's the area code?"

"Two one three."

"That's Los Angeles."

"Oh…" Mae's voice sounded like a moan. "No L.A. cleaner is going to be in the Bijou neighborhood."

"If you can take a picture of the pickup from your window, do so. If it drives by again and you can zoom in and get the license plate, do that, too. But try to stay inconspicuous. I don't want you to be seen by the driver. I'm on my way. You'll know it's me by my old Jeep."

Mae gave me directions.

I opened the door. Spot got up and trotted through the opening, banging against the door jamb as if his balance needed adjustment after his upside-down meditation. We hurried down the stairs and out to the Jeep.

I drove partway across town and turned into the Bijou neighborhood on Rufus Allen Boulevard, watching for any maroon pickup. I saw none.

I drove past the library. Several turns later, I pulled up in front of two clapboard bungalows that were probably built back in the 1960s. They couldn't be more than 600 square feet each, almost as small as my log cabin. I parked behind a white pickup truck with a roof rack that held two ladders. The pickup's bed had custom tool boxes built into the sidewalls.

Mae had said there were two matching houses. She lived in the left house, and Daniel Callahan lived in the right one. There was a carpenter working on a broken front door at the right house.

The houses were twins with mirror-image floor plans. One was painted dark brown and the other dark green. Both had cream-colored doors and window trim. The doors were a traditional style with inset panels. The buildings appeared to be in perfect repair except for the broken door.

The front door of the left one opened, and a woman leaned her head out. She looked up and down the street and then stared at Spot, who pushed his head out the rear window. His tail thumped against the back of my seat.

She came out of the house and walked toward us.

My first thought about Mae O'Sullivan was that, while she wasn't old, she was old-fashioned. I'm not clothing fluent, but even I could tell that this woman, who seemed in her mid-forties like me, had nevertheless time-traveled from the 1960s, an era before she was born. She wore a light blue-green paisley cotton shirt tucked into baggy blue jeans with bulging pockets spacious enough to haul any cargo a person would need to get through a decade or more without reporting back to base camp. The pants were cinched up high with a macrame belt made of hemp or baling twine. She was 5' 8" or more, and her pant cuffs were high enough to show a lot of bare ankle. On her sockless feet were flat sandals with soles made from car tires, with thick wide leather straps that reminded me of horse bridles. Her strawberry blonde hair was long and wavy and held in place by a headband made of the same denim fabric as her pants. The one part of her wardrobe that was out of place was a large techy-looking watch on her right wrist. But even that was anchored in the '60s by a brown leather watch band that was heavier than my belt. Mae wore no makeup that I could see. And the few strands of gray hair interwoven with the dark blonde revealed that she used no hair dye. Her skin looked Irish, ruddy like not-quite-ripe tomatoes with lots of freckles.

I got out of the Jeep and walked toward her. "You must be Mae," I called out. "I'm Owen McKenna."

"Thank you for coming by." She walked over with a long athletic stride, reached out, and shook my hand. She didn't crush my fingers, but I sensed that she could put on a serious squeeze if she wanted to. She probably weighed around 140 and telegraphed the physicality of an athlete. But the confidence that often accompanies an athletic demeanor was countered by emotional stress, her brow furrowed with worry lines. Her eyes were viridian green speckled with yellow flecks and surrounded with swollen, pink lids. It looked like she'd recently been crying and was still on the verge of tears.

Mae made a nervous glance down the street as if checking for the maroon pickup she'd described on the phone. Then she looked at the Jeep. Spot had his giant head out the window. But the levity that his presence normally creates had no effect on Mae.

"No more sightings of the maroon pickup?" I asked. "Any luck getting a photo?"

"No. I've been watching at the window since we talked on the phone. It never came back down the street. I can't help but think its appearance is connected to Daniel getting beat up. I'm so worried."

"Does Daniel still seem okay?" I asked.

"I think so. He's kind of dozing. I told him I'd keep an eye on Ed, the carpenter, so Daniel could shut his bedroom door and sleep. I hired Ed to fix the door because I know he's reliable. But I keep peeking into the bedroom to check on Daniel. Sometimes, he's asleep. Sometimes, he opens his eyes and looks at me and says, 'I'm fine.'"

"You know Daniel well?"

"We're not close in the sense of confiding in each other. But I probably know him better than anyone else. I've lived in his rental now for two and a half years."

"He owns both matching houses," I said.

"Yes. House rich, cash poor. I get the sense that he doesn't have much savings. I think the rent I pay and Social Security make up his entire income."

"Does Daniel have family?"

She shook her head. "Not that I know of. He had a sister who died young."

"No kids?"

Another head shake. "No. Never married. That's all I know about his relatives. He's very private."

"Do you still think this wasn't an accident? That Daniel didn't really fall and break the door?"

"No chance. Nothing about what happened or his story makes sense. And his morose, angry mood wouldn't fit, either. It only makes sense as a reaction to being assaulted." Mae gestured toward the carpenter and the broken door. "Just look at the door. It's strong. Daniel is light and frail. Even if he threw himself at the door with all his strength, he couldn't break it like that. It was obviously kicked in by someone strong. That's why I want you to investigate."

I nodded. "How do you envision this going?" I asked. "Do you want to take me into his house and bring me into his bedroom?"

"No, no. I could never do that. I'm the only one allowed into his house. If I brought you in, he'd get very stern."

"Should you bring him outside to meet me?"

"No, he wouldn't have that, either. I thought about it after speaking to you on the phone, but I haven't come up with a way to get him to open up to a stranger."

"My dog Spot is in my car. He can soften the defenses of most people. Does Daniel like dogs?" I asked.

Mae frowned and shot a glance back toward the Jeep. Spot's giant tongue did the little flick at the tip with each breath. From this distance, one couldn't see the tiny drop of saliva that typically arced into the air with each tongue flip.

"No, I'm sorry to say Daniel hates dogs. He's afraid of them. I think he was bitten by a dog when he was young. Even little chihuahuas make him nervous. I don't really know how to get Daniel to talk. Maybe you could act official like you're a social worker investigating injuries or something?"

"If he wouldn't speak to the police, he won't speak to me in that capacity."

Mae nodded. "I guess you're right. What do you think?" She turned and looked up at me with searching eyes. "You must have interviewed reluctant victims or witnesses before."

"I think we should take a straightforward approach. We tell the truth, although perhaps we don't volunteer all of the details."

"But what if he refuses to talk?"

"If you can get me into his house, I'll take it from there."

Mae made a slow nod. "Okay. But I don't see how this is going to work."

I looked at the carpenter who had the broken door lying across two sawhorses. Instead of replacing the door with a stock exterior door, he was repairing the damaged one, a laborious job that would maintain the original architectural integrity. He'd removed the panel that had been broken to gain access to the lock, and he was fitting a new piece of wood into the opening. He leaned over, his thick glasses nearly touching the wood as he studied the fit.

"Here's a plan," I said. "The front door opening still has no door. You go inside and somehow get Daniel into the living room. I show up at the door opening. I knock on the door frame. You see me and say hi. I introduce myself and tell Daniel that I'm a private investigator and I understand he had a break-in. Then I'll just step a little inside the doorway and see where I can go from there."

"He'll be upset. He's very set in his ways, stubborn as a mule."

"I can be stubborn, too."

She thought about it. "Okay, I'll see what I can do."

We walked up to Daniel's front door.

"Hi Ed," Mae said. "No need to move your tools. We'll just slip past you."

I nodded at Ed. Ed didn't seem to notice me. He stayed silent.

Mae stepped into an entry room that was inset into the corner of the living room. It was small with just enough room for a vintage armoire closet and a coat rack. Hanging on the rack were several canes. Two were the lightweight type I'd seen blind people use, straight, lightweight rods, white with red bands. Two others were heavier wood, designed for taking weight. I hovered to the side of the door, out of sight from the living room, but close enough that I could hear Mae going back to Daniel's bedroom and calling out his name.

The bedroom door must have shut because her voice became muted.

After a few minutes of mumbled sounds, Mae's voice became clear once again.

"I'll bring you a mug of Irish tea and some Irish soda bread, so you can just sit in your chair. That will be most comfortable for you."

I heard some movements and then kitchen sounds. I knocked on the door jamb.

"Hello? Anyone home?"

"Just a minute," I heard Mae call out.

I stepped in through the doorway.

"Who are you?" a man's voice rasped.

I turned and saw a tiny frail man sitting in a rocker. He wore brown trousers, with black socks and polished black shoes such as one would wear to an important meeting in a big city. He had on a white cotton shirt with button-down collar and over it a buttoned-up cardigan sweater, gray with brown designs that looked a bit like long, slender boats. The man's face was scarred around the eyes as if from a severe childhood burn. The scars were mottled with bruising, red with deep purple marks, which made his wispy white hair and eyebrows stand out like cirrus clouds in a sunset sky. His cloudy eyes looked a bit like flying saucers of the UFO type, the cornea of the right one larger and whiter than the left. A fresh scab showed where his flesh had popped open over one of his cheekbones. The purple had spread from a thick swollen area below his cheekbone and was radiating down into his neck. His left hand, which he cradled in the crook of his right arm, was purple and swollen and scabbed as if someone had stomped it.

"Hello, sir. My name is Owen McKenna. Your name is Daniel Callahan, correct?"

"That is my business, and this house is my castle. I'm not inviting you in."

"I'm a private investigator. I'd like to ask you some questions."

"I don't care who you are. Obviously, you don't understand privacy. You're not welcome in my house. Please leave."

THREE

I ignored Callahan's command to leave and took a step into his living room. Just behind the living room was a small dining room, and behind that a galley kitchen. The kitchen was visible through a wide window opening in the rear dining wall, similar to what I'd seen in old cafes where short-order cooks could pass food through.

The old man shouted at me. "I said leave. At once! Or I'll call the police!"

"Be my guest, please, Mr. Callahan. Commander Mallory will be relieved to hear that I'm stepping up from the private sector to attempt to talk some sense into you. Public servants sometimes worry they'll be accused of malfeasance. An elderly man refuses to follow their common-sense recommendation to get medical treatment following a home invasion and assault. Then, when his injuries turn out to be life-threatening and he ends up on life support, he sues, or, after he dies, his heirs sue, saying, reasonably, that the authorities should have followed their instincts. They should have ignored his wishes and taken him to the hospital. Now I'm giving the police another line of defense in front of the jury. 'See, the old gentleman even ignored the private investigator. The case against the police is groundless.'"

Mae appeared. She held a steaming mug.

"Here's some hot tea, Daniel. This will calm you." The sincerity combined with her woodwind vocal tones was sweet and touching.

He waved his arm through the air as if to bat her away. "Oh, go away, Mae. Leave me alone and stop with your eternal fussing!"

Mae's reddish complexion colored a deeper red, and tears came to her eyes.

"Tell you what, Mae," I said. "Because Mr. Callahan insists on being abrasive and dismissive, why don't you go home and leave him to me. I may not be able to get him to see reason. But either way, there's no point in you putting up with such abuse."

Mae's embarrassment at Callahan's rude comments seemed to give way to alarm at my statement, which probably sounded combative. She looked at me with wide eyes. I nodded at her and made a little jerk toward the door with my head.

"I saw that movement," Callahan said. "I may be legally blind, but I saw that. You two are conspiring against me."

Mae set the mug of tea down on the fireplace mantel next to a framed black-and-white photo of a young woman, then walked around to stand in front of the man.

"Daniel, Owen McKenna may be moving his head and trying to get me to leave. But I'm not conspiring with him. I just called him because I'm worried sick about you. And I'm so afraid you're hurt really bad. But you're too stubborn to do anything about it. That poem I told you about, 'No man is an island' is true, even if you don't believe it. You can sit here in this house and die for lack of care. But the result wouldn't just stay with you. It would probably bring joy to the guy who beat you up. But it would bring great sadness to your neighbors and the people you know. The people who sell you your morning donut and coffee every day. The woman who cuts your hair, and your dentist, and the guy who clears the snow, and the young man who cleans your house. And it would affect me." Mae's voice was wavering and cracking. "Greatly. More than you'll ever believe. More than you want, I know. And I'm sorry about that. But there it is, and there's nothing you can do to stop it."

Mae turned, held her head high, and walked out of the house.

Daniel turned his cloudy eyes to me and said, "Mae O'Sullivan is my one buffer zone protecting me from the world. Now she's working with you. So I'm stuck here with you badgering me. This is what I get after a lifetime of minding my own business. This is what happens when I've hurt nobody, when I've committed no crimes and caused no strife beyond the trivial nonsense reactions that come from people who don't like it that my approach is matter-of-fact instead of ingratiating and fawning." He made a little jerk as if something startled him. He immediately used his hand to feel around his lap and the seat of the rocker. Not finding what he was looking for, he moved his hand to the arm of the rocker and slid his fingers from the end back to where the rocker arm joined the chair back. His hand hit a pair of sunglasses that hung there. He lifted the glasses to his face and put them on. Then he used his hand to smooth his hair.

The effect was surprising and charming. The old blind man was vain enough to try to look good even when the only person who could see him was a pesky intrusive investigator he didn't invite in or want to talk to.

Daniel Callahan's hair was white and cut to a medium length. It looked stylish. But the glasses really stood out. They were the metal aviator style favored by pilots and some movie stars, and their lenses were mirrors of metallic gold.

"I better talk to Mae," I said. I turned and followed Mae as if I were going to talk to her outside. But once I was through the front door, I paused. Mae had stepped past the carpenter and his sawhorses and was heading back to her house. Spot still had his head out the Jeep's window. He watched her. Then he looked at me. I peeked back into the living room.

Daniel Callahan was bent forward in his rocker, the palm of his uninjured right hand to his forehead. He bounced it against his head, making a muted slapping noise. He seemed to float away from the moment, his attention on something else. He smacked his forehead again. And again. With each blow he made a kind of painful vocalization, heavy exhalations combined with grunting, like a child having a temper tantrum. Instead, it was an outburst of frustration from a man in his 90s who seemed about to lose his sanity. I thought he was going to have a stroke from pressure buildup. Then his repetitive grunts became more like the beginnings of a word trying, but unable, to escape his mouth. Finally, he stopped hitting his hand against his forehead and spoke under his breath, through clenched teeth, his voice a hiss of anger that I only heard because I was close and the room was quiet. "You think you can break me?" he said. "Fine. Just try it."

I stepped back into his living room. "What's that, Mr. Callahan?" I asked.

He gave himself a little shake as if coming out of a trance. "What's what? You're back. Go away."

"You said, 'You think you can break me? Fine. Just try it.' What does that mean?"

Callahan lifted his face and the aviator mirrors toward the ceiling, the details of which he couldn't see. His face was a map of stress and worry lines.

Callahan reminded me of past times when I'd dealt with innocent victims of violence. A sudden wave of anger went through me.

"I know this is difficult, Mr. Callahan. Having someone use you for a punching bag is profoundly disturbing. Having someone break into your house and threaten you will drive you to do whatever it takes to make it go away. You also want revenge. You want to punish the bastard who assaulted you. I can probably help."

"No. Go away. I shouldn't have to repeat myself."

"No, sir. I won't go away. You're going to have to listen to me. I was on the San Francisco Police Department for twenty years. At the end, I was a Homicide Inspector. I put away some really vile, disgusting people. And when I caught them, it was like slaking an appetite. I got the chance to hold them down for a minute, and I felt the power of right versus wrong.

"So when I see your broken front door and, much worse, your bruises... When I see you wince as you move injured joints, it brings back that hunger. I want to track this dirtball down and put him away for a long time. But before I ease up on him, he and I will have an understanding. That he is done being a predator.

"Those are the feelings that drive me into this, Mr. Callahan. You should know that the ones who threaten never let up until you give them what they want. So this man is, no doubt, coming back to torture you some more. But the bigger problem is that after he extracts that last bit of information from you, it will give him cause to kill you because you will be of no more use to him."

I pushed an upholstered footstool over in front of Daniel's rocking chair. I sat down on it and leaned toward Daniel.

His face turned left and right. In spite of the sunglasses, he was no doubt assessing the gray essence of my shape and size.

I waited, silent. Daniel didn't respond. The man had been on his life tour for twice as long as I'd been on mine. Like most old people, he knew more than I did about most things. One of those things would be the balance between patience and action, calm and fury.

"What do you say?" I asked. "Will you let me go after the man who tormented you? All I need is for you to tell me what happened." I said. "I already know the basics. Someone forced himself into your house. Nothing significant was taken. So that suggests that he demanded you give him information. When you didn't acquiesce, he hit you, over and over. When you still didn't bend to his wishes, he threatened you. There are lots of ways to intimidate victims. The easiest is to threaten to maim those you care about. He probably said, 'Tell me or I hurt your family members. Or your neighbor Mae.'"

Daniel Callahan was shaking with fear. I hated making him revisit the terror. But I knew it might be the only way to save him. "If you don't do what he says, he will try to do what he's threatened. Maybe I can prevent that. Maybe not. But the problem is you're trapped. Even if you do exactly what he says, he's likely to silence you after you give him what he wants. There's just too much risk for him. He knows that you may remember something that will allow law enforcement to track him down. And it's easy to rationalize killing you. You're old. You don't have that much time left. Yes, that sounds harsh. But it's how psychopaths think. They do whatever it takes to get what they want. And they do whatever they can to cover their tracks afterward."

I expected him to rally his previous bluster and yell at me again to get out of his house.

Instead, he was silent.

I stood up. "You said 'You think you can break me? Fine. Just try it.' That implies the man tormenting you will come back to pressure you more. And you're going to be tough and not give in. But what if he follows through on his threat? You're probably assuming he won't hurt Mae or anyone else. You think he'll come back to pressure you first. You might be right. But what if you're not?"

Daniel made shallow, fast rocking motions in his chair. His head shook. He didn't speak.

"I know some techniques for undermining tough guys who want to pressure you. They're effective, but they take time to put in place. So we can't dawdle. I'll come back in, let's say, two hours. That'll give you time to gather your thoughts. Okay?"

Daniel Callahan didn't respond. He lowered his face as if to stare at the floor. He seemed as broken as a person can be. He was likely wrestling with a maelstrom of fear, images of Mae or someone else being beat up or worse. It was a tough dilemma. If Callahan talked to me, he would worry that the retribution on the part of the assailant might be severe. But if he didn't talk to me and instead told the assailant what the man wanted to know, the guy might still maim and kill to cover his tracks.

There was a third possibility, which was that Daniel Callahan might not have the information or whatever it was the assailant wanted. Callahan might think he could convince the man of that fact. But Callahan would eventually realize the folly of that idea.

Each of the choices was as dark as a person can face, the knowledge that their actions could lead to murderous violence. It would take time.

"See you in a couple of hours," I said. "You and I will talk. Then we'll make a plan to take this guy down."

FOUR

I walked back out through Daniel Callahan's front door. Ed, the carpenter, had the replacement panel fitted into the door. He was holding the door up into the door frame. I paused to help him position the door. He leaned in very close, his eyes just an inch from the top of the three hinges, trying to see the position. His glasses were as thick as ashtrays.

When the door came into alignment, he slid the pin down an inch or two until friction stopped it. Then he bent down to fit the bottom hinge, again almost touching the hinge with his nose in order to see what he was doing. Once all three pins were positioned, he started tapping them down with his hammer.

Ed straightened up, glanced very briefly at me, his eyes magnified by his glasses. He made a nod of acknowledgment but didn't speak. As he turned back to the door, I noticed that his right knee seemed very thick inside of his jeans. His leg was a little bent, and he hobbled a bit. Maybe his knee had been damaged at the same time his vision was compromised.

I stepped onto the small landing and walked down the three front steps.

I glanced around at the yard and saw the broken wood panel that had been shattered by the intruder's well-placed kick. The panel had been just below the doorknob. An easy height to kick in, and it was close enough to the doorknob to reach in through the opening to open the door.

The wood used for the door panels was plywood with beveled edges. Because of the alternating plies, the broken piece hadn't split into separate pieces, but had folded at a 30-degree angle, bent where the shoe had stuck and gone through the panel. From the damage, it seemed the person kicking the door had succeeded in plunging his shoe most of the way through the panel. Maybe all the way.

I leaned over, picked up the broken wood, and held it up to the daylight. On the splinters of broken wood were some white threads and fuzz. Maybe it was nothing. But I visualized the assailant's sock catching on the wood splinters as the man kicked through the door and then pulled back to extract his foot. Or the fibers could have come from the man's sleeve when he reached in to unlock the door. Maybe Mallory's crew had already processed it. Maybe not.

"You don't need this broken wood, right?" I said to the carpenter.

Ed turned toward me. It didn't seem that he could see what I was holding up.

"This piece of broken wood was on the ground. It's not useful for anything except as kindling. Mind if I take it?"

He frowned at me for making a strange request, but shook his head no, he didn't mind.

"Thanks," I said. I walked to the Jeep, thinking about the carpenter's silence. It could be he was just focused on his job and didn't feel the need to talk. Or maybe he was mute. Either way, it seemed fitting that Mae had given work to a hobbled carpenter who had trouble seeing and the work was to fix the door at a blind man's house.

Spot was wagging, his tail thumping the confines of the back seat as I opened the tailgate. I lifted up the rubber cargo mat, slid the broken plywood under it, and lowered the mat over it. "Sorry I couldn't bring you in, Largeness. But the resident has a problem with dogs. I know, hard to imagine." I gave Spot a rough rub. I shut the tailgate and walked to the matching house where Mae lived.

She answered the door a moment after my knock. "I was watching for you. It's not like I can relax with tea after that jerk was so rude."

"Not the easiest guy to get along with," I said.

She made a big sigh of frustration. "I try to tell myself that he's old and I should give him a break. But the truth is that while he sometimes plays the role of an ornery old man, he's very sweet most of the time. But when he's stressed, it feels like he takes it all out on me." She paused for a bit as she looked at me. "Now that you've talked to him, do you agree that he wasn't just the victim of a random assault? That someone targeted him for a specific reason?"

"Yes," I said. "That seems clear. Nothing about the house would tempt an ordinary burglar. So I assume the assailant wanted something specific to Callahan."

"When you were acting firm with him, that was just an act, right?"

"Yeah. I wanted him off-center. I wanted him to realize that he couldn't have everything his way. Having me crowd into his space was unsettling for him. It may be that something will eventually come of it. In the meantime, I'd like to talk to you a bit, if you have time."

"Outside of my daily swim and working four days a week at the library, I have nothing but time. Except in the evening. I'm a big reader." She walked into a living room that was, in shape and size, a replica of Daniel's living room but in reverse orientation. In front of two walls were bookcases filled with books, mostly hardbacks, mostly older, probably a high percentage of first editions. She gestured toward two chairs that faced a small couch.

I followed Mae in past a coat rack that was similar to the one in Daniel's house. Instead of canes, Mae's coat rack held a neoprene wetsuit and two face masks of the type that scuba divers use.

"Have a seat," Mae said. "Would you like some tea or coffee?"

"No thanks." I sat. Next to my elbow was a techy-looking reading light that had a heavy chrome base on the floor. Hanging on the top arm of the lamp was another face mask. I touched it and set it swinging. "You are obviously a diver."

"Diver and swimmer. Pools and lake. When I got serious about swimming, I wanted to always have a face mask so I could see. It hangs there as a reminder to me about my focus. My purpose. Instead of watching TV, I read and I dive."

"This is a good neighborhood for it," I said, "with the rec center pool a block one way and the lake a block the other way. Is there a reason you have more than one mask?"

"There are advantages to each type of mask. But the multiple sets is just because I'm kind of a diving freak. I buy every new model that comes out." She gestured over to a set of clothes hooks behind the front door, hooks I hadn't seen when I came in. There were more face masks on the hooks.

Mae continued, "I always carry a face mask in my day pack just in case I end up at a different part of the lake."

"I only see face masks. No swim goggles."

"That's because I'm a freediver. I need to be able to blow into the mask to equalize pressure when I go deep. You can't do that with goggles."

"What's a freediver?"

"There are lots of variations. But basically, freediving means diving while holding your breath."

"No scuba tanks."

Mae nodded.

"Like pearl divers or sponge divers," I said.

Mae made a sudden smile, the first I'd seen. "Exactly!" she said.

"So when other people are searching out a new beach on the lake, you're looking for the perfect dive spot instead."

She nodded.

"How did you meet Mr. Callahan?"

Mae took a seat opposite me. She sat primly, back straight, and ankles and knees together. "It's a long story. But I'm paying you for your time. So if you think it's worth it..."

"The more I know about Daniel, the more likely I am to find out what motivated the assault on him."

Mae nodded. "I ended up meeting him because of freediving. I started freediving in Monterey near the Bay Area. I heard about a group of scuba divers who've been exploring the big sunken ship in Tahoe. You've probably heard of the Tahoe Steamer."

"Sure. The longest boat to ever cruise Tahoe. But it's at the bottom of the lake. Do the divers go that deep?"

"Actually, the Steamer was sunk in Glenbrook Bay back in nineteen forty. So even though it's around four hundred feet down, that's nothing compared to the bottom at sixteen hundred feet deep."

"You said this led you to Callahan."

"Yeah. I got to thinking that it might be cool to get involved with high-altitude divers. Of course, there's a big difference between the divers with air tanks and the divers who just hold their breath. But there are similarities, too. So I came up here on vacation and went to a talk that was hosted by some divers who were focused on the Tahoe Steamer. These were some of the first guys to actually dive down to the wreck. It was very cool hearing about new diving experiences while seeing pictures of a boat almost no one's ever seen before. Later, three of the guys were talking about an old guy who had actually witnessed the sinking of the Tahoe Steamer."

"Daniel Callahan?" I said.

"Right. Daniel is kind of a legend among the divers, even though he's never dived and most of them have never met him. Daniel was something like twelve or fourteen when the Steamer was scuttled. So I looked him up and came and knocked on his door. He was like you saw, a curmudgeon. But I managed to befriend him a little bit. That was when I found out he had this rental and the tenants had given notice. So I offered to rent it on the condition that I could get a job. As it happened, a position opened up at the South Lake Tahoe Library, which is just three blocks away. That was a little over two years ago. In many ways, they've been the best years of my life.

Getting to know Daniel Callahan hasn't been easy. But it's been worth it. Despite his bad attitude, he's a good guy, and he's a good role model for being steadfast and reliable and not swayed by the temperamental day-to-day changes of life. I've often thought that he's like a crooked old oak tree. He's seen a lot of storms, and he's got the physical and mental scars that come with that. But he's still strong in the important ways. He's constant, and you can trust him absolutely."

"As you've come to know him, what seems like the likeliest

reason for this situation, for someone assaulting him?"

"I have no idea. I can't imagine he's ever done anything that would make someone want to hurt him. So it must be that he's got something that someone wants."

"Any idea what that would be?"

She stared vacantly at the wall and shook her head. "No. He's not poor. He's got his house and this rental. But even though houses in Tahoe have value, it's not like he owns something really valuable. I'm certain there's no gold or diamonds hidden in his house."

"Maybe he knows something that someone wants," I said. "Some valuable information."

"But what could that be?"

"When you think of everything you know about Daniel Callahan, what's the most remarkable thing that comes to mind?"

She thought a moment. "That trust. I've learned that a lot of people will say one thing and do another if they are tempted strongly enough. But not Daniel. You could trust him with your life."

I pondered what she'd said. "I can't connect that good quality to his assault. I need a different way he's remarkable."

"Well, the only other thing that comes to mind is that he witnessed the scuttling of the Tahoe Steamer. I mean, that's no big deal, right? Anyone could have seen that. But most of the people who did - maybe all of them but Daniel - are gone now. So, while it's no achievement, maybe there's some aspect to it that has value to the guy who broke into his house and beat him up."

"Maybe something valuable went down with the ship and Daniel saw it."

Mae made a single nod. We were silent awhile.

I said, "I'm wondering why someone would kick in Callahan's door. Why not just knock and then push in the door when Daniel opened it?"

"Daniel doesn't open his door when someone knocks unless it's a woman."

"But how does he know? He's blind."

"First of all, if it's daylight, then Daniel can tell a person's gender. You'd be amazed at what he can tell even though he's blind. He looks through the window, and he can tell if it's a man or woman by their posture and how they walk. I know it sounds crazy. But he says attitude and posture are revealed even in vague shapes. He says it's as distinct as handwriting. Of course, he can't see handwriting. But he's read about it."

"He reads Braille?"

"Yes. There are lots of books printed in Braille and some journals. Now there are Braille computer printers. And of course, with books on CDs and downloads and computers that can read, blind people have more options than ever." Mae pointed over to a desk and a large printer next to a computer. "That's a Braille printer. Daniel says he has no desire to learn about computers. But he paid for the printer and he sometimes has me look stuff up on the computer and print it out in Braille format for him to read. But back to people knocking. Even if he can tell the gender, he still always asks, 'Who's there?' If a man answers, he won't open the door. He tells them to go away. It's kind of a gutsy response. But I've witnessed it."

"You think that's what happened when his attacker kicked in the door?"

"Probably."

My cell phone rang. I looked at the readout. "Sorry for the interruption, but I should take this. It's Mallory, the police commander."

Mae nodded.

"Owen McKenna," I answered.

"Mallory, here. First, I gave your name to a woman named Mae O'Sullivan." The commander's rough voice was mixed with road noises.

"I'm currently in her house, talking to her about the assault on her blind neighbor. She said you don't believe that Mr. Callahan injured himself by falling."

"No, I don't. What's your take?"

"I've spoken to the man, and I agree with you. I think he

isn't talking because he was threatened. He's very shook up as if something bad would happen if he told anyone about it. Like maybe his attacker tried to swear him to secrecy."

Mae looked out the window toward Daniel's house.

"And he made a revealing verbal stumble." As I said it, I saw Mae turn from the window and look at me.

"A verbal stumble?" Mallory said. "Fancy talk for an ex-cop."

"Oh, that probably comes from hanging around with Street," I said.

"Ms. Casey is a smart one. Sergeant Diamond Martinez, too," Mallory said. "So what was it the old man said?"

"He was stressing, and he didn't think anyone was near, and he went into a kind of a temper-tantrum trance and said, 'You think you can break me? Fine. Just try it.'"

As I said it, I saw Mae jerk slightly and frown.

"Interesting. What happened after this so-called stumble?" Mallory asked.

"Nothing. He caught himself and stopped talking. I'm wondering what you think."

"It's a clear case of battery." Mallory said it like there was no doubt about it. "The old man was beat up, no question. If only he was a cooperative victim. If only we'd found obvious incriminating evidence that pointed to a suspect or a witness. I'd love to get something to take to the DA. I don't like it when somebody beats on an old guy. But without any of those, it isn't worth pursuing."

I heard the growing whoop of a siren in the background over the phone.

"It sounds like you need to go," I said.

"I'm just waiting on the coroner. That's a county deputy bringing him now."

"You've got a body?" I asked.

"Yeah. El Dorado Beach. Near the bottom of the new stairs. That's why I called you. If you could swing by, you could maybe help us."

"What's it about?"

"The body has an unusual tattoo. But it's not like any tattoo I've seen before. Kind of looks like a painting. And you're sort of a painting expert, right?" he said.

"I'm no art expert."

"I heard otherwise." Mallory sounded distracted. Probably the approaching siren.

"I like to look at art. But I'm like an eight-year-old kid listening to music. The kid dances and grooves with the beat. But that doesn't mean he knows anything about the music."

"Even so, can you come look at this tattoo and tell us if it means anything to you?"

"Mae's house is five minutes away," I said.

"I'm sure the coroner will still be here. We can talk about the old man after they remove the body."

"On my way," I said.

I hung up and turned to Mae. "I need to go, but I'll be back. By the way, the carpenter who's fixing Daniel's door? I think you said his name was Ed."

"Yes."

"Is he always so quiet?"

Mae nodded. "Yeah. He rents a room in a house down the street. I heard he was a good handyman. So I've had him fix a few things here and there. At first, I thought he was deaf and mute. But he'll say a few things. Especially when you call him on the phone and he can't answer you by nodding or shaking his head. Mostly, he's just very quiet. Like an extreme example of the strong and silent type."

"Does he know Daniel?"

"Not really. But he's done Daniel's yard work for the last few months. And when Daniel's washing machine died, Ed replaced it. You may have noticed that Ed doesn't have the best vision. I think it helps him to help a blind man. It probably makes him feel fortunate that he can see as well as he does."

"Any chance Ed saw the maroon pickup or anyone watching Daniel's house in the last week or so?"

"Good question. I'll ask him."

I said goodbye and left.

FIVE

Great Danes like car rides almost as much as popcorn. So, even though we'd already driven from my office to the Bijou neighborhood, the moment I slid into the driver's seat, Spot's tail was banging about like a teenager learning to play the bongos.

El Dorado Beach is only a few blocks west of Bijou, where the Al Tahoe neighborhood, the main drag, and the beach all come together. There were two South Lake Tahoe PD patrol cars, two El Dorado County Sheriff SUVs, one fire truck, and one ambulance parked on the edge of the crowded boulevard. I drove past the official vehicles, turned right on Lakeview Avenue, and drove down a block. The summer tourist crush had filled every available parking place. I parked in a no-parking zone. I left Spot with his head out the rear window, and I jogged back to the Lakeview Commons park, where picnickers had interrupted their barbecues to stare at the corpse down by the water's edge.

There was a large half-circle of crime scene tape arcing from the water's edge, around the body, and then back to the water. Its purpose was more to keep away tourists than to preserve evidence. It looked like the body had washed ashore. Other than the body itself, there would be little if any evidence to protect.

The victim was a caucasian male, with buzz-cut black hair, a thick mat of dark chest hair, wearing nothing beyond tight, boxer-style, red swim trunks. A gold neck chain glinted in the sunlight. The victim lay on his back and was surrounded by several men and one woman in uniform, both the SLTPD's blues and the El Dorado Sheriff's browns.

A female sheriff's deputy held up her hand as I approached.

"Owen McKenna here at Commander Mallory's request."

The woman frowned, then relaxed. "Now I remember. You're

the Bay Area cop who went private, right?"

I nodded.

She lifted the tape, and I ducked under.

"I was thinking of doing that," she called after me. "Is it hard?"

"Going private? Only if you think doing your job without any authority or backup or uniform for credibility or regular paycheck or retirement program or benefits would be hard."

She frowned. I kept walking.

Mallory raised his can of Coke and nodded at me as I approached. The other cops - only one of whom I knew - saw him nod and realized I was okay. I stopped behind the cops and stood silently, watching.

The dead man appeared to be a drowning victim. The coroner leaned over the corpse. The paramedics pointed. They spoke in low tones.

After a minute, Mallory stepped over to me. "In addition to the tattoo, this body might be of interest to your professional curiosity. The victim looks like what I imagine aliens to look like."

"I've always wondered how you visualize aliens."

"Funny guy," Mallory said with no trace of mirth. He leaned his head toward the body. "Tell me what you think."

Up close, the victim appeared to be in his mid-thirties. He had the waxy look of the dead. His eyes were open, but they were dull.

Bent down next to the body was the coroner, wearing gray slacks and a white shirt. Next to the body was a bag like a doctor would carry. But he held no instruments in his gloved hands. Instead he was pressing his blue latex-gloved fingertips to the victim's chest in several places. The chest flesh looked very firm as if in full rigor. Then the coroner moved his hands to the body's abdomen and pressed in a similar fashion. The abdominal flesh moved easily. No rigor.

With the coroner's hands off the victim's chest, I now saw what Mallory meant when he said the victim looked like an alien. The body's chest was huge. Yet there were no appreciable muscles. It was as if he had an oversized rib cage, with the rib bones pushing out against the skin. The top of the man's abdomen bulged out, but the rest of his midsection was slim with no apparent belly fat. His arms and legs were thin, almost scrawny.

"I could be mistaken," the coroner said. "But I think this man died of tension pneumothorax." He ran his fingertips over a distended vein in the victim's neck.

Mallory was sipping from his can of Coke. "What's that?" he said.

"I think this man's chest is full of air. When the pathologist gets him on the table, she can get a better sense."

"Can you guess what happened?"

The coroner shook his head. "If it were a standard case, maybe. But this guy's chest is rock hard. Like the air is under serious pressure. You don't get that from a normal accident. I've seen cases where there is bloat from decomposition. Bloat can produce real pressure."

Mallory frowned. "Like that dead whale I read about? It decomposed on a beach in Alaska and eventually exploded?"

The coroner winced. "That would be an extreme case. You don't need to worry about that here. This victim hasn't been dead longer than... I'd guess twelve to eighteen hours. And he's been in the cold water for some time, maybe since he died. Tahoe's water is cold enough to slow decomposition almost to a stop."

"So the guy has air in his chest," Mallory said. "Is that what killed him?"

"Could be."

"Air usually gets into the chest through a puncture wound, right?"

"Correct. A gunshot or a knife. Once you have a sucking wound, each time the victim tries to inhale, air can get pulled in through the wound and trapped inside the chest. Wounded flesh can be like a one-way flap valve, letting air in but preventing it from escaping. But an air leak, coming in during an attempt at inhalation, can't produce this pressure. Also, I see no wound, front or back, so we have a conundrum. The other strange thing is that tension pneumothorax is usually just on one side of the chest. From the looks of it, this is on both sides. I have no idea how that could happen. I've seen enough. You can remove the body."

"Just as soon as we get a consultation on the tattoo," Mallory said.

The coroner made a small nod, picked up a clipboard, made some notes, and then walked away.

Mallory turned to me. "Come look at the tattoo. It's on the man's back."

"I know nothing about tattoos," I said as I walked over.

Mallory turned to two of the officers. "Can you roll the victim over so we can see the back?"

Two officers, also wearing latex gloves, bent down and did as asked.

Mallory pointed. "Just take a look. Tell me if anything comes to mind." Mallory stayed some distance away as if he were uncomfortable with the sight.

I squatted on my toes and looked up close. The man's back was covered in a dramatic and colorful tattoo of geometric shapes, mostly triangles. There was a dusting of sand on the skin. But the tattoo was so dramatic that the sand didn't obscure much. I stared at it, thinking it looked familiar.

After a bit, I stood up and stepped back to see if the image looked any different from a distance.

Mallory watched me look at the dead body. "It's not a normal tattoo, right?" he said. "More arty."

A young officer in South Lake Tahoe PD dress blues walked up to Mallory. He was holding a radio, something Mallory rarely carried. "Commander, the Ink Maestro is here." He pointed up toward the steps that descended from Lake Tahoe Boulevard.

"Send him down," Mallory said. Then to me, he said, "We called a tattoo expert, too."

The officer spoke into his radio. Another officer at the top of the steps accompanied another man down the steps. The man looked the opposite of the uniformed officer. He wore torn jeans and a flowing cream-colored shirt with three-quarter-length sleeves and a band collar. The shirt was open halfway down the front of his hairless chest. Long, bleached-blond hair draped over his shoulders. He was quite thin and almost as tall as me and had wide-open eyes that showed the whites. His black eyebrows jumped out from the blond hair. Even from a distance, his dramatic looks were obvious. He radiated intensity and charisma and looked like a kind of an ancient, mythical god.

"The Ink Maestro?" I said to Mallory.

"His name is Ivan Manfred. But the guy's business name is the Ink Maestro," Mallory said. "My boy Holden, here, has his body tatted up. Lucky for his employment, he didn't continue the ink onto his face and hands. He says Ink Maestro is the best tattoo artist on the South Shore. Isn't that right, Holden?"

The young officer looked very serious. "No question," he said. "He charges a fortune but has to constantly turn away business because he's too busy. He's a real intellectual. An art genius."

"Ivan Manfred helped us once before when we had a gunshot victim with what looked like a gang tattoo. The Ink Maestro knows the circles where inkers hang out. He made some calls and found out what the tattoo meant and which gang it signified. Turned out, the vic belonged to a gang in Omaha, Nebraska. Go figure why he ended up in Tahoe."

"Prospecting for possible gang recruits?" I said.

"Maybe. Or maybe just on vacation. Anyway, Manfred's a nice guy, and he helped us solve the case. Let's hope he can do a repeat."

The man they called the Ink Maestro got down the steps to the sand and, unlike most beach goers who step carefully to avoid filling their shoes with sand, he strolled across the beach with the same gait that he used on the steps above, no doubt filling his leather flip flops in the process but not risking his image of confidence and control and swagger. As he approached, he said, "Hey dudes," in a deep resonant voice and then looked at Holden with a familiarity that suggested they knew each other well. Holden turned to Mallory as if directing Manfred's attention to his boss.

Mallory made a little nod.

Without speaking, Holden looked at The Ink Maestro and

gestured toward the body.

The man looked at the victim. "This is the art you're wondering about?" he said. "Wow, that's some totally rad ink work."

Holden nodded.

Mallory said, "We'd like to know whatever you can tell us about the tattoo."

Manfred put his hands to his knees, bent forward and leaned in close, an intense frown creasing his forehead. His hair swung forward, framing his handsome face.

Some distance away were two teenaged girls wearing sheer wraps that did little to disguise their bikinis and ankle tattoos. They stared at Manfred, their mouths parted, as if he were their favorite rock star.

Ivan Manfred straightened up, turned to Mallory, and spoke. He had one hand on his hip and gestured dramatically with the other like a practiced orator.

"It's an obvious watercolor style with a broad color palette. Strong color saturation, though. Impressive. The inker knows what he's doing. Didn't use any template that I've seen. It looks freehand. Done with a coil machine."

"What about the picture?" Mallory asked. "Do you recognize it? Does it mean anything?"

Manfred shrugged. "As I said, the tattooing technique is expert. But the image... Hard to say." He looked at Mallory. "That's all I know in a just-the-facts ma'am kind of knowledge. Do you also want what I think?"

"Yeah."

"What I think is this pic is a poor attempt at a modern abstract. The repetitive triangles, the deep space, the value contrast. They make me think it's a noble effort, but it's weak artistic execution. I think this design comes from one of a group of new inkers who fancy themselves academic artists. The problem is that they focus so hard on something new and bold but end up with a result that has no there there."

"No there there?" Mallory said.

Ivan Manfred made a little grin. "My new favorite saying. Gertrude Stein was a famous writer who lived in Paris and referred to her childhood town of Oakland, California by saying there's no there there."

"You going to take up writing now that you've mastered tattooing?" Mallory said.

"No. My writer friends don't make any money. Whereas a good inker can make real money. I just know about Gertrude Stein because she hung out with artists. Picasso, Matisse, Renoir, guys like that."

"Any way to tell who this inker was?"

Ivan shook his head. "L.A. maybe. Or New York. One of those places where an artist-wannabe can indulge pretensions. The opposite of Tahoe. We hike and bike and ski and soak up Mama Nature's grand scheme, while the city inkers pose and flirt and fuss about their pedicures in a man-made world of glass and steel."

"Okay, thanks," Mallory said.

Ivan Manfred paused. "Holden said that consultants might receive a fee."

Mallory frowned and looked over at Holden, whose face reddened. Mallory turned to Manfred. "I never authorized that. But in this little mountain town, we tend to send referrals to local businesses that help us. Right?"

The Ink Maesto's face was placid on the outside. But one got the sense that gears of frustration were turning on the inside. He probably could have done another profitable tattoo in the time it took to come and look at the body. "Right on," he finally said. "Referrals are the milk of mountain dudes. I didn't get a fee the last time I helped you all. But it never hurts to ask, right? Anyway, I can probably put my normal per-hour fee down as a deductible charitable contribution on my income tax. Helping the police, right?"

Mallory nodded. "Sounds good to me."

The Ink Maestro walked away, striding, scuffling his flip flops, puffing up clouds of sand. The teenaged girls were still watching him.

Mallory turned to me. "So what does an art buff like you think? Is that tattoo a weak execution of a modern abstract?"

I gave Mallory a small grin. "Maybe. But it looks to me like something I've seen in one of my art books. I think this tattoo might be a copy of a famous painting by Caspar David Friedrich, a painter who is considered a German master. One of the Romantic Landscape painters. If I remember correctly, the painting is called The Sea Of Ice. It's also known as The Wreck Of Hope."

"That doesn't sound like an abstract," Mallory said.

"No. Friedrich painted quite realistically." I pointed to the body's tattoo. "In the painting, these jagged triangles aren't abstract shapes but giant, broken slabs of arctic ice surrounding a shipwreck." I pointed toward the right side of the dead man's back. "This darker area is the stern of the ship."

"So it isn't abstract, and it doesn't sound modern, either," Mallory said.

"No. Friedrich lived in the early nineteenth century. I think he painted this in the eighteen twenties."

"So it's a painting of a tragedy."

I nodded. "Yeah. Some expedition to the North Pole that didn't end well. I forget the details."

"How sure are you about this?"

"Not very. But you could Google it on your phone."

"Good idea," Mallory said. He pulled out his phone.

I repeated Friedrich's name and the title of the painting.

A minute later, Mallory said, "Here it is. Wow, that's quite a pic. Let's compare."

He walked over to the body and held out his phone next to the man's back.

"Good call, McKenna. It's got to be a copy of the painting. There's no question that the lines match up even if the tattoo doesn't show the same detail as the painting. I'd guess that The Ink Maestro probably knows ink technique. But he doesn't know art." He stared some more at the phone and the body's tattoo. "Does the painting have a particular meaning?"

"I have no idea."

"But you knew the name of it."

"The dancing eight-year-old probably knows the name of the

song, too."

Mallory grunted. "You have to wonder why a guy would have a tattoo of a shipwreck painting."

"Maybe he's a treasure hunter who's focused on sunken ships," I said, remembering Mae's comment about the divers who were interested in the Tahoe Steamer wreck.

"Yeah, maybe," Mallory said. He sipped some Coke.

"What's your thought on how this body got here on the beach?" I asked.

"No idea. Except he isn't wearing a wetsuit, so he couldn't have swum from very far. Either he came to this beach by car or he was dropped off by a boat. The only other way he could have come from a significant distance is if he died somewhere else on the lake and the waves washed him to this beach. The wind's been out of the north for the last couple of days. So he could have floated from many places on the lake."

"Most bodies sink," I said. "But this one's full of air, so that makes sense. One more thing you probably noticed."

Mallory raised his eyebrows.

"The body's neck has red abrasions."

Mallory turned toward the man's neck, the back of which was facing us. "I thought it might have come from his gold chain. But the abrasions go all the way around the neck. You got a speculation on that?"

"Nope. But if the air in the man's chest was put there as part of an assault, maybe the perpetrator held onto the victim's neck chain, abrading the man's neck. If the victim rotated, that could extend the abrasion to all sides of his neck."

"Kind of what I was thinking," Mallory said.

We both looked down at the body.

"So you talked to the old, blind man," Mallory said, changing the subject.

"Yeah. I told Mr. Callahan that I was a private investigator and that if he rejected my recommendation to get medical treatment, that would strengthen the police case in the event they should be accused of malfeasance in not forcing him to go to the hospital."

"You were protecting me," Mallory said, his tone sarcastic.

"Of course. I said that it certainly looked like someone had broken down his front door and beat him up. It was after that when he made his 'just try it' comment."

"What was it again?

"He said, 'You think you can break me? Fine. Just try it.'"

Mallory frowned.

I said, "It seemed that the 'try it' comment was like an internal dare. He wasn't just talking to his tormentor, but to his demons. When I asked him about it, it would have been very simple for him to explain why he said it. But going silent indicated that he regretted making a statement I could overhear. He didn't want to risk making it worse."

"What do you imagine he's going to do?"

"No idea," I said.

"You think the guy has all his nuts and bolts?" Mallory asked.

I nodded. "He's maybe got some age issues and some anger stuff regarding the man who assaulted him, but yeah."

"I've got some age issues and anger stuff, too," Mallory said. He drank the last of his Coke, sucking hard to get out the last few drops. "He say anything else?"

"No."

"Sounds like he was threatened. And the perp is coming back," Mallory said.

"That's what I thought."

Mallory turned and looked across the lake toward the entrance to Emerald Bay six miles to the west, a narrow break in the forest that couldn't be directly seen from the South Shore. "Seems like crime victims lie as often as crime perps. Makes you wonder why."

"Because they're afraid?" I said.

"Probably." Mallory crushed his Coke can in his fist. He turned toward the two paramedics who were still waiting near the body. "We're finished, here. You can pack up the body."

They spread out a long black bag and lifted the body onto it.

As they began to zip it up, I said, "Oh, I forgot to ask the obvious. I assume there was no ID on the victim."

Mallory shook his head. "Like a pouch around the neck? No. And those swim trunks are snug. They pretty much reveal all of this vic's assets."

I looked at the body's shiny red boxer shorts. "The waistband is low, but wide and darker than the rest of the fabric. No chance it could contain a pocket of sorts?"

Mallory turned and looked at me, then looked back at the corpse. "Holden? Check the corpse's swim trunks, would you?"

Holden looked as though he'd been given a distasteful duty normally reserved for rookies. He made a show of pulling on blue latex gloves and then walked over and squatted down next to the body. Very gingerly, he fingered the waistband of the victim's trunks, flexing it, running his finger under the top edge. "Nothing here, boss," he said.

"What about inside?" I asked. "Did anyone take a look?"

Now both Mallory and Holden looked uncomfortable. Holden shot Mallory a questioning look.

"Give it a look," Mallory said.

Holden pulled out on the waistband and peered underneath. "The vic is wearing a jockstrap under the trunks," he said.

"With the temperature of this water, I would too," Mallory said. "Be double sure there is nothing but his equipment in that jockstrap."

Holden made a face. He reached in and seemed to run his forefinger around the waistband of the jockstrap. "I feel nothing, sir. The victim is…" he stopped talking just as his hand stopped searching. "Maybe there is something here, sir." He looked more closely. "The jockstrap waistband is thick. It seems there is a double layer of fabric. Let me see if this has an opening." He re-traced his finger movement, then flexed the waistband and turned it inside out. He caught an edge of fabric and pulled it out farther.

It was a pouch of sorts, nearly invisible, perfect for stowing an ID and a credit card.

Which it did.

Holden pulled out two pieces of plastic and made a show of holding them out as he walked over to Mallory.

Mallory wore no gloves and showed no indication that he was about to pull some on. He kept his hands at his sides.

"What, Mr. Holden, sir, do the plastic cards reveal?"

"This one is a Visa credit card."

"And the other card?"

Holden turned the other card over twice, reading. "This one's a driver's license, and it appears that the photo matches the victim. Let me do the math. The corpse's age would be thirty-seven. And the name of the deceased appears to be Colin Callahan."

"And the address?"

"Nine-one-zero Nocturne Street, Citrus Heights."

I pulled out my pen and notebook and wrote it down.

"Okay. Put the cards in an evidence bag," Mallory said.

SIX

Mallory turned to me. "The victim had the same last name as the old man who got beat up. What's the chance of that if they're not connected?"

"Not much."

Mallory nodded.

We walked up the stairs to the boulevard, both of us quiet. Mallory opened the door of his unmarked Chevy and got in. He leaned out the window. "Assuming the dead man is related to old man Callahan, maybe you could do the honors? Let him know? Technically, it should be one of our officers. But you used to be an officer of the law."

"According to the private investigator law, I'm still pretty much an officer of the law. And according to what you told Mae O'Sullivan, I'm a pretty good investigator. Pretty good might be good enough to tackle such a task. If I make some notes first, I might even remember to ask the old Callahan if he's related to the young Callahan."

Mallory looked at me, his face unmoving. He was probably wondering if there was an appropriate sarcastic response. Or maybe he was just thinking about going home and having a beer. After a bit, he said, "Let me know what you find out." He drove away.

As I walked toward the Jeep, I thought about Colin Callahan's shipwreck tattoo and what I'd said about the dead man possibly being interested in sunken ships. It had sounded a bit ridiculous at the time. But with Daniel having witnessed the sinking of Tahoe's greatest ship back in 1940, it seemed like sinking ships were more than another unusual coincidence. It was an axiom of law enforcement. Assume that what looks like an unusual coincidence is probably no coincidence at all.

I drove back to the Bijou neighborhood and pulled up in front of the matching houses. Ed the carpenter was gone. The repaired door was hung, closed, and, no doubt locked. It had a fresh coat of paint. A sign to the side of the door had printing large enough to see from the street.

"WET PAINT"

I knocked on Mae's door. This time it took her much longer to open.

"You're back," she said. "Is your investigation going well or not?"

"It's going well in that the investigation is proceeding along the lines I expected. Not so well in that Daniel Callahan is probably in more danger than I thought."

"What is it?" Mae asked, her green eyes wide with worry.

"Let's go talk to Daniel." I stood.

She nodded. We stepped outside, and she shut her door.

We walked the short distance to Daniel's house.

Mae knocked long and loud.

After a minute, she knocked again. "It's Mae, Daniel. Please let me in."

"I'm coming. I'm coming."

The door opened. Daniel Callahan gripped a heavy wooden cane in his right hand and leaned on it. I gathered that, while he used a support cane in his right hand, his left hand typically held one of the lightweight white canes for navigation. "Oh, it's you two again. Here to team up and badger me." His opaque eyes scanned left and right, taking in whatever he could discern through what must be like heavily-frosted windows.

"I have some news that concerns you, Mr. Callahan," I said. "News you'll want to hear. May we come in and talk?"

Daniel Callahan stood a long time, leaning on his cane. Then he made a slow rotation, walked into the living room, and sat on his rocker. He reached for his aviator shades and put them on. Mae and I sat on the small couch across from him. Daniel frowned, his white eyebrows dipping partly behind the sunglasses. I glanced up at the mantel and the framed picture of the young woman. I realized that she looked a bit like Daniel.

"Daniel, do you know a man named Colin Callahan?"

Daniel continued to frown.

"He's thirty-seven," I said. "Thin like you. Mae told me you don't have children. But I'm guessing he's related to you in some fashion. The grandson of a sibling or a cousin."

Daniel Callahan paused. I couldn't sense why. "Why would you think he's related to me? There are a million Callahans."

"Because you were assaulted last night. And it appears that Colin Callahan was murdered last night. Here in Tahoe."

Mae gasped.

I watched Daniel closely. He showed no surprise or shock, just resignation. He sighed and leaned back in the rocker, his head making a thump against the top rail of wood. The silence that followed was long. Mae started to say something but then realized it was best to wait for Daniel's response.

Eventually, Daniel said, "So this is my attacker's way of letting me know he can get to anyone I might know. This is how he shows me he's serious."

There was no point in commenting that Daniel was finally admitting what had really happened.

Mae started to speak again, and I raised my hand to stop her.

We waited a long minute. I could tell that Daniel was running scenarios through his head. Possibly the things I'd said in my earlier visit about how his attacker would continue to torment him and, even if Daniel gave him what he wanted, maybe kill Daniel as well.

"To my knowledge, I've never met this Colin Callahan," Daniel finally said. "I don't think I've ever even heard his name. But if he's related to me, I'm guessing he is descended from my cousin Astor. The reason is my other two cousins were female, so they didn't have the Callahan name after they married. Astor's father was my father's brother. Astor was closer in age to my sister Nora. Which made him about ten years older than I am. So I didn't know him nearly as well as she did. Last I heard, cousin Astor lived back east. He went to Princeton as an undergraduate, which made for some jokes because Astor was a stuffed shirt with a stuffed-shirt name, and the crowd I hung with at Sac State considered Princeton to be the world headquarters of stuffed shirts. I think Astor got a law degree from Yale but ended up working for the State Department as a foreign affairs bigwig. Astor would now be one hundred and five or so, so he's likely long since dead. This dead man named Colin... You said he was thirty-seven? Then he could be Astor's grandson or even his great grandson. But grandson is most likely. How did Colin die?"

"We don't know yet. But his body washed up on El Dorado Beach, and there are signs that he didn't drown. It doesn't look like a natural death, but I shouldn't be presumptuous. I'll wait for the pathologist's report."

Daniel paused again. "I'd heard way back that Astor had three sons and that he crowed about it as if having three sons was some great accomplishment instead of the commonplace result of sex. And according to Christmas cards and the like over the years, Astor also fussed over the fact that one of the sons had committed the cardinal sin of moving west to California. When I heard that, my first thought was, who wouldn't move three thousand miles away from a stuffed-shirt father like Astor? Anyway, maybe that Eastern transplant to the West sired Colin. That would be a fitting insult to the overbearing grandfather, a grandson who had the audacity to be born in California. Tell me, does this dead man have thick black hair?"

"Yes."

Daniel Callahan made a little knowing nod. "Astor's wife was of Spanish descent. My sister said that the woman's family's most notable physical characteristic was amazing hair, pelts like you'd expect on a black bear."

Callahan took a deep breath. "So now we know that my attacker is willing to kill to motivate my cooperation. I assume that means that Mae is in great danger."

Mae, still silent, inhaled again. "What do you mean?"

Daniel turned to Mae. "I'm sorry, but you, my dear, are the closest person to me. Yes, I'm irascible at times. But don't let that mislead you. Without you, I'd be in trouble. Oh hell, I may as well say the truth. Without you helping me, and without your companionship, I'd be adrift. I suspect this isn't a hard concept to deduce from the outside. Am I right about that, Mr. Investigator?"

"Yes, it's obvious. Daniel is right, Mae. You are at risk. Daniel's attacker is probably Colin Callahan's murderer. The message he's sending is that he can track down a distant relative of Daniel's and kill him to show that he means business. It would be easy for him to grab you."

"You mean kidnap me?!"

"Anything he thinks might motivate Daniel to cooperate. Which means your safety is a main priority."

"Are you saying I can't even stay in my house?"

"There is no clear best approach in a situation like this. If safety were your only concern, you'd leave this afternoon for an extended stay in Europe."

"But that doesn't help find Daniel's attacker."

"Right. There are other concerns. The same applies to Daniel."

Daniel nodded, an interesting gesture from a blind person. Maybe nodding and shaking one's head was hardwired and not a trait that was learned by seeing people. "If you hide me away," he said, "you lose your bait for tempting the killer to approach, right?"

"Correct," I said. "We should do whatever we can to ensure the safety of both of you. But from the standpoint of catching your assailant and Colin Callahan's killer, it's best to make you available. We can try to keep people near you. And you both can make certain you keep doors and windows locked."

"That didn't work before," he said.

"Right. So you can hide and be safer. Or, as you've said, the best way to catch the killer is probably to make it so he can come to you."

Daniel's landline phone rang, startling all of us with its loud, old-fashioned jangle.

"Shall I get it?" Mae asked.

Daniel nodded.

Mae stood up, went over to a sidebar, and picked up the

receiver.

"Hello?" Pause. "Who's calling, please?" she said. Another pause. She put her hand over the mouthpiece and turned to us.

"It's a man talking in a weird voice as if to disguise it. He wants to talk to you, Daniel."

"That could be my attacker. He had something in his mouth when he beat me up. Dental cotton or something."

She turned to me. "Is that the right thing to do? Let Daniel talk to him?"

I nodded.

She handed the phone to Daniel.

"Hello?" he said in a soft voice. There was a long pause. Daniel listened for what seemed like a full minute. "Go to hell," Daniel finally said and hung up.

Mae put her hand on Daniel's shoulder.

All the landlines I knew in Tahoe were AT&T. I took the phone from Daniel and dialed *57, one way to activate call trace on the last caller. A synthetic voice said that the call was untraceable. Probably the caller was using a call anonymizer to hide its number.

Mae watched me hang up the phone. "It didn't work?"

"No. There are web services that can sometimes pull the history." I turned to Daniel. "Did it sound like the person who attacked you?"

"Yes."

"What did the caller say?" I asked.

"He said that Colin Callahan was a warning. The caller said he could get to everyone I know and do the same thing. He also said there was no point in me calling the police or a private detective like Owen McKenna because he wasn't going to show up. He was only going to call on the phone."

"Did he say my name, or did he just refer to a private detective in a generic way?"

"He said your name. He said if I don't tell him what he wants, the next death would be someone I know and care about."

"When he beat you up or when he called just now, did he say what he wants to know from you?"

"Yes," Daniel said, his voice soft, his tone somber.

"Can you tell us what it is?"

Daniel nodded. "He was asking about the Tahoe Steamer. He said, 'I want to know what really went down with the ship.' Then he said to stay in my house, by the phone."

SEVEN

I called Mallory on my cell.

"You got something?" he said when they connected me.

"Daniel Callahan does not know the victim on the beach. But he thinks it's possible that Colin Callahan is a distant relation and was killed as a warning to him."

"So now the old man admits he was attacked."

"Yeah. I'm pretty sure he was resisting because he'd been threatened." I looked at Daniel as I said it. He had taken off his sunglasses and was rubbing his eyes. "He didn't want to give in to some thug who threatened him." Daniel nodded.

I continued, "Daniel just got a call from man identifying himself as Colin Callahan's murderer."

"Callahan recognized the voice?"

"Only to the extent that it was the same man who assaulted him. The attacker disguised his voice both in person and on the phone. When Daniel was attacked, he thought the man had something like dental cotton stuffed in his cheeks and it matched the sound on the phone just now. The caller said he wants Daniel to think about how vulnerable he is. Same for other people Daniel knows. The implication being that he can hurt any of them. He said he'll call back soon for information."

"Why is the creep calling back?" Mallory asked. "Why not just demand the answer now?"

"I don't know. I suspect the caller thinks Daniel will continue to resist. So he wants Daniel to ponder the risk to other people who might face Colin Callahan's fate."

"And more pondering will result in a more truthful response?"

"I think that's the idea, yeah. Like priming the pump of

distress," I said.

"Now you're a poet?" Mallory said.

"Even pretty good private investigators do what we have to."

"Can Callahan guess what the caller wants to know?"

"The attacker already told him. He wants to know what went down on the Tahoe Steamer when they scuttled it in nineteen forty."

"I don't get it," Mallory said.

"Turns out Daniel Callahan is possibly the only person still living who witnessed the scuttling of the Steamer. The man who claims to be Colin Callahan's killer thinks Daniel saw something significant."

"What does Callahan say now?"

"I'm putting my phone on speaker." I turned to Daniel Callahan. "Mr. Callahan, Commander Mallory wants to know what really went down on the Steamer."

Daniel shook his head. "Nothing. It was towed from Tahoe City to Glenbrook Bay. Then it was sunk. It went down fast. Word was the tow boat captain had trouble with towing a boat so much larger than his, and he was worried about the Steamer dragging his boat down. So he cut the line and opened the seacocks sooner than necessary." As Daniel spoke, I wasn't convinced he was telling the whole truth.

"And you saw all this even though you're blind." Mallory's voice sounded scratchy through the little speaker on my cell phone.

"I'm mostly blind," Daniel said. "But not totally blind. I can see enough to pick up movement and sense what's going on."

I said, "Commander, the caller said he's calling back. Daniel has a landline. But star fifty-seven says the last call was untraceable. I don't know where law enforcement currently is with landline call tracing..." I let the statement drift off.

"The Supreme Court is still wavering," Mallory said. "Too bad it's a landline. Cell phone tracing is like the wild west. Anything goes if you know the numbers involved. What's Callahan's number? I'll see what I can do."

Daniel Callahan recited the number. His voice was soft, so I repeated it to Mallory.

"Got it." Mallory hung up.

I looked at Daniel. "Your phone could ring at any time. There are some questions I'd like you to try to ask. The first one is…"

I was interrupted by a phone ringing. But it wasn't the sharp jangle from Daniel's old phone. Nor was it my cell. The ring was an electronic chirp like from a cell phone, and it was muffled. Mae inhaled. I looked at her, wondering if it was her phone. She shook her head.

"What's that?" Daniel said as I stood up, turning, wondering.

The chirping ring came again. The sound was below me. I got down and looked under the couch. Swept my hand through the darker areas. Mae was on her knees, peering into the shadows.

Another chirp. Now it didn't seem to be on the floor. I pushed up.

"I think it's in the couch!" Mae said. She reached under the cushion that she'd been sitting on.

I lifted the other cushion and flung it aside.

There was a small, black phone, cheap, prepaid burner style. No frills. No easy way to track the number when we didn't know what it was. It made a slight motion as it rang again.

The whole point of a burner phone was to be anonymous, so I knew immediately that it would be wiped of prints. I pressed its speaker button so Daniel and Mae could hear as well. I set the phone on the little table next to Daniel's rocker.

"Clever," I said loud enough for all to hear, "leaving a phone in Callahan's couch."

"Listen real careful." The words were garbled just enough to obscure the voice even though we could still make out the words. "First, I'm in control. All of your lives. If you wanna live you're gonna do jus' what I say. If you don't believe me, look at the picture on the mantle."

We all turned to look at the small framed photo. A wavering green laser light dot appeared.

"What is it?" Callahan said.

The light dot disappeared.

I turned around to try to see which window the laser had shone through. It could have been the main window in the living room or one in the dining area. There were several houses at a diagonal across the street, groups of trees, and some thick plantings of bushes. But it was also possible that it came in the side window.

"Tell me!" Callahan said.

"There was a green dot of light," I said. "Like what a laser rifle scope produces. Either the caller has a rifle pointed at your house, or it's a laser pointer and he wants you to realize that it would have been possible to have a rifle pointed at us."

"See?" the caller mumbled. "You better tell me the truth. Now. Callahan, what went down on the Steamer?"

Mae and I watched as the green laser dot reappeared, dropped off the framed picture, and traced over to her, settling on Mae's chest. She cried out, putting her hand over the dot, which of course illuminated the back of her hand. Then the green dot jumped away to the side. She jerked away, bumped the wall, and slid down until she sat on the floor. She trembled with terror.

Daniel Callahan's white eyes were wide with fear. His body trembled. He turned toward me and then Mae. His mouth opened and shut twice, silently, like a fish trying to push water through its gills.

"I'm waiting," the voice said. "I can tell if you're lying. If you lie, Mae O'Sullivan dies. Yeah, I know her name. I know she lives next door to you. I know she's a librarian from Monterey. I know she came from Bakersfield. She's got dirty blonde hair and green eyes. She's wearing jeans and a jeans headband. You wanna save her life? Then you tell me the whole truth. What went down on the Steamer? TELL ME NOW!"

When the garbled voice shouted, Daniel jerked as if under electric shock.

"What…" Daniel started to talk and then stopped as if choking on the words. He swallowed and made mouth movements as if trying to generate saliva. "My…"

"FIVE MORE SECONDS, GEEZER MAN, OR MAE DIES!"

There was a popping sound, and the large living room window exploded.

A thousand chunks of glass rained down onto the floor.

The green laser dot reappeared on the wall. It tracked over to Mae. She was sitting frozen in place, immobilized with shock. I took two fast steps toward her. I pulled her down until she was lying on the floor and then pulled her to where she would be out of sight from the window.

"What's happening!" she yelled.

"Stay down," I said. "Daniel!" I shouted. "Get down on the floor!"

"Wha..." He was quaking. He had to use both hands on the rocker arms to get down. From his movements, I could tell he couldn't kneel. He leaned sideways and half-fell onto his left hip.

"Stay down!"

I got out my cell phone. I used minimal movement in the event that I could be seen by the shooter. Nevertheless, Mae saw me. I looked at her and made a little shake of my head. The only speed dial number I had other than Street Casey's was for Sergeant Diamond Martinez's cell. South Lake Tahoe wasn't in the Douglas County Sheriff's Office jurisdiction, but I thought he'd be most likely to get the drift of what was happening without me giving him a long explanation. And I wouldn't have to go through a receptionist. As if scratching the side of my head, I cupped my phone in my palm and raised it to my ear so Diamond's voice wouldn't project. When he answered, I quietly said, "Listen." Then I moved my phone near Daniel's table, keeping the phone in my hand. From the killer's view, it might look like I was leaning on my hand. I wanted it close to the burner phone so Diamond could hear the conversation.

"OKAY, TIME'S UP!" the caller on the burner phone shouted. "WHAT WENT DOWN ON THE STEAMER?!"

Callahan jerked in fear and screamed. Then he gathered his focus and shouted, his voice shaking. "My sister Nora murdered her boyfriend and left his body on the Steamer when they scuttled it!"

EIGHT

"What is your sis's name?"

"Nora."

"Where does she live?" the garbled caller asked.

"Her name was Nora. She died when she was young. Twenty-eight. That was about seventy-seven years ago."

The voice on the burner phone was now less abrasive. I shifted my hand to bring my cell phone closer. I hoped Diamond was still listening on the other end of the line.

"What's her last name?" the caller asked.

"Callahan, like me. Nora Miriam Callahan."

"What was her boyfriend's name?"

"Frank. I never knew his last name."

"Where did he live?"

"I don't know. Near the coast, I think. My family always took a summer vacation in Tahoe. That year, nineteen forty, Frank came up to Tahoe. He camped someplace nearby. Frank became Nora's summer boyfriend."

"Why'd your sister kill 'im?" the garbled voice said.

"I have no idea," Callahan said. "But I think it might be that he was seeing another girl named Jenny. I heard some things. I couldn't say for sure. But I think he was in love with Jenny. Nora was prone to moods. Something like that could make Nora crazy."

"Did you see her kill him?"

"No. They were walking in Tahoe City. I was nearby, trying out my new binoculars."

"You could see back then?"

"No. I was always blind. But I can see shapes. And sense movement. Binoculars bring those vague shapes closer. It was Nora and Frank. I'm sure of it. They walked by me, and I heard their voices. They walked to the marina and got in a rowboat and rowed out to the Steamer where it was moored."

"Did you go with them out to the Steamer?"

"No. I saw them. Both went out. Only Nora came back."

"How d'you know she killed him?"

"I don't technically know. And she never confessed to me. But they were talking about murdering someone else. Nora was going to show how they could kill the other person and where they could dispose of his body. When she came back in the rowboat alone, I realized that previous talk was probably a ruse to get Frank out on the Steamer."

"She planned all along..." The garbled voice got a bit more clear halfway through the question. Then it seemed as if he rearranged what was in his cheeks, and the last words were more mumbled than ever. "She was gonna kill Frank all along?"

"I don't know if she planned that," Callahan said. "She was impulsive and tempestuous. It might have been spur of the moment. But it may have been planned from the beginning."

"Why would she kill him?"

"I don't know. They seemed to get along."

"Make a guess," the garbled voice demanded. "You coulda thought of why for a lot of years. Separate from Jenny, what would be a reason why Nora would kill Frank? What's your best guess?"

Callahan hesitated. I couldn't tell if he was reluctant or simply didn't have a guess.

"TALK, MAN! Gimme your guess or Mae dies!"

"It's just a guess. But I think they were going to steal something valuable. After they figured out how to steal it, I think Nora decided she couldn't trust Frank. If she thought he was planning to double cross her, then she might have decided to double cross him instead."

"After she killed 'im, did she steal what they wanted?"

"I don't know." Callahan was staring, unseeing, at the wall and shaking his head.

"There would be some way to tell!"

"I don't know what you mean," Callahan sounded

desperate.

"After the Steamer was sunk! Was she planning to steal something big time? Was she, you know, happy? Or was she sad?"

Callahan paused. I expected the caller to get mad at his silence.

Callahan said, "At first she seemed elated. Then she seemed distraught and anxious. After a week she went into a long depression."

"What's that mean?"

"I don't know," Callahan said.

"GUESS!"

Daniel Callahan jerked.

"My best guess is convoluted."

"I'm waiting."

Callahan spoke carefully. "At the time, I came to think that Frank wasn't just planning to double cross her. I think he already did. Before they went out to the Steamer."

"And...?"

Callahan was shaking. "At first I thought they were planning a theft of something valuable. Something they'd both do. Then I wondered if maybe Frank had already stolen it himself. And maybe he was planning to kill Nora. But she surprised him and did what he hadn't anticipated, killing him instead."

"So she'd get depressed?"

"Maybe. But I wondered if he had the stolen item on him when she left his body on the Steamer."

This time the garbled voice paused. "And the stolen item went down with the ship?"

"That occurred to me, yes." Callahan said.

"What do you know about this guy Frank?"

"Almost nothing. He'd spent some time as a barnstorming pilot. He was charismatic. But after I got to know him a little, he seemed shifty. I didn't trust him. One time when I heard Nora talking to him, he said someone named Jack Questman had killed someone and stolen something valuable. And Frank thought he might steal what Questman stole."

"Did Frank have brothers and sisters?"

Callahan paused. "I don't think so."

"How old was he?"

"A little older than my sister. She was twenty-two in nineteen forty. He was maybe twenty-five. Or twenty-six."

The garbled voice said, "Okay. I might call back. I'll be watching. If you've lied to me, you die. Mae first. Then you, McKenna. Callahan, you're gonna be last. You got that?"

"Yes," Callahan said.

"How 'bout you, McKenna? If you mess with me, I'm gonna stick you where it hurts."

"Your message is loud and clear," I said. Then, thinking fast, I thought of a way to get some breathing space with regard to the subject. "Before you hang up, there's something I should say." I was thinking fast, improvising.

"Say it."

"You probably already know about the Steamer Festival," I said. "But I don't want you to think we had anything to do with it or that we're talking to anyone about the Steamer."

"What's this about?" The garbled voice sounded guarded, wary, and dangerous.

"Just that Commander Mallory of the SLTPD had me come to El Dorado Beach so he could ask me about the tattoo on Colin Callahan's back." I was thinking fast, making stuff up on the fly. "When I told him it was a replica of a Caspar David Friedrich painting about a shipwreck, he said that was a funny coincidence because he'd heard about something called the Steamer shipwreck and some festival."

"What's that?"

"I don't know. I got the idea that it was in the planning stages. Some kind of celebration. Scuba divers or something."

"How'd you know about the tattoo?"

"Pure luck. Mallory knows I like art and had me look at it. I recognized the image."

Another pause. "Okay. We never talked. You never heard me. You tell the cops about me, I come back and pick you off, one by one. McKenna, you go home and forget this ever happened.

If you don't back off, I can kill you easy. But first, you're gonna suffer big time. I know where you live and where you work. I know you drive an ugly old Jeep. I know where your girlfriend works and where she lives. I know you got a big dog that will chow down a ball of burger, nevermind what poison might be in it. So you go away and you don't come back."

The man hung up.

NINE

Still holding my phone in my hand, I grabbed the burner
phone with my other hand and clicked it off. I didn't want
the shooter to fake hanging up just so he could hear what we said
afterward.

I shifted a bit, then lowered down next to Mae, thinking
I was out of the shooter's line of sight. The shooter could see
through the broken window, but I didn't think he could see me
down on the floor.

"Diamond, you still there?" I said into my phone.

"Sí. Are you all okay?"

"Yes. Mae O'Sullivan and I are at Daniel Callahan's house.
Can you hold while I use Daniel's landline to call nine, one,
one?"

"Of course."

I scooted over to Daniel's landline phone and dialed 9-1-1.

"Nine, one, one emergency," a woman said. "State your
address and name."

"Owen McKenna reporting a shooter at Daniel Callahan's
address in the Bijou neighborhood. I'm on a landline that will
show you the address."

"Please stay on the line. We'll have officers enroute
immediately."

"I just spoke to Commander Mallory. He will want to know."
I handed the phone to Mae, whose ruddy face was blue-white
pale. "The dispatcher may have questions."

She looked numb and in shock. But she took the phone and
held it near her ear.

I picked up my cell. "Could you make out what happened?"
I said to Diamond in a low voice that couldn't be heard from any
distance.

"Yeah," Diamond said. "A threat, a bad guy, a potential murder from back when the Steamer was scuttled."

"Hold those thoughts. I need to deal with this situation. Call you later?"

"Sí."

I hung up.

I sat down on the floor next to Daniel. He was leaning against the wall. His jaw muscles bulged with tension.

"Are you okay?"

"Sure. I get beat up and shot at every ninety years, like it or not."

"Your sense of humor will keep you going for another ninety. Sit tight. The cavalry will be here soon."

I slid across the floor to Mae. She was hunched up in a corner, knees raised, arms around her shins. She'd dropped the phone handset. It lay on the floor, no dial tone because the dispatcher was still connected.

"Not what you bargained for, huh?" I said. I put my hand on her knee and squeezed.

She was shaking. She didn't reply.

"It gets easier, the more you get shot at," I said.

I noticed tears on her cheeks.

"Sorry," I said. "Taking my cue from your friend, here. Sarcastic humor works for some, seems insensitive for others."

"No," she said, crying. "I mean, yes." She tried to take a deep breath. "You're trying. I appreciate that."

"Wait 'til you see me at open mike night. Seriously, I haven't a clue how to comfort. But I want to comfort."

"Keep trying. It works."

I heard sirens growing in the distance.

An hour later, there were lots of SLTPD uniforms in the house, in the vacant lot across the street, talking to Mae and Daniel. Mallory had me in the middle of the street going over details.

Just down a few vehicle spaces, Spot had his head out the window of the Jeep. His ears were up and focused toward me, the faux diamond ear stud sparkling. I wished I could send him on a search. But I had nothing to scent him on. He'd no doubt heard the shot and smelled the perpetrator. But our communications with dogs, useful as they are, do not allow us to send dogs on suspect searches with English descriptions alone.

After the cops left, I escorted Mae and Daniel over to Mae's house. Getting away from the broken glass calmed them somewhat. Mae tended to Daniel with food and liquids, which seemed to help them both.

I stepped out her front door and dialed Diamond back.

"You okay to talk?" I asked when he answered.

"You and your clients have been assaulted and shot at, and you're concerned about my work schedule?" Diamond said. "Sensitive cop mode taken to extreme."

"I'm not being sensitive. I just want to know I've got your full attention." I figured sarcasm didn't have to be limited to dealing with crime victims.

"Right," Diamond said.

I told Diamond what had happened since Mae had first called me that morning. "What you heard earlier was us talking on a burner phone that the killer planted in Daniel Callahan's couch," I said. "I've always heard that tracing cell phones was like the Wild West. Is that still your impression?"

"Pretty much," Diamond said. "But if you don't know the number of the calling phone or the receiving phone, you're probably out of luck. Maybe a cell-phone hacker geek could backtrack the number."

"Here's another question," I said. "The shooter called Callahan's landline first, then called back on the burner phone he'd hidden in the couch. Why do you suppose he called on the landline in the first place?"

Diamond took his time answering. "One possible explanation is that he wanted to establish that Daniel was in fact at the house before he called on the burner phone. If he'd called the burner first, a stranger to him might have heard it ringing. Let's say a house cleaner was there alone. If they hear a phone ringing in the couch, they might pull it out and carry it away to wherever Daniel was, returning what they assume was his lost phone. If you want to ensure that the burner stays hidden in the couch until you're positive Daniel is there to answer it, you don't call its number until you've already established that Daniel is present."

"Makes sense," I said. "But there was still the landline to call on. Why put the burner there at all, when there is a landline?"

Diamond continued, "You said the caller had already beaten up Daniel. So the caller might think that law enforcement's response would be to put a recorder on the landline. The caller doesn't want to say anything significant over that connection. He calls, talks to Daniel, verifies that Daniel is there. Then he calls back on the cell so that he can't be recorded."

"Ah, thanks. One more question you might know about," I said. "Daniel Callahan's big picture window was shot out. But I heard no shot. Thoughts?"

"Other noises masked the shot? A silencer?"

"My sense was the shooter would have been some distance away and used a rifle."

"Silencers on rifles are less common than those on pistols, but still sometimes used. Or maybe it was a PCP gun."

"It's a familiar term that I can't immediately place," I said.

"Pre-charged pneumatic gun," Diamond said. "A compressed air gun that fires pellets instead of bullets. When there is no conventional cartridge in a weapon, there is no explosion of gunpowder. No explosion means little noise. A PCP gun makes a relatively soft pop."

"Now it comes back to me. The pellet guns of my youth. But they weren't capable of sniping at a distance and taking out large picture windows."

"Your youth was misspent. Compressed air guns go back to the middle ages. They were configured to shoot all sizes of rounds, even up to what we now call fifty caliber. Enough to kill an elephant or shatter typical barricades. Today, they come in all calibers. They are as serious as any other weapons."

"I didn't realize big PCP guns were still in use. The compression cylinders must be difficult to pump."

"Most don't pump at all," Diamond said. "These guns use compressed air tanks. They carry up to four thousand pounds per square inch."

"That's like a scuba tank."

"Exactly. Scuba tanks with a hose that connects to the gun. They fill a small compression chamber on the gun, sometimes within the stock."

"If we can find the pellet that broke the window, can it be traced to the gun? Do pellets pick up rifling marks like bullets?"

"Some air guns have rifling spirals to give pellets a spin. But it's not so dramatic as with bullets. And the science of detection is not so rigorous, either."

"And you know this how?"

"Cop magazines on the tables in our lunchrooms. Douglas County law enforcement officers are up to speed on weapons science."

"I see. Maybe I'll call on your expertise in the future. Bring you cerveza for your time."

"For payment, I take Pacifico, Carte Blanche, and even Corona in a pinch."

TEN

I went back inside Mae's house.

She was sitting next to Daniel on her couch.

"What do we do next?" she asked.

"My official recommendation is that you and Daniel should stay with someone else."

"No," Daniel said. "My home is my castle. I won't give someone the satisfaction of driving me out of it."

"The window's gone," I said. "It would be dangerous."

"We'll get that carpenter - what's his name - to fix it." Daniel was shaking his head. "Anyway, the man wasn't trying to kill me. He was trying to scare me. He succeeded in getting me to tell everything I know. There is no reason he would want to kill me now."

"Daniel," Mae said. "It will take a day or two for Ed to board up the window. You can stay here with me at this house. I know the food you like. It will be the least disruptive."

Daniel didn't immediately object.

"Good compromise, Mae," I said. "But I think you should stay somewhere else as well."

She thought about it. "I'm in the same situation as Daniel. I don't want to cave in to threats. And now that Daniel has told them what he knows, why would they come after me?" She paused. "Yes, it's scary. But if Daniel is brave enough to face it, I can be too."

Daniel said, "I only need a few things. Toothbrush. Pajamas. My comb and glasses and canes."

"I'll be right back." Mae immediately went out the door and over to his house as if she wanted to act before he could change his mind.

Daniel and I sat and waited. I tried to make conversation

but he didn't respond. Even though he was blind, it seemed he glowered at me. After a bit, he feigned sleep, leaning back on Mae's couch.

Mae was back in a few minutes. She handed Daniel his sunglasses and comb. He put the glasses on and ran the comb through his hair, using his other hand to smooth the result. "Come, Daniel," Mae said. "Let's get you set up in my bedroom. I'll sleep on the couch." Mae led Daniel the short distance to her bedroom.

I waited in Mae's living room as bits of conversation came from the bedroom. I noticed that, like Daniel, Mae's living room had no TV. Maybe Daniel, being blind, only listened to the radio. Or maybe they both had small TV sets in their bedrooms.

On Mae's mantle was a framed picture. It sat in nearly the same spot as a picture that was on Daniel's mantle.

The photo was of a woman - possibly Mae - in a boat. She wore a blue wetsuit and a white swim cap.

Mae was gone a long time before she reappeared in the living room. "He's in my bed, trying to nap," she said in a whisper. "This stress has taken all his energy."

She sat down on her couch and leaned forward, elbows on her knees, her palms cradling her face. She was taking deep breaths. "That shooter..." her voice trailed off.

I could sense her stress. I walked over and sat near her.

"I don't mean to be upset," she said, her face buried in her hands. "I'm sorry." Her body started to shake.

"It's okay to be upset," I said.

"I didn't know if... I thought..." her voice dissolved into spasms and sobs.

I put my hand on her shoulder. "When someone shoots at you, it shakes you to the core."

Her chest was heaving.

I rubbed her back. "You get such a surge of adrenaline that it takes over your actions. And when the threat is gone, that adrenaline drops off. That's when it hits you what you've been through. You lose control."

She was unable to speak, shaking and shivering and crying.

"Everyone who's been through a shooting goes through this. Cops too. Your world tips up on edge, and you feel yourself sliding off. And when the ground finally levels out again, you collapse, unable to make the stress go away for a long time."

Mae couldn't get enough air. She was gasping and eventually she lost her strength to sit up. She melted, falling sideways, her shoulder hitting the couch, her head landing on my thigh.

I didn't know what to do beyond gently rubbing her shoulder and arm.

In time, her shaking slowed. I pulled her hair back from her eyes. The strands were wet and cold with tears.

Her breathing deepened, forceful inhalations of someone trying to calm themself.

I kept rubbing her, very lightly. Not a massage but a comforting touch.

After ten minutes I wondered if she'd fallen asleep. But she tensed and slowly pushed herself up to a sitting position. She wiped her eyes and her face, and then stood up and walked to the back of the house.

I heard a door close and water running. Five minutes passed before she returned, looking traumatized and red-faced. But her look revealed a determination to be strong.

I had picked up the picture off her mantle.

"That was taken of me in Roatan, Honduras," she said. "I went there to try warm-water freediving." She sniffled, found a tissue, blew her nose.

"You mentioned freediving before," I said. "That it's basically diving while holding your breath. But what does it entail?"

"Freediving is what we call an apnea discipline. And yes, I know your next question will be, what's an apnea discipline?"

"Indeed," I said.

"Basically, apnea is a word that describes the act of holding your breath. You've probably heard of sleep apnea. That happens to be a kind of involuntary breath holding when you're asleep. After a bit, the person gasps for air and starts breathing again. Sleep apnea can be bad for people's health because people need their sleep, and sleep apnea disrupts the normal sleep process.

But when people do voluntary breath holding, that's different."

"Is freediving competitive?" I asked.

"It can be. There are all kinds of challenges and competitions based on doing stuff while holding your breath. One is simply holding your breath underwater. Another is seeing how far you can swim while holding your breath. There is every category of diving you can imagine."

"All while holding your breath," I said. "I suppose it makes sense to do breath-holding stuff underwater because then there is no cheating."

"Actually, that's not why people do it. It turns out that going underwater slows a person's heartbeat and lowers their blood pressure and metabolism."

"Is that because water calms you? Or is it some other aspect of physiology?"

"Both," Mae said. "The apnea scientists don't fully understand it. But the basic principle is that being underwater helps you hold your breath longer."

"So if I can hold my breath above water for, let's say, one minute, how long could I hold it underwater?"

"Hard to say. Maybe a minute and twenty seconds. It seems to have something to do with cool water on your face. That's a trigger that lowers your metabolism. The colder the water, the more dramatic the improvement in breath holding. It also seems to be connected to water pressure on your body. A slower metabolism means your air supply lasts longer."

"What's the effect on you?" I asked.

"You mean, how long can I hold my breath above water versus below water?"

I nodded.

"Above water, with proper preparation, I can go two minutes. Below water, two and a half minutes. I believe I'll eventually get to three."

"You said 'proper preparation' for holding your breath. What's that?"

"You breathe deeply for a few minutes. That helps get rid of excess CO-two - carbon dioxide - which is the gas our metabolism produces. Carbon dioxide is also the gas that produces our breathing response, what's known in the business as respiratory drive. When we have more carbon dioxide in our system, we have a stronger desire to breathe."

"I thought breathing was all about getting oxygen."

"Well, yes, we have to get enough oxygen or we pass out. But lack of oxygen doesn't give us the urge to breathe. It's some kind of quirk of evolution. It's the buildup of carbon dioxide that makes us crave more air. If we were to breathe air without oxygen, we'd still get rid of carbon dioxide, which would make us feel comfortable. For example, we'd feel comfortable breathing pure nitrogen, the main component of air, because we'd still get rid of our CO-two. But we'd pass out from no oxygen. And then we'd eventually die."

"Interesting," I said. "The mechanism that drives us to breathe isn't about taking in oxygen, it's about getting rid of carbon dioxide. So diving brought you to meet Daniel Callahan."

"Yeah. I was working as a librarian in Monterey, which, it turns out, is where Daniel is from. Anyway, I got notice that the branch library I was in had lost sufficient funding and would be closing. They thought most of us could find jobs at other libraries, but I thought it might be a good time for a major life change. I'd been reading philosophy, and there's this thing in philosophy about transformative experiences, which basically says that you can't think your way to a major life change. You have to have the actual experience. And I… Oh, never mind. I get off on these tangents. Anyway, I'd gotten involved in freediving. Mostly in Monterey Bay. I wondered about finding new diving territory. And I realized that of all the freediving places and competitions, there's almost nothing going on with high-altitude diving. So I got to thinking about Tahoe. Like maybe I could be on the cutting edge of something for once in my life. I did a little research and learned about these specialty scuba divers who use new techniques to go deeper than ever before, especially at high altitude."

"That makes me remember something," I said. "I once had a case that involved a scuba diver in Tahoe. She talked about how the bends happen more readily at high altitude. The metaphor was that when you open a Coke at high altitude, it bubbles more than when you open it at sea level."

Mae nodded. "Less atmospheric pressure makes it so more dissolved gas bubbles out of the Coke. The same thing happens with your blood. It's supposed to be a very painful way to die."

"As a freediver, you're not breathing compressed air. So you wouldn't end up with much dissolved gas from only one lungful, right?"

"Right. As a result, we don't have to make decompression stops. We're down and back so fast, there isn't much time for air to dissolve in our blood. A single deep breath doesn't put us at risk for the bends. But the other problem with deep diving does affect us. And that is Nitrogen Narcosis."

"What they call the rapture of the deep, right?"

Mae smiled. "Right. When you go very deep, more nitrogen dissolves in your blood, and too much nitrogen in your brain causes you to lose your ability to think clearly. They refer to it as rapture because nitrogen narcosis makes you happy as you die. To prevent that, scuba divers who go really deep use exotic air mixtures with helium and other gases that replace nitrogen. But freedivers don't get to use exotic air mixtures. I've heard some scary stories from freedivers who lost all common sense and couldn't figure out how to pull the cord that inflates the flotation vest that brings them back up. Or maybe they didn't even care if they came back up."

"So you came to Tahoe to learn about diving at high altitude?"

"Yes. I'm embarrassed to say I haven't done more than a few dives in Tahoe. You can't just go and do free dives by yourself. You need a group. People to trade off tasks. You need a boat. People to run the boat. You need to set up the lines and the markers. Timing and watching. It's not safe to freedive by yourself. And there are very few freedivers up here to work with."

"Have you dived the Tahoe Steamer wreck?"

"No. Actually, the only people who've done that are just those few elite scuba divers I mentioned. No freediver to my knowledge has been down to the wreck. It's too deep and the water's too cold. I'm not saying it couldn't be done. But it would take a tremendous focus and dedication. And a large financial commitment, too."

There was a sound from the bedroom.

"I better check on Daniel," Mae said.

ELEVEN

Mae held Daniel's hand as he came out and sat on Mae's couch. It was as if he had suddenly become more frail. But having someone shoot at you and take out your picture window would make anyone feel frail.

Mae went into her kitchen while I sat in one of the opposing chairs. Daniel's breathing was labored. It seemed he had no extra energy for talking. Mae brought out a tray with tea and a plate of small bread slices. I would have thought Mae would use an aluminum camping cookpot. Instead, the teapot was old-fashioned china, like something Mae might have gotten from a grandmother. It was white ceramic with pink roses and gold metallic decorative lines. The tabs of two tea bag strings hung out from the edge of the teapot lid. On the tray were three matching cups and saucers. The bread slices were aligned on a small plate from the same set. The slices were very small and looked crunchy.

"Your favorite Irish tea and Irish soda bread," Mae said. It was a touching surprise gesture for Daniel from his '60s flower-child, time-traveler renter.

She poured a cup of tea and guided Daniel's hand to its edge. He picked it up, held it high, and said, "Sláinte." The word sounded like 'slawn-che.'

"Is that 'cheers' in Irish?" I asked.

"Sort of," he said. "It's a traditional Irish toast to your health."

"I'm part Irish," I said. "Someday I'd like to go there."

"Me too," Daniel said, a nice sentiment from someone in his mid-nineties. "But my trip on this planet is coming to a conclusion, so Ireland probably isn't in my future."

"Don't say that, Daniel," Mae said. "You could be around for a very long time to come."

"I could. But I'd be a fool if I didn't look at the calendar and notice my age. Not a lot of people go much farther than me."

"Well, that may be. But let's focus on what we have now."

We all sipped tea and had soda bread. We took our time.

Eventually, Daniel turned toward me and said, "When my window was shot out, do you think the shooter was trying to kill us?"

"No. He had a laser scope. It would have been easy to kill any one of us. That suggests he was just trying to terrorize you. He wanted you off balance so that you would tell him what you know."

"It worked," Daniel said. "All that glass breaking was so loud, it upset me. Or as you young people say, it freaked me out. I didn't even hear the rifle shot."

"Yes, the breaking glass was loud," I said. "But it may be that we didn't hear the rifle shot because the shooter didn't use a firearm. It could be the shooter used an air gun."

"What's the difference?" Daniel asked.

"Most rifles use bullets propelled by explosive gunpowder. Exploding gunpowder is very loud. An air gun uses compressed air. They're sometimes called pellet guns. They can be just as deadly as firearms. But they don't make a loud crack. More of a pop."

"I remember hearing about pellet guns as a kid. You have to pump them dozens of times to build up the pressure, right?"

"On some, yes," I said. "But many modern air guns use compressed air from a cylinder."

"Like a scuba tank?" Mae said.

"Yes." I pointed out Mae's living room window. "Across the street from your house is a vacant lot," I said. "Manzanita bushes, trees, lots of cover. To the left of it is a public utility building. There's lots of places someone could hide. The softer sound of an airgun might be almost completely absorbed by the foliage."

I stood up, walked over to the big window, and looked left and right. "Can you tell me about the neighbors?"

"Mae knows them better than I do," Daniel said. "Even

though I've been here for forty years."

Mae said, "If you stand in the street and face Daniel's house, on the right is an old log cabin from way back. The owner comes up from the Bay Area. Just one week in August, mostly. His name is John something. To the right of that cabin is the Birklands'. They're retired. Kind of old. Sixties or seventies. They're pretty normal. But they argue a lot. Mostly about money. To the left of my house are two vacation rentals, mostly empty in the spring and fall, and mostly rented by young people summer and winter. Past them is a blue house where Carter Sampson and Ed Filusch live. Ed is the guy you saw fixing Daniel's door. Ed and Carter are roommates. A little younger than me. Renters like me."

Because they were in the common age demographic for violent crimes, I was interested.

"What does Carter do?" I asked.

"Carter is a mechanic at Heavenly. He fixes chairlifts and such. A prime job from what I've heard. And while being a handyman like Ed sounds like a bare-bones living, he does pretty well."

"Hobbies or other interests?"

"Carter is a sports guy. Any sport, all the time. He's real big. Actually, as you probably noticed, Ed is big too. But Carter is pro-football big, moves fast, has an aggressive manner. Whereas Ed is help-you-move-your-couch big. Strong but not coordinated like an athlete. Carter is kind of a hothead, always provoking. Ed is mellower. He likes to watch movies on his laptop. Carter calls him Eddy. Ed doesn't seem to mind. Or maybe he does, but he realizes that with a guy like Carter, it's best to do whatever it takes to get along."

"Are they buddies?"

"Not really. Carter's buddies are all sports guys. Most of Carter's buddies ride Harleys like Carter. Whereas, I don't think Ed has any friends. And because he's so quiet and a loner, it makes sense. Who'd want to hang around with a guy who won't talk?"

Mae sipped some tea. "Ed once told me that the only sport he could ever imagine doing was swimming, because it doesn't require so much eye-hand coordination. Recreational swimming. So I invited him to come to the rec pool with me. He said no, because he didn't know how to swim. That was a surprise. I pointed out that lots of the people at the pool aren't good swimmers, so he could just have fun in the water. Then he admitted he was afraid of the water. Just like Daniel."

Daniel made a dismissive wave of his hand. "I'm not afraid of water. Unless you put me in a pool or lake."

Mae made a little, forced chuckle. "Oh, Daniel, you're funny. That's like saying you're not afraid of dogs unless someone brings you next to one."

"That's true, too. Anyway, I don't call it fear. It's reasonable precaution. Water can kill you. Dogs can too."

Mae turned back to me. "I became a little pushy with Ed and encouraged him to sign up for the learn-to-swim class. He resisted because he said he didn't want to take a class with little kids. But when I explained that they have a class for adults, he signed up."

"I notice that Ed has a knee problem of some kind. Does that make it harder to learn swimming?"

"I don't think so. His knee looks okay to me. But apparently it hurts from some old injury. So Ed wears an ace bandage to give extra support. It's like his vision. He struggles to see, but it doesn't prevent him from doing anything."

"Is he swimming now?"

"Not quite. He's gone to class three times. He told me it was like following my lead as a freediver because they had everyone practice holding their breaths and going underwater. It's all about getting comfortable with water and realizing that it won't hurt you."

We talked some more, getting to know each other. All three of us probably saw the situation as an effort to make Daniel feel more comfortable after the life-changing effects of a home invasion and physical assault, and now the shooting of his window.

Mae said she'd call neighbor Ed in the morning and see how soon he can get to Daniel's window. "He's one of those types that gets up real early. In the meantime," she added, "I can go over and find something to cover up the window."

"I'll help."

"Is that okay, Daniel? It shouldn't take long."

"Yes. Thank you. I'll be right here in this chair."

Mae and I went back to Daniel's. We spent some time sweeping up all the glass. The only possible window covering that Mae could find was a bedspread. So we used a staple gun to attach it around the perimeter of the window. If the breeze wasn't too strong, it would possibly keep out bats and other critters. Multiple times, Mae looked out toward her house, no doubt worrying about Daniel.

When we walked back to Mae's, it was early evening. I said I'd be in touch and left her with Daniel.

I thought I'd see if Carter and Ed were home.

I remembered that Ed had a white pickup with built-in tool boxes, and Mae had said that Carter Sampson rode a Harley. I walked to the Jeep, pet Spot, told him I had one more stop to make, and continued to their house. Both the Harley and Ed's pickup were parked on the street.

The house where Carter Sampson and Ed Filusch lived was a narrow, blue two-story in the shape of an L. There was a covered porch at the inside corner. On the porch were two old wicker chairs and a Weber barbecue. A large black cat was perched on the railing of the porch. It watched me as I walked up to the house. As I approached, I expected the cat to run and hide. Instead, it got down in a crouch as if to leap and attack me. Its jade green eyes looked so intense that I kept my eyes on it as I knocked on the door.

From inside came the sound of a baseball game, the crowd cheering, and the announcer calling the play by play.

The door opened. A large man with short, spiked, blond hair said, "Yeah?" He was as tall as me and half again as thick and looked as tough and fit as a jaguar. He held a bottle of Miller beer in his left hand. His breath suggested there were many empties somewhere nearby.

"Hi," I said. "Are you Carter Sampson?"

He nodded.

"I'm Owen McKenna. I'm an investigator looking into an assault on your neighbor down the street. I'd like to ask you and your roommate some questions, please."

He frowned.

"Routine neighbor stuff," I said. "People or vehicles you may have noticed in the neighborhood. Like that."

"This would be about Mr. Callahan, the old blind guy?"

"Yes."

Sampson glanced over his shoulder. He called out, "Yo, Eddy, wake up. We've got a guy out here wants to ask some questions about your house repair client. Never mind it's the bottom of the ninth for me and beauty-rest time for you." Sampson lifted his bottle and drained it. He turned his head back toward the house, lifted his chin and made a sound not unlike a howling wolf. "Eddeeeeeeeeee!"

The cat jumped off the railing and disappeared around the back of the house.

"Gimme a sec," Sampson said. He walked inside, leaving the door open. Across the living room was a giant TV. The White Sox pitcher threw a fastball. The Yankees' batter hit it deep into left field. "Eddy!" Carter shouted from the kitchen. "Get your butt out of bed and come down here. Y'all got civic duty calling. When the cop man wants info, you best 'fess up to your crimes."

I heard some noises. Sampson returned with a full beer, walked past me down to the end of the porch and sat on one of the wicker chairs. "I don't need to watch the Yankees earn another kill notch on their belts." He took a long draw of beer, his throat making cartoonish glug, glug, glug sounds.

Ed appeared in the doorway. He was wearing a T-shirt and boxer shorts and black socks inside slip-on Vans. His eyes were obscured by the thick glasses, but they looked very sleepy.

"Hi, Ed," I said. "You and I met at Daniel Callahan's. I'd like to ask some questions."

He nodded, walked over, and sat in the other wicker chair.

I hitched my hip on the porch railing, one leg up and bent.

"I'm wondering about anything unusual in the neighborhood these last few days," I said.

Carter shrugged. "Ain't seen nothin,'" he said.

"A neighborhood has a routine and a standard cast of

characters. I'm looking for the odd item. Persons. Vehicles. Arrivals and departures at unusual times. Sounds in the middle of the night."

I watched both of them. Ed was silent and impassive. Carter Sampson drank beer.

"Sorry, dude," Sampson said. "This neighborhood is like a dead zone in the ocean. There's fish jumping everywhere else. But this reef is a bleached out reef. Nothing ever happens."

"Are you a diver?"

Sampson shrugged again. "Tried it a few times. Took a lesson in Grand Cayman once. Saw these monster rays with ten-foot wingspans."

"Have you ever dived in Tahoe?"

"Once. Went down at Emerald Bay State Park. It's like, one of the only underwater state parks. I saw an ancient pickup sitting on the bottom. Trust me, seeing a sunken pickup is not worth freezing your ass off."

"Do you know any divers who are interested in the Tahoe Steamer?"

"The shipwreck? No. What's the point? Someone said it's down so far, it's dark down there. Nothing to see in the dark."

"Mr. Callahan witnessed the scuttling of the Tahoe Steamer in nineteen forty. Can either of you think of anyone who has mentioned Mr. Callahan?"

Sampson shook his head and drank more beer. Ed Filusch had no reaction.

"Ed knows Mr. Callahan," I said. "What about you, Carter? You know of him. But have you ever met him?"

"Sort of. The library lady was talking to me on the sidewalk one day when the blind dude came out of his house. She told him my name and said I was a neighbor. He just walked on by."

"Did you get an impression of him?"

Sampson shrugged. "Just an old guy. Life is easy street for him. Being blind makes things pretty sweet. Everybody looks out for you. People have sympathy. He probably gets some kind of government handout. Plus rent money from the library lady. He never has to work a real job."

"I bet he worked a job for decades," I said.

"No, I mean real work," Sampson said. "Climbing chairlift towers. Hauling cable. Lubricating bullwheels. Replacing chair cushions on thousands of chairs."

"Does either of you hunt?" I asked, changing the subject.

"You mean, shoot Bambis?" Sampson asked. He pointed toward Ed, jabbing his finger repeatedly. "Just ask Eddy, the great hunter. He can kill those furry critters faster than you can spell 'em. Go on, Eddy. Tell the cop man about your big kills."

I turned to Ed. "What kind of gun do you use, Ed?"

Ed was slow to respond.

"It's a weird gun," Sampson answered for him. "Doesn't even use bullets. Compressed air. Who'd a thunk?"

"A pre-charged pneumatic gun?" I said, looking at Ed.

He nodded.

"We think it was a PCP that was used to shoot out Daniel's window."

Ed's face showed no reaction.

"Can you think of anyone besides you who knows Mr. Callahan and also has a PCP gun?"

Ed shook his head.

Sampson said, "Takes time to get used to Mr. Talkative, here. A never-ending stream of words is Eddy."

Ed turned his head toward Sampson. For a brief moment, he had a murderous look on his face. It was so full of emotion that I could visualize him shooting Sampson.

"Ed, what kind of PCP gun do you have?"

He took his time and then mumbled some words.

"Did you say, 'Benjamin Marauder?'"

Ed nodded.

"Caliber?"

"Twenty-five."

"How do you refill it?"

"A scuba tank. Three thousand PSI."

"You can shoot a lot with the air from a scuba tank, right?"

"One scuba fill gives me fifteen rifle fills. Each rifle fill shoots twenty-four shots. That's three hundred sixty rounds."

"Is your rifle registered?"

"Yeah."

"Why'd you choose that model?"

"It's real quiet. I don't like loud noises."

"Have you fired your gun recently?"

Another nod. "There's lots of places where you can shoot in Nevada."

"Do you keep it here at this house?"

He nodded.

"When you've done work for Daniel Callahan, has he treated you fairly? Paid you promptly?"

Ed looked at the floorboards of the front porch.

"Callahan treats Ed like crapola, like he doesn't matter," Sampson said. "Give me a new door, here's your money. No neighborly love there."

I spoke to Ed. "Was Mr. Callahan mean or rude to you?"

Ed didn't respond.

"Not so much mean," Sampson said, once again answering for Ed. "He just ignores him. Ed stops everything to fix his house, but Callahan acts like, of course he should."

I turned toward Sampson. "Carter, have you ever fired Ed's gun?"

"What, now I'm a suspect?"

"It's a simple question."

"And if I don't answer, you'll tell the other cops, and they'll think it suspicious and haul me in for questioning?"

"Something like that," I said.

"Yes, I've fired Ed's gun. And a sweet piece of equipment it is, too. Laser sights make it accurate as hell. Quiet as squishing a Robin's egg. And the air tank lasts the better part of forever."

"What color is the laser sight?"

"Green, natch. The red ones are practically obsolete these days. And no, I wouldn't know how to rig an air tank to shoot a guy full of air."

That was a surprise. "You know about the body on the beach? How did you hear?"

Sampson gave me a snide smile. "I've got contacts in this

town. People talk, something like that happens."

"Who told you?"

Carter thought about it. "I don't remember. I was at a bar, I think. Guys were trading gross stories. Someone mentioned a body all blown up like a beachball."

I turned to go. "Thanks, guys. You've answered my questions. Ed, it would be good not to dispose of your rifle or any related compressed air tanks or hoses in the near future. And both of you should stay in the area. Don't suddenly decide to move away or take a long trip without telling the SLTPD about your intentions."

"So now we're suspects?" Carter said.

"No. But if you leave without notice or get rid of the rifle or accessories, you will be."

TWELVE

I called Street Casey. "Any chance you are available for a consultation this afternoon?"

"What kind would that be?" she asked, a bit of mischief in her voice.

"Well, it's been a long, hard day, and it's almost cocktail hour. I miss your warmth and intelligence and your common sense."

"Common sense...," Street said. "Every woman's dream description."

"Did I mention your sensuous beauty and animal heat radiating like a hot star, your gravity pulling me irresistibly closer and closer until my orbit is doomed to fall into your clutches?"

There was a pause. "Better," she said. "You could come to my place for hors d'oeuvres. I've just got a few more insect samples to label and refrigerate."

"Just to be sure... You're not talking chocolate-covered grasshoppers, are you?"

"No. Although insects have more protein and fiber than other snacks by far, something some cultures around the world know."

"Good for them," I said.

"You're not enthusiastic. That makes me think you're coming for work, not insect treats."

"Possibly. Not a lot of work. But a question. Something that might utilize your microscope."

"Definitely work. Okay. Fifteen minutes?"

I stopped at my office to check for messages and then drove the short distance down Kingsbury Grade and pulled into the lot where Street had her entomology laboratory. Spot and I got out, and I retrieved the broken piece of wood from under the Jeep's cargo mat.

As Spot and I approached her lab door, Street's Yellow Lab, Blondie, started a frenetic barking. Not the warning kind but the anticipation kind. She couldn't see Spot coming, but she knew anyway. For his part, Spot was doing the little bounce on his toes.

The door opened before I reached it, and Blondie shot out. She jumped up on her rear legs, hit Spot hard with her paws to his chest, and then ran into the forest knowing that Spot would give chase. Blondie also knew that despite Spot's high speed on a straightaway, he couldn't catch her dodging through the woods.

I gave Street a kiss and hug, and we went inside.

"Busy day?" she asked as she lifted a tray of little glass jars and carried it over to one of her fridges.

"Traumatic, actually." I told her about meeting Mae and Daniel, and then, later, how I went to see Mallory at El Dorado Beach. I mentioned the tattooed body that turned out to be Daniel's relative.

"And when I went back to Daniel's house to ask about the dead man, his assailant called on a burner phone that he'd left in the couch. In order to get Daniel to talk, he threatened Daniel and then shot out his living room window while..."

"Owen! What are you saying?! You've been shot at!"

"Just one shot that we know of."

"My God, Owen, is everyone okay? Daniel and the woman? Mae? Is she okay?"

"Yes. They were both pretty upset. But I think she and Daniel are both okay. He's staying at her house."

"What about his house?"

"The local handyman fixed his door. I imagine he will replace the window as well."

Street looked traumatized herself, her brow a deep network of lines.

I hugged her for a long minute.

"The shooter could have followed you!" she suddenly said. "Blondie and Spot are in the woods! We should get them inside!"

"I don't think you need to worry," I said as I walked to her door. "The whole point of the shooting was to scare Daniel into telling what he knows. It worked. Daniel explained all that he remembered. Nevertheless, we can bring our animal friends closer to the cave entrance."

I stepped outside and used the whistle that means treats. There was no response. I walked to the edge of the building and whistled again.

This time, Spot and Blondie came running up. They were panting from effort, but still had plenty of energy. Blondie was jumping up and giving Spot double-paw hits to his chest.

Once inside, I shut and locked Street's door. Street got the dogs calmed a bit.

"I'm so sorry for all of you," Street said. "Maybe you should just sit and have a drink and a hot shower."

"Yeah."

"But first, what did you want to check out?" Street asked.

I picked up the broken wood from where I'd set it on the floor just inside her door. "This is a piece of Daniel Callahan's front door. It's from where the door was kicked in." I held up the wood, angling it so Street's ceiling lights would give it illumination. "I noticed that there are a couple of threads caught in the broken wood splinters. From their placement, it occurred to me that they could be from the assailant's sock or pants cuff. I wondered if you could look at the threads under one of your microscopes. If you could get a closeup photo of the threads, maybe I could show them to a person who knows fabric. I doubt it could lead anywhere, but you never know."

Street reached for the wood and looked at it up close. She frowned. "I see. Let me have a look under the scope."

Street took the broken wood over to one of her microscopes, a type with two eyepieces for a 3D image so she could see insects in glorious magnification. She had other microscopes that she used to look at slides with invisible cells, amoebas or whatever. This microscope was for the bigger little stuff. She rolled back the lens device so that it wouldn't get damaged, and positioned the frayed, splintered wood under it. Bit by bit, she turned the knob that brought the lens closer.

"I see some wood splinters," she said. "And some threads." She turned another knob. "Zooming in, I see they are fabric threads. Let me go closer." She turned the knob another notch. "Lots of stuff, here. Mostly, it's detritus. Lint and chunks of organic matter. Ah, here we are. I've found a bug."

"Insects in the wood? From the burglar's sock, maybe."

"Maybe. But it's not an insect. It looks like a mite."

I had heard the word before, but I didn't know what it meant. "What's a mite?"

"A mite is an arachnid. Not an insect. It's distantly related to spiders and scorpions. This guy looks like a type of mite that attacks citrus. It's called a Silver mite." She stared through the binocular eyepieces, adjusting another knob.

"Because it's silver colored?"

"No. Silver mites attack lemons. They get their name because they cause the lemon peel to become silvery."

"So this is one of the infamous bugs that attacks our food supply," I said.

"Yeah. They are a problem, but not as bad as their cousins, the Rust mites."

"Named because they make lemon peels rusty?"

"You could be an arachnid specialist," she said.

"Are they ugly?"

"Well, you're talking to an entomologist," she said. "So my idea of beauty is not shared by many."

"But you could still make a judgement. Are these mites ugly?"

"Yes."

"I can't imagine spending much time near something like mites." I said.

"Don't be too turned off. Most people have mites living on them. Demodex mites live in your eyelash follicles."

"Live in them?" I said.

"Yeah."

"You're saying I have bugs living in my eyelids? Or they live in other people's eyelids?"

"In most people's eyelids. You probably wouldn't want to know the details."

"Sure, I would."

"I'm not so sure," Street said.

"Try me."

"Is this a dare?" Street stared at me.

"Yeah."

"Okay. First I should say that Demodex mites are very small."

"I figured as much. So nothing they do could be that unsettling."

"The mites can leave your eyelash follicles and crawl around on your eyelids. Especially at night when you sleep. They like the dark. But mostly they live inside your eyelash follicles."

"Inside."

Street nodded. "Right."

"Which means what, exactly?"

"It means that while inside your eyelash follicles, they do all the stuff of living. They eat. Dead skin cells, mostly. They excrete in your follicles. They mate, lay their eggs, all that sort of stuff."

"Wait. You're saying that mites have sex while they are inside my eyelash follicles."

Street made a solemn nod.

"You're right. I didn't want to know all that."

"That's what I said. But you told me to tell you," Street said.

"I shouldn't have," I said. "As a scientist, you must have shockproof, titanium armor. If you want to be happy, it's better to have an ignorant view of the world. Where all is sunny, and the grass is green, and the flowers and hummingbirds cavort as if in a Disney movie, and there are no critters having sex inside of me."

"You won't find a Disney fantasy with mites," Street said.

"So I gather. The inside of my eyelash follicles is not sunny."

"No. Neither are mine."

"So we carry these critters around with us," I said. "Do they harm us?"

"Not much, as far as we've been able to tell."

"Except emotionally."

Street took her time responding. "Just knowing about them makes you, what?"

"Queasy."

She nodded. "Me, too. A little bit. But I remind myself of all the other parasites that live on and in us. Arachnids and insects, too."

"Which you won't tell me about, now," I said.

"Now that I know you get queasy over a few little mites, maybe not."

"Thanks."

Street reached a tweezer toward the splintered wood, carefully pulled out the threads, and put them in a vile. She labeled the vile and added it to her fridge.

When she was done, I said, "One thing I should mention is that the shooter threatened me over the phone. He mentioned you."

"In what way?"

"He said he knew where you lived and worked."

Street started as if she'd experienced a slap. "But of course, you won't drop your investigation."

"I will if you want me to. And I don't mean that to seem like a baited statement. I would go for the idea, but I might be able to capture this guy, which would be a very good thing. If I don't pursue him, this bad guy might go on wreaking destruction."

"Then you should keep going."

"Are you sure?"

"I have Blondie. You and Spot come by frequently. I keep my doors locked. At night I pull the blinds. During the day, I pull the sheer drapes. I've been through this before. It comes with the territory."

"The territory being a boyfriend in law enforcement?"

"Yeah."

"You could go away. Take a vacation."

"I appreciate it, but I've got work. You've warned me. That's enough to make me prepared."

"Do you want Spot and me to stay?"

"Thanks, but no. I'll be careful. I promise."

I stood up to go. "Thanks so much for your help. I now have a lead in the form of a mite found in Daniel Callahan's door, a mite that attacks lemon trees. But I'm not sure how to follow it."

"I know of an arachnid specialist. I'll contact him tomorrow and see what he thinks."

"This bug science is pretty hot stuff, huh?" I said.

"Like - what were your words - something like animal heat and gravity pulling you closer and closer until you fall into my clutches?"

"Yeah. Like that. Maybe we should do something about that."

"When you next stop by."

THIRTEEN

The next morning, I called Street and told her I was headed off to learn about the dead man, Colin Callahan, whose body had washed up on El Dorado Beach.

"You'll still be careful about locking doors and such," I said.

"Yes. But I am heading out. I called the woman you told me about, Daniel's neighbor Mae. I've been thinking how she's sort of all alone in helping Daniel. That would be no big deal in normal times. But with this violent assault, these are extraordinary times for her. I thought it would be good for her to get some support. So we're having lunch at Artemis, a little Greek restaurant over by the "Y" in South Lake Tahoe."

"Good idea. And kind of you. Be vigilant."

We said our 'I love you's' and hung up.

I'd gotten Colin Callahan's address off his driver's license: 910 Nocturne St., Citrus Heights, which was a residential area in the urban/suburban area east of Sacramento.

From my cabin on the East Shore of Tahoe, I thought the fastest route was Truckee to Interstate 80, up and over Donner Summit, then down the west slope of the Sierra. As always, traffic was heavy, with enough big rigs and summer tourists to fill eight lanes even though there were only four.

I turned off on Sunrise, drove south a couple of miles, and then zig-zagged over to Nocturne.

Colin's address was on a block filled with townhouse buildings laid out such that the connecting walkways ambled this way and that through plantings of bushes and trees and around patios outfitted with barbecues in case the residents wanted to have cookouts. It reminded me of a condo-style hotel, not fancy, but nice and with a homey feel.

Each building had eight units. Unit 910 was on the lower level of building H. I drove to a distant corner of the closest lot, where there were three parking spaces partially under the convenient shade of a large oak. I parked so that I was two-thirds in one space and one-third in another and completely in the shade. I hoped to leave before the residents all came home from work. I left all the windows open. It wasn't the standard security procedure to protect your vehicle from smash-and-grab break-ins, but my old Jeep posed no temptation except possibly the excitement of petting a dog that was substantially bigger than a mountain lion.

When I got out, Spot looked at me with droopy bedroom eyes, then lay his head down on his front paws.

Colin Callahan's door was inset into a corner and tucked under the deck of the entrance of the unit above. Despite the sun of midday, the light didn't penetrate to the door. I knocked.

After a minute, the door opened. A man in his early thirties stood there wearing shorts, flip flops, and a rolled towel wrapped over his bare shoulders. His hair and skin were wet as if he'd just gotten out of the shower or a pool. He was holding a Monster Energy drink.

"Yeah, what?" he said. "I ain't buyin' nothin'."

The man had a hard body, electric blue eyes, and cheekbones sharp enough to cut your knuckles if you struck him. He looked like a movie star. But his squeaky voice and bad diction made him sound like he wasn't smart enough to run a vacuum cleaner.

"Hi, I'm Owen McKenna and you are…" I held out my hand to shake.

He scowled at me. I couldn't tell if he was excessively dense or calculating.

I waited.

"Brand."

"Brand," I repeated.

"Jay Brandon Morse. My friends jus' call me Brand." He shook my hand.

"Hi, Brand. I'm looking into the death of Colin Callahan. I have this as his address. Was he your roommate?"

The man stared at me as if he didn't comprehend. "Whoa, Colin died?"

I made a single nod.

"Really? Dead? That's real bad for me. Now I'll never get paid. I can't believe it."

"Colin owes you money? How much did you lend him?"

"Three hundred seven dollars. But I didn't borrow him the money. That would be dumb. I invested it. He said I'd double my money. It was guaranteed."

"Doubling your money?" I said.

"Yeah. I'm getting six hundred seven dollars back. 'Cept, now I pro'bly won't get it."

"If your money doubled, you'd get six hundred fourteen dollars back."

The man frowned and squinted like he thought I'd said something suspicious.

"Anyway, I need that money. I get twelve hundred a month as manager, but I have to make it pay for everything."

"That would be hard, paying rent and all."

"Not counting rent. I get free rent as manager. It's the bonus for my responsibility. That's the management package. The free-rent bonus and my salary."

"You manage this condo complex?"

"No. There's eight condos in the building. I just take care of this one and the one next door." He pointed at the wall behind the TV. "I have my roommates and there's three renters next door. I collect the rent, and I do the chores."

"No doubt that's a lot of work," I said even though it didn't seem like much.

"Just taking out the trash is a big job. My roommates fill garbage cans full of beer cans and pizza boxes and other stuff. They're supposed to help. But they're always off at work. Or too tired 'cuz they just got home from work."

I looked past him at the condo. The living room was dominated by the giant TV screen. An aged, puffy, faux-leather couch sprawled along the longest wall of the room. One squat leg was broken and had been replaced by a red brick. Two worn metal folding chairs were at the end of the room. Between them was an overturned cardboard box with some car magazines on it. On one of the chairs were some dirty socks.

"Where do your roommates work?"

The man stared off, visualizing. "Tom works construction. He's a framing carpenter. Jordan works yard maintenance. He says it's back-breaking. And I'm thinking, it's carpenters who do real work. Lumber is heavy, right? But anyone can push a mower and rake leaves."

"Probably still back-breaking," I said. "What did Colin do?"

Brand rolled his eyes. "Yer gonna laugh. Colin was a treasure hunter. He'd track down stuff that was cheap. He had a word for it. Undervalued. How's that for fancy speak? He'd buy it and then resell it on Craigslist and eBay."

"He didn't have a job?"

"No. He said jobs tied your hands and took up all your time. You couldn't do stuff if you were stuck in a job. As long as he pays the rent, I don't care. Jacky Wormack stopped paying the rent. I raised it twenty-five bucks, and he takes a walk. Moves to Merced to live with his old man. All to save twenty-five bucks a month. Now I got Jordan. I hope he stays."

"Where do you work?"

"I just told you. I'm the manager. It's a big responsibility."

"What company do you work for?" I'd never heard of a manager who just managed two condos.

He shook his head. "No company. Jus' my ma. She owns these two condos. She's a tough boss to work for. She calls herself a real tough nut. Says I better be a tough nut with the renters, too. Now with Colin dead, I'll have to clean out his room and show the place to other renters. I jus' did that with Wormack's stuff. Talk about chores. So how'd Colin die? Pro'bly drown-ded to death searching for sunken treasure. Am I right?"

"I don't know. His body was found washed up on a beach in Tahoe."

"Wow, that's like a creep-out movie."

"Was Colin looking for a particular treasure?" I asked.

"Yeah. He found some letters from his aunt. No, not his aunt.

His aunt's aunt. How's that for weird?"

"Yeah, that's weird," I agreed. "But an aunt's aunt would be the aunt of one of his parents, right?"

Brand frowned. "I never heard Colin talk about any parent. I don't think he had parents. Maybe they died when he was really young. At least, he never said anything about them."

"How'd he get letters from his aunt's aunt?"

"Someone sent him a footlocker from some relative who died. So Colin reads the stuff and starts talkin' about sunken treasure. He said he was going to find it."

"What gave him an idea about treasure? Did you see what the letters said?"

"No way. Colin was all about privacy."

"But he told you about the sunken treasure."

Brand looked confused. "Yeah. That wasn't part of privacy. That was like a guy bragging on a secret."

"Is that when he got his shipwreck tattoo?"

"Yeah."

"You knew the tattoo was about a shipwreck?"

Brand hesitated, and his sharp cheekbones flushed. "Yeah. That's what he said."

"Who was the tattoo artist?"

"I dunno. Colin went away for a few days and came back acting all sore. I asked why. So he took off his shirt and showed me. Man, what a dumb tattoo. All these colors that look weird on skin. He said it was a picture of a shipwreck. But all I saw was weird shapes. He had this tube of ointment, and he wanted me to rub it on his back. Talk about gross."

"Why'd he get the tattoo?" I asked.

"How would I know? He was jus' into everything 'bout shipwrecks."

"What was the ship?" I asked.

"I dunno. But it wasn't an ocean ship. It was a lake ship. You said his body was on a Tahoe beach. So the shipwreck is pro'bly in Lake Tahoe, right?"

"What kind of car does Colin drive?"

"A brown, ninety-seven Volvo." Brand started nodding his

head. "I know. A regular guy most likely drives a used pickup, right? Ford or Chevy. Mine's a two thousand four Silverado. Four-wheel-drive. White. Chrome wheels. I've almost got it paid off. But Colin is pretty weird that way, driving a Volvo. Go figure."

"I drive an old Jeep," I said. "Is that weird?"

"No, that's not weird. That's pretty cool. At least you've got four-wheel. Like if you go up to Tahoe in the winter."

Behind Brand, on the side of the kitchen counter, was a book. The title on the spine said, 'Sanford Meisner on Acting.'

I asked, "Who's the actor?"

Brand was slow on the uptake. "What do you mean?"

I pointed behind him. "That book about acting."

Brand turned around. "Oh. That's Colin's. He was, like, a dreamer. He thought maybe he'd go to Hollywood after he found his sunken treasure. He could use the treasure money to pay for a movie. And he'd be the star. He even took acting lessons way back."

"Where did Colin park his car?"

"In the condo lot. Where else?"

"Can you show me where?"

"No. You don't get a regular space here. You park wherever you can find a space."

"Have you looked for Colin's car?"

"Why would I do that?"

"Because he hasn't come home for awhile," I said.

"Colin never came home for awhile. That was what he did. Go away for awhile. Come back, pay rent, go away again. It's a treasure hunter thing."

"Did you and Colin get along?"

"Sure. Why not?"

"Because you sound removed about him," I said. "You don't sound like he's a buddy."

"These guys are my roommates, not my homeboys. And I already said that Colin was weird. But we got along. Like, brothers can argue but still be brothers, right? You always got your bros."

Brand took a deep breath. He clenched and relaxed his fists as if following a relaxation exercise he'd learned in a class.

FOURTEEN

I watched the man with the movie star looks, trying to sense whether he was stupid and sincere, or smart and deceptive. I wondered why he hadn't thrown me out of his house.

I asked, "When did Colin get the tattoo?"

"A couple of weeks ago. Colin isn't into going shirtless, so what's the point of having his back tatted up, anyway? When I first saw it, I thought, 'dude, you've got the art display and you ain't ugly, so show it off.' But he's shy. It's kind of pointless. If I had a tat, I'd show it off. But I'm saving my body for the future. Pretty soon, it will be cool to not have tats."

"Did Colin ever mention Ivan Manfred? He goes by the name Ink Maestro?"

"No. What's a maestro?"

"It's like a master. He presents himself as a tattoo master."

"That's weird. Why not jus' say tattoo master?"

"Good question," I said. "Where do you think Colin might have gone to find tattoo artists?"

Brand shrugged his shoulders. "They're on every corner. There's one a half block from here. Or maybe he went to one of the tattoo expos. I heard about a big one in Oregon. Then you could meet them and see if they're real."

"What's that mean, real?" I asked.

"Like, if they're good. One guy told me about motel inkers."

I raised my eyebrows.

"Tat lowlifes. They haul their machines in their pickups. They go from place to place, and sell their ink cheap. I heard you get killer diseases from those guys. My body is my temple. I don't want a disease."

"Do you think Colin went to one of those motel inkers?"

"Naw. Colin was always spending like he was upscale. Lots

of money. He pro'bly went to a real artist with a clean studio and extra clean needles. What's that called. Sterilized."

"Can you give me the names of his friends?"

Brand guffawed. "Colin didn't have friends. He knew some shipwreck hunters. I wouldn't call them friends. More like scammers trying to get you to give them money so they could go scuba diving and search for treasure."

"Like you giving Colin money?"

"I told you, that was an investment."

"Did he ever find sunken treasure?"

"Naw. Well, him and a bunch of other guys went diving off Cabo. There was something there. Maybe a wreck. The other guys thought it was nothing. Colin said it was special. But all he brought up from the bottom was a chunk of wood. He called it Spanish galleon wood. That's a ocean ship. He dried out the wood and cut it up into pieces and varnished them and sold them on eBay. Genuine galleon paperweights, he called them."

"When did you last see him?"

Brand thought about it. "A few days ago. He comes and goes. Mostly goes. I don't think he slept here barely at all in the last month."

"Where has he been?"

"I don't know. I s'pose he was looking for the treasure in the aunt's aunt's letters."

"If you had to guess at the treasure," I said, "what do you think it was?"

"'I don't know. But I could tell it was about a sunken ship because I can detect stuff. I'm like those TV detectives."

I couldn't tell if Brand was putting me on or not. But if he wasn't sincere, he did a good job of acting.

"Did Colin mention the names of his aunt? Or her aunt?"

Brand shook his head.

"You said some relative shipped Colin a footlocker that had the letters inside. Did Colin keep the letters in the footlocker?"

"No. Colin kept them in his little briefcase. It's made of cloth. He called it his purse. Far as I can tell, he slept with it under his pillow. So there must have been some kind of treasure in those letters. Or maybe a treasure map!"

"What about the names of any people in the letters? Did Colin mention their names?"

The man shook his head in an exaggerated motion. "Nope. No names. Wait. He did say the aunt's aunt had a boyfriend named Frank. So how would he know that? It would have to be in one of the letters, right?"

"Makes sense," I said. "Was there anything else Colin said that you can remember?"

Brand screwed up his face, trying, apparently, to think.

"Bakersfield," he said.

"What about it?"

"Colin said something about Bakersfield."

"You don't remember what it was about?" I asked.

"No. But maybe Bakersfield was where the aunt's aunt lived. Or maybe her boyfriend Frank lived there."

"Can I see the footlocker?"

Brand stepped back and regarded me carefully. "What's your name again?"

"Owen McKenna. I'm a private investigator."

Brand's eyes got wide. "Like a TV detective?"

"Sort of."

"On TV, they have to have a warrant to look at stuff. A warrant signed by a judge."

"I don't need a warrant if you show me the trunk."

"Why?"

"Because a warrant isn't necessary when you give consent to my search. And if you give me your consent, I'll tell you where the treasure is."

Brand frowned. "That sounds like a bribe."

"It is a bribe. You let me look at the footlocker, I tell you where the treasure is."

"So there really is treasure?"

"From what we can tell. We don't know what it is. And we haven't gotten to it, yet. It's in a hard-to-reach place."

"I don't get it. It's hard to reach? How could that be? A locked safe?"

"Sort of."

He looked puzzled, like a little kid trying to do long division in his head.

"I'll tell you," I said again. "But it's a trade. You show me the footlocker first."

Brand frowned, thinking hard. "Okay. But you gotta promise."

"I promise." I was trying to think of reasons why Brand would agree to show me the footlocker. Did he really want to know what I might tell him? Or was he just an eager provider of privileged information, showing off to whatever audience he could find, no matter if it was just a stranger?

Brand turned and walked through the living room, down a short hallway. The muscles of his back rippled as he walked. They weren't bulky steroid muscles, but the kind that only come from exercise.

We went past one bedroom with an open door. "That's Tom's room. He gets his own room because he pays an extra hundred bucks a month. Easy for him because of his carpenter pay."

Brand continued to the next bedroom.

This room had two twin beds. One was unmade, sheets and blanket twisted and hanging onto the floor. The blanket on the other bed was taut as a trampoline.

"Which bed is Colin's?" I asked.

Brand pointed to the bed that was made. "That's Colin's." He swung his arm around to the messy bed. "That's Jordan's. The beds look like the guys. Jorden doesn't tuck in his shirt. His hair is like an old mop. But Colin doesn't go out without taking a shower and dressing nice. And he always combs his hair."

I thought of the way Daniel Callahan combed his hair, even though he couldn't see it.

At the end of Colin's bed was a small, low rectangular object covered with a cloth. The cloth was printed with sailing ships. Square riggers. Brand pulled off the cloth and tossed it on the bed.

The footlocker was an old, military-green metal box of the kind that soldiers put at the foot of their bunk.

"The footlocker ain't locked 'cuz there's nothing valuable in it."

"You say that with confidence as if you've personally looked through Colin's things."

Brand gave me a severe look. "I'm the manager. I have to make sure my renters are safe from meth and drugs and ninja knives and stuff like that. And no ammo. If you wanna rent from me, you can't have ammo."

"Just ammo? What about guns?"

He paused. "Guns, too."

I got down on my knees in front of the footlocker and opened it. Inside was a variety of items, some hand-embroidered linen towels, a lap blanket with an elaborate monogram, a jewelry box.

I opened the box. There were a handful of war-time, 1943 steel pennies, some necklaces and bracelets that would be nothing more than cheap costume jewelry except that some of the items were engraved with the name Elsie Callahan. There was a little velvet bag that contained a woman's high school class ring. In an envelope were several wallet-sized black-and-white photos of girls and one of a boy, all of whom looked like high school kids.

Under the linen towels was a small leather chapbook with handwritten poems. Inside the front cover was a loose slip of paper that said, 'Auntie Nora's poems.' Also tucked under the chapbook cover was a newspaper clipping about barnstorming pilots. The grainy picture showed a pilot wearing a leather helmet and goggles and standing in front of his plane. As a pilot myself, I recognized the plane as a Curtiss JN-4 biplane, known as a "Jenny," a famous World War I plane that had been produced in large numbers. The Jenny was later used by barnstorming pilots because they could take off and land from dirt runways. I recalled that Charles Lindbergh learned to fly in a Jenny before he made the first solo flight across the Atlantic, a mission partly financed by Tahoe's Vikingsholm Castle owner Lora Knight.

Under the blanket was an old picture frame with a high school diploma. The glass had a single crack that ran diagonally from corner to corner. The name on the diploma was Elsie Callahan.

The date was 1957.

There was a cloth bag and in it a small silver cup of a ceremonial design used for awards and such. The cup was engraved with a floral script.

Elsie Callahan
Valedictorian
Class of 1957
Valley High School
Bakersfield, CA

As I expected, there was nothing of value in the footlocker. Had there been - like treasure information in letters - Colin would have taken it out. As Brand looked on, I continued to recheck the items in the footlocker while I pondered the barnstorming article about Jenny airplanes.

"How long was it from the time he got the footlocker until you last saw him?"

Brand screwed up his face, apparently thinking. "The freight company delivered the footlocker on a Friday. I knew because that's the day Jordan gets off early from his yard maintenance, and he was here to sign for it. The next three nights, the footlocker was all Colin talked about. I know because we watched TV on Sunday, and Colin was like a space case. Like he didn't even see the TV. The next morning, he was gone. I haven't seen him since."

"You said Colin was studying to be an actor?" I said.

"Oh, that's just…" Brand stopped. "Yeah. He was all about, you know, doing accents and - what's it called - impressions and stuff."

"What about you? Are you an actor?"

Brand frowned. "That's funny. Someone told me that I look like an actor. But I know a guy, he acted in a car dealer commercial. And he does stand-up. You know what they pay him? Nothing. That's how much he makes. He said the commercial was an intern thing. I think that's the word when you don't get paid. So I'm going to act? I don't think so. Even if I look like an actor, it's a no brainer. I'll be a real estate manager. That way I can make real money."

"Taking care of this apartment," I said.

"And the one next door. My ma calls it a skill set. I'm like, who cares about a skill set. It's what you know how to do that counts. But she's pro'bly right. Pretty soon, I can get big bucks with a big company."

"Where did Colin hang out?"

Brand shook his head. "He doesn't hang out. Not his style. He just looks stuff up on his computer. All the time. Buried treasure. Lost treasure."

"Did he travel?"

"I don't know about travel. But he was pretty much always gone. I guess that means travel, right?"

"Does he have family? Brothers, sisters? Parents?"

"Naw. I think he said he was an only kid. Or it could be he was an orphan kid."

"Do you think that's true? Or was he just estranged from his family?"

"Strange from his family? What's that?"

"Forget it. Tell me this," I said. "Did Colin live here last Christmas?"

Brand nodded.

"Where did he go for Christmas?"

"No place. He said he didn't have a place to go. So me and him went to my ma's and then the Sacto improv. Oh, I get it. If he had a family, he'd go to their place."

My turn to nod. "Did you watch comedians at the improv?"

Brand nodded.

"Comedians are pretty much like actors, right?"

Brand shrugged. "If you say so." He paused. "So where is it?"

"What?"

"The treasure."

"Oh," I said. "It's a sunken treasure."

"Really? Just like Colin is always talking about! Where is it sunk?"

"There's a steamship at the bottom of Lake Tahoe. The

treasure is on the ship."

"What kind of treasure is it? Gold or somethin'?"

"I don't know what it is."

"Then how're you gonna get it if you don't even know what you're looking for?"

"I'm not."

"Oh, I see. You're not after the loot, you're just after his killer."

"Who said anything about a killer? I just said Colin died."

Brand was very good at his reaction. "I jus' figured that if Colin was after treasure and people like you come asking about him and treasure and then it turns out he died, that would pro'bly mean he got aced. Am I wrong?"

I regarded him for any "tells" that would suggest prevarication. His face was blank.

"No, you're not wrong. Colin was killed."

Brand made a small nod. "Figures."

I slipped the newspaper article on barnstorming back into the chapbook of Nora's poems and was replacing the stuff in the footlocker when I dropped the framed diploma.

"Oh, sorry," I said.

Brand reached down and picked it up.

As Brand's attention was diverted, I slipped the chapbook and article into my pocket.

Brand straightened, holding the diploma.

"The glass was already cracked," I said.

Brand looked at it, then looked at me as if wondering if I'd told the truth.

"I know," he finally said.

We closed the footlocker, I thanked Brand for his time, and left.

Spot was standing, head out the window, wagging. Thankfully, he was still in the shade.

"Sorry for the wait, Largeness. That's what gumshoes do. We mostly just wait."

I got in the Jeep and headed back to Tahoe.

My conversation with Brand was one of those inconclusive ones. Lots of inputs, but not necessarily reliable.

I'd heard about a kind of acting practice where the actor puts on a fictional persona and carries it to extreme. The goal is to spin a tale and create a world that is completely false yet convincing to others. The idea is that if you're employing good acting techniques, other people believe your tale.

In Brand's case, I believed some of what he told me about Colin's letters and tattoo and treasure hunting. But I didn't believe Brand was who he said he was.

As I drove, I went over what I'd learned.

Colin and Daniel Callahan both had a relative named Elsie Callahan. She was Colin's aunt, and she was Nora and Daniel's niece. Thus Daniel's sister Nora was twice removed from Colin, his aunt's aunt. However, Daniel had said Nora was his only sibling and he and Nora had no kids. So Elsie's relationship must have been another step removed. She was probably the daughter of one of Daniel's cousins. Close enough to think of the mysterious, prematurely deceased Nora as her aunt.

Elsie had kept some mementos.

Among them were the letters that had eventually come to her from Aunt Nora after Nora died. Perhaps they were handed down by one of Elsie's parents, a cousin of Nora's. Those letters suggested intrigue and possible treasure to Colin, and they probably remained hidden in Colin's purse, wherever he'd left it before he was murdered.

The chapbook of Nora's poems might contain intrigue. But it was likely they were valuable only for sentimental reasons.

I didn't feel bad about stealing the mementos from Jay Brandon Morse, the actor/landlord who went by Brand.

Daniel had more right to them than anyone else.

The most fascinating item was the newspaper article about barnstorming pilots, an article that showed a pilot in front of a Jenny plane.

Daniel had also told us that he felt that Frank was two-timing her with another girl. A girl named Jenny. Was Frank's other love a girl named Jenny? Or was it an airplane named Jenny?

The notable thing I knew about Jenny planes wasn't about the plane itself, but about an unusual postage stamp I'd read about some years before. Back in 1918, the Post Office had produced a 24-cent stamp with a picture of the airplane. But the printer had mistakenly printed a sheet of 100 with the image turned upside down. Because of their rarity, the Inverted Jenny, as the stamp is called, is very valuable.

FIFTEEN

I drove back to Tahoe. Spot and Blondie raced around in the woods behind Street's condo while I talked to Street. She was at the kitchen counter, working on food prep as we spoke.

"How did your lunch with Mae go?"

"It was good. We're alike in several ways, spending much of our lives alone, pursuing non-typical goals. And while library science seems a long way from insect science, there is common ground, a science undercurrent that operates on research and principles of knowledge and the pursuit of non-material value. Mae is, of course, much more robust than I am in physical ways, what with her freediving and such. But intellectually, we share a lot. I think we both enjoyed our lunch and will likely do it again."

I was grinning.

"What?"

"Just that when most people get together for lunch, they chat about people they know and their favorite entertainment and topical news and, dare I say, sometimes even gossip. But you and Mae find 'common ground in science that operates on research and principles of knowledge.'"

"I agree, it was not your typical lunch gossip," Street said. "I think Mae is a little like me, not very good at social skills. But we had silly fun, too."

"What was that?" Street was not given to silly fun.

"Mae told me about a phrase that is sort of the equivalent of saying 'Break a leg' to an actor before they go out on stage. When she goes freediving, and she's done her prep breathing, she shouts, 'May the devil drown!' just before she jumps in. So we riffed on that at lunch, dreaming up other scenarios for 'May the devil drown!'"

"Like dealing with a difficult boss or client?"

"Yeah." Street grinned like a young girl who's confessed to mischief. "And pretty soon, other diners were staring at us, wondering what strange people we were, shouting, 'May the devil drown!'"

"I'll remember that. It's a good banishment of evil."

"What about your day?" Street said.

I told Street about Brand and how he came across as a dumb guy who was movie-star handsome. In this case, it may have been a movie-star act. I explained about finding a book on acting in his condo, which had no other books.

"I love the concept," Street said as she worked in her kitchen, chopping vegetables for dinner. "The secret actor. Maybe he's part of a group. Maybe there are several of them doing the same thing, carrying their craft to the limit, which would include murder!"

"You have a twisted imagination."

"I know. I could be a novelist."

I showed her the chapbook of Nora's poems and the article on barnstorming pilots.

Street studied them. "When I had lunch with Mae, she told me about Daniel and how his sister Nora had a boyfriend named Frank," Street said. "Frank was a barnstorming pilot. Could this guy in the helmet and goggles be Frank?"

"That's my thought. Otherwise, it would be too much of a coincidence."

"If so, the plot has just gotten very viscous."

"Science speak for thick?"

She grinned.

I was sitting on one of the two barstools at the short counter that divided Street's kitchen from her dining nook. She was on the kitchen side, stir-frying onions. She cut up three kinds of peppers and set them next to the pan.

"While you're cooking, I could make an exploratory mission looking for wine," I said.

Street said, "I'm pleased to report that this bug scientist recently acquired a bottle of top-drawer syrah."

"Yeah?"

"Windwalker. One of those foothill wineries in the Fair Play appellation. Supposed to be very good. I've been saving it in my wine cellar."

"I could test it if I knew the location of your wine cellar."

She pointed. "In the cupboard next to the fridge is a paper grocery bag."

I opened the cupboard door and lifted out a paper bag with a wine bottle in it. "An entomologist's wine cellar," I said. "Why am I not surprised?"

"All of my premium spaces are used for storing bugs," she said.

"Of course." I got busy with her corkscrew, popped the cork, and poured the deep purple elixir into two glasses. Swirled it around and drank. It was a taste explosion.

"Here is a reason to become a wino," I said.

I held the wine out and turned, holding the glass to the light, admiring the color. My sleeve bumped Street's pepper shaker off onto the floor.

"Oh, so sorry," I said. I bent down, picked it up, and the metallic top fell off. By comparing the broken edges, I saw that the glass had sheared neatly, no chips. The top rim of the glass shaker was still screwed into the inside of the metallic top. I moistened a paper towel, mopped up the small amount of spilled pepper, and then set the shaker back on Street's counter. I balanced the metal top and its enclosed glass shaker rim on top of the jar. I slid it next to Street's fire extinguisher, the position making it less vulnerable to being bumped off.

"There. All better," I said. "No one would ever know that this pepper shaker is broken, lying in wait for the unsuspecting diner."

Street looked at the shaker as she stirred onions. "It'll be a memory test for me. The next time I want pepper, will I tip it over and dump the broken top into my food? Or will I think to set the top aside and then pour the pepper out?"

"A memory test, indeed," I said.

She sipped her wine. "Ah, good. My palate is naive, but I rate it a ninety-nine. Anyway, you think the Brand fellow is hiding something? That he's an actor playing you?"

"Maybe. But if so, he has tremendous follow through. He never once cracked."

I sipped more syrah. "I was thinking about the mite you found in those fibers from Daniel Callahan's door," I said. "You said the mite was a kind of citrus mite that attacks lemons. Does that mean it's found on lemon trees, or lemon fruit? Because if a person could get it from fruit, that could happen in thousands of places, like a grocery store. But if those little buggers are only on the trees, that would imply that the person who kicked in Daniel's door was at a citrus orchard not too long before Daniel's assault."

Street said, "That particular mite infests both lemon trees and fruit," Street said. She lifted the fry pan off the stovetop. She leaned forward and set the pan on a trivet in front of me, then handed me a fork.

"Maybe you shouldn't do that," I said.

"I just want you to test the onions and make sure they're cooked enough for the veggie stir fry I'm making."

"No, I mean you shouldn't lean forward like that. Or else fasten your top two shirt buttons. That shirt is too fitted and too undone for me to think clearly."

"You know I don't carry around a lot of distracting feminine assets."

"Shows what you know. It's not about dimension. How can I judge onions when I'm preoccupied?"

There was a bark at the door. I walked over and let the dogs in.

Spot immediately lay down. Blondie went to Street, reached her nose toward the counter, and wagged. Was she interested in cooking veggies or human amore? Her tail hit the nearest kitchen cabinet. Unlike Spot's rock 'n roll bass-drum tail, Blondie's furry tail was like the swish of a jazz drummer's brush.

"See, Blondie's not distracted," Street said. "She wants to be my onion tester, not my modesty judge." Street looked down as if to make her own judgment. She fastened one more button, stabbed a piece of onion with a fork, and handed it to me.

I ate it. "Perfect."

"I should put it in the sauce now?"

"A few more minutes on the fire. Then add it to the sauce."

"I thought you said it's perfect now."

"A few more minutes will make it perfecter."

Street put the fry pan back on the stove top. "You were saying..."

"Let me think. Maybe you should pull on a baggy sweatshirt. Now I remember. Lemon groves are mostly in the San Diego region, right? I could go there to search for the man who assaulted Daniel Callahan."

"Lemons are all over California. That's how California produces more lemons than all of Spain, France, and Italy combined. And the mites that infest lemon trees are found all over the state as well. But this particular mite may have a narrower range. Just to be sure I was on the right track, I sent a photo of the mite to an arachnologist named Marcelo Nogales at Fresno State. He's kind of known as the mite guy. Professor Nogales says this mite species is less pernicious than others, and it's quite localized. He says it turns up primarily in a long narrow strip of orchards just up from the Central Valley floor, on the west side of the valley."

"Can you show me on a map?"

Street's laptop was at the end of the counter. She opened it, tapped some keys, and brought up a map. She pointed to an area southwest of Fresno. "He said the region is on the east-facing slopes of the coastal range and stretches for a hundred miles or so."

"Based on your sense of how mites can get distributed, would it be crazy for me to drive there and poke around, hoping it was picked up in that particular area? Or do you think that mite just blew in on the wind? Or maybe it was in a grocery store?"

"I would guess there's a decent chance that the mite was picked up in the area where it lives and was brought to Tahoe by the person who kicked in Callahan's door. You're thinking of going to the orchards and asking if any Central Valley locals went to Tahoe in search of treasure on the sunken Tahoe Steamer?"

I smiled. "Something like that."

Street frowned, thinking. "You've gotten results from crazier ideas," she said.

"But you're not enthusiastic about the idea."

Street said, "I suppose you could apply that upside/downside test of yours."

"Good point. The upside of going is that there is a chance, however slight, that I get a lead on the killer. The downside is that I have to spend a day or two taking a pleasant drive through orchard country."

"Sounds like you found your answer. It would be a search that, however unlikely, could eventually lead to treasure."

"Maybe you should undo that button again. I could make a different search."

"What would you find?"

"Treasure, of course."

SIXTEEN

When my dinner with Street was over, Spot and I headed up the mountain to my cabin.

I was thinking about Colin Callahan and the stressful way he died. It occurred to me that the pathologist must have finished with the autopsy by now. But it was too late to get a report from Mallory.

My friend Doc Lee is an ER doctor at the South Shore hospital. I didn't know what his schedule was, but I knew he worked all hours, sometimes all night. I called his cell expecting to leave a message.

"Hello, Owen McKenna," he answered, getting my name off his caller ID.

"Wow, I didn't think you actually answered your phone. Are you home reading a book or something?"

"I'm on break, eating a turkey cheese bean spinach burrito in the hospital parking lot."

"I have a medical question about the autopsy on the body found at El Dorado Beach. I figured you may have heard something."

"I have. But my break isn't that long. Maybe come by at midnight when my shift is over. Remember, sometimes I get delayed an hour or two, depending on business."

"Of course. I'll find your car and wait for you there."

"I should tell you it's a new one, new color. A red Panamera."

"That's a Porsche, right?"

"That's right. You drive a Jeep. All you care about is utility. No awareness of style or beauty or poetry."

"But I spend my free time with Street."

"Good point."

"See you tonight," I said.

Spot and I were in the hospital parking lot at midnight. I let Spot out of the Jeep. We did a slow walk around the lot.

Spot always becomes hyper alert on nighttime missions. He instinctively understands the risks of night, a time when darkness renders humans vulnerable. His nose and ears were on overtime, nostrils flexing, ears turning, sampling the night scents and sounds. For a time, he focused on a dark group of trees behind the hospital. I looked to see what might have caught his attention. But I saw nothing. When I gave him a soft tug, he resisted, still watching, listening, sniffing.

Eventually, I coaxed him away toward a red Panamera in the far corner of the lot. No doubt Doc Lee placed it there in hopes of minimizing scrapes from other vehicles. Of course, dark corners in parking lots maximize the likelihood of theft or vandalism. But knowing Doc Lee, anyone who touched his ride would probably be photographed from all angles by hidden webcams, their DNA would be sampled by some surreptitious process, and the data would be uploaded to facial and DNA recognition websites. Do more than touch his car and there would be a serious response from a security team. Doc Lee was tech savvy, and he had friends in law enforcement and government, a combination that made him the wrong guy to cross.

I brought Spot over to Doc Lee's Porsche. The flashy car was low enough that Spot could rest his jaw on the roof if he wanted to. "What do you think, Largeness? Even if I could afford one of these, I don't think you'd fit inside."

"He's not going to drool on my ride, right?"

I turned and saw Doc Lee walk up.

"Maybe. Nice wheels."

"This doctor business is getting less fun. Too many rules made by bureaucrats who don't know anything about doctoring. Too many insurance requirements made by companies who care only about profits. One of the few benefits of the job is enough income for a red sports car."

"I'm surprised you got out when your shift was over."

He shrugged. "We just got a call on a rollover with injuries up on Echo Summit. So I can't go home. But I can talk until the ambulance gets here."

"Then what?"

"Then I go back under the stage lights, make some fast assessments, stabilize the wounded, then dive in."

"What's the dive part?" I asked.

"Slice and dice, stitch and sew, the usual steps."

"You say that like it's a dance performance."

Doc Lee paused. "Actually, it kind of is like a dance performance. Except I don't wear tights."

"Tights on an ER doc. There's an image to savor."

"Actually, I look good in tights. What did you call about?"

"I had a question. Commander Mallory and his crew had a body at El Dorado Beach. I was there. The body was a male, mid-thirties, with a chest blown up like a hard beach ball. The coroner was a guy I don't know. He thought the person died of something called tension pneumothorax. Can you explain?"

"Actually, I heard about it because the circumstances and details were interesting. The El Dorado County coroner is John Mercer. Smart guy and a knowledgeable sheriff's detective, but not a pathologist. The autopsy was done by Benicia Train, a pathologist who recently came to El Dorado County from San Luis Obispo. She performed the post-mortem late this afternoon. The circumstances were unusual. Yes, the victim died from tension pneumothorax. Normally, that's something that happens on one side of the body. But this was in both pleural cavities."

"Sorry, I don't know about pleural cavities."

"The pleural cavities are the compartments in the chest that contain the lungs. When a person breathes, they expand their chests. Air gets sucked in through the throat and rushes into the lungs. But if the pleural cavity gets air from another source - like air that leaks in through a hole in the chest that was caused by a bullet or a knife wound - that can keep the lung from inflating. The person is trying to breathe, but air gets pulled in through the sucking wound and ends up outside of the lung instead of inside. When that happens, it collapses the lung on that side.

Both pleural cavities? Both lungs. No working lungs means no oxygen, and you die. The air also presses against the heart and veins leading to it, preventing the heart from expanding and filling with blood to pump out to the rest of the body."

"If you get to the victim in time, what's the treatment?"

"You do a needle thoracostomy and aspirate the gas."

"Meaning you stick him with a needle and let the air out."

Doc Lee nodded.

"And when the victim is dead?" I asked.

"Same thing. In this case, Dr. Train probably collected the air in a gas sampling bag. Once the lab identifies what the gas components are, they'll have a better chance of understanding how he died."

"So the corpse I saw, rock hard with air pressure, would be like a normal corpse after Dr. Train let the air pressure out?"

"Yeah."

"Is tension pneumothorax a quick death?" I asked.

"Depends. But fast or slow, it's painful."

"Did the pathologist find anything indicating the cause of the tension pneumothorax?"

"Maybe. The victim had thick chest hair. Train found two tiny punctures on the man's chest. They were effectively hidden by the chest hair."

"What does that mean?" I asked, not sure I was understanding.

"Merely that the puncture wounds could be the source of the air in the man's pleural cavities. In fact, Dr. Train does believe that's how the air got into the man's chest."

"But tiny wounds wouldn't be a sufficient source for more than a tiny amount of air, right?"

"True, unless the air was introduced under pressure."

I thought about what he said. "How does Dr. Train think that could happen?"

Doc Lee held his hand out in the dark, his thumb and forefinger spaced about an inch and a half apart. "You know those air inflation needles that are used to put air into basketballs and such?"

"Sure."

"If you had a pressurized source of air attached to a basketball inflation needle…"

Now I understood. "Dr. Train thinks the man died from having an air inflation needle stuck into his chest."

"Two needles," Doc Lee said. "A needle into each pleural cavity. If you stuck an inflation needle into both sides of the victim's chest and blew a large quantity of compressed air into both pleural cavities, the lungs would collapse, the heart would be unable to fill with blood, and death would come very fast."

"Train thinks this was murder."

Doc Lee nodded.

"Did Dr. Train speculate on the source of pressurized air?"

I saw Doc Lee nod in the dark. "Train thought that those air inflation needles had such small passages that any volume of compressed air would require high pressure to be effective in a short amount of time. And if someone were stuck with needles, they would immediately push them away, pulling them out of their chests, right?"

My turn to nod.

"So Dr. Train thought the air source would have to be both voluminous and under high pressure. She said a scuba tank might do the job."

I thought about it. "I'm thinking of a rigid metal pipe with two air inflation needles spaced about six or eight inches apart. The pipe would be attached by a pressure hose to a scuba tank at a pressure of about three thousand pounds per square inch. I open the tank pressure valve and swing the tube at the victim, stabbing him with both needles. The air rushes out of the little needles, collapsing both lungs. When I pull the needles back out of the body, the chest tissue presses back together, sealing the puncture wounds and trapping the pressurized air inside the chest. Does that sound about right?"

"Yes, exactly!" Doc Lee seemed a little too enthusiastic about the whole macabre enterprise. But his business was medicine, and a twisted way to kill was probably an interesting break from routine.

SEVENTEEN

The next day, I had breakfast with Street, and we purposely chatted about fun subjects, dream beach vacations, San Francisco restaurants, New York theater, sailboat cruises in the Mediterranean. Two hours later, Spot and I said goodbye to Street and Blondie. "May the devil drown," Street said as she shut the door.

Because we were headed to the southern half of the Central Valley, we went around the South Shore, out to Hope Valley, over Carson Pass, and down to the Central Valley.

The transition from high altitude to low isn't as dramatic in the summer as it is in the winter. But still it surprises. Tahoe's sunshine is relentlessly searing in July, despite comfortably cool air in the shade. By the time I'd dropped 8600 feet from Carson Pass to the valley floor, which is very close to sea level, the sun's rays, filtered through much more air and farm dust, were softer and didn't feel like they'd broil one's skin quite so fast. But the air temps had climbed from the high 70s to the low 100s. The green of manzanita and conifer-covered mountain slopes gave way to the gold of dried grasses in the foothills and on the valley floor.

Spot decided to stop baking his brains and pulled his head in from the open window. I rolled it up and turned the A/C on high.

I angled my way southwest across the Central Valley and turned south on I-5 near the two huge aqueducts that carry water from NorCal to SoCal. Eventually, I exited onto a back-country road that wound through citrus orchards, lemons, oranges, and grapefruit. Seeing the trees stretch off for miles made me realize the flaw in my plan. It could take all day just to track down a single farm manager, and that person might not be willing to talk to me or might not have answers to my questions.

I stopped on the side of the road and used my phone to find the closest county sheriff. There was an address located five miles away in a nearby farm town called Lemon Hills.

The Sheriff's Office website referred to the farm town location as a branch office. But that turned out to be a grand description. The office was in a small rundown trailer home. I parked in the shade of a malformed oak tree, left the windows cracked, the engine running, and the air conditioner on high. I told Spot to be good, got out, knocked on a rickety door, and opened it a bit.

"Anybody home?"

"C'mon in," a woman's voice said.

I ducked under a door opening sized for hobbits, stepped inside, and shut the door behind me to keep the warm, humid inside air from mixing with the broiling, dry outside air. Just an inch above my head was an old air conditioner mounted in the wall above the door jamb. It shook and rattled and wheezed. Anyone would guess its remaining life expectancy at ten minutes or less. Although it had probably been running since the 1970s, so expectations of its demise might be premature.

In one corner, lit by two small corner windows and a fluorescent light above was a small potted lemon tree. The tree sported several diminutive lemons, brilliant yellow. It was an alchemy that still amazed. Give a plant water and light - whether manmade or nature-made - and the plant, if self-pollinating, makes fruit.

Next to the tree was a cluttered desk. There was a woman behind the desk. She wore a tan sheriff's deputy uniform and a belt with her radio and weapons, the things that some cops put in their desk drawer when they're on desk duty. On her face was a look that, while not mean, was very much no nonsense. She looked strong of body and stronger of attitude. This was not a woman you would want to have an altercation with, mental or physical.

"Good afternoon, my name is Owen McKenna. I'm a private investigator from Tahoe."

"Tahoe P I, huh? Euphemism for skiing in the morning, golf

in the afternoon, and handling party security at rich people's lakeside mansions?"

"Not quite..." I leaned in a little closer to read her name tag, "Ms. Havlick," I added. "I used to be with the SFPD, twenty years."

"Sorry. Deputy Tanna Havlick, at your service." She leaned forward in her desk chair and shook my hand. "What brings you to lemon country? You got a taste for Meyer lemons? I've got one right here at arm's reach." She extended her arm and touched one of the little lemons on the potted tree. It swung back and forth.

"I'm actually tracking a suspect who may be from lemon country, who kicked in a door and assaulted a ninety-some-year-old blind man in an effort to learn about what is probably a phony sunken treasure. The perpetrator thought the old blind man knew something about this so-called treasure. He beat the man almost to unconsciousness. After the assault, another man, who was related to the old man, was murdered. We think the killer was likely the same thug and the killing was probably a warning to the old guy. A sort of 'Tell me what I want or I kill you next' thing. "

"Oh, mister, you want me to believe that story?" She'd been chewing gum, and her chomping sped up.

"The story gets even more involved. Where the broken door was kicked in, there were some textile fibers as if from a man's sock. In those fibers was a lemon mite, which I learned is a tiny bug. Not an insect. But a bug nevertheless. An entomologist identified the mite as a Silver mite, a variety that's found on lemon trees on the west side of the Central Valley." I held my arms out and gestured toward the low-elevation mountains immediately out her trailer window.

The woman stopped chewing gum and looked at me with disbelief. She didn't speak.

I said, "You could think on it, and, if you get an idea, you could call me at one of the Tahoe mansions where I hang out poolside, drinking mite-free lemonade and chatting up tech titans. Google, Apple... You get the idea."

"A real smartypants," she said. "You've been practicing your

Philip Marlowe."

I used her silent approach back at her.

"This citrus mite," she eventually said. "Is it one of those no-see-ums?"

"Kind of. Microscopic or almost. But I don't think they bite. No see ums bite, right?"

"Bet your ass, they do. If these mites don't bite, what do they do?"

"I don't know the details, but they attack lemon trees."

She eventually said, "You think, what, that you could drive around to orchards, collect microscopic mites, and see if you can find a match? And then what? Interview all the farm workers and see if any show undue interest in sunken treasure? I hope you can describe it in Spanglish."

"I wondered about that," I said. "But I'm thinking of a different approach. Because the assault was bold, I thought perhaps the local Meyer lemon constabulary could tell me about any local boys who have a history of making bold trouble. The type I'm thinking of is the schemer who dreams up the big scam and isn't above beating on old blind men to pursue it."

As I said it, I thought I saw a twitch of her eye, a hint of some idea flickering back in the cop part of her brain.

I waited again.

"I'm thinking through some possibilities," she said. "I can ignore the ones currently in prison. And the ones who disappeared over the years and are probably dead. And the ones whose evil is only directed at children. The most likely possibility in these parts that comes to mind is the Bosstro brothers. Bad asses in every way. But they're not schemers who could dream up something elaborate. They're enforcers. You go much beyond knocking heads together, you're out of their league."

"Two brothers? Both bad?"

She nodded. "Yes and yes. It's like they've always had a competition to see who could be the worst."

"Mean enough to beat up an old man?"

"Mean enough to stomp bunny rabbits to death," she said. "One is smart mean, the other is stupid mean. They grew up in one of the subdivision houses on the north side of town. It was long enough ago that I was young. But from what I remember people saying, their mother Harriet was twisted enough to whip those boys with a willow branch if they looked at her wrong. And when she worked her gas station job, grandmom Hattie came to babysit. Grandmom was even meaner. From what the boys said, she would whip them just for fun. One day, the boys walloped back. But where the women used the lady-like switch, the boys used garden hoses. By the time they were done, grandmom was dead and mom died two days later. The boys were only around eight and ten at the time, so their time in Juvie was only until foster homes could be found." She paused. "When society spectacularly fails with children, those children sometimes grow up to be spectacular failures."

"First names?"

"I'll have to think on that. The whole town just knows them as the Bosstro brothers. They have regular names. Something like Carlos. Carlos and Jim. No, Carlos and Jeff. That's it. Pretty sure, anyway. Cops call them Chinless and Flyboy. Though not to their faces."

The woman unwrapped a new stick of gum and substituted it for the one in her mouth, wrapped the old one up, and tossed it into the wastebasket.

"They have a father?"

She nodded. "For a short time. Mathias Bosstro. He went to prison on a Murder One a month before the second boy was born, and he was killed in a prison brawl a month after that boy was born. The boy never saw his daddy. And the first boy never saw him enough to remember him. Not the best beginning."

"How old are these guys, now?"

The woman stared up at the highest branch on her lemon tree. Its leaves rubbed on the fluorescent light. "I remember that I was in middle school when Mathias Bosstro killed his boss in the back of the tractor dealership. So, figuring that Mathias went to prison not long after his crime, that would make me about thirteen years older than the youngest brother. Which would mean the Bosstro brothers are about thirty-four and thirty-six.

Or close to that, anyway."

"Do these Bosstro brothers live or work near a lemon orchard?"

"McKenna, this is lemon country." She glanced at her lemon tree. "You can't even walk into a sheriff's office without coming into contact with lemons. They're in the fields, at roadside stands, in the markets, spilling out of passing trucks. Every farm worker has lemon detritus falling out of their pant cuffs. When the wind is strong, lemon twigs and leaves are blowing through the air. I've probably got lemon mites on me as I speak." She made a little shiver and reached to scratch her sides. I decided not to pass along what Street had told me about mites having sex in people's eyelash follicles.

"Can you remember when was the last time you saw either of the Bosstro brothers?"

She shook her head.

"Do they live around here?" I asked.

"In a twist of fate, the boys do farm work for Harly Gardino, the man who owns the house they grew up in, the house in which they did away with mom and grandmom. Harly had a hard time finding renters for that house because of the taint from the carnage that took place in there. So when the boys got older, Harly rented it to them in exchange for farm labor. Word is that they don't provide much labor, but Harly is too kind to crack down on them. Or maybe he's afraid to demand fair value for their rent. Harly's gotta be about eighty-five now, so he might not be too tough these days. So the answer to your question is that when the brothers are around, they're either in their house - probably cooking meth - or they're out on Harly's farm, maybe driving a pickup or tractor. Both places are private. Unless they're driving through town, we can't keep track of them."

"Can you see them trying to find a sunken treasure and killing and beating to get it?"

"Chinless Carlos - he's the smart one - I can see him getting excited about treasure. But like I said, I don't think he's enough of a schemer to do much more than get excited. As for Flyboy Jeff - the dumb one - he couldn't imagine a scheme if it came packaged as a Victoria's Secret Angel. He just does whatever Carlos says. Mostly, that means swinging a baseball bat at anyone unfortunate enough to get in the way. The problem with your idea is that your old blind guy is still alive, right? Maybe even lucid."

I nodded.

"So that shows an unusual restraint on their part. Restraint is not the Bosstro brothers' strong suit. Even if they attempted to go easy, I would still expect the old guy to be dead. Also, you said another man was killed?"

"Yeah."

"How?"

"It was unusual. He died from a compressed air injection."

Tanna frowned. "Your story gets better and better. How does a compressed air injection work?"

"We think the man was stabbed with two basketball inflation needles. Or something like that. The needles were attached to a source of highly compressed air, like what you'd have in a scuba tank. Turns out that if you inject air into a body, it can't easily find a way out. The compressed air filled the victim's chest with enough pressure to crush his lungs and stop his heart."

Tanna winced. "Okay, that's not the Bosstro brothers," she said. "At least not anything I can imagine them perpetrating. I don't think they could plan a complicated killing."

"What you're saying makes sense," I said. "A guy who swings a club or hits with his fist is unlikely to dream up and employ an air pressure weapon. Is it possible they aren't engaging in such nasty stuff anymore? Could they have gone legit?"

"Nasty is their business. If you're willing to pay their fee for intimidation services, they will likely take on the job. If they want to kill someone, they beat him to death. Or they torture him with choke collars and then beat him to death. "

"Wait. Choke collars?"

She looked out one of the little windows and took a deep breath. She was probably trying to decide if it was worth it to go into detail or not.

I said, "The compressed air murder victim had abrasion marks around his neck consistent with a noose. You can understand my interest."

Deputy Tanna let out her breath in a long sigh. "It first came up about ten years ago," she said. "A witness said that the Bosstro brothers were hired to coerce a drug dealer to reveal where he'd stashed money. The witness said the Bosstro boys tied his hands behind his back and put a choke collar on his neck, the kind you'd use for a huge dog like a Mastiff. They tied a rope to the collar and tossed the rope up and over a beam in an old barn. They pulled down on the rope, which lifted up on the collar, until the dealer couldn't breathe. Just before he passed out, they loosened it a bit to let him talk. The witness snuck away unnoticed while the dealer was screaming. He was later found dead."

"Were charges brought against the brothers?"

"Yeah. The DA put together a good case. He even had the witness under lock and key. But when the trial started, the witness had a change of heart and refused to testify."

"So the case fell apart," I said.

Tanna took another deep breath. "Bottom line is these boys are world champion scum. There's nothing they won't do to cause pain and death while they earn a fee."

"Are they expensive?"

"Long ago, an informant told us they charged five K for a serious beating and twenty K for a killing."

"Who do they work for?"

"Well, they don't specialize for the Mob or drug kingpins, if that's what you're wondering. They hire out to anyone with the bucks."

"Do you have descriptors on these boys?"

"Got them memorized, which should tell you something. Six three or four and two-sixty on the big one, which would be Chinless, the smart, older one. Six one and two-thirty on the younger one, which would be Flyboy. Although Flyboy is a bit less imposing than his brother, you should remember that he's the most dangerous. You look away at the wrong moment, your head is mashed potatoes under his baseball bat. More important to remember is he needs no provocation. Just your presence and his whim, and you're dead."

She tapped on her computer, waited, tapped some more. "Here's their latest mugshots." She turned the monitor toward me.

The photos were side by side on the screen. The only common characteristic of the brothers was that they were white. They looked nothing alike in facial structure. One was bald and clean shaven and had eyes pinched very close together. Beneath his mouth was a micro chin, nothing more than a little bump on the way to his throat. His face just seemed to end at his buck teeth. His jaw was wide, but his neck was wider. He had skulls tattooed on both cheekbones. The tops of his ears had been altered to be pointed like Mr. Spock in Star Trek. The pointy ears looked rough and uneven, like the surgery was a homemade ear-cropping effort with a pruning shears during a serious drunk.

The other man was megacephalic, with dramatic cheekbones and a Neanderthal brow that projected out over his eyes by an inch and a half. He wasn't grinning, but his open-mouth stare was sufficient to show that he had fewer teeth than tattoos, several of which decorated his face and forehead, disappearing into his hair. One tattoo was a marijuana leaf, centered on his left cheek. A leaflet traveled across to the bulbous nose, the point of the leaf ending at the tip of his nose. Perched on the end of the tattooed leaf was a tattooed fly. It was big and black like a champion horse fly.

"Now I get the nicknames," I said. "Handsome devils, aren't they?"

"Yeah. We joked about uploading their pics to one of the dating services. How many women would swipe left vs right?"

"What's that mean, swipe?"

Tanna looked at me with shock on her face. "Now you're going to tell me you met the love of your life in person and she's a dream and you've never used an online dating service or posted photos of yourself online."

I thought about it. "Well, sure, we met face to face, and we don't have an online relationship, if that's the appropriate description. But we email back and forth now and then. So that shows I have some computer skills. But I wouldn't know how to post a photo or where. How does it get from a camera onto the internet, anyway?"

Tanna was speechless.

"Anyway, it's a lot easier to call on the phone," I added. "Especially a landline," I said. "The quality is better."

Tanna Havlick scribbled something on a Post-it Note. She paused, then looked up at me. "Sorry. Sometimes, when I hear something incredible… I just have to make a note. I'll have something fun to tell the girls at the range."

I pointed at the mugshots. "These guys spend much time inside?"

"Uh huh." Tanna made a small nod. "They've each been guests at the state's bad-boy hostels. Four years for Flyboy Jeff and three for Chinless Carlos. Felony assault in both cases. Flyboy, especially, taunts people he doesn't like. According to a victim's testimony in court, he points to the tattoo on his nose and says, 'Try to swat the fly. If you don't try to swat the fly, I try my fly swatter on you.' Turns out he's very quick at ducking and dodging, and his fly swatter is his Louisville Slugger."

"They've stayed out of trouble since they got out?"

Tanna did the lemon-tree stare again. "How do I put this… We've dealt with six murders that look like Bosstro work. The DA had enough evidence to prosecute on one of them and made it a joint trial for the brothers. They were both charged with a hate crime of murdering a gay man in a bar. The defense claimed the victim looked like one of their grade school teachers, a man who was mean, and that the victim taunted them and made them afraid for their lives. A witness for the defense claimed that when the Bosstro brothers shoved the man around, he pulled out a Boy Scout pocket knife. So the brothers beat him to death. The defense claimed the men killed in self-defense, that they were terrified of the man they killed, and that he reminded them of their abusive teachers, that they cried like babies after the killings, so horrified were they by what they'd done. The jury acquitted. While the defense was handled surprisingly well, there was speculation that jurors were bought off."

"Can you direct me to their house and Harly's farm?"

The sheriff's deputy looked at me with a stone face. "And you would go out there and try to find them, and if you did, you would try to get them to talk?"

I shrugged. "You know that's what we investigators do. Shake trees. See what falls out."

The woman made a little grin. "Only thing that falls out of our trees is lemons."

EIGHTEEN

Tanna Havlick said, "Let me draw you a little map." She pulled a piece of copy paper out of her printer and drew on it with a ballpoint pen. "This is where you are now. Over here is Main Street, which runs the entire one-block stretch of downtown Lemon Hills. At this end of Main Street is a biker bar called Reds, no apostrophe. The road you want is a left turn at that bar. You take it about two miles out. Where the pavement turns to dirt, there's a Y. Take the left fork and drive another mile. You'll come to a rise, and there'll be lemon orchards as far as you can see. In a little valley are Harly's farm buildings. Now, if instead of going left at the Y, you went right, you'd come to The Ranch Estates, which is the subdivision where the Bosstro boys grew up and still live. The development is twenty-four two-bed-one-bath houses on a half acre each and set in dirt so tough you can't tell the driveways from the front yards. Unless, of course, you're visiting one of the estates that has old tires marking the driveway." She made an X with the pen. "Here, at the left-rear corner of the estates, is a house once painted red but now faded to pink. It's missing part of the roof from storm damage a few years back. Harly never had it repaired. The boys just cover the opening with plastic held down with tires. They replace it every year or so when the sun turns the plastic to crispy chips. I think the house is probably rotten where the rain seeps in. But it dries during the summer."

She handed me the paper.

"Any advice before I go out there?"

"Bring your sidearm with a round in the chamber."

I nodded. "Thanks much."

"One more thing," she said. "Let's just say you were to roust a Bosstro. Neither them or their biker friends would hesitate at using you for target practice."

"So I should be careful," I said.

"Very."

"Of their biker friends, is there anyone in particular I should know about?"

Tanna shook her head. "No one is close to the Bosstro boys. But everyone wants to court favor with them, if only to avoid their wrath."

"You said their mother and maternal grandmother and father are all dead. Do they have any other relatives? Aunts? Uncles?"

"The only other sort-of relative I'm aware of is a foster step brother. Because of what happened, the Bosstro family was a regular topic in town around the time when I graduated from high school. I remember some of the details. Back when Bosstro's mom was selling cigs and sodas at the gas station, her hours were reduced to part time. So she and grandmom talked the foster care placement folks into certifying them to take on a male child. The extra eight hundred a month made up for mom's lost wages. They were given a boy who was maybe six. According to the state rules, the foster boy was supposed to have his own room in the house. But of course, that was not an option in a two-bedroom house with two other boys and a mother and grandmother. There was a little pantry-type room off the kitchen. When the social worker went out to check, mom had made up the pantry to look like a miniature bedroom. The social worker thought it was window dressing and that the foster boy was sleeping on the floor in the same bedroom as the other two boys. She was going to remove him from the house, but the mom had a little talk with her, and the social worker retracted her concern. Don't ask me what kind of threats that talk may have consisted of."

"Got it. What happened to the boy?"

"I never heard. If I recall correctly, he was there less than a year before the Bosstro brothers killed mom and grandmom. The foster boy was taken away, and I never heard about his whereabouts."

"Less than a year in the Bosstro home is enough time that he could have bonded with the brothers, right?"

"Maybe. More like, he could have been twisted by the brothers. The thing is, the foster boy was strange in his own way. He never spoke. It was something that people talked about around town, people who'd never even met the boy. They referred to him as The Silent One."

"Was he real shy? Or deaf?"

"I don't think he was deaf," Tanna said. "If so, people would refer to that. They'd say, 'He's deaf, so he doesn't talk.' Right? As for being shy, even the shyest people still talk. So there was something else going on."

"Maybe he was nonverbal because of some kind of brain damage?"

Tanna shrugged. "Maybe. The armchair shrink in me would say that he had witnessed things so traumatic, he went silent for psychological reasons. Maybe the women beat on the foster boy just like the brothers. Or maybe he watched Chinless and Flyboy beat the mom and grandmom to death. That would chill a boy's soul."

"Do you remember his name?"

"No. It's probably in the foster records somewhere. But that was - let's see - about 30 years ago. Unless you could find a teacher or someone who happens to remember the boy's name, it would be very hard to extract it from official records. You'd have to know just where to look, and get a court order, and be a diligent investigator."

"Did you ever meet the foster boy?"

"Not that I recall. I was heading off to cop school. I had my first boyfriend. There was a lot of excitement in my life at the time. Foster kids were not something I paid attention to."

"Would anyone you know have met the silent foster kid? Or remember his name? Or where he was sent after the mother/grandmother murders?"

"I doubt it. I'll keep it in mind. If something comes to me, I'll call."

"Here's my number." I handed her my card, took one of hers out of the plastic holder on her desk, thanked her, and left.

NINETEEN

I drove out to Harly's lemon farm and parked under another, lone, malformed oak. Maybe it was a metaphor for my investigation.

This time, I turned off the engine, opened all the windows, and let Spot out.

He ran around, a loping gait I'd seen before. It's a combination of stretching his limbs and gauging the heat along with a general reconnaissance.

When we see a dog doing a slow run, getting some air, investigating a new landscape, we think it's just a dog running, making a simple assessment of the territory. But the dog perceives whether or not there are people around and, if so, how many and whether the people are clean or not. The dog knows what the people last ate and if their main focus is drugs or sex or beef stew. The dog can tell if this new world contains gunpowder or garlic. The dog smells fear or bravado and adjusts his attitude accordingly. In one of the most important perceptions of all, the dog understands the difference between encampments with only men and those that include women and children. At a base level, the dog is on hyper alert with the former group and is on casual observation with the latter group.

None of these perceptions is revealed in the dog's manner. But all affect how the dog responds to play or stress or violence.

From the moment we got out of the Jeep, the place seemed unnaturally quiet. I looked around, visualizing snipers under camo netting over the nearby rises.

While Spot loped large ovals, I walked zig zags. I looked through windows into a dirt-floored pole barn that had huge, locked, sliding doors. Yet the windows, which were large enough for a horse to jump through, were wide open. All I could see in the barn were empty horse stalls on one end and a large open area on the other end. In the large area was a flat-bed trailer with wooden pallets on it. To the side of the pallets were stacks of flattened corrugated boxes. For lemons? I didn't know.

At the end of the room was a workbench and on it several tanks. They looked like scuba tanks, except that unlike the scuba tanks I'd seen, these varied in size. There were also thin hoses and small metallic devices, like the components of scuba regulators for breathing. There was a machine that seemed familiar.

I realized it was an air compressor.

The various components looked like equipment for constructing compressed air devices.

Near the barn was a small shed surrounded by a perimeter of chicken wire. From what I could see, the shed had compartments that might be perfect for chickens. But there were no chickens.

It seemed clear that the farm used to be set up to house animals. Now, the farm was only for orchard produce. Or maybe the orchards had been retired. Maybe the farmer was too old to take care of animals and trees. Or maybe there was an easier way to make money.

Some distance away was an old farmhouse. I hiked over to it, the hot sun burning into the back of my neck. I knocked and got no answer. There were windows with no drapes. I cupped my hands around my face to see inside. There was some old furniture, some piled newspapers, an old TV on a rolling metal cart, and a wide-brimmed straw sun hat, the kind worn by old men who've had some cancerous growths nipped off. It was not a hat that dirtball enforcers wear.

I left and drove to the Bosstro house in the corner of The Ranch Estates.

I'd thought Tanna was exaggerating when she described driveways delineated by rows of old tires. I saw three such houses before I turned into the street that included the Bosstro home.

I parked in the street, at a bit of an angle, just far enough from the Bosstro house that the residents would not be able to easily see my license plate number. I pulled my baseball cap down low over my face, got out, and let Spot out of the back.

My goal wasn't to be completely incognito. After all, a tall man with a Harlequin Great Dane arriving in a Jeep was easy to notice and remember. But that doesn't constitute identification, should anyone try to prove it was me at a later date. It was a small distinction, but one worth paying attention to.

The house was as Tanna described, unkempt, with a storm-damaged roof draped in plastic that had darkened from the original clear to a chalky gray. The anchoring tire weights which once held the plastic in place had ceased to be useful as the plastic had been shredded into strips by the blowing wind. The strips now waved like streamers. In today's calm air, the streamers drooped, almost motionless, down to the ground.

Spot and I walked up the red dirt drive. There was a sidewalk of sorts made of paving stones. Maybe they had a limited number and wanted the pretense of a walkway, so the pavers had been set with ten-inch gaps. If you walked carefully, you could step from paver to paver. But the red dirt between the pavers still came through, coating each paver and blowing up against the house so that the lower courses of the peeling pink siding were a deeper red.

I knocked on the door. There was no response. I listened for movement inside the house. But the only sound was a distant rustle of overly dried bushes in an arroyo behind the back yard.

I walked around the house, peering in through the few dirty windows. I could see almost nothing. When I came to a sliding glass door, the inside view was a little better, revealing some out-sized Nike shoes, one lying upside down, another tossed onto its side. There was a sweatshirt hanging over a chair.

The only interesting thing was a tattered couch. Someone had drained a Budweiser beer bottle and then stuffed it, base down, between the seat cushion and the back of the couch. When the person had drained a second bottle, they shifted a few inches to the side and then stuffed that bottle behind the cushion next to its neighbor. The person or persons were evidently fond of Budweiser, for they had proceeded down the couch. The result was a long row of 40 or 50 beer bottles all standing up like shiny brown soldiers at attention, guarding the boundary between the cushions and the seat backs. A person could still sit on the couch. But they couldn't lean back without a row of bottles pushing into their back.

It was an inspired decorating idea, and I imagined that a portion of visitors to the Bosstro residence would admire the concept and go home to see if they, too, could decorate their abodes with a spread of beer bottles.

When I'd circumnavigated the house and arrived back at the front door, I had seen no sign of occupants. I didn't want to leave without checking out the inside. Because no one was there to let me in, it was necessary for me to let myself in.

I didn't want to be too obvious to any cameras that might be recording.

So I made a show of knocking again, smiling all the while, then walked with Spot back to the Jeep and drove away.

This time I drove a half mile down to where the dry arroyo intersected with the street. Apparently enough rainwater periodically channeled through the ravine to feed many groups of tall bushes. I found a place to park my Jeep off the street in behind some of the bushes and under the shade of a wispy pine that was sage green in color. My vehicle wasn't invisible, but it was obscured. This time I left Spot in the Jeep with the windows down. It would be too warm for him to remain there for long, but I didn't intend to be long. If he got too hot, he would jump out the window and come calling. As it was, he seemed happy to snooze for the time being.

I walked back to the Bosstro house, keeping under the odd trees, and staying down among the bushes of the ravine.

My hat was still down low over my face as I came up from behind the house. I kept my head down and chose my path so that I wouldn't be obvious to any cameras mounted under the eaves.

Normally, I'd take the time to use a home invasion technique that would cause the least damage to the building and, thus, to the occupants' psyches, as well. However, I was thinking about how Deputy Tanna had described the abusive activities of

Chinless and Flyboy. Without thinking about it much, I decided it was acceptable to act with a lack of respect for the Bosstro boys, considering their lack of respect toward the people they victimized.

So I picked up a rock that sat at the back of the house near the sliding glass door. I sensed something shiny under the rock, something I belatedly recognized as a key. But before I was burdened by that realization, I used the rock to smash the big sliding glass door.

Unfortunately, smashing tempered glass makes a large crashing sound not unlike a small bomb.

More unfortunately, an alarm went off, a shrieking whoop whoop whoop that could be heard from a half mile away.

TWENTY

When the burglar alarm went off, two or three neighborhood dogs started a commotion so loud they would alert anybody who may have been too deaf to hear the alarm. They would certainly alert Spot as well, and I wondered if he'd stay put. He was used to me leaving him in the Jeep, so he knew that I'd likely return soon. Perhaps that would keep him in place for a few minutes.

As an ex-cop, I had learned to pause before I had a dramatic reaction. During that short pause, I realized that running back to the Jeep and racing away would confirm anyone's suspicions.

Instead, I took the time to do what a friend of the Bosstro brothers would do. Figure out how to turn off the alarm, which neighbors might interpret as demonstrating that I was a legitimate visitor rather than a criminal intruder.

Tempered glass is hard to break. But when it does break, it shatters into a million diamonds rather than shards. Except for bits of broken glass at the perimeter of the window, the door was now a large opening. I was able to step through into the living room.

I trotted toward the front door. There was no alarm panel that I saw. In one way that might indicate a good thing, because no panel possibly meant an unsophisticated alarm, maybe even a do-it-yourself installation. As I looked around at the doors and window edges, I saw no visible electrical contacts, and no wires that I could follow to the control box of the alarm system. Keeping my head down so my face wasn't visible to any cameras in the upper corners of the room, I turned, trying to see the likely camera locations with my peripheral vision. I saw no cameras and no glowing red lights, which might indicate a motion sensor. But there had to be sensors somewhere...

The alarm was still shrieking at a decibel level that would damage hearing if left on for long. It was loud enough that I had a hard time thinking.

I tried to force a kind of concentration. The power for an alarm was electrical. Cut that power, the alarm would go off unless it switched to a backup power source, like a battery, which could be small and well hidden. I had to find both. Or, I could find the alarm noisemaker and cut the wires powering it. Then I would at least be in blessed silence even if hidden webcams continued to broadcast my movements to the internet and send messages to an alarm company and the police.

I looked in all the obvious locations. I found nothing. No panel. No humming laptop running the system. No obvious power source.

I started looking for the house power. It would probably be a gray electrical panel with a row or two of circuit breakers. I trotted through the house, the alarm howling in my ears, but found nothing.

I trotted out the front door and resumed my search.

The electrical panel was at the right front corner of the house. I opened it. There was one row of breakers, 20-amp on the upper half and 15-amp on the bottom half. At the top was the master, a 100-amp breaker. I flipped it, shutting off power to the house.

The alarm went silent.

The total time elapsed had been at least a minute. Maybe two. Too much time to come off as a legitimate visitor. But here I was. I heard no police sirens. May as well take advantage.

Back inside, I made a slower tour of the house. My heart was still pumping with vigor, blood pressure pounding in my head. I paused, took two deep breaths, and continued, my ears numbed from the alarm but somewhat tuned to possible sounds from someone approaching from outside, about to burst in through the front door.

The two bedrooms were as I expected and almost duplicates of each other. There were multiple piles of dirty clothes and stray dirty clothes tossed everywhere. Empty beer cans littered the room corners. Each room had a mattress on the floor. There were no sheets or blankets, just sleeping bags, one in each room. Maybe the bags had been washed in the last year. Maybe not. In one bedroom were wall posters of basketball players, in the other bedroom, wall posters of pin-up girls caressing and sprawling across motorcycles. In a moment of what might be misplaced sympathy, I felt bad for the girls who may have needed the modeling fee for rent money or baby formula but didn't realize that it would be someone like Chinless or Flyboy who would be looking at them night and day for years to come.

The single bathroom looked like someone had carefully rubbed black dirt into the corners at the tub and wall, toilet and floor, sink and faucet. There was no bar of soap in the shower and just half of a motel-sized mini soap at the sink. There were some aerosol deodorant cans. Instead of standard towels with terry-cloth nubbing, there were two crumpled blue work towels of the type that auto garages get from a weekly linen service.

I went into the small kitchen, opening the cupboards and fridge, finding most of what I expected, boxed pasta dinners with powdered cheese flavoring, orange juice, and bottles of cheap vodka, multiple bags of barbecue-flavored corn chips. In the garbage were empty plastic burger packages. On top of the fridge was an open package of hamburger buns.

Off the kitchen was a pantry room full of shelves sparsely populated with canned goods. A folding closet door. This would be the room that Tanna had spoken of, presented to the social worker as a bedroom for the foster kid who was silent. I tried to imagine it as a bedroom. It didn't have a window. It didn't even have a light. But in one of the dark corners was a rolled-up sleeping bag and a small pillow in an Army camo pillow case. That made three sleeping bags in the house.

The house had nothing of note, nothing of interest, nothing unexpected.

I realized I'd hurried, constantly listening for the sound of motorcycles or pickup trucks pulling up out front.

I went back through the house, slower this time. I found something of note in the closet of the smaller bedroom.

Up on the shelf was a rifle. On the floor was a dirty T-shirt. I used the shirt to pull out the rifle, trying not to smudge the areas where one would typically find fingerprints.

It was a PCP rifle, a pre-charged pneumatic gun, the kind of gun Diamond had suggested might have been used to shoot out Daniel Callahan's window. If it was, how did it get to lemon country? Or was it brought from lemon country and then brought back to hide it?

It gave me a new understanding of the compressor and hoses and regulators in Harly's barn. If you wanted to make custom air weapons and have a ready source of compressed air supply, you wouldn't want to make frequent visits to a scuba shop where the workers would notice. And you wouldn't want a compressor and other equipment in your house, where the neighbors would hear it running.

I now could see a connection between the compressed air murder and Daniel's window being shot out.

I put the gun back on the closet shelf and was walking out of the bedroom when I heard a car door slam.

In a moment, someone would walk through the front door. Once inside, they'd see the pile of broken glass in the living room. And they'd block my escape route out the sliding glass door.

I did a soft-footed run to the living room, and jumped through the broken glass door as I heard the front door open behind me. I sprinted across the back yard, angry words trailing after me.

"What the hell is this?!"

"Dude! Someone busted into our pad! Check your stash! Check your rifle!"

I rushed into the arroyo, then slowed, ducked down, and darted from bush to bush. I expected to hear shots, even if the muffled variety that came from a PCP rifle. But no shots were fired.

I got back to the Jeep. Spot put his nose all over me as I started the Jeep and drove up and out of the ravine. I was careful not to rev the engine. Instead, I eased up onto the dirt road and cruised away at a slow speed.

TWENTY-ONE

I drove back to the corner where I'd turned at the bar, which I now saw had a small red neon sign that said, 'Reds Place.' As Deputy Tanna Havlick had mentioned, there was no apostrophe between the d and the s.

There was a gap in the boulders and bushes that defined the perimeter of the property. I drove in. There was no obvious parking lot. The bar was surrounded by dirt, and many vehicles - mostly motorcycles - were parked around it, some lined up in groups of three or four, others in a scattershot pattern.

The number of vehicles suggested that bike cruisers on nearby I-5 had learned that not far off the interstate was a hangout where they could spend some time with their own kind. Either that, or three-fourths of the town had taken the day off and was spending the afternoon at Reds.

Some of the vehicles were pickups, older Fords and Chevys mixed in with a few Dodge Ram. Among the working trucks were a few of the new, out-sized type, washed and polished four-wheel-drives on high suspensions with over-sized tires that had a gloss coating to make the black tire rubber as shiny as blackberry syrup. These were the trucks that had never hauled a load of manure or hay or gravel or concrete block or two-by-eight treated lumber. Nor had they ventured into a field where an errant small boulder or fallen tree might dent a fender. But they looked sharp.

The motorcycles were 90% Harleys, the rest Harley lookalikes. The only odd bike was a single orange Japanese race bike, a modern iconoclast among the old guard of noise makers. Maybe some kid wanted to see where his uncle hung out. As performance goes, there is no comparison. The race bike is superlative by every normal measure, maneuvering, acceleration, braking, and nearly twice the top speed. It costs less, gets better gas mileage, has better reliability, and still carries two riders like the big hogs. Just not with as much comfort. Unless you value your hearing, which, on any Harley, is at serious risk. But as a guy once told me, just because it's got two wheels with an engine between them doesn't make it a motorcycle. A Harley is a motorcycle, he said. A race bike is a toy. Fast, but who cares.

My old rusted Jeep with the bullet-hole ventilation didn't fit with the group, either, so I parked next to the orange toy. I let Spot out of the back, and we walked through rows and knots of Harleys leaned over onto their kickstands. A few of the Harleys had center stands, a more secure way to keep your bike from tipping over. But no one used them. It could be because the Harleys were too heavy for their owners to do the small lift required to rock the bike onto the center stand. More likely, they weren't used because a bike on a center stand sits up straight and tall and looks as square as a first grade teacher. Whereas a bike leaned over onto its kickstand looks rakish and fast and ready for action.

The Reds Place bar building was similar in construction to the pole barn out at Harly's lemon farm, a simple rectangular building with metal siding and few windows. It could have been put up by the same builder, although the bar likely had a better floor than dirt.

There were six men near the front door. Most held cigarettes or beer or both. Some leaned forward, elbows on the top rail of a fence designed as if for hitching horses. Those same men each had a single boot heel hooked up on the lower fence rail. Half of the men wore bluejeans, and most of the others wore leather pants. One guy had jeans but with leather chaps over them, cowboy style. Never know when you need to ride your Harley through a field of manzanita. All the pants - blue jeans or leather - were either held up with suspenders or were overalls with shoulder straps, because the men didn't have any place in their mid-section around which to hitch a belt. The men all wore black leather vests adorned with embroidered biker gang names across the back and gang trinkets and fringe hanging at the edges. The men had bare arms, fat as those of sumo wrestlers, and most of the exposed skin was covered with blue and red tattoos.

The tattoos and biker vest had become the universal bad-boy uniform. It was worn by everyone from doctors and professors out to escape the confines of their stuffy jobs to the men who had developed and perfected the look.

However, as I looked at these guys, I didn't see any candidates for doctor or professor. Men who used the ten-day rule for personal hygiene - either take a shower or put on deodorant at least once every ten days - weren't usually doctors or professors.

I remembered what a cultural anthropologist once told me. The best way to learn about a people and their culture is to keep quiet and observe the natives in their environment. Uniforms - biker vests or business suits - reveal more than eating and drinking habits, more than speech mannerisms, more than most anything else.

Uniforms convey membership, cultural acceptance, and power. It's usually men who are drawn to a uniform's power. Pick your uniform: sporting, soldiering, farming, hunting, doctoring. Whether marching band members or cops, firefighters, or gangs, all use the uniform as a type of communication, a wordless language. Even the non-uniform uniforms, like the power ties that investment bankers and lawyers wear, serve the same purpose. It identifies the person as belonging to a particular group. In the viewer's eyes, the uniform imbues the wearer as having the qualities of the group.

It is this feature that figures so prominently in the biker persona. Your average guy, struggling with the insecurities that come from lack of career success and a marriage that doesn't excite, and kids that make him feel poor but don't make him proud, can put on the biker gear and suddenly be somebody. The guy now projects an aura and, possibly, a sense that he is indeed someone to be reckoned with.

If he really buys into the cult of bad-boy toughness, he adopts the beer and chips and fast-food diet to extreme, puts on 100 pounds, and becomes a "big" guy who, while not able to move fast, can intimidate through size alone. It's an instinct that permeates all animals, grizzly or elk, tiger or cows. We give wide berth to the guy who, if he sat on your chest, would crack your ribs and choke the breath out of you.

Of course, some women join in and don the uniform. But their presence just emphasizes their small numbers.

The men all turned their attention to us as Spot and I walked up. But they played it with a pilot's cool. They saw us, but they didn't react. Never mind my dog's unusual size. It's not cool to reveal any kind of surprise. Nothing fazes the true bad boy.

I nodded at them and pulled open the door. As Spot and I walked into the dark interior, I heard one of the men speak from behind me.

"Watch what happen. Red don't like no dog in his crib."

The inside of the bar was cooler than outside but still palpably warm and humid, and filled with the odors of unwashed men and the loud bass thump of Led Zeppelin. Crowds of bikers bellied up to the bar with beer bottles in one hand and Beer Nuts in the other, and cigs in their mouths or tucked between fingers. More men sat at plain tables, their metal chairs pulled back from the table edges to allow space for their girth. Some played pool at two billiard tables in one corner. Above each table was an old-fashioned fluorescent light hanging on chains. One fixture had two greenish bulbs. The other had one tube that was creamy white and another tube that was more blue. The cream-colored tube flickered. Over behind the most distant pool table sat a group of three women, self-ostracized from the men despite their embrace of the same behavior and uniform and physical body characteristics.

The bar was about 50 feet long. It was of homemade construction, heavily-varnished plywood with a thick front edge that protruded a quarter inch above the bar surface as if designed to stop drinks from sliding off onto the floor. Behind the bar were shelves and bins, also homemade. The main lighting came from multiple signs advertising beer and booze manufacturers, some signs with neon tubes, others fancier with metallic gold logos on smoky-mirrored glass. Two men worked the bar, each wearing the biker uniform. They were not as fat as most of the patrons. The reason why was clear. They were working fast and hard, sweating with exertion. Combine constant movement and no time to eat snacks, and you stay leaner.

The bar was clearly a huge success and an example of service trumping decor. If you provided drinks with good value, poured them reliably, kept long hours, learned your customers' names, and competently performed all the other tasks of running a business, you developed what is often called a cash cow. This place was bringing in the kind of dollars that made car dealership owners wonder why they'd ever passed up alcohol for vehicles.

One reason might be the air quality, which, despite California law that forbids smoking indoors, was filled with a blue haze of smoke. Based on the smell, Reds' smoke was mostly a mix of cigarette and pot with just a bit of the heavier seasoning of cigars. Through the haze I saw a big man with reddish orange hair and beard rolling a two-wheeler hand truck with a huge beer keg on it. He stopped near a big cubby close to the end of the bar, then wrestled the keg off the two-wheeler and started switching out the empty keg that it was to replace.

As Spot and I approached, the music had shifted to Twisted Sister, and the general ambient noise began to shift from a dull roar of shouting and yelling to a quieter conversation. Men began elbowing their companions and pointing at Spot. As the relative hush reached the man I assumed was Red, he unbent himself from his beer keg and raised up to see what the sudden drop in commotion was all about.

He saw me and called out. "I don't allow dogs in my bar."

"He's a service dog," I said.

The man looked at me with steel gray eyes. He was only a couple of inches short of my six-six, but about 40 pounds over my 215. His weight wasn't biker fat, but keg-hauling muscle.

"What's your disability?" he asked.

"I'm nuts. This dog is my psychiatric therapy dog." I looked down at Spot and gave him a little scratch on the crown of his head. I raised my voice up high. "Isn't that right, Largeness? You're my nutcase helper dude, right?" I looked back at Red and said, "Federal law allows psychiatric service dogs to enter any public establishment."

"You don't look crazy to me," Red said.

"Looks deceive," I said. "If something happens to push my buttons, I go pretty wacko. Post traumatic stress going way back to the time I was in high school and some drunks beat me up back of a bar. A place kind of like this. I might be having flashbacks already." I spoke down toward Spot's ears. "We call 'em psycho triggers in our support group, don't we, boy?"

He wagged.

Twisted Sister was replaced by Judas Priest.

I pulled Spot up to the bar. Two men moved apart to let us fit. The bar was higher than normal. But Spot lifted his head at an upward angle, set the end of his jaw on the bar lip, and sniffed, nostrils flexing, taking in what must have been a dramatic assortment of powerful odors.

"You got Sierra Nevada Pale Ale on tap?" I said.

Red ignored my question. His eyes were narrowed, the gray having disappeared behind slit openings. He gestured toward Spot. "So what's he doing right now to help you not go wacko?"

"He's doing an olfactory room search, so if I have a dissociative episode he can lead me to safety before I act out."

"What do you do when you act out?"

"Oh, you know, like in the movies. Bust up the place. Break some bones. Make a mess. One of my triggers is being denied service."

Red sighed as if he knew he was being played but felt he should go along with it for the moment. "I don't sell fancy beer. You wanna Bud?"

"Yeah, sure. I forgot about Bud for a moment. Yes, sir. Gimme a Bud."

Red tipped a glass under a tap and filled it with sudsy amber. He set it on the bar in front of me with enough force that the head slopped over the edge and ran down the side. I picked it up, took a sip, set a $10 bill on the bartop.

"I'm looking for the Bosstro brothers," I said. "I've heard they hang out in this kind of place."

Red's expression went from tolerance to interest.

"What's that mean, 'this kind of place?'"

"You know. Charming decor, soft music, upscale clientele, sophisticated menu."

The man next to me called out, his speech slurred. "Don't say nothin' about the Bosstro brothers, Red! They got a right to privacy. It's American."

"Shut up, Mo. There is no substantial American legal right to privacy." The specificity and out-of-character aspect of the statement made me think maybe Red was a closet intellectual who read books or pursued some other equally deviant activity.

Red turned back to me. "I haven't seen the Bosstro brothers in a long time. What'd they do this time?"

"I don't know. But I'd like to ask them about a ninety-some-year-old man who got beat up a few nights ago. The person who did the beating was looking for information about a sunken treasure. I've heard that would be just the kind of thing the Bosstro brothers might get excited about."

Reds eyes twitched just like the lady cop's had.

"Red! You don't wanna go there. Flyboy'll bust up your place. He just don't listen to Chinless anymore." The man's sour breath and acrid body odor flowed over me, making it difficult to breathe.

"I said to shut up, Mo!" Red said a second time.

"Flyboy told me..."

I turned toward Mo and leaned over close to his face, which was pink and puffy and scarred in several places. A tattoo of a King Cobra snake wrapped over one ear and then down and around his neck. Mo was huge, and if he hadn't been so drunk, I would have backed off.

I said, "Red and I are having a conversation, Mo. One of my triggers is when people interrupt me."

"So wachu gonna do, tall boy? The last guy who got in my face still has two casts on. I don't care about your episodes or whatever you call 'em."

"Let me show you a dog trick," I said. I tugged at Spot's collar. "See this man, Largeness?"

Spot swung his head around and lifted his nose toward the

man.

The man held his ground. Although my dog was 170 pounds, the man was at least twice that. No dog, however large, could scare him.

I rested my hand on Spot's neck as I spoke to the man. "If I point my dog toward you and then touch his throat and tell him to growl, he'll growl at you."

"So? He can growl all he wants. I can still put a round through his head with my pocket Glock. If your dog assaults me, I'm within my rights to shoot both of you dead."

"He won't assault you. He's just going to show you a dog trick. No cause for pulling a gun. But if you pulled a gun anyway, the problem is that if he's growling at you, it will unnerve you. And if you're unnerved, you won't be very smooth getting your piece out. But worst of all is that if you pull a gun on me or my dog, that will in fact be assault, and my dog and I will have to defend ourselves. My dog could possibly bite. And then I'll have one of my episodes, and Red will wish you'd never come into his fine establishment. He'll probably ban you for life."

The man looked at me as if he'd been holding his breath and couldn't go much longer without bursting.

I touched Spot's throat. "Go ahead, boy. Show him your trick."

Spot looked up at me as if he didn't understand.

"I mean it. Growl at this man."

Spot looked at the man then back at me.

I bent down and made a growling sound in Spot's ear, soft enough that only Spot could hear me.

Spot growled. Low-pitched and soft at first. I touched his throat again. He upped the growl, not so low and not so soft. He lifted his lips enough to show some fang.

The big man stiffened.

I touched Spot on the top of his nose and he stopped growling. "See, Mo, that's his trick," I said. "Pretty good, huh?" I looked at Spot. "Good boy!" I pulled a dog biscuit out of my pocket and gave it to him. Spot munched once, then swallowed. He looked at my pocket where I keep the doggie treats and wagged.

I turned back to Mo.

"You try that again, I'll shoot," Mo said.

"No, you wouldn't be that stupid. Then again, maybe you would be. Spot, let's do another trick and show..."

I saw Mo reach for his pistol and jerk it up and out. "Spot! Weapon hand!"

I waited a half second to see if Spot would react. As he swung his head toward Mo, I turned, anticipating how Red would react, and leaped toward the bar.

Red was pulling an ancient sawed-off, double-barreled, shotgun out from under the bar.

TWENTY-TWO

I didn't know if Red was going to use his shotgun on me or Spot, or maybe Mo. Maybe he only intended to wave it for intimidation. But I couldn't take a chance.

I slid halfway across the bar and reached for the barrel. But I was too slow. He jerked it away from me and fired it toward the ceiling. His speed was such that I thought he'd probably done that before.

People see shotguns in movies and TV shows, and they realize they are wicked weapons. But what video doesn't show is a shotgun's sound volume.

When Red's gun went off in the confines of the bar, it was like a bomb blast. Several people dropped to the floor in shock, not even realizing that it was a gun that had gone off. Others jerked so hard they dropped their beer bottles.

I'd seen the shooting unfold, so I was prepared. Even so, the blast was a powerful shock to my ears and no doubt Spot's as well. Fortunately, he was down on the floor, where he'd pulled Mo down. The bar had protected them both from the worst of the sound.

Red was swinging the gun toward me.

I grabbed a glass off the bartop and hurled it his way as I slid across the bar's surface. The glass slammed Red on his right hand, hitting the knuckles near his trigger finger. He jerked in pain but didn't fire. I landed on my feet on the other side of the bar. Red recovered his focus and resumed bringing his gun toward me, but I grabbed the gun by its barrel.

"No more!" I shouted at Red as I jerked the gun.

Because he was slowed by the pain of the glass strike, he lost his grip on the shotgun. Red flinched, probably stunned that I'd launched over the bar at him. No doubt he was also wondering if in fact I really was unhinged, and that this was the beginning of my "episode," and that I was about to shoot up the bar and his patrons and maybe him, too.

As Red backed away from me, I pointed the shotgun to his side, and said, "Are you going for another weapon?"

He shook his head. It looked sincere.

I held the second hammer back, pulled the trigger, and let the hammer down gently. I snapped his gun open, and ejected the two shells, one empty, the other still fresh. I opened one of his chest coolers, dropped the shells inside, and shut the lid.

The crowd in the bar was back to a loud volume of commotion. Men rushing about, at least one of them waving a gun. Still holding the shotgun, I put one foot onto a plastic crate near the beer keg, used it to step up onto the edge of the keg, and from there stepped up onto the bar. The ceiling was high enough that I could stand up.

I held the shotgun but didn't point it. I shouted, "Listen up everybody! Everything is okay and under control! Isn't that right, Red?"

I looked at him. He was leaning forward, both hands on the bar. A flashing neon sign on his left lit the left side of his face in pulsing orange. Red nodded.

Directly below me, Spot was on the floor, chest down, elbows spread, his jaws around Mo's forearm. Mo lay on his back, arms and legs both spread-eagled. The pocket Glock was nowhere in sight. His face was a grimace of pain.

I continued. "Sorry for the commotion. I came in here for some simple information." I pointed down at the floor. "But Mo, here, picked a fight. Big mistake. I'm an investigator pursuing a murder and a separate assault on an old man." I didn't say any more about the crime, because any details obtained from an informant, if accurate, will indicate the likely truth or falseness of their information when compared to the known facts.

I thought about an appropriate white lie to keep the calm and possibly motivate some help. "The sheriff's office and the state Bureau of Investigation are coordinating this investigation. As I speak, there are fourteen law enforcement officers staked out around the parking lot outside this bar. If you run out, you will be detained and brought in for questioning, maybe held overnight. And of course, if there are any outstanding warrants for you, your freedom is up. Unless…" I paused. The room went relatively quiet. "If you stay calm and listen to me, you will be left alone and free to go when I'm done." I glanced back at Red. He hadn't moved.

I said, "Our investigation has led us here because we want to question the Bosstro brothers."

There was a sudden rise of voices.

"Mo knows something about the Bosstro brothers," I said. "He could have given me help. Instead, he went for his gun and was taken down by my patrol dog. I'm hoping no one else is that stupid. If you are, my dog will be happy to chew on you as well. I have a question for all of you. If any single person answers it, I go away and none of you will ever see me again. I won't even charge Mo with assault."

I paused to take a deep breath to slow my heart. "Mo's reaction to my mention of the Bosstro brothers tells me that they are my target. I went out to their house and Harly's farm, but saw no sign of them. I assume that somebody here knows their phone number and where they are. That's all I ask. There's a reward for the information."

Everyone seemed to talk to each other in subdued voices. But no one spoke up that I could hear.

I waited.

A voice from over by the billiard tables said, "How much is the reward?"

I got out my wallet, pulled out two $100 bills that I'd brought for the purpose of buying favors, and held them up. "Two hundred dollars. The Bosstro brothers' phone number and current location. You don't need to give me your name. Oh, one more thing. I'll give you an extra hundred if you give me the name of the inker who did the Bosstro tattoos." Another pause before I continued. "Red is going to close early tonight, right, Red?"

He frowned, then nodded, probably thinking about potential

trouble with the law and the hope that I would make that go away.

I bent over and spoke to Red in a low voice. "Give me your card. I'll call and tell you where I leave your gun."

He made a single nod and handed me a card.

I stood up and spoke to the crowd. "When I get outside, I'm going to call the commander of the LEOs surrounding this place and tell them to pull back. Mo will be my bodyguard. I'll park my Jeep near the exit. As you exit, you'll drive by me. Give me the information, I hand you the money. Mo will be facing the other way, so he won't see who told me."

I jumped down off the bar.

"Spot, release the suspect."

He didn't immediately respond. Like all dogs, his natural instinct was to hang onto his prey, whether it be a frisbee or a smelly man.

"It's okay, Largeness." I pet him. "Let go. Mo is coming with us." I put my hand on Spot's snout and eased his jaws off of Mo's arm.

I pointed the shotgun at Mo, reached for his uninjured arm, and tugged. "Time to get up, Mo. We're going out to the parking lot."

With a significant upward heave from me, Mo was able to sit up without first turning over onto his hands and knees. I saw his Glock on the floor where he'd been half lying on it. I picked up his weapon and put it in my pocket. Then I tugged him up onto his feet.

"Your dog wrecked my arm," Mo said, his voice that of a gruff, tough guy who was trying not to whimper. He held his right arm slightly bent, his hand hanging limp.

"Yeah, he tends to do that when someone pulls a gun on me."

"I'm going to need a doctor. I'm going to need surgery."

"Good idea," I said. I kept the shotgun on Mo and held onto his good arm with my left hand.

"You're gonna pay for this. I'll sue you for everything you've got."

"Then I'll have you booked for assault with a deadly weapon. I have a hundred witnesses. You can't collect damages for injuries obtained in the commission of a felony. And how many felonies would this assault give you? Three? That would put you inside for a very long time. Could be you'll go to Granite Bay. I hope you're good at making friends with those gangbangers. Even though you're fat and ugly, they'll still make you their sex toy."

Mo hobbled toward the front door. He was holding his right arm with his left hand. Some blood dripped down the back of his ring finger, but it didn't look like a dangerous volume. I used my foot to push the door open. Spot followed us through.

We walked out into the parking lot. I let Spot in the back door of the Jeep.

"Mo, you get in the front passenger seat."

It took Mo some effort to get in the Jeep. He completely filled the space. There wasn't enough room to keep the shotgun on him. So I got his pistol out of my pocket and held it pointing up under his chin, the barrel against his throat. Mo was rigid with fear as I drove one-handed over to the entrance and parked so that the tailgate would face the traffic as it exited the parking lot. Mo would not be able to see the vehicles as they drove past the rear of the Jeep.

"I'm going to get out and stand next to the passenger door. You're going to sit looking straight ahead so you don't see who pulls up to collect the reward."

"Flyboy and his bro are up at Lake Tahoe," Mo said.

"Why Tahoe?"

"There's some kind of treasure. Sunk in the lake. Their boss wants it, and they're helping him."

"Who's their boss."

"I dunno."

"How do they think they'll get it?"

"I dunno."

"What's Flyboy's number?" I asked.

"I've got it written down."

I continued to hold the gun under his jaw. "Where?"

"In my wallet. But I can't reach it. This car's too small. I'll have to get out of the car to pull it out."

I got out of the Jeep and stepped away. When Mo got out, I once again leveled the shotgun at his chest. Mo was probably too dumb to realize it was unloaded and I hadn't cocked either of the hammers.

"Pull it out," I said. "Slowly."

He reached behind him with his good hand and pulled out his wallet. He held it out. "I can't get it out one-handed."

"Yes, you can."

Mo struggled with it, trying not to drop the wallet, holding it against his body as his thick fingers worked into the folds. He eventually got a piece of paper out, holding it like a cigarette between his index and middle fingers.

I took the paper. It was blank except for a phone number written in blue ballpoint pen. "This is Flyboy's?"

Mo nodded. "That's my only copy of the number. I should write it down on something. You could write it for me."

I ignored his request. "Flyboy is otherwise known as…"

"Jeff Bosstro."

"Why do you have his number?"

"'Cuz sometimes I like him to help me on jobs."

"What kind of jobs?" I asked.

"You know. Deliveries. Collections. Regular job stuff."

"The regular stuff of what business? Cooking meth?"

Mo shrugged.

"Where does Flyboy stay in Tahoe?" I asked.

"I dunno."

"Is he there with his brother?"

"Yeah. Flyboy couldn't put on his shoes without Chinless… Without Carlos telling him which goes on the right and which goes on the left."

"What kind of weapons do Chinless and Flyboy carry?"

"Chinless like a Concealed-Carry Ruger. But Chinless say a baseball bat is more Flyboy's speed. Less chance Flyboy hit himself with it."

"Flyboy does everything Chinless says?"

"Pretty much ever one does whatever Chinless say. He's big

and he's mean. Smart, too. It's just, you know, in your interest to keep Chinless happy."

I held up the two bills I'd brandished in the bar. "Who's the inker who did the Bosstro tats?"

Mo shook his head. "Don't know."

I stared at him.

"What?"

"I'm trying to decide if it's really 'don't know' or 'won't tell.'" I raised the shotgun so the barrel was under his throat. Then I lifted it so the metal made a hard connection to his jawbone.

"I don't know. Honest truth."

I pushed the shotgun barrel onto his Adam's apple.

"Honest!"

I eased back on the gun barrel pressure.

"What about my pocket Glock?" Mo asked.

"Its new home is my pocket," I said. I handed him one bill.

"You said two bills." Mo was almost whining.

"The other is the cost of your recalcitrance." I got in the Jeep.

"My re-what?"

I drove away.

As I turned right onto the local road, I swerved over into the tall grass and weeds on the shoulder, and opened the driver's door a few inches. Without slowing, I eased the shotgun down onto the dirt, shut the door and drove on. A few blocks down, I got out the card Red had given me, dialed the number, and told him where I'd put his shotgun.

I wondered about Mo's comment that the card with Flyboy's number was the only one he had. If that wasn't true, he could be calling Flyboy, warning him that I had his number and that I knew he was in Tahoe with Carlos. In which case, this entire trip would be a waste. But Mo might have been telling the truth that the number in ballpoint pen was the only copy he had.

When I was back on the interstate and some distance north of Reds, I pulled off on an east/west farm road. I called Diamond and got his voicemail.

I said, "Sergeant, I have what looks like a cell number I'd like to trace." I looked at the card and read off the digits. "Not long ago," I continued, "you said that the world of tracing cell numbers is like the Wild West in the nineteenth century. Websites that trace numbers with no court order, sites that are pretty much out of reach of the law. Do you have a recommendation? Thanks."

I continued to drive east until I got to the first aqueduct. The road went up the incline to the bridge. In the middle of the bridge, I tossed Mo's Glock out the window. It arced away and fell down into the water. The rules about the aqueducts were related to hygiene. No swimming or bathing or boating or dumping. But I wasn't aware of any fine print that said Los Angelenos didn't like drinking water with a little gunpowder smell in it.

I turned around and was heading back to I-5 when my phone rang.

"Owen McKenna," I said.

"Burner phone," Diamond said. "Nothing you can do."

"Did you call the number?"

"No. That would limit your options. I just put it in the search bar on a website I've learned about. Gotta go."

"Thanks very much." I clicked off.

I thought about my approach as I drove back to Tahoe. If someone had already warned off Flyboy Jeff Bosstro, I was out of luck. But if not... Well, maybe I could construct a scenario that might entice him.

Four hours later, I crested Carson Pass. Despite the heat of the Central Valley and the warmth of summer across the foothills, I had to roll up the windows because the early evening air above 8000 feet was in the 30s. Spot had long since pulled his head in from the open window and lay down on the back seat to conserve warmth.

I drove through Hope Valley and started down into the Tahoe Basin. It was early evening, and the necklace of lights around the lake was just becoming visible from up on the pass. The lake was deep indigo with what looked like a few lightning bugs crawling across its surface.

I stopped at my office on Kingsbury Grade to check messages. There were none. I was about to use my office landline to dial the number in blue ballpoint pen when it rang. I picked it up.

"Owen, it's me," Street said.

"Street, my sweet. You sound stressed."

"First, I'm okay. But I was sort of run over."

TWENTY-THREE

"What happened?! Are you really okay?"

"Yes. I'm in the parking lot at the doctor's office on Kingsbury Grade. I was at Heavenly Village meeting the new Forest Service supervisor/basin manager for coffee. Afterward, we were walking along the sidewalk and a guy bumped me. I fell off the curb and tumbled into the road."

"I'm so sorry! You were obviously injured if you sought medical attention."

"Well, it could have been much worse. I held my arms out as I went down and kind of skidded to a stop on my stomach. Like a belly flop."

"You probably took the skin off your palms. Did you hit your chin or face?"

"Palms, yes, face, just a little bit. But the reason I went to see the doctor was that the fingers of my left hand were run over."

"What? A car's tires went over your hand?!"

"A truck. It was just the tips of my ring finger and middle finger. So I worried that maybe they got badly smashed. It turns out, they were just lightly smashed."

"Street, this is serious. Where are you now? I'll come over."

"The clinic on Kingsbury Grade. In the parking lot. Mason drove me here, so I don't have my car. I'd walk over to your office or my lab, but I'm a little shaky."

"Stay put. I'll be there in a minute."

When we pulled into the doctor's office lot, I got out and ran to the clinic entry where Street stood.

Her left hand was bandaged. She held it up. She frowned and her jaw shook with shivering despite the warm weather. She had a bandage on her left cheek bone. The skin near her left ear was abraded, with red scrapes going from her ear down to her jaw.

She'd clearly slid with her left hand out in front and then turned her head to the right as her left cheek hit the pavement.

I kissed her forehead and gave her a light hug. "Thank God you're alive." I held her gently but close.

"Can you take me to my lab? Blondie is there."

"Yes, of course. Are you okay to walk to the Jeep?"

"I'm fine. The doctor took several x-rays. She said the worst injury was to my psyche. It's a bit upsetting to come so close to being killed. It could have been my head under that truck tire."

I walked Street to the Jeep. Spot was eager to explore the scents of bandages and other doctor office aromas.

I had Street inside her lab just minutes later. For the first time in memory, Blondie ignored Spot. She must have sensed the level of Street's stress. Her tail was tucked down and she made crying noises. As Street sat in her lab chair, Blondie stood next to Street with her head in Street's lap.

I got a cup of tea going in Street's microwave, handed it to her, and pulled up another chair. I asked her for the details.

"Mason Krato, the new Forest Service guy, wanted to go over my proposal for a change in their bark beetle strategy. So we met at a cafe in Heavenly Village. Afterward, we were walking up Park Avenue toward the parking ramp when a man bumped into me with substantial force. Later, Mason said the man was a big guy wearing sweats and running shoes, and that the man had been out for a run. Mason thought he was weaving recklessly through the tourists on the sidewalk. Mason said the man may not have realized that a little bump from a big guy could be more like a body slam for a small woman like me." She paused to take a deep breath.

"I might have caught myself and not fallen. But I was near the curb and, as my foot went out to stabilize me, it slid off the edge of the curb and down to the road. I stumbled and sprawled out on the roadway, skidding toward a delivery truck. I don't think the driver ever knew what happened. My arm went out and I never had a chance to pull it back from the truck's rear tires."

Street shivered again as she described the incident.

"The doctor thinks your hand is going to be okay?"

"Yeah. She was quite clear about that. The x-ray showed no damage. She thinks I was really lucky in that my fingers probably meshed perfectly with the indentations of the tire tread. She also said the scrape on my cheek was just a surface abrasion and that I should heal completely in a couple of weeks." Street chuckled, which seemed strange considering she'd just had a very serious close call.

"What?" I asked.

"Oh, just that I joked with the doctor. I said maybe the face abrasion would scrape away some of my acne scars and that I might end up pretty without the cost of plastic surgery."

"Street, stop that kind of thinking. You're not just beautiful to me. You're beautiful, period. You don't have to look like a model to be beautiful."

Street nodded solemnly.

I bent over, put my arms around Street's shoulders, and hugged her again, careful not to squeeze too much. "I'm so glad you're okay."

Street rested her bandaged hand on Blondie's head. "Even though I'm okay, the experience creeps me out."

"How do you mean?" I asked.

"You're going to think I'm paranoid."

"No, I won't. What is it?"

She paused. "I have no reason to think this, but..."

"Think what?"

"I have the sense that the running man hit me on purpose."

I immediately thought about what Daniel's attacker had said on the phone. "I was afraid of this," I said.

"Why?"

"When Daniel Callahan's attacker called and shot out his living room window and made his threats, he added one for me. He said, 'I know where you and your girlfriend live and work.' He wanted me to go away and not come back."

Street looked horrified. "So it's not just me having creepy thoughts because I'm traumatized. It could be this bad guy wants me dead to get at you."

"That's my worst fear," I said. "I'm so sorry."

"Then what do we do?" Something about Street's tone made Blondie lift her head and cry some more.

"When the caller threatened Mae, Callahan's neighbor, I told her that the safest thing would be for her to go away."

"I couldn't do that," Street said, immediately shaking her head. "I have too many commitments. And even if I could go away, what would it solve? The killer could just wait until I come back."

"If you can't go away, we need to think through every possible situation where you're vulnerable. Then we have to address each one."

"You mean, we do like when my father wanted to kill me… I don't go anywhere without Blondie at my side."

Blondie looked up at Street's face at the mention of her name.

Street continued, "I never get out of my car without letting Blondie out first. I never go into my condo without Blondie at my side, so we can't get separated on opposite sides of the door."

I nodded. I stepped behind Street's chair and rubbed her neck and shoulders.

"You said yourself that a Yellow Lab is no great protector," Street said.

"Not like a Dane, no. But any dog is hugely better than no dog. Blondie would bark and alert others. A bad guy would know that if he attacked you, even a Yellow Lab would bite. The best thing would be to stay away from places where you might be vulnerable. Any situation where you think Blondie might not be enough deterrent is a situation where you should have Spot with you. Or me."

Street reached her uninjured right hand up behind her head and gripped my arm.

"I'm sure I'll be okay," she said. "I'll do like you say and stay away from any risky situations. So I'm sure you can leave me alone."

"You know I'm happy to stay with you, be with you, never let you out of my sight," I said.

"Thanks, but I wouldn't be happy with that."

So at Street's insistence, Spot and I left her and Blondie alone. It was hard to leave. But I remembered what Sergeant Diamond Martinez had recently reminded me about the rights of individuals and the ethics of intervening in their lives. Diamond explained it was like an ethical law, and that great philosophers had written about it. We have the right to cross a person's desire if we are preventing them from harming others. But we have no right to intervene in a person's life against their wishes if we are merely trying to prevent harm from coming to them.

This didn't prevent society from doing just that. But ethicists found fault with it. More importantly, Street was fiercely independent. To not respect her wishes would be to dismiss the value of her judgments. If I did that, she would stay away from me permanently.

Street had given me Mason Krato's phone number. I went back to my office and dialed, not expecting an answer because the Forest Service would be closed.

But Krato must have been working late.

"Forest Service."

"Owen McKenna calling for Mason Krato, please."

"Hi Owen, Mason here. Street mentioned you. No doubt she told you about the accident. How is she? I'm worried."

"She seems physically fine. The doctor couldn't find anything wrong beyond scrapes and such. But Street is quite distressed."

"I should think she'd be very upset. If that had happened to me, I'd be sitting at home in the dark with my back to a corner, on my third martini, trying to talk myself down from the frights."

"Yeah. I'd like to ask you some questions."

"Of course."

"Did you get a look at the runner?"

"Just a glance. We were walking up Park Avenue. The road was to our right. The oncoming traffic was close to us. I was next to the curb, Street was to my left, and the runner came up from behind, on her left side. When he hit her, she was a half step in front of me. So the blow shoved her in front of me toward the road. If I'd been more alert, I might have caught her. I feel terrible about that. Anyway, because she stumbled in front of me and fell while she was moving to my right, I didn't really notice the runner, who was off to my left. My sense of him was just from my peripheral vision."

"So you didn't see his face."

"No. It may be he never looked back. But if he did, I never saw it."

"What was your sense of his size and shape?"

"Only that he was a big guy, probably an athlete. Broad through the shoulders. I didn't sense a skinny waist like on a body builder. But he seemed fit."

"If you had to guess at his height and weight?"

"Hmmm, let me think. Maybe six-four and two fifty. But that's just a guess."

"Understood," I said. "Was he running fast or just jogging?"

"I think pretty fast. Not a sprint but fast. He was either in a real hurry or he was very serious about staying in shape. Although that wouldn't make a lot of sense."

"Why?" I said.

"Anyone running hard for physical fitness would be a regular runner and have one or two regular routes, right? But no runner would choose to run on the sidewalk of that busy road during tourist season."

"Good point. What about his clothes?"

Mason paused. He began talking slowly. "I think he was wearing gray. Like gray sweats. But it's just a sense. I don't have an image of him in my mind."

"Sweat shorts?"

"No. I think I'd remember shorts. So I think he had on long pants. And a sweatshirt. Probably long-sleeved. Although maybe the sleeves were pulled up a bit."

"Hair color?"

Another pause. "You know, Owen, these questions point out just how poorly we observe things. I'm sorry, but I can't recall anything about his hair."

"That's common. Did you get any sense of where he went?"

"No. I was focused on Street. I bent down next to her. I'm

embarrassed to say that I had no idea what to do. Like, what if she'd had a spinal injury or something else serious. I didn't even think to call nine-one-one for a pretty long time. And when I finally did have the thought, Street told me not to, that she thought she was okay. So she walked with me to my car and had me drive her to the doctor's office on Kingsbury Grade. I didn't get the name, but maybe you know where it is."

"I do. I met her there and took her to her lab."

"Good. I was afraid to leave her there, but she said she'd be fine."

"Thanks for your help."

"You're welcome. Oh, one more thing."

"What's that?"

"I had a sense about something else. It's so ridiculous that I'm almost embarrassed to say it. Like it's probably just my wild imagination."

"I'll keep that in mind," I said. "I'd like all of your thoughts."

"After the incident was over, I had a feeling that something about the man's head was very strange."

"In what way?"

"Again, you're going to think I'm nuts. But I feel like he had strange ears. I don't recall even looking at them. But that's the feeling I came away with."

"In what way were they strange?" I asked.

"My sense is that they were pointed."

"Pointed ears?"

"Yeah. Like they were cropped."

TWENTY-FOUR

After I hung up, I thought about what Deputy Tanna Havlick had shown me. The mugshot of Carlos Bosstro showing that his ears had been cropped to be pointed like Mr. Spock's. Knowing that he was in town as Mo at Reds Place had said, was disconcerting. Knowing he'd already targeted Street made me feel murderous toward him and terrified for Street.

I tried to think about something else, like what Doc Lee had explained about the compressed air weapon. I remembered the tanks and other gear I'd seen in Harly's barn, equipment that may have been used to create a compressed air weapon.

I remembered that Mae had talked about being a freediver. That freediving didn't involve scuba tanks and compressed air. But she said she'd met some local scuba divers, people who were very familiar with the characteristics of compressed air and compressed air equipment.

I drove to the Bijou neighborhood and knocked on Mae's door. She didn't answer.

"Just coming home from my library shift."

I turned around to see her walking up.

"Any news?" she asked.

I told her that I'd been to lemon country tracking a mite that Street had found.

"Street told me! The one stuck in Daniel's broken door."

"Yes."

"Was it a good lead? Did you find where it came from?"

"Maybe."

Mae opened the door and went inside. "Neighbor Ed was able to replace the broken window in Daniel's house. So Daniel's back in his home." She set her things down. "Can I get you something to drink?"

"No, thanks. I just have some questions."

"Of course." Mae sat down on the couch.

"When you mentioned that you were a freediver, you made it clear that the sport doesn't involve the use of scuba tanks. But you mentioned meeting scuba divers when you moved up to Tahoe. I'm wondering if any of them stand out in your mind?"

"In what way?"

"Just in the sense that you noticed them. Maybe they have a high profile in the diving community. Or maybe you noticed a diver who was a bit strange or seemed to have motivations that were different from the other divers."

"So you're looking for the oddball diver," Mae said.

"Yeah."

She seemed to think about it. After a bit, she shook her head and said, "No. No one comes to mind."

It was the typical reaction a person has in this situation. Maybe if I could keep her talking on the subject, something would occur to her.

"Can you tell me more about freediving? What the experience is like? I've been scuba diving, and I thought it was great. But I think it would be scary to go more than a few feet underwater without a source of air. Do freedivers go very deep?"

"Actually, there are many versions of freediving. But they all involve taking a big breath and seeing what you can do underwater. The sport evolved from people who have always dived while holding their breath, sponge divers and pearl divers. In the old days, before scuba diving was invented, freedivers also went down to retrieve items from shipwrecks that weren't too deep."

"You told me about the term apnea and the various disciplines that freedivers pursue," I said.

"Right. For example, we have categories like Dynamic Apnea, where we see how far we can swim horizontally. Constant Weight Apnea is when we see how deep we can go under our own power. And both of those disciplines have categories with swim fins and without. The freediving category that often gets the most attention is No Limit Diving, where we hang onto a weight that pulls us down and we ride an inflatable vest that pulls us back up. That's the version I've been doing."

"Why did you choose it?"

Mae looked embarrassed. "I guess it's because it's the most exciting. There's the speed. The weight pulls you down fast, and the vest pulls you back up fast. There's also the sheer depth. No Limit divers go the deepest by far. The good ones get down so far that light can't even penetrate. In just a minute or two, you go from sunlight to blackness and back. It's a foreign world. I sometimes think it must be like going into outer space."

"But not all divers do it," I said. "Why?"

"Several reasons. One is that many elite divers think it isn't pure to dive with mechanical aids. It's like racing a motor boat instead of a sailboat. Some elite divers feel that there's more skill required when you swim down and up. And I agree that's true. You earn your dive more by swimming under your own power. Getting dragged down and then back up seems like cheating by comparison. They think that anyone could hold their breath and do that. But the truth is that while No Limit diving may not require the skills of super-efficient swimming technique, it still requires breathing skill and psychological skill, and the courage to try something that will kill you if you misjudge your capabilities. But the main reason for No Limit diving is the excitement. Sailing and canoeing and bicycling are great. And there is a kind of purity to them. But I admit to being thrilled by a motorboat or motorcycle."

I walked over to the mantle and picked up the same picture I'd looked at before, one that showed Mae in her diving gear. "This turquoise water is amazing," I said. "It looks like there's an underwater cliff that goes down very deep."

"It does. It's not as deep as Tahoe's underwater cliff at Rubicon Point. That drops one thousand feet. But Roatan has warm water, and it still goes down over one hundred fifty feet."

"Did you go that far?"

"Oh, no. My goal is to one day go one hundred feet down. In Roatan, I started doing shallow dives. At the end of the first day, I was up to ten meters, which is a little over thirty feet.

The next day, the guides gradually set the marker deeper and I eventually went down to twenty-five meters, which is eighty-two feet. I was scared to death. I almost chickened out. But it helped that the water was so clear and blue. I could almost see my goal marker from up in the boat. So I did my preparation breathing like a meditation. Eyes closed, getting very calm. Then I went. It was… spectacular. I hit the marker, pulled my vest cord, and shot back up to the surface. The entire dive only took one minute, forty seconds, so I had air in my lungs to spare." Mae grinned. "Honest, Owen, it was one of the greatest experiences of my life, going that deep just holding my breath. I'm going back next winter. I hope to go to thirty-one meters, which is one hundred feet."

"And that would be what you called a transformative experience."

"Right. It's something I read about in the Monterey library. For an experience to be truly transformative, you have to experience something new. You can't just learn about it and think about it and take classes about it or watch videos. Skiing, ziplining, skydiving, childbirth, mountain climbing, skydiving, performing on stage, whether singing, acting, or standup are all transformative experiences. There are mental ones, too, writing a novel, composing a song or a score, making a scientific discovery, painting a landscape or still life or portrait. All these things have to be experienced to make their mark. You can't just imagine your way there."

Mae's enthusiasm was infectious.

"You've thought about this a lot," I said.

She nodded. "All the time. And even though you have to have the experience to get the full level of transformation, you can still plan for it, visualize it in advance." She held up her wrist with the large high-tech watch.

"That looks like one of those fitness watches, heartbeat monitor and such."

"Actually, it does some of that stuff. But the main reason I have it is because it's a depth gauge."

"For when you dive," I said. "It tells you how deep you go."

"Yes. Records it, too." She pointed to the watch face. "I keep visualizing thirty-one meters. One hundred feet. I'll do it eventually. And it will be forever displayed on the face of this gauge."

"Until you go deeper."

She smiled. "Right. Who knows? Maybe I'll go to a hundred feet and then deeper still."

"What drew you to freediving?"

Mae thought about it. "I think it was the fact that it's something where you test yourself, discover your limits. And while you can compete with others, the main drive is to see if you can best your previous experience. You're mostly competing with yourself. It's completely internal. There is no reward for freediving other than your own sense of accomplishment."

"Which fits with being a loner scientist?" I said.

Mae made what seemed like a small grin of embarrassment. "I suppose so. Street Casey and I talked about that at lunch. We each pursue work that is primarily about our relationship to a science, not to other people. At one point we were talking about movies we like, and Street said something I found interesting. She said that she likes a medium where you observe people on the other side of the movie screen. In other words, a carefully edited version of people with all the non-essential minutia taken out."

"Yeah, I've witnessed that with Street."

"I realized that I feel similarly, except that my preferred medium is books. Novels, especially. Instead of dealing with people in person, I like them once removed, characters in stories. Characters in books go through the full range of human experience without the gossip and the kinds of activity that serve no obvious purpose, activity that, in hindsight, seems like wasted time."

"You sound just like Street," I said.

"I suppose I am."

We were silent for a moment.

I said, "I was thinking I'd like to try to get Daniel to spend some time talking to me. If I can get him in a new environment away from the recent stress, I might learn something. I wondered if you thought he'd be amenable to coming with me someplace else? And I wondered if I might need you to help facilitate it."

"I think it's a great idea. No, he won't be amenable to it. Not at first, anyway. But I'd try it. And while I might be a good facilitator, I think he relies too much on me. I think you should try to approach him when I'm at the library."

"When is your next work day?"

"I'm on tomorrow morning at nine. It would be good if he doesn't know in advance. That way it's harder for him to get his defenses up. So I won't tell him you're coming."

"Thanks. May I ask my earlier question again?"

"I forget what it was."

"Can you think of any scuba divers who stand out. Anyone I should talk to about Daniel or the Steamer?"

She shook her head. "Sorry."

TWENTY-FIVE

The next morning, I stopped by Daniel Callahan's house at 9 a.m.

Mae had previously explained that Daniel wouldn't answer the door.

As I walked up to the door, I saw that the living room window had been replaced with attention to detail. The moulding and adjacent siding had all been painted. The window caulking bead was very smooth. Ed Filusch had done a professional job.

I knocked on the door, and, as predicted, Daniel didn't answer. I could hear Ray Charles singing Georgia. I knocked again. And again. When Ray was done, Boz Scaggs came in with Sophisticated Ladies. The volume was turned up loud, but I thought Daniel would still hear me knocking. I knocked again. Several times.

After a couple of minutes, I decided I'd given him fair notice. So I began knocking continuously. Queen Latifah pushed out Scaggs with Lush Life. The volume went louder. I knocked harder. Hard enough that I had to switch hands after a few minutes to keep from permanently damaging the knuckles on my right hand.

The thing about knocking is that if you don't stop, and if there is someone inside who is not deaf, you'll eventually get a response. It might be a shotgun blast through the door. But it's more likely that the frustrated resident will finally throw open the door in exasperation and yell at you.

I knocked for ten minutes. The music shut off, the door finally opened, and Daniel, shaking with frustration, yelled at me.

"What is wrong with you! Don't you realize how rude you are being! I have a right to privacy! Go away and leave me alone!" I couldn't see his eyes behind his aviator glasses. But his body language was so aggressive, it seemed he might try to hit me.

"Hi, Daniel. Owen McKenna, here."

"I know who you are! The manly cowboy walk is as clear an ID as there is."

"I'm sorry to bother you. But I need to talk to you."

"No. I don't like agitation. I need calm. Doctor's orders."

"Talking can help bring calm. You will recall that when we met before, things weren't very calm. I may have saved you and Mae from being shot to death. You owe me for that. And now you're going to repay me by answering questions."

Daniel swung the door shut. I stopped it with the toe of my hiking boot, then gently swung it back open.

"This is an illegal intrusion! I'll call the police!"

"Please do. They consider you an obstructionist crime victim, unwilling to help them do their job. They'll be very glad to find out that I'm intruding into your life."

"You are infuriating."

"Your grand nephew is dead. Years ago, it appeared that your sister's boyfriend was killed, which is probably what set all of this off. Mae was nearly killed in your living room. She can rightfully consider that you have an obligation to help law enforcement find the shooter. And right now, my sympathies lie more with her than you, in spite of the fact that you were assaulted."

"You are a pest!"

"Yes. And I'm going to pester you into talking to me."

Daniel's chest was rising and falling with the effort of breathing and raising his voice to me. I felt bad that he seemed so unhappy. But I'd been in this situation enough times to believe that his best chance of reducing his stress was to let me help him.

Daniel backed up across his small living room, reaching one hand behind him until his palm landed on the arm of his rocker, an impressive feat of navigation. He sat down.

I stepped inside the entryway and shut the door behind me. I stayed where I was. I didn't want to encroach on Daniel's space any more than I already had.

Van Morrison started singing Brown-Eyed Girl. Daniel picked up a remote and dialed it down to a soft volume. He leaned his head back against the top rail of the rocker. He took a deep breath, his small chest rising. He exhaled slowly. Repeated. It was a good relaxation exercise.

As he calmed, I noticed how his house was very neat. I understood that a blind person would need items all put in their place so they could be easily found again. But Daniel's house went beyond that to a kind of visual neatness, with everything lined up just so. Like his vanity about his personal appearance, his home's neatness seemed ironic considering he couldn't see the results.

In time, Ella Fitzgerald started singing It Don't Mean A Thing If It Ain't Got That Swing.

"You like the classic jazz standards," I said, hoping it could be a conversational opener.

Daniel nodded. "Forties, especially. Obviously, Van Morrison's songs don't fit the bill. But he's Irish, so I make an exception."

"I like mix tapes," I said.

"This is something different. I told Mae what songs I liked, and she put them on one of the new players. She did this thing where I can hit shuffle, and it plays them in a different order each time."

"How do you know about these new artists like Queen Latifah?"

"You think I just sit around and watch reality shows on TV in my spare time?" Daniel said, without trying to be funny. "I listen to NPR. They have interview programs with musician guests."

Eventually, I said, "I have several questions I need to ask you if..."

He interrupted, "No, I don't want to talk here. We should go somewhere else."

At least, that was an improvement. Now he was willing to talk.

I said, "Mae said that you walk to the supermarket every morning. Why don't we talk while we walk? We can head over to the Bijou golf course. There are nice walking paths."

"No. I got hit by a golf ball there. Someplace else."

"Your choice," I said.

"Take me out to Emerald Bay. It's always been my reset place."

"What's that mean?"

"When I need to clear my head. You stand on the beach with the castle behind you and the roar of the falls behind it. It makes your problems seem small."

"I'm happy to take you there. But my dog is in the car. I know you are afr…" I caught myself. "I know that you prefer not to be near dogs."

"Is he in the back seat?"

"Yes."

"Can you make him stay in the back seat?"

"Yeah, but he likes to sniff a little. Especially when strangers come into his space. He has a cold, wet nose. I'm pretty sure you won't like it. But I can guarantee that he won't hurt you. He's very friendly."

"I've heard that before."

"I see your point. It's good to be skeptical of other people's claims. I'll open the front passenger door, and you can get in without confronting Spot. He'll sniff the back of your head, but I'll try to hold him off."

Daniel thought about it. "Okay," he finally said.

I waited while he put on a pair of hiking shoes. He lifted a floppy cloth sun hat off the coat rack. It had a large brim and a safari-style neck flap that draped the sides and back of his neck.

Then he lifted a windbreaker off the coat rack. I helped him pull it on. He took both the white navigation cane and the heavier support cane off his coat rack.

Just before he walked outside, he walked back to the fireplace mantle, kissed his index finger, and used it to touch the framed picture of the young woman.

Outside, he stopped some distance from the Jeep. Spot had his head out the back window. He seemed to stretch himself out toward Daniel.

Daniel faced Spot from ten feet away, his head covered by the hat and his face obscured by the aviators.

Beyond Daniel, half a block down, a maroon Chevy pickup

pulled to a stop, and its running lights turned off. I would never have registered its presence but for the fact that no one got out and Mae had talked about a maroon pickup cruising the neighborhood. But it could very well be someone who was pausing to hear the last of a radio program. Or someone who had arrived early to meet one of the Bijou residents.

I focused on Daniel and said, "If you reach out your hand and give my dog a pet and let him sniff you, he will think you're wonderful. Dogs become less curious when they get familiar with your scent." As I said it, I thought that Spot would not lose his curiosity about a man shrouded in a hooded hat on a warm summer day, especially if the man would not even hold out his hand for a sniff.

Daniel didn't react. I thought that perhaps he, too, was sniffing the air. "I can tell he's very large. What's his name?"

"Spot."

Daniel made the smallest of nods. "Just let me into the car. I don't need to get cozy with your dog."

"Okay. You have your hat with its neck flap. That will keep you from too much contact."

Daniel nodded, reached up and snugged the neck flap around the top of his shoulders and around to his cheeks. He did a little sweep with his white cane and took a step toward the car.

I opened the front passenger door and told Spot to stay back, holding my hand out as a barrier. I got Daniel inside, ran around and got in the driver's side. Spot was putting his nose all over the back of Daniel's Safari hat. Daniel was hunched forward. His hands gripped the edges of the hat brim and pulled them down. He was no doubt worried, if not terrified. I pushed Spot back again.

I started the Jeep, and we drove away.

Daniel stayed hunched most of the way to Emerald Bay. When Spot gave up and lay down on the back seat, I told Daniel so he could relax a bit. But he remained tense.

The Vikingsholm parking lot was full of summer tourists. There was an attendant to prevent people from trying to squeeze in. I stopped and explained that I was dropping off a blind person and that I would park down the road and come back. The attendant was very concerned that I was adding to the traffic overload.

So, moving very fast, I helped Daniel out and directed him over near a large boulder where he would be protected from drivers who weren't paying attention as they jockeyed in and out of tight parking spaces. I told him I'd be right back.

As I drove away with Spot, I glanced back at Daniel, standing in the sun, jacket zipped, safari hat cinched down tight, one cane in each hand, waiting for me, a relative stranger, to return. It was likely a familiar situation for blind people. But it demonstrated the dependence on others that people with disabilities sometimes have. It also reminded me that there is more than one kind of loneliness. People like me think of loneliness as an unfulfilled desire for companionship. But for blind people, there is another version. He was standing in one of the world's most beautiful places, but was unable to see it. I thought that must produce a powerful longing. To not be able to access that most fundamental perception - to look at your surroundings - would be very sad for me. For those of us who weren't blind, if we suddenly experienced it, it might be heart wrenching.

Because most tourists try to find parking at the head of the bay, I went the opposite direction and drove up the slope to the northeast. Every available place off the side of the road had a parked car. I continued on the highway. About a half-mile up, I found a steeply-sloped place between two trees. I shifted into four-wheel-drive and ground up the embankment until I was off the highway.

I let Spot out, and we jogged back toward the Vikingsholm lot, a half mile away. As we ran, a maroon Chevy pickup cruised past us, coming from the direction of the Vikingsholm lot. The truck's windows were smoked, so I couldn't see the driver. Just after the pickup went past us, I heard the sliding grit of hard braking. I turned and saw that the pickup was turning around in the middle of the highway. It made an abrupt K-turn, then raced past us, back down the slope toward the parking lot where I'd left Daniel.

TWENTY-SIX

There was no way to know if the maroon pickup was the same one that had pulled up near Daniel's house. But its actions suggested the possibility that the driver was following us at a distance, saw us pull off the road, and realized that we must have dropped Daniel off someplace, like in the parking lot.

The concept was possibly far-fetched. But if the pickup hurried, the driver or the driver's companions could grab the old blind man and get away before Spot and I got there. We'd have to run back to where we'd parked. The delay would make it impossible for us to catch the pickup.

I sped up my trot to a full run. Spot, of course, thought that was fun. The human was running full out. But humans were so slow...

I knew I couldn't maintain a sprint for the entire distance. It was too far, and I wasn't in that kind of shape. But I could try.

The traffic was heavy. I had to stay on the shoulder to avoid being hit. In places, the road edge dropped off to a slope too steep to get decent footing. Gravel is hazardous on a slope, like running on ball bearings. I veered down to where the ground was less steep only to have to slalom around trees and manzanita bushes. Spot kept glancing behind to gauge my direction, easily anticipating my movements.

My lungs were at their limit of pain, gasping for breath, trying to keep up my fastest run. We emerged from the forest edge at the upper edge of the parking lot. I rushed onto the asphalt, dodging through cars, both parked and moving. There was a maroon pickup over near the entrance to the lot. It was cruising slowly along the gravel shoulder.

I couldn't see Daniel. But if the pickup driver had wanted him and had already found him, he would have raced off.

The pickup stopped. The passenger door opened up.

I pushed faster, pumping my legs beyond what I thought I could do.

I still couldn't see Daniel. The boulder was to the side of the entrance, not far from the pickup. Even if I saw someone come out of the pickup, I couldn't send Spot after him. If Spot doesn't have a scent and hasn't witnessed previous aggressive behavior from a suspect, and if there are lots of other people in the vicinity, there is no effective option.

When I got closer, I yelled, "Hey! You with the pickup!"

Maybe someone saw me. Maybe not. The passenger door closed. As I ran closer to the boulder where I'd left Daniel, the pickup made a 180-degree turn and started moving forward. When it cleared a group of people walking along the highway toward the parking entrance, it sped away, tires squealing on the pavement.

"Daniel!" I shouted. "Daniel! Where are you?!"

I spun around to the back side of the boulder. There he was, sitting on the ground, leaning back against the boulder.

"Right here," he said. "I'm right where you left me."

"Good." I was breathing hard.

"Where's your dog?"

"Over there. Sorry. About twenty feet to your right."

"I don't want him on me. You've obviously been running. All this excitement. I've read about that. Dogs, when they run, they can fall into pack behavior. It might stimulate his prey drive." Even though his sunglasses hid his eyes, Daniel looked very worried.

"No, it won't. But I'll get him." I walked to Spot, took hold of his collar, came back.

"What's wrong?" Daniel said.

"Nothing."

"Don't lie to me," Daniel said. "I may be blind. But I can still tell you're lying. You don't want me to lie to you."

"You're right," I said between breaths. "I'm sorry. I had to drive well up the highway to find a place to park. As Spot and I were walking back, I saw a maroon Chevy pickup driving up the highway, the same way we'd come. It looked just like a pickup I saw down the street from your house as we left. Maroon is not a common color for a pickup. As soon as the pickup went by us, it made a fast turn and rushed back to this parking lot. That made me worry. What if someone wanted to grab you, away from your house, someone who might think you still had more to say about the sinking of the Steamer. That person could see Spot and me trotting toward this lot, and they could figure out I'd left you waiting here alone."

"You were worried I'd be kidnapped. I'd set the world's record for the oldest kidnap victim."

"Yeah."

"Are they gone now?"

"Yes. The pickup left as Spot and I ran closer. Maybe they saw us and that caused them to leave."

"Or there could be no connection," he said.

"True. It could be coincidence."

Daniel shifted both of his canes to his left hand. "Help me up? I can still get down on the ground without hurting myself. But I can't get up off of anything lower than a chair."

I took his free arm and gently lifted. When he was standing, he switched the white navigation cane to his right hand and kept the support cane in his left.

"Can you hold your dog with your left hand while we walk down the path to the castle? Because then I could hold your right elbow. I don't want to be next to your dog."

"Yes, that's fine."

"Then you could hold my support cane as well?"

"Yes."

Daniel handed me the cane. I held it in my right hand with my arm bent. Daniel held onto my elbow. I took Spot's collar with my left hand. We started across the parking lot and headed down the asphalt path. Daniel was very deft with the navigation cane, moving it gently back and forth in front of him. He walked without hesitation. Although that may have been partly because he assumed I would steer him away from obstacles.

Mostly, I had to steer Spot away from the passersby who

wanted to pet him.

After we'd gone a few hundred feet, Daniel said, "I can walk faster. It's a mile down to the castle. At this speed, we won't get there until tomorrow."

"Okay." I sped up a bit. "You're a very good walker."

"One of the only things I'm good at," he said.

At the faster rate, Daniel limped with every step of his left foot.

"Your foot is hurting?" I said.

"Leg."

"Should we slow?"

"No. It just takes a bit for someone my age to get moving. Find a car or a building or anything else my age, it will have lots of mechanical problems."

"No doubt. Have you done this hike recently? It's a good mile down, and another back up. The elevation gain coming back up is substantial. Especially when the parking lot is close to seven thousand feet above sea level."

"You're wondering if my mechanics will hold out?"

"I just don't want you to have any regrets."

We walked for a hundred yards without talking. Daniel still limped. But he moved at a fast pace.

"You should know that, at my age, every day, every hour has a potential for regret," he said. "Most times, something won't go as I hoped. But even when it does, my brain starts worrying over something in my past, and the regrets are a flood. I'm not the easiest person for me to spend time with."

I had wanted to develop a comfortable conversation before I started asking questions about his assailant and threats and suspects. But it wasn't going especially well. I tried a new subject. "Daniel, you've often referred to things you've read, books and articles. That makes me curious. Are all those available in Braille?"

"Some are. Braille books can be very expensive, so I get them from the library. Some are books on tape. I used to listen to lots of those. But it hasn't been tape for years. It's CDs. The library also has special machines for listening to books. I've even been listening to this mystery series set in Tahoe. They come from Nevada Talking Books. And ever since Mae moved into my rental, she's been getting me audiobooks on downloads. She gets the downloads on her computer, puts them on a player, and I listen to them that way. And it's not just books. She gets articles and other things that are like radio shows. I forget what they're called. Pods or something."

"Podcasts."

"That's it. I go over to Mae's house. She looks on her computer, and she tells me the different choices. I pick what I want. Biographies. History. Novels. Current events. More than I could ever listen to in my lifetime. Which, of course, at my age, could end any day."

Daniel slowed and then stopped walking. He tilted his head as if listening. It reminded me of the way dogs tilt their heads to focus on a particular sound.

"Must have been warm last night," Daniel said as he resumed walking.

"What makes you think that?" I asked.

"The roar of the falls is especially loud. That means a warm night that melted more snow than normal. More water over the falls."

I listened. "That's cool," I said, "sensing last night's temperature with your ears."

"I would think anybody would do that," Daniel said.

We continued walking.

"You said the pickup's color was maroon," Daniel said. "What does the color maroon look like?" Daniel asked. "I've heard the word, but I never really knew what it was." Daniel said.

I smiled. "It's rare that someone asks you a question that you've never thought of before. Thank you. Let me think. Maroon is a dark reddish color."

"Like purple?"

"No. I would think of purple as red mixed with blue. Maroon is red mixed with a bit of orange. Except that adding orange would make the red lighter, and maroon is darker than red. So maroon must have some brown in it. Although if an artist heard me describe maroon, they would probably wince. But I think I'm going in the right direction."

"What's maroon feel like?"

That stopped me. "Well, it's a rich tone, more presence than, say, a brown of the same darkness."

"Can you name some things that are maroon? Other than bad-guy pickup trucks?"

"Well, I should probably point out that pickup trucks are rarely maroon. They are usually silver or white or black or sometimes dark green or red."

"Colors men like," Daniel said.

"Yes, exactly. You won't see many pickups that are baby blue. That wouldn't look macho enough. Okay, things that are maroon… Leather furniture is often stained maroon. Lots of woods are stained maroon, and some woods, like mahogany or manzanita, are naturally maroon. Often fabrics are maroon. Especially in elegant surroundings. Banquet tablecloths in hotels. The big curtain in theaters and showrooms." I paused. I thought of dried blood, but I had the sense not to say it. "This is fun. Thanks."

"My pleasure," Daniel said.

"Were you ever able to see colors?"

"When I was very young. Three years old, I think. But the only color I have a memory of is yellow. I had a stuffed monkey that was yellow. Don't ask me why. But it was my favorite toy. Yellow with black eyes that were shiny smooth. Like rocks. His name was Felix. My family had come up from the valley to vacation at the lake. One day I was at the shore, spinning in circles, swinging Felix around, and I lost my grip. Felix flew into the water and floated, gradually moving out away from the shore. So I ran after him. I didn't think about it. Maybe I assumed I'd float too.

"The neighbors at the cabin next door had a dog. The dog ran into the water and grabbed Felix. I was horrified. But as I charged into the water to save Felix, I didn't float. I sank. My last memory of that incident was that dog racing away with Felix in his teeth and me about to drown. The next thing I knew, my sister Nora yanked me out of the water. She held me up and patted my back.

I coughed water. Nora saved my life. But I cried for Felix. Nora said they'd find Felix. But they never did. That dog ate him. Or buried him in the forest. Or maybe just left him to drown. I don't know. I've been terrified of dogs and water ever since."

We walked in silence.

"Nora was a fair amount older than you," I said.

"Yes. Eleven years older. She was my protector and my vision guide and my support. My parents did the basics. Food. Shelter. Clothing. But Nora was the person who gave me emotional and intellectual sustenance."

"Nora isn't still alive."

"Oh, God no. She'd be one hundred and - let me think - one hundred and six or so. No, Nora died young. In her twenties. A terrible tragedy."

The way Daniel said it, I did not dare ask about it. Instead, I said, "Were you born blind? No, of course not. You just described Felix as being yellow."

"I was born with normal vision." Daniel's words were slow and measured.

I didn't respond.

"I had a bad accident that ruined my eyes."

He also said that in a way that made me think that was the end of that subject.

Daniel tilted his head again. "A hawk," he said.

"I didn't hear one. Did you hear a call?"

"No. It's the Steller's Jays. Listen. Three of them. Sending out their alarm call."

Only after he said it, did I hear it.

"That call means raptor. There are a few possibilities, but I'm thinking Goshawk. They nest around here."

"Are they the main raptor that nests at Emerald Bay?" I asked.

"No. There are lots of raptors around here. Eagles and ospreys. But Steller's are medium-sized birds, favored food for Goshawks or the larger falcons like the Peregrine. If the tiny birds were sounding alarms, we'd look for small falcons." Daniel paused, lifted his head toward the sky, a few puffy clouds reflecting in his aviators. "There. Hear it. A keee-rrrr sound. That's the bird that's even more feared than the Goshawk. A Red-Tailed Hawk."

I looked up toward the sky. But I saw nothing.

"I'm impressed," I said. "You sense temperature with your ears. Now, you predict hawk species by listening to Steller's Jays. Is there anything else you can do that the rest of us, handicapped by our vision, cannot?"

I said it as a bit of a joke. But Daniel remained serious. He made a little shake on my arm and then spoke in a soft voice. "There are several things that legally blind people notice that normal people do not. Remember, I can see vague shapes. That allows me to observe movement in a way that you probably don't. For example, a few decades ago I was an independent consultant doing gait analysis."

"What does that mean?"

"It means looking at the way people walk. They called me a kinesthetics expert."

"What's it for?"

It took several seconds for Daniel to respond. It seemed as if he was looking down the path, toward the trees and rocks and lake in the distance.

"Do you see those people coming up the path toward us?" he said. "There are three of them, right? No wait, maybe there's a fourth person behind them."

It was obvious to me that the group was four people, two women and two men. One of the men trailed behind a bit, huffing his breaths, trying to get enough oxygen in the high-altitude air.

"Yes, it's a group of four," I said.

"Look at the man who's going to come closest to us as we pass by them."

I looked. "What makes you think that's a man? The person is short and has a feminine shape, albeit overweight, and the person is wearing a large sunhat. I think that's a woman."

"I can't see those details. I just see the movement. I know he's a man because he walks like a man."

"What does a man walk like?" I asked.

"It's not my specialty to describe it in words. I just know it by the look. Men and women have differently-shaped pelvises, right? Maybe that's the difference. All I know is that he walks like a man."

"Okay. I believe you. Why do you bring him up?"

"Because..." and now Daniel lowered his voice even more. "Because he's in the early stages of Parkinson's Disease."

For some reason the statement shocked me. "You think that based on the way he walks?"

"I know it. I did a study for IBM. They were trying to figure out a better way to analyze future company medical expenses. They hired me to put together a study that would analyze the way people moved and identify motor-control diseases that would impact the company's bottom line ten or more years out. Basically, I sat in the building lobbies as employees streamed in on their way to work and streamed out when they left to go home. IBM had an early closed-circuit TV system that would record the flow of people. I had a button that I clicked when a person with motor dysfunction came along. I also had a note-taking system so I could record where they were in the crowd and what gender they were. If any questions arose, they could go through the TV tape and double check which person I was referring to."

The concept seemed outlandish to me. We were about to pass the group of four people. I spoke in a soft voice. "So if I walked up to that person approaching us and asked him, he might admit that he has Parkinson's?"

"Oh, no. This is early stage. Almost for sure, the person doesn't know it. His spouse has, no doubt, recognized changes in his movement. But it probably isn't significant enough that he's agreed to go to the doctor about it."

"Wait a moment." Now I was even more surprised. "It sounds like you're saying you know when a person has Parkinson's before they know it."

"Yes, of course." Daniel was matter-of-fact about it. "That was my job. Years down the road, IBM's analysis proved that I was right. All the people I identified from their gait eventually were determined to have Parkinson's."

"That's amazing."

"I don't think so," Daniel said. "It's a devastating and heartbreaking disease that strikes even the most physically fit people. Because I'm able to focus on movement, I can see the hints that some other people miss.

I watched as the group went past us. The person Daniel was referring to showed no distinctive movements that I could see. He - assuming it was a he - was in his late sixties or early seventies. He obviously did not have an athletic walk. But it wasn't a halting or difficult walk, either.

After we passed them, I said, "How did you learn to recognize a Parkinson's patient by their walk?"

"My grandfather on my mother's side would sometimes join us when we vacationed in Tahoe. This was after my accident. Even though I could only see vague shapes, I always noticed that he moved differently from other people. Especially when he walked. Later, they determined that he had Parkinson's. Over the next many years, I met other people who showed similar characteristics in their movement. Sometimes I found out that those people had Parkinson's, too."

"I don't really know about Parkinson's. Has your ability to diagnose the disease saved any people?"

"There isn't a cure for Parkinson's. At least not that I know of. So, no, I haven't saved any lives. But IBM was able to encourage certain people to get a checkup, which then enabled their doctors to help them cope with the disease."

"Is this… I don't want to pry. But is this something you did for a job?"

"Sure. I did real well for many years. I bought the two houses in Tahoe. I also did part-time consulting for law enforcement in the Bay Area. I was their bank robber guy."

"How did that work?"

"You know how often the bank camera gets the bank robber but his hat hides his face?"

"Ah, you're one of the guys who watches the camera footage. Then they have the suspects walk back and forth in the lineup."

"That was me. I was really good at it. Of course, to a blind guy, video footage of a person is just a vague blur moving this way and that. But to me, it's practically like fingerprint evidence. Maybe just as good. Of course, not all judges will accept forensic gait analysis. Especially when it's done by a blind guy. But us blind guys are much better at it than people with normal vision. And it's becoming more accepted. Especially as supporting evidence. It can be one more thing for a jury to consider. It's hard to describe how it works."

"You're not distracted by how pretty the girl's face is, so you can focus on her movement patterns."

Daniel walked several steps before responding. "That's actually a good metaphor. Blindness cuts out the visual distractions."

"Gait analysis sounds like a cool job," I said.

Daniel shook his head. "It was. Now they use computers. Artificial intelligence. The computer looks at the video and analyzes the suspect's walk."

We came down to where the path neared the castle and the bay. I'd said nothing about where we were. But Daniel obviously knew.

"This is my favorite place on Earth," Daniel said. "I used to ask my parents to bring me here on my birthdays. We'd go very early so I could be here at dawn. In the early days, my scars were extremely sensitive to the sun. But at dawn, I could feel the sun's warmth with no burning pain. We'd sit on the beach and wait for the sun to poke up above the East Shore mountains."

"Some people are leaving a bench over there," I said. "Should I grab it?"

Daniel nodded.

I handed Daniel his support cane, pulled Spot, and we ran across the sand. I patted the bench. "Sit on the bench, Largeness."

He looked at me doubtfully, his tail on slow wag.

"Seriously. You sit on the bench." I turned him and pulled him back until the backs of his rear legs hit the bench. He tucked his tail between his legs and sat on the bench. It wasn't unlike the way a human sits except that Spot's front paws were still on the ground.

"Stay," I said, putting my palm on the end of his nose. "I'll be right back.

Several groups of people were nearby, staring at Spot. They immediately pulled out their phones and started taking pictures. I got the sense that Spot enjoyed it. He stayed put while I trotted back to Daniel and brought him over.

I sat in the middle, with Spot to my left and Daniel sat to my right.

I reached into my cargo pocket, pulled out a dog biscuit, and gave it to Spot. He chomped once, swallowed, and turned his head down and back toward me to look at the pocket where I keep the treats.

"That was one trick," I said to him. "One treat for one trick."

Spot kept looking at my pocket. With his head down, his jowls drooped open.

"What's that?" Daniel asked.

"Dog treat. My hound will sometimes do what I want if the reward is praise. But he will nearly always do what I want if the reward is food." I took off my daypack and set it in my lap. "I brought peanuts and water for us," I said. I reached into my day pack and pulled out a jar of peanuts. I gave it a little shake so Daniel would understand it was a jar.

Daniel took the jar of peanuts. "Is this my treat for a trick? I haven't performed a trick, yet."

I chuckled. "You are a funny guy, Mr. Callahan."

Daniel shook peanuts out into his hand, tipped his head back and used his hand like a funnel to direct the peanuts into his mouth.

After he carefully chewed and swallowed, he said, "You said you had questions for me."

"Yeah. I'm trying to figure out a way to catch the man who beat you up. I believe it's the same man who murdered your grand nephew, Colin Callahan."

Daniel poured more peanuts from the jar and ate them.

I continued, "I'd love it if you can help me think of a way to find this man. The man found you. I don't know how. I assume it was through Colin. The connection from him to you should seem more clear to you than to me."

"I don't have a clue about the connection," Daniel said.

"Then why are you eating my peanuts?" I asked.

"Now you're the funny guy. However, I do know how to catch him."

"How's that?"

"You figure out how to get the suspects in front of me. I don't know how. That's your expertise. But if you do it, I'll use my expertise."

I saw where he was going with it. "What a great idea! I parade possible suspects in front of you and you watch how they walk."

"Like I said, gait analysis," Daniel said, "is practically like fingerprints."

"I'll work on that. That's definitely worth peanuts."

Daniel nodded, chewed his peanuts, and washed them down with delicate sips of water.

"Do you know what a triquetra is?" he asked.

"No, I'm sorry I don't."

"It's an ancient Pagan Celtic symbol of interlocking arcs that look vaguely like three leaves. Some people think of it as a good luck shamrock. The triquetra symbolizes lots of things, from Celtic culture to goddesses to affection. When you give someone a triquetra, it says you think they are special. For many years, I've been weaving triquetras with flat, green leather cord. I give them to people as gifts. And I want to give you one."

Daniel reached inside his windbreaker, unzipped an inner pocket, and pulled out a beautiful woven leatherwork, about two inches in diameter. It was comprised of an intricate type of three-lobed knot with an intersecting circle running through it. Attached to it was a long cord of the same green leather so that it could be worn as a necklace. He handed it to me.

"Daniel, this is beautiful. I'm very touched." I put it over my head. The triquetra symbol hung at my chest. "I have to admit that I don't see how you would go from hating me when I knocked relentlessly at your door, to giving me a handmade gift."

"I could say that we are all a mass of contradictions," he said.

"But the truth of it is that I'm impressed with your persistence. I tried hard to send you away, yet you were stubbornly insistent. As we talked on the way down to this beach, I realized that I'm lucky that anyone would care enough about me to pound on my door until I gave in and talked to them. That makes you special. And this triquetra symbolizes that."

"Thank you, Daniel. This means a lot to me."

"You're welcome." He paused. "But next time, call before you visit."

TWENTY-SEVEN

Daniel still limped with pain, but he showed surprising stamina as we walked back up to the Vikingsholm parking lot, a rise of several hundred feet.

When we got back to his house, it was nearing the end of the afternoon. Daniel rested in his rocker.

"Mae will be home from work, soon," he said. "Maybe you would like to stay until then?"

"I'd be happy to."

A few minutes later, I saw Mae walking down the street. "Here she is now," I said.

I got up, opened Daniel's front door, and waved.

Mae came up the walk and into Daniel's house.

"I see you two are visiting," she said, no doubt remembering that I had planned to talk to Daniel even if I had to badger him into it.

"Yes," I said.

Daniel spoke up. "He forced me to walk down to Emerald Bay where we had to sit in the sun and listen to the noisy birds and smell too much fresh air."

Mae grinned. She reached out and touched my triquetra necklace. "And so you gave Owen a triquetra to symbolize your displeasure."

Daniel nodded.

"Maybe I'll make some tea and you can tell me about it."

Without waiting for either of us to respond, Mae went into the galley kitchen and put on water. In a few minutes she came out with tea, this time in Daniel's old aluminum pot and some heavy ceramic mugs.

"I poured boiling water into the mugs to pre-warm them," she said.

She served tea. We lifted our mugs, and all said, "Sláinte."

I glanced at Daniel's mantle.

"I've noticed your special picture," I said. "May I ask who it is?"

Daniel stood, took three careful steps and reached out his arm to put his hand on the mantle. He slid his hand to the left, came in contact with the picture frame, and picked it up. He touched the glass with his fingertips as if revisiting the image in some way. He handed the framed photo to me. "My sister Nora. She gave this to me a few weeks before she died. I don't know exactly when it was taken. But I always had the idea it was a recent photo. She knew she was my best friend. Even so, I liked that she'd give a picture to her blind kid brother. She knew that I see in other ways. To have the photo has always meant a great deal. After she died, it became even more important."

I took the picture from him. It was a black-and-white headshot. The young woman had just a hint of a smile with just a tiny reflection of teeth showing. She didn't look especially happy, but she seemed knowing in some way. She had feminine curls of dark hair around her face, and there was a bit of fire in her dark eyes. Her eyebrows were thin and delicate and arched in dramatic parabolas.

She wasn't beautiful, but she somehow looked angelic. "A guy could fall in love with that face," I said. In my peripheral vision I saw Mae turn to look at me.

"Lots did," Daniel said. "I learned that's as much a curse as a blessing."

"You said Nora died young," I said.

"Yes. Worst day of my life."

Mae and I didn't ask the obvious questions.

Instead, I asked, "What was Nora like?"

"Do you know of the writer Virginia Woolf?" Daniel asked.

Mae responded. "My women friends all know of her. She wrote A Room Of One's Own."

Daniel nodded. His white eyes seemed to stare vacantly into space. "Nora always wanted to be a writer. She was quite fixated on Virginia Woolf. I got one of Woolf's books in a Braille version, and I couldn't make anything out of it. But she inspired Nora, and that was good. Nora wrote several short stories and started a novel or two. When Virginia Woolf wrote that to be a writer, a woman needed a small regular income and a room of her own, Nora chose that as her goal. She was convinced that was all that stood between her and a successful writing career. But even though she made a little money and eventually got her own apartment, she couldn't make a writing career work. It was, I think, a great disappointment, to come to accept that, for whatever reason, she didn't have what it took."

I was still holding Nora's photo. I turned the frame over to see if there was an inscription. The frame's backing paper had no writing on it. But it was covered with dots. It took me a moment to realize the obvious.

"There's an inscription in Braille," I said.

"Yes. My family got one of the earliest Braille machines. Nora would use it to transcribe things for me to read."

Mae reached for the frame. I handed it to her.

"What does it say?" I asked.

"It's from the song Danny Boy," Daniel said. "When I was very young, I had lots of bad dreams. My mother would try to comfort me. My dad tried, too, although he was awkward at such things. Nora was the only one who could calm me down. She did it by singing Danny Boy to me. When I cried out in the night, she'd come to my bed, crawl under the covers with me, and sing the song. She did that more times than I could count, and she kept it up for years. Long after I'd become a bit of a tough boy, too hard for casual sentimentality, we still had that close relationship. When she wanted to be nice, she'd come into my room and sing. It was the nicest thing anyone ever did for me." He reached for the picture, and Mae handed it to him. He held it close.

"And what does it say in Braille?" I asked.

"The last lines of the song."

Daniel cleared his throat and sang in a surprisingly clear voice, high and sweet. He ran his fingertips over the Braille dots as he sang.

"'Oh Danny Boy, Oh Danny Boy, I love you so.'"

TWENTY-EIGHT

B ack at my office, I dialed the local newspaper.
   A woman answered, "Tahoe Herald."

"Glennie, I'm so glad you haven't become a victim of the incredible shrinking newspaper business."

"Is that Owen McKenna?" she said with delight. "It's been so long I don't even know if your cape is the same color!"

"Same color, same logo. But it's getting threadbare and very faded. Today's bad guys laugh in my face. Maybe I should start a new career. I could be a rapper or something."

There was a short pause before Glennie replied. I thought she was probably thinking I was nuts.

She finally said,

"If you ever grouse,

waiting for your bug lady to be your spouse,

I wouldn't be a louse and say you were to blame

But maybe I should try to dowse your flame."

"I guess you're the one who should be a rapper," I said.

"What brings you calling?"

"I'm feeling my way here. I'm trying to catch a murderer, and I've got an unusual idea of how to trap him. It would involve a newspaper article under your esteemed byline."

"My curiosity is piqued!"

"Here's my thought. I believe the murder has something to do with the Tahoe Steamer."

"Wait. The Steamer was sunk way back in…"

"In nineteen forty," I said. "August twenty-ninth. I've met someone who witnessed the ship being scuttled."

"Nineteen forty? That would make this witness old."

"Right. Mid-nineties. Anyway, a person I believe is a grand nephew of this witness was recently killed at the lake."

"Are you talking about the body on El Dorado Beach?"

"Yes."

"The one that was ruled a homicide by pneumo something?"

"Tension pneumothorax. Pressurized gas in the chest."

"Owen, this is real news! I'm so tired of writing for tourists. The ten best places to go hiking. The five best pizza restaurants."

"Glad to be of service. But the main thing I'm bringing you isn't news. It's a fishing expedition."

"That might catch a murderer? With the right angle, that could be journalism."

"Will you be in your office for a bit?"

"Yes, please come over and be quick about it. I haven't seen you in forever. And bring His Largeness."

I knocked on the door of the down-scaled Herald office twenty minutes later. Glennie was grinning when she opened the door. She hugged Spot first. Then I bent down, and she reached up and gave me an enthusiastic hug.

Glennie hadn't changed since I'd last seen her. She still exuded the happy buoyancy of a cheerleader but with a gravitas that few of them had. She still had the earnest desire to write good, informative stories but with little of the cynicism that infects journalists at big-city newspapers. She still had the palpable charisma and feminine charm of a celebrity but with none of the self-absorbed ego and focus.

Glennie was in many ways the opposite of Street Casey. Where Street was an introverted scientist who focused on her insect research and was happy to be alone, Glennie was an outgoing reporter, excellent at getting people to open up and spill their secrets. Where Street experienced and telegraphed a full range of moods including the darker end of the spectrum, Glennie was eternally sunny, the kind of person around whom it was impossible to be a curmudgeon. Where Street was, by most measures, too thin and had a countenance that, with her acne scars and tendency to wear dark makeup, sometimes seemed more severe than pretty, Glennie was the smiley, curvaceous, and often stunning woman who was pursued by countless men.

I was flattered to receive Glennie's attentions. And yet, to Glennie's often-stated regret, I was much more drawn to the complicated, intellectual scientist who few other than me would call beautiful, a woman who had barely spent five minutes goofing off in her entire life and who focused on a never-ending quest to produce valuable science. Glennie's goal was a happy life. Street's goal was a productive life.

We sat at a small conference table, Glennie across from me, and Spot next to her, his giant head at the same level as hers, panting as she pet him. After a bit, he lowered it down to rest his jaw on the table. Glennie ran her hand along his head and neck.

"So what's on your mind?" she said.

"I mentioned the man who witnessed the scuttling of the Tahoe Steamer."

She nodded.

"Another man recently assaulted that witness in an attempt to gain information about something valuable that might have gone down with the Tahoe Steamer when it was scuttled."

"Treasure on the sunken ship?"

"Treasure or something. We don't know what."

"In all that I've read about the Steamer over the years, I've never come across any mention of a treasure, gold or whatever."

"If it's treasure, it would be private, something only one or two people knew about. If so, those people are probably long dead. But instead of treasure, it could also be valuable information."

Glennie's eyes got wide. "The proverbial treasure map!"

"Maybe." I had a question that I wasn't sure how to ask. "I'm wondering if you have to have multiple sources to corroborate everything you write?"

Glennie paused. "If I want to present something as a likely fact, yes. Two sources minimum."

"And if not?"

"If I can't verify a story, I can present it anecdotally. 'A source close to the situation claims that…' Like that."

"And I could be your source," I said.

"Right."

"Okay. Tell me what you think about this idea." I chose my words carefully. "I'm thinking about a treasure recovery mission, a mission that the organizers want to keep under wraps if not totally secret."

"Recovery of whatever went down on the Steamer," Glennie said. It was notable that she didn't ask if the recovery mission was real or something I'd dreamed up.

"Yeah," I said. "There's a question as to who might try to acquire this treasure, whatever it is."

"People fighting to get to it first," Glennie said.

I nodded.

"I don't know maritime law," she said, "but isn't there some kind of rule that says that treasure that's been lost a certain length of time belongs to the person who finds it?"

"Probably," I said. "But in this case the person who is out to find it may well be a murderer. And the act of retrieving the treasure would possibly connect him with the murder."

"Got it. So you need to stake out the treasure recovery mission in order to entice your murderer to come and steal the goods. Then you can catch him. Or her."

"Exactly."

"And my story would bring other people to observe, making it less obvious that you are in the crowd."

"You could be a detective. Then again, you are a journalist, which is a kind of detective."

Glennie leaned over and wrapped her arms around Spot. "Did you hear that, Largeness? I'm a detective, too."

Spot lifted his head off the table, started panting again, and then walked his front paws down until he was lying on the floor.

Glennie looked at me. "Can you give me any particulars to add to the story? Specific detail is what gives a story verisimilitude."

"Vera what?"

"Oh, sorry, writer's jargon. It's the quality of seeming like real life. The more specific the detail, the more believable the story."

"Okay," I said. "Your story could talk about ROVs, remote operated vehicles sent down with lights and cameras and a robot arm to pick up items. Several groups have sent ROVs down into the lake."

"Are ROVs like drones?"

"Yes, they are. Underwater drones."

"And when is this mission happening?"

That was a question I hadn't planned for. I thought fast. "From what I understand, the mission is next Sunday."

"When would you like the story to run?"

Another thing I hadn't thought about. "As soon as possible, I suppose. And if you followed up with more information in a subsequent edition, your story would produce a good turnout for the event. Divers would show up to see if they could join in or swim along. Tourist boats would probably plan special trips. Maybe other ROV operators would bring their underwater drones."

Glennie asked some questions about the details of the mission, the location, the time, etc. I made up answers that seemed most reasonable and useful. All along, I got the clear idea that she understood that the mission was no more than a ruse designed to draw out the murderer, an event that would be created by her reporting of it.

When we were nearly done, Glennie made an unusual face, a grin and a frown at the same time. "The person who started this by pressuring the witness about what went down on the ship… What gave them the idea of treasure in the first place?"

"I don't know. But I think they saw some letters that were written back then, and those letters had hints of treasure."

"Have you had your assault victim look at suspect photos?"

"No, he's blind."

"Oh, wow, it gets better. I mean, it's not good he's blind. But it will make for a great story. Will you reveal the witness's name?"

"I'd prefer we keep him incognito. And I wouldn't want you to describe him as blind, either, because that would make it easy for people to figure out his identity. The assault was a serious trauma, physically and psychologically. I don't want him to have to fend off curiosity seekers, or worse, more toughs trying to squeeze him for info."

"Okay, one more question," Glennie said. "Do you believe that there is treasure of some kind on that ship?"

"I don't know. Even though I have no evidence for it, I believe it's possible. But I do know that something unusual happened the day or two before the ship was scuttled. But I can't say more than that at this time."

Glennie raised her eyebrows. "'Something unusual!' Whoa, that's a couple of intriguing words." Glennie stared into space. "The headline could lay out the hook, and the story could bait it."

I nodded. "Yes, perfect." I stood up. "Thanks so much. And call with questions."

"You know it." Glennie raised up on tiptoes and gave me a peck on the cheek. Then she made the grin that was a touch maniacal. She was clearly excited. "Say hi to your bug lady. She's a lucky girl."

The next morning, the headline was huge.

POTENTIAL SECRET TREASURE ON TAHOE STEAMER SHIPWRECK
80 Years After Tahoe Steamer Scuttled, A Treasure May Be Revealed

The grandest ship to ever sail our magical mountain lake was the S.S. Tahoe, known to most simply as The Tahoe Steamer. It was built by lumber baron D.L. Bliss and launched in 1896. It plied Tahoe's waters for decades, delivering people and building supplies and mail around the lake. Unfortunately, the highways that were eventually built around the lake put the ship out of business, and it was scuttled in 1940, sunk where it was originally launched, in Glenbrook Bay.

According to a reliable source, there are new rumors of treasure aboard the Steamer. While the nature of this potential treasure hasn't been described, the source says that a dive team with remote operated vehicles (ROV) and other high-tech gear is after that treasure.

As of this writing, maritime law applicable to sunken treasure in Tahoe is not clear. However, because the location of the ship is 400 feet below the surface, and because the ship has been sunk in public waters for eight decades, and someone claiming a connection to this particular shipwreck is a murder suspect, this newspaper believes that the public should be informed of any operation that would plunder the contents of the Tahoe Steamer wreckage.

The dive team is planning a treasure-recovery journey to the sunken ship on the second Sunday in July, whether by human dive or robot dive. It should be noted that a previous team of highly-regarded professional divers in Reno is the only group that has ever been proven to visit the Steamer wreck in person. Because of the great depth of the wreck, specialized technique and gear and gas mixtures are required to make such a deep descent.

Because of these difficulties, it may be that these other divers are doing their work entirely by ROV. Divers may still be in the water. Perhaps they will want to transfer any ROV cargo into a duffel bag or two underwater and out of the scrutiny of onlookers.

The article seemed ideal for my purposes.

I thought it was a masterful story, a baited hook that would have all of the Tahoe Basin and many people elsewhere focused on the Steamer and waiting to see what would happen on the day of the Steamer Festival.

Now I had just a few more pieces to put in place for my trap.

TWENTY-NINE

I looked up the number for the Mountain Belle tour boat and dialed. After two transfers, I was speaking to Patty, the booking manager.

"Hi, Patty. I was just reading in the Herald about this Tahoe Steamer event on Sunday. It sounds pretty cool. I know that you mostly do Emerald Bay cruises, but I'm wondering if you might be putting together a special event cruise to Glenbrook Bay for this treasure raising."

"You know, I was just talking about that with Matt, our GM. He's definitely onboard with the idea but he hasn't worked up a plan yet. Oh, wait, he's waving at me. Hold on."

I held.

"Hey, man, Matt Bronsky here. Sorry, I stole the phone from Patty. Reason is, I'd like to do a Tahoe Steamer cruise. Because you're the first call we've had, I realized I should ask you your preferences, if that's okay."

"Fine by me."

"Typically, our questions are cruise length time-wise, start time, party size, food, and drink. And of course the cruise objective."

"I'm not sure I have a plan, yet. I'm just curious about this whole Steamer thing. They say they might be bringing up treasure that went down with the Steamer when it was scuttled. That would be exciting, right?"

"It'd make history," Matt said.

"I'd like to be there to witness it. But I would only have a small group."

"Okay, so this wouldn't be a private tour," Matt said. "We'll sell tickets to the general public."

"Yeah, I think that makes sense," I said. "But I'm not sure of

- what did you call it - the cruise objective."

"Okay, lemme mention the typical range of interests for such an event and see if these are idea generators for you. Our guests usually fall into these categories. A romantic cruise for you and the missus? A party for your friends? A gathering of professional photographers? Drone operators who bring their own drones? Scuba divers who want to use our onboard compressor and other gear? History buffs who want a docent to give a talk? Foodies who want barbecue and craft beers? Am I getting close?"

"That's a lot of choices," I said. "Let me think. It wouldn't be a party so much as a group that's curious about the Steamer and whatever is happening with that. Photos, a chance to witness something exciting, an appreciation for Tahoe Steamer history. Stuff like that. I'd like it if we could get to Glenbrook Bay early, maybe an hour before any expected action. And we'd possibly stay for three or four hours."

"Getting there early is a smart idea," Matt said. "We could beat the crowd, if there is one. That way we can get good placement. There's not much public beach where we could make a beach stop like we do in Emerald Bay. But, depending on the wind, we may be able to anchor not too far away."

"I don't know about what's involved in anchoring. I do know the Steamer is more than four hundred feet down. And I'd like to be above it or close, if you can arrange that."

"We can try to get close, but not above it. The steamer is too deep to anchor above it."

"Can you just float above the Steamer? Hovering?"

Matt made a little laugh. "The short answer is, yes, in some situations. It sounds simple, doesn't it? Drive to the spot and use our engine to keep us in position. The Mountain Belle is quite maneuverable. But those big twin screws still only go forward or reverse. Accurate maneuvering requires we move forward at a minimum speed. For hovering, the Mountain Belle has what's called a Dynamic Positioning System that's pegged to GPS. It uses bow and stern thrusters and works great for keeping us in place over a fixed spot on the bottom. The problem is, it only works in very light wind and no current. If we get any more wind than a light breeze, then the positioning system gets overwhelmed. Plus, the Steamer is part of the National Register of Historic Places. They have lots of rules about not messing with the wreck. We've got eight hundred feet of anchor chain, which, following the one-to-eight rule, means our anchor can be at one hundred feet of depth. It would be best if we anchored in whatever is the shallowest place upwind of the wreck. Then the wind would drift us toward the wreck until the anchor chain grabs. Make sense?"

"Perfect. I suppose I'd need some price range before I commit," I said.

"Tell you what. I'm going to make the decision to do this right now."

"Great." I was counting in my head, Mae and Daniel, Street and me. "Figure it for four people and two dogs. I'd like some kind of table. Something inside and out of the sun and wind?"

"Sure. We have a lounge amidships. It accommodates about a dozen passengers and is divided into quarters. I could put you down for a quarter lounge space. The setup is like at a casino showroom. Nice chairs, your own table, and wait service. Let me put you on hold, and I'll get back on the line in a minute with some pricing."

I waited five minutes. Matt eventually returned and quoted me a price that was probably reasonable for his business but seemed like the cost of a Hawaiian vacation.

I thought about it. "Okay," I finally said. I gave him my phone number, and he said he'd get back to me with details about departure times and such. I thanked him, and hung up.

THIRTY

Next, I called our local radio station.

"KXcellence radio, where our excellence is your life," a young man answered. "How can we make your day excellent?" Not only was there no enthusiasm in his voice, he sounded so weary that I wondered if he'd make it through another hour.

"My name's Owen McKenna. I'm interested in purchasing a custom sponsorship that would involve some creative writing."

"For that you'd need to talk to Andrew."

"The guy who calls himself Airwaves Andy?"

"One and the same. He's currently off the air, so I can connect you. Hold on."

After a minute, there was a click. The resonant radio voice that most people in Tahoe recognize said, "Airwaves Andy speaking."

I introduced myself again. "As I explained to your secretary, I'm looking for a custom sponsorship possibility."

"Maybe you can explain it to me again. My intern is not the most thorough. Of course, what can I expect for free, heh, heh."

I repeated what I'd told the young man. "Does this seem like the kind of thing you'd be interested in?"

"Yes, definitely. Custom programming is my specialty."

"Great. But before we invest time in this, I should ask about your cost range."

Andy said, "It would be dependent on how extensive the work would be. Typically, even with the most custom work, we try to fit it into one of our packages. For example, let's say you want to run our twenty-twenty campaign. That would be twenty spots of twenty seconds each. As long as the spots are all the same, the writing is included. We have two time frames. Drive time and dead time, heh, heh. As you can imagine, the dead time is real cheap, and the drive time will cost you."

"Let's start with the drive time package."

"That would set you back seven hundred ninety-five dollars. Don't worry, I can do the math for you. That's less than forty bucks a spot, which is a monster bargain compared to the city markets. Not only that, but I throw the writing in for free. In the city, that would be many thousands."

I refrained from commenting that city stations probably had thousands of times the listeners. The main thing I got from Andy's pitch was that he was eager, no small thing in purchasing any small business services.

"Can we meet?" I said. "I'm looking for something unusual. I'd like to explain it in person."

"Of course. I'm leaving for an appointment but will be back in the studio later this morning. Would eleven-thirty work?"

I found the KX Radio office on the back side of a tacky strip center. The door was dented steel with peeling red paint. On either side was a garbage dumpster. The smell was not pleasant.

I knocked.

A guy with a big belly on a small frame opened it. "Hey, bud. You must be McKenna. Sorry for the lack of spit polish. Interns are supposed to do it. You can imagine, heh, heh."

"It's the voice and the presentation from the car dash that counts," I said.

"Oh, you are so right. Let's talk in my conference room." He walked over to a Costco folding table that was jammed between a rack of electronic gear and a wall that was painted black but covered with scuff marks. I stepped over a thick group of electric cables. Andy pulled out two metal chairs. We sat. From my position, I could see through a dusty window into the sound room, which had dark gray, egg-crate, sound-absorption foam on the wall. There was a table stacked high with papers and CDs. Behind the CDs was an old computer and a large microphone with an eight-inch circular pop filter in front of it.

An unseen monitor speaker was playing the current broadcast, a canned mix of music and pre-loaded advertisements. The volume was low, just sufficient for Andy to tell if things were going as planned.

Andy had a pad of yellow paper and a Bic ballpoint pen. He set his phone next to that.

"I want to do a kind of radio play," I said when he seemed ready to concentrate.

His eyebrows went up. "How 'bout you grab a guy's attention with your first sentence. Does this mean a play like something made up? Fiction? Or are you selling something real?"

"A mix. I'm a private investigator trying to solve a real murder and a real assault."

Andy's eyebrows went higher. "Sweet."

It was an unusual reaction. But I understood that the media is always looking for an attention grabber.

"I'm taking something real and enhancing it," I said. "Think of it like fiction based on a true story."

Andy was taking notes at a furious pace.

I continued. "This Sunday, beginning late morning, there's going to be an on-water event at Glenbrook Bay. It's called the Tahoe Steamer Festival. The focus is the possible retrieval of treasure from the Tahoe Steamer four hundred feet down at the bottom of the bay. I think I would like your package of twenty spots, providing advance promotion of the festival."

"I saw the article about it in the Herald," he said.

"I'd also love to have you do an on-location broadcast about the festival, preferably from a boat."

"Like when I do on-slope broadcasts for ski and mountain bike championships."

"Exactly. I think it will be good promotion for KExcellence Radio. The Tahoe Herald will be running additional stories about it, and they'll also do a followup mention or two. I'm willing to give you an exclusive for on-the-water reporting in return for a discounted price on the advance spots. It could be a prize opportunity, bringing the world the story of valuables hidden for eight decades on Tahoe's most famous shipwreck."

Andy nodded. "I'm sure we can work something out. Tell me more."

"The treasure retrieval attempt will likely be made by what

are called underwater ROVs."

"Remote operated vehicles," Andy said. "I know about them."

"We don't know exactly which ROV companies will be involved. Unfortunately, the ROV action is underwater."

"Which is where I come in," Andy said. "Not much excitement to witness from a boat, heh, heh. But I bet I could do something exciting."

"Right. I'm thinking you could build up the hype by reporting the ascent of a particular ROV run by a company called Deep Recovery. As the ROV approaches the surface, I'm hoping that your reportage would draw the attention of the murderer."

"Wait. Let me make sure I'm clear. You don't want to draw attention to the murderer. You want to draw the attention of the murderer. Because he's after the treasure." Andy's eyes were wide with excitement.

"Yeah. We don't want people to even know about the murder. Hopefully, the murderer will think that he's just one more spectator. Your angle could be that you have a connection to the Deep Recovery company. That's what would rivet people's attention to KXcellence Radio. You would be able to work the question of whether or not the ROV is carrying anything as it approaches the surface. You could create suspense around that concept."

"Teasing it out, dragging it out," Andy said. He added, "But I wouldn't really have a connection to the company. Because it doesn't exist, right?"

"It exists as part of a law enforcement concept to catch a killer. I'm hoping that your work will be instrumental in this plan. If we're successful, you can add that to your list of testimonials. KXcellence Radio, the only station to ever help catch a killer."

Andy beamed.

"Your story angle could be all about the ROV's depth. The crushing pressure four hundred feet down, then three hundred, and so on. Why divers can't go that deep without special air mixtures and special training. And, will the ROV come up empty-handed or with fabulous treasure?"

"I've got the patter in my head already."

"Can you do this from a boat?"

"Absolutely. My buddy owns The Black Jack Pot. He lets me borrow it. It's just a twenty-four-foot runabout. But it will give me on-the-scene accuracy. I have a battery-powered satellite uplink I can bring along. As long as it doesn't get wet, I'm king of the airwaves."

He paused, thinking, frowning. "Here's my first idea already. I know a guy who has one of those ROVs. He's not real speedy on the tech stuff. But he's had it in the water. And he's put it through some dives, testing the lights, the video cam, the control features. How 'bout I call him. He could have his drone in the water and give us an underwater video feed. We could patch his video into an internet presentation. Would that be great or what!"

I liked that Andy was so enthusiastic. It seemed that he'd already started thinking of himself as running the whole show, for which he'd get a reasonable fee and, more importantly, the buzz that comes from reporting something the local community would think was big.

He continued, "I could do a radio/video simulcast. People could watch and listen in real time as the ROV is coming up from the depths. They could tweet their friends while they're throwing treasure-hunting parties. This could be the most exciting thing to happen on Tahoe's waters in years! And all the while I'll pump the "Deep Recovery" label. People won't be able to find info on it through traditional channels. So it will be all Airwaves Andy!"

He made some more notes on his pad, then looked up at me, his eyes crinkling with excitement.

"Let me see if I'm imagining this the way you are," Andy said, trying to sum up. "In essence, what you're after is a theatrical event. Using the power of radio and internet, you want me to create theater about a treasure that - in the listener's ears - is going to be brought up from the Tahoe Steamer by an underwater ROV. That ROV will carry a package that looks like something that's been four hundred feet down for eighty years. The presentation will be so enticing that numerous divers will want to be underwater to witness this incredible find. And some of those divers may try to steal the package." Andy's lower eyelids were raised, making him look crazed.

"Exactly," I said. "And if a diver tries to take the package, other divers may intervene, trying to stop him or attack him or maybe steal the package from him. Even though your video feed will seem official, people will wonder if other ROV companies might try to get in on the action with their own robots. So no one will know for sure which ROV is bringing up treasure."

"Wow," Andy said. "This is like the old west when rumors came down about a stagecoach hauling a secret load of gold through the desert wilderness!"

"I'm hoping you'll get uncountable benefits from having the whole world of Tahoe and the world of shipwreck diving all tuned to you."

Andy grinned as if I'd just convinced his bank to cancel foreclosure proceedings on his house.

"You bet, McKenna. You're gonna be amazed at what I can do. Thanks for this opportunity."

We shook, and I left.

THIRTY-ONE

Before the festival started, I wanted to track down the artist who did the elaborate shipwreck tattoo on Colin's back.

I spent some time visiting tattoo artists' websites and looking at tattoos. I saw nothing that was reminiscent of the shipwreck tattoo based on the Caspar David Friedrich shipwreck painting. I Googled the words "shipwreck tattoos" and found nothing useful. I needed to talk to tattoo artists.

The first artist who came to mind was the man that Mallory had called to look at Colin's body on the beach. I remembered that the man, Ivan Manfred, went by the business name of Ink Maestro. He hadn't recognized the Caspar David Friedrich painting that Colin's tattoo was based on, but he might know how to track down other tattoo artists.

When I Googled his name, I clicked through to his website and looked through his library of images. There was a large number of images and a large variety of styles. His rep as a master inker seemed justified by his impressive range of work. I remembered that he had disparaging comments to make about tattoos made from paintings. And nowhere on his website were there images with the feel of paintings, famous or not. Despite Ivan Manfred's far-ranging abilities, his tattoos seemed, to my naive eyes, quite traditional.

That was probably where the money was.

I looked up his business address and drove there with Spot.

The Ink Maestro's studio was one block off Lake Tahoe Boulevard in South Lake Tahoe in what looked to be an old, brick, auto repair garage that had been painted white inside and out, and fitted with new large windows.

I parked in the shade of a thick stand of Jeffrey Pine, gave Spot a pet, and walked over.

The inside of the converted garage was visible through the windows. It was well lit, as if from unseen skylights above and track lights that shined on the white walls. Painted on the walls were huge black lines with rough edges. They formed abstract shapes as if they were a new type of Kanji, American instead of Japanese.

The effect was commanding. No one could turn down the street without being riveted by the view inside the windows. Something about the pattern seemed familiar. But I couldn't identify it.

In one corner of the single spacious room were a table and two chairs, one on each side as if comprising a mini conference area. On the table were three-ring binders, perhaps with tattoo designs that customers could flip through. In the center of the room was a techy recliner similar to a dentist's chair, and articulated lights like those a dentist might use. On a nearby workbench was some machinery that I took to be tattooing equipment.

Ivan Manfred appeared to be alone. He was pacing back and forth, talking on his cell phone. His blond hair flowed behind him. When he made his about-face turns, his hair flew out like the mane of a palomino horse in a barrel race.

I pushed open the door. Ivan turned and looked at me, made a little wave, and kept pacing and talking.

"Eight o'clock? No, I don't do evening appointments." Pause. "Sorry, but I'm a professional. You wouldn't ask your doctor for an evening appointment. Same with me." Pause. "Noon? No, I'm at lunch from noon to two. You wouldn't ask your doctor to interrupt lunch. So either we fill in for my cancellation at three-thirty on Thursday, or we pick a time during the month after next. If you prefer, I can refer you to another artist."

"You'll call back? Okay." He hung up and turned to me.

"I know you from someplace, right?" he said. "But I haven't inked you. I remember all of my clients."

"You saw me briefly when the South Lake Tahoe cops called you to look at an unusual tattoo on a body at El Dorado Beach. I was there as well."

Ivan frowned. "Oh, yeah. The abstract on the man's back.

Unusual for a tattoo, that's for sure."

"Because abstract tattoos are uncommon?"

"So much so that they don't exist in any measurable way. Lots of tattoos are non-literal. They can be really fantastical. But they are almost always recognizable pictures of something. Not abstracts."

I decided not to explain what I'd told Commander Mallory on the beach, that the tattoo was in fact a recognizable picture of a famous painting and not abstract at all.

I reached out my hand. "Owen McKenna. I'm a private investigator. Those same cops called me for help as well."

"Ah. I provide the intellectual artistic input. You provide the gumshoe, street-crime input. An interesting dichotomy. Which suggests that you are here to ask something about art or tattoos or... Dead bodies?"

I gestured toward his big wall. "Would this kind of image be good for tattoos? Or is this too abstract as well?"

"You like abstract expressionism?"

"Not especially. But I do like Franz Kline more than most of the New York School. De Kooning's idea that Kline take a rough sketch and blow it up wall-sized so that it loses all connection to the original object he drew was brilliant, don't you think?"

Ivan Manfred didn't respond. He studied me, a strong frown on his face. It was one of those expressions you see when someone realizes they had misjudged a person. Eventually, he gestured toward the wall and spoke slowly.

"No, I don't think these marks would make a good tattoo. They are special, however. Maybe you'll figure them out with time."

I stared at the wall.

"Have you learned anything about the person who died on the beach?" Manfred asked.

"No. But I thought that if I could track down the tattoo artist, that would be informative. So I came here to ask you how one would find a particular tattoo artist. To my knowledge, there was no identifier on the tattoo, no artist signature."

"Some Japanese inkers sign their work, especially on large,

full-body art. But they sign with Kanji, so people who don't know Japanese just see it as part of the art, not as a signature."

"American artists don't put their signature on their work?"

"Not generally. People look down on artists signing their names as if it is crass commercialism. But some inkers have sly ways of identifying themselves. For example, they'll add a tiny image that is associated with them to every large tattoo they do. It becomes a kind of trademark."

"What kind of image?" I asked.

"Anything. It could be a small valentine heart or a skull or an eye or a cat's head. The customer just thinks it's an artistic style. And on a complicated tattoo, the customer might not even notice the image if it's small enough."

"Do you remember noticing such an image on the dead body's abstract?"

Ivan shook his head. "I specifically looked for one. But no."

"How else might I track down the artist?"

"You could post the image online. There are uncountable tattoo sites and tattoo threads. Someone might recognize the tattoo or, more likely, the style that would suggest a particular artist."

"Good idea. Although I would have no idea how to do that. Because I don't know the business at all, I'm curious about something else. You are a celebrated tattoo artist. Why is it that you don't have tattoos yourself? Or if you do, they're not in visible locations."

He frowned and glanced at his watch as if very squeezed for time. "I'll give you a couple of quick answers. First, I keep getting better at my art. And tattoos are hard to remove. So I don't want to put a work of art on my own body because I imagine that some day I will think it's not up to my new standards. Another reason is, frankly, that I'm a bit of a snob. Most tattoos are done in a way or a location that makes it hard or impossible to ink yourself. And I don't think other inkers are as good as I am. So I'm reluctant to have the work of other inkers on my body, even if I design the tattoo."

"Ah," I said.

"There's one more reason. If you think of other kinds of artists, say, oil painters, you'll find that some of them have blank walls in their houses. Their studios will be full of their art and the art of other artists. But their living room walls are often bare or at least not cluttered with art. It's a kind of respite from work. When you leave your studio after working on an image all day, you sometimes want to go home to the calm of no images. Well, that's the way I feel about my body. I spend my entire working day putting images on bodies. When I get out of the shower and look in the mirror, I like to feel like I'm on a mini-vacation from my work life."

"A good point," I said. "One more question, if I may. How did you learn tattooing?"

"Not like a lot of other artists, I can tell you that. Most inkers learn by apprenticing under a successful inker. Then they get a machine, tattoo their own ankle, move on to their friends and so forth. I went the more formal way. I got my BFA degree at San Jose State, a school which has a really good art department. Then I got my MFA at CalArts in Santa Clarita. I considered getting a doctorate in art history because the Masters of Fine Arts is a terminal degree for practicing artists. You can't go any higher. And, well, I always wanted to have a Ph.D. Ivan Manfred, Ph.D. It sounds good. But I realized that painting was my fated oeuvre."

"Yet you became a tattoo artist."

Manfred looked insulted. "Tattooing is not a step down, despite what ivory tower academics think. Those are the same people who used to think that photography was a step down. Some still think it. You can make serious art in nearly any medium. When I saw that tattooing was the new frontier for art, I apprenticed under a well-known inker in Southern California. I think I'm now one of the pioneers in great tattoo art."

"You probably are," I said. I handed him a card. "Please call if you hear anything that might lead me to the person who did the dead man's tattoo."

"Will do."

I opened the Ink Maestro's door and headed over to where

I'd parked.

Spot had his head out the window. He was panting, the huge tongue flopping. I could see his tail wagging across the back seat. As I got close, I said, "Eager to see me, huh? Hard to go without your master, isn't it?"

Then I realized that he wasn't looking at me. He was looking past me toward the tattoo studio. I turned.

Ink Maestro was trotting after me. "I'm sorry to bother," he said. "But I realized you are heading toward this Jeep, which means that Harlequin Dane is yours. Am I right?"

"Correct. Although a closer analysis of our relationship might suggest that I'm his rather than he being mine."

Ivan slowed as he got closer. "Could I... Would it be okay if..."

"Yes, feel free to pet him. He's friendly. So much so that he might like to go home with you."

Ivan didn't seem to hear me. He was transfixed as he got closer to Spot. He had both hands out as if to walk up and cradle the face of a religious icon. Ivan's transformation from arrogant artist to Great Dane groupie was immediate. Gone was the holier-than-thou attitude. In its place was childlike wonder.

Spot stopped panting just long enough to sniff Ivan's hands, then resumed panting.

Ivan put his hands on Spot's cheeks and pushed back across his ears. Then he used one hand to pet the top of Spot's head while his other hand gently cupped underneath Spot's jaw.

It was obvious that Spot loved it.

It was also obvious that Ivan was breathing more deeply, a common relaxation that happens to people around Spot. They lose their ability to focus on what previously had them tense, and they become completely lost in the new world of His Largeness.

After ten seconds, I said, "Okay, you're getting perilously close to the rescue dog transfer threshold," I said.

"What's that?"

"A person at a shelter once explained it. If a person pets a homeless dog for more than thirty seconds and the dog keeps loving it, then the shelter can invoke the rescue dog transfer statute .

and require the person to take the dog home with them."

"You're joking, right?" Ivan still hadn't taken his eyes off Spot. He sidled backward up to the Jeep and next to Spot, and put his arm around Spot's neck. Spot shut his eyes and leaned into the headlock.

"Maybe not," I said.

"Sorry, I'm monopolizing your dog. What's his name?"

"He answers to Spot or His Largeness as much as any other."

Spot turned and glanced at me for the briefest moment, then went back to concentrating on the new man in his life.

Ivan didn't hesitate. His voice was a mezzo soprano squeak. "Oh Largeness! What a giant head you have. You want to come home with me?"

Spot wagged.

Ivan said, "In grad school, there was a girl named Barbie who had a Harlequin Dane named Brutus. Brutus, like Largeness here, was beyond regal. Beyond imposing. Even beyond Barbie who was no slouch herself. So we started calling him Brutus Beyond. Then we made it a phrase. If we had any experience that was really incredible, it was 'Brutus Beyond Barbie.' I became fixated on the black-and-white patterning of Harlequin Great Danes. That's why I developed a fascination with Franz Kline and decided to take his concept in a new direction. Most people don't see it, even after I point it out. But now that I've said it, you will."

I must have frowned.

Ivan pointed back at his studio. "Look through the window at the black marks on the inside wall. You can see the resemblance from here."

I turned and saw it immediately. The bold, black, kanji-type figures were an abstracted version of a Harlequin Great Dane's blotchy black marks. There was no specific outline of a dog. But once I saw it, the image emerged. Legs, chest, an ear, the snout, the black nose.

"Wow, impressive."

"Do you think Largeness would sit for me?"

"Sit for you like an artist's model?"

"Yes. What do you think?" Ivan sounded very eager. "I've been hoping to start a new painting series. He could be immortalized on canvas. Although they'd have to be big canvases."

"Well, first of all, he wouldn't stay sitting for very long. Too much work to hold up one hundred-seventy pounds. But he can lie down for a long time. We could maybe work out a date. But it will cost you a lot in dog treats."

"No problem. I could talk to my agent and get you a licensing cut. And I'll definitely look for that abstract tattoo artist who did the dead man's back."

I thanked him for his time, said I'd call, and left. As we drove away, Spot looked longingly back toward the man with the flowing blond hair.

I told Street about it over wine. "Spot fell in love with another man today, a tattoo artist. And now the man wants Spot to be his artist's model."

Street made a little grin, then bent over to reach Spot, who was lying on her bare floor near Blondie, who was on her dog bed. "Oh, Spot, you should know that there is a long history of artists taking advantage of their models." Street turned to me. "Maybe Spot should be accompanied by a chaperone."

"A common dilemma for the guardians of artist's models," I said. "Do you have a suggestion?"

"What about Blondie? If this artist took both at once, you and I could go on a romantic getaway."

"And I could search for more treasure."

Street narrowed her eyes and gave me a demonic grin.

THIRTY-TWO

That night after I left Street and Blondie, Spot and I sat out on my deck. I drank a beer. Spot watched me.

"Sorry, boy. I know you love the stuff, but I only brought out this one."

The evening chill at 7200 feet of elevation is remarkable, so I was wearing my leather jacket. I looked across the vast expanse of lake and thought about how the Tahoe Steamer Festival was shaping up. Despite its potential, it seemed I should be doing something else. I'd been charging around asking questions, but it didn't seem like I'd made much progress.

I was thinking about my visit to lemon country when I realized I hadn't ever called the number I'd gotten for Flyboy Jeff Bosstro when I was at Reds Place.

I dug it out and dialed.

After five rings a generic robot voice came on asking me to leave a message.

"Owen McKenna calling," I said. "I'm looking for Jeff Bosstro. I believe we have a mutual desire about a certain valuable item. We could join forces and help each other. I help you. You help me. You could get rich. So call me back." I left my number and hung up.

I tried to look at it from the Bosstro side of things. They, or maybe the man who hired them, had already hurt Daniel and Mae by scaring them to death. They'd hurt Street by pushing her into a truck. Maybe next time they'd want to hurt me directly. If so, they might want to stake me out. What better way than to watch me and follow me to pick a good spot for doing the hurting?

Maybe they even staked me out late into the evening. I thought about how fishermen caught big predator fish. They baited a hook and went trolling. Perhaps my phone call was the bait.

Time to troll.

It was 10 p.m. when I let Spot into the Jeep. I drove down the mountain and turned south toward Cave Rock. I kept a close watch on the rearview mirror. They could be parked anywhere. When they saw me, they could pull out and follow me from way back. Or they could vary their distance and, if there was any other traffic, move farther forward or back to confuse me. Or they could be sleeping off a drunk in a campsite, planning to take me down the next day.

The late evening light of July had faded to nothing more than a memory of a dark orange glow across the lake as I approached the Cave Rock tunnel, which was illuminated inside with its new modern lighting. As I got near the entrance, I saw a pickup up ahead, possibly maroon, going my direction, though much slower, and weaving as if the driver was only one drink short of passing out.

Well, look at that. You try to entice a fish into following you, and you end up following him.

I slowed a bit and came up to within ten car lengths, close enough that I could see well, but the driver wouldn't be able to see much of me in the rearview mirror.

The pickup went into the tunnel, taking up both southbound lanes. In the lights of the tunnel it seemed that the pickup had smoked windows like the one I'd seen before. But I had no way of knowing if it was the same truck.

The pickup went through the tunnel, still weaving. It had a pattern where it slowly veered to the left, and just before it went off the road, it made a sudden over-correction to the right and came back into its lane. Then the process repeated.

When the pickup emerged from the tunnel, it went the equivalent of a long block and then made a quick turn into the Cave Rock State Park parking lot entrance. The driver misjudged the road, clipped a sign, ran off the pavement, then jerked back. The pickup made a sudden stop.

If I was careful, it was an opportunity for me to engage a man who might be Daniel's tormentor and maybe Colin's murderer. In addition, an advantage was that drunks are easy to subdue, especially if they aren't armed and firing.

I pulled over on the highway, shut off my engine and the Jeep's lights. I opened Spot's door, took his collar, and shut the doors quietly.

The driver's door of the pickup opened, and a man stumbled out, leaving the pickup's engine running. The man tripped and almost went down, then caught himself. He slammed his door in a dramatic gesture. The parking lot was sloped. The man did a lurching run down the incline, got to the side, bent over hands on his knees, and vomited long and hard.

The park was closed and there were no lights. The ambient light from distant houses was very dim. But I could see that the pickup's driver was a big enough guy that it must have taken a lot of beers to get him in this state.

Spot and I walked slowly into the trees to the side of the parking lot. Then we came out well away from the running pickup and angled across the lot toward the man.

From what I'd seen, I was fairly certain the drunk was one of the Bosstro brothers.

Spot was tense at my side, his rigid muscles transmitting high-alert status through his neck and up my arm. He knew that this type of drunk man in an empty parking lot at this time of night was highly unusual. I knew it, too.

But it wasn't until we'd gotten closer to the man, far enough from the pickup that its engine noise wasn't filling the air, that I heard its passenger door open and shut. I knew then I'd been incredibly stupid and fallen for an ancient trick.

The drunk man straightened up, no longer drunk. He turned a tactical flashlight toward me, its beam like the high beam on a modern car. The light shined in my eyes before I could look away or block it with my hand. I quickly looked down, but not before my night vision was temporarily destroyed.

I too had one of the super-bright lights in my pocket, but it was of little advantage when you're outnumbered.

Another light came from behind me. I turned just enough

to perceive the second man's position and size, which was larger than the first. Two Bosstro brothers, here to beat me to a pulp or death or both.

The breeze off the lake became brisk in a moment, the kind of crispy cold that made for runny noses. It smelled less like a lake and more like an approaching snowstorm. But I knew the real reason for my chill was my fear. Two men, armed at the minimum with baseball bats, were going to crush my skull and maybe fill me with enough compressed air to crush my organs from the inside.

I tried to take a long, deep breath, a calming technique to still the fear and minimize the panic.

"You were warned, McKenna," a voice from behind me said. "You were told to go away. But you didn't. Now you learn what happens."

"Good luck with that," I said as I quickly pulled my tactical light out. I figured I was as good as dead, which meant I had nothing to lose. That gave me license for bluster that I didn't feel. I turned my light on with one hand and, while shading my eyes with the other hand, looked up and shined my light toward the Bosstro below me. Then, my eyes still shaded by my hand, I quickly spun and shined my light toward the Bosstro above and behind me. I couldn't see anything clearly. But I hoped that my light may have returned the visual assault. The men might now be compromised like me. The light behind me wavered. I kept mine shining at eye level and moved it back and forth.

Through the camera-flash purple dots that comprised my impaired vision, I sensed no guns raised. Of course, it's nowhere near as much fun to shoot a guy as it is to break his bones with a club. In the sweep of my flashlight, I saw that the man below me was huge and held some kind of club. It seemed about the heft and size of a baseball bat. He no doubt had held it in front of him as he performed his weaving walk, shielding the bat from my view. And the man behind me also had a club.

I said, "The Bosstro brothers from Lemon Hills, right?" I called out. "You in front of me are the big one, right? Lemme think. Chinless or some dumb name to go with your size. And you behind me is Flyboy."

The man in front of me said, "It's unfortunate for you that you said that. Because we don't leave witnesses who know our identity. And my bro, up there, has a little thing about using his fly swatter, which has the word Slugger burned into it."

"Maybe I got your ID wrong," I said as I turned a second time, sweeping my light toward their eyes. "I heard the big bro was supposed to be smart. That would be you, Chinless. But clearly you're an idiot, going around with your enforcer brother and his bat like some kind of TV show bad guy. Smart people are more inventive than that."

He shouted up at me. "I'll make sure to invent some new ways for you to enjoy severe pain before I'm done."

It seemed that the light shining on me wavered. I got the sense that both men were advancing on me, one coming up from below, one coming down from above. That meant that my life was dependent on how Spot and I acted in the next few seconds.

Time makes weird compressions and expansions in moments of life-or-death stress. In the space of a few seconds, I realized that when I want Spot to be aggressive, I normally point him toward a suspect. But I didn't have the suspect's clothes to scent him on. I couldn't see with the blinding lights shining on me. Most of all, the men had baseball bats. And a club breaks a dog as easily as it does a person.

My instinctive calculation had me thinking that I had to get between Spot and the baseball bats before I started my defense.

Like most animals, dogs understand aggression. They react differently to a friendly approach than they do to a tense, combative approach. Spot was already taut with tension, a quality I could feel with my hand that held his collar.

Instead of Spot running out in front of me, I wanted Spot to run with me. If he watched my lead, he would sense my trouble and respond accordingly. My hope was that I could draw the swing of the bat before Spot got to the man.

I bent down next to Spot's head and used a low, rough voice.

"Ready, boy?" I stopped shading my eyes, pushed my

fingertips down into his neck, and vibrated my hand to give him a sense of agitation. "Let's go!"

I ran toward the man down below us. I held tight to Spot's collar so he couldn't get ahead of me. Spot pulled me as I sprinted, forcing me to go faster than I thought possible. I concentrated on not looking at the blinding flashlight. Instead, I focused on where I thought the man was. For no particular reason, I imagined the man as right-handed. Which meant he held the light with his left hand.

Or with his teeth.

I held my light up above my head as I ran, and I shined the beam where I thought the man's eyes would be. My goal was for him to think that I was higher above him than reality and that he should swing higher.

I wanted him to swing the bat horizontally instead of vertically. So I ran with a tall, awkward posture, hoping I could get the man to swing for left field.

When I sensed that I was close, I made a running leap, trying to gain enough height to make him swing higher still. I hoped I was just in front of the man when I landed. I collapsed my legs and pulled Spot down with me. I released Spot as I hit the ground rolling. I used my arms to continue the roll. I heard a grunt of effort. My side ribs struck shin bone just as wood swished the air above both me and Spot.

I heard a growl. Then came a man's scream, followed by a thud of a body hitting the ground. I knew that Spot would hang onto the man he grabbed unless the man played dead and another person attacked Spot. If the man moved or raised his other leg to kick at Spot, Spot would bite down harder, crushing the bones.

I shot my arms out, flailing in the dark. My forearm hit the bat. I pulled my arms in to the side, got a grip on the bat, and jerked it away. I jumped to my feet.

Spot had the man on the ground just as he had with Mo in Reds Place. There was another grunt. The man kicked up into the air and landed a hard blow on my hip bone. My upper body went numb. I lost my grip on the bat and it clattered away across the parking lot.

The brother raced down from above us. He shined his light as he ran toward the loose bat. I jumped up and ran limping after him. The man reached down and scooped up the wayward bat. It was a big mistake trying to hold two bats. He should have tossed it into the lake. Instead, the second bat slowed his moves.

I launched and landed a flying kick on the side of the man's knee. Tissue squeaked and a bone snapped. The man screamed. He fell, twisting, dropping the second bat, which clattered toward the lake. He swung his remaining bat with ferocious intensity. The wood hit a glancing blow on my upper quadriceps. If it had been a direct blow, it would have crushed the muscle over the femur. Even so, it was my turn to holler. The pain was electric.

I grabbed for his bat. But his grip on it was like a vice. So I did a half-fall, half-jump onto his writhing body. I landed butt first on his abdomen. His breath went out in a big whoosh. His grip on the bat loosened. I jerked it away and scrambled to my feet, the tremor in my leg still making it jump. Incredibly, the big man kicked out with his good leg and struck me just to the side of my groin. It wasn't completely incapacitating, but it was brutal. I bent over in a partial collapse. I was unable to breathe. My balance was off, and I knew I was falling. But as I went down, I managed to make a small rotation. He still held his light, pointed at distant trees. I used the reflected glow to guide me as I made a hard swipe with the bat, angling low.

My bat hit the ankle of the same leg with the knee I'd kicked, crushing Bosstro's bone and tissue and maybe denting the asphalt as I went down.

This time his scream was tighter and shorter and eventually morphed to a growling, angry threat escaping through gritted teeth. "You're dead, McKenna. You are so dead."

My turning fall took me seven or eight feet away from the man. I kneeled on the pavement, still paralyzed from his kick to my groin. I still couldn't get air. Vertigo seemed to haunt my perceptions. I couldn't tell up from down.

Somehow, the man got up, hopping on his good leg, and hit me from the side like an NFL tackle. My body folded like a rag doll around the blow. It blew me to the side. My head hit asphalt.

My ears were singing a high note, obscuring all inputs. I tried to hear through it, sensing the world. I couldn't see and couldn't hear. I felt the man grab the bat from my hands. I sensed him standing up tall, hopping on his good leg.

I knew he was going to deliver a death blow. Yet some ancient perception gave me warning that he wasn't going to use the bat. He was leaning on the bat like a cane and lifting his good leg to stomp my head. He was unable to resist the desire to feel his foot crushing through my face and back to my brain.

Without any clear focus, but with the barest sense of movement from his raised foot, I made a sudden contraction and pulled my head and body into a strong fetal contraction. The man's foot stomped where my head had been half a second earlier. I heard his foot hit the pavement. He roared. You can't stomp pavement without causing damage.

I got to my feet.

The man was an arm's length away, doing a dance of pain, one foot broken from hitting pavement, the other ankle broken from the blow of my bat. It was only a matter of moments before he collapsed to the pavement.

I moved in close. His reaction was slow. I set up an elbow punch with all the time in the world. Brought my closed fist to my chest for support, twisted as I lifted my elbow up and out, and spun fast. My elbow struck his nose. Hot blood sprayed through the dark onto my face before he even had a chance to sound his anguish. He went down in a fast spiral, writhing on the pavement, hands to his face as he gauged how many facial bones were shattered. He'd probably live. But he'd never again look the way his friends remembered him.

I grabbed the bat and advanced on the even bigger man that Spot had been holding.

"Let go, Spot," I said as I approached. I held the bat up, ready to swing.

Spot hung on.

"It's okay, boy," I said. I reached down with my other hand, took Spot's collar. I tensed my grip on the bat as I pulled Spot off.

The man rolled away ten times faster than I would have thought possible. I tried to shine my light, but I couldn't put the beam on the man. He sprinted away. Other than where Spot had bit him, the man was not very wounded. I thought of sending Spot, but I worried that the man would have a knife or other weapon on him.

Now I'd lost him.

I shined my light toward the man on the pavement. He was sitting up holding his knee.

I heard the roar of the pickup engine revving. The vehicle's headlights swept the trees at the edge of the parking lot and swung around to Spot and me.

"C'mon, boy. Time for you and me to make our escape."

We trotted. I was still dizzy so I leaned on Spot. We got into the trees where the man couldn't drive over us with his pickup. He turned again, and I saw him drive toward his brother sitting on the pavement. Then something gave him second thoughts. He spun around, drove up out of the parking area, squealed tires as he raced away toward the south.

Spot and I hustled up to the Jeep. I started it, pulled into the entrance to the lot, and faced so my headlights illuminated the man sitting on the pavement.

I called Diamond on my cell and explained that there was drama at Cave Rock.

Diamond and one of his Douglas County deputies showed up 15 minutes later. They trotted down to the man in my headlights.

I got out and hobbled over to Diamond.

"You okay?" he asked.

"Bruised but okay." I pointed to the man on the ground. "This guy is Jeff Bosstro," I said. "A career dirtball from Lemon Hills, California. The man who got away was his brother Carlos Bosstro. Jeff is substantially wounded. Carlos is banged up, more to his ego than his body. He apparently realized that his only escape opportunity was at the expense of leaving his brother."

"What was their intention with you?" Diamond asked.

"Their plan was to beat me to death with baseball bats."

"Are they the guys who tormented Daniel Callahan?"

"I don't know. Maybe not. That guy garbled his voice with stones or something in his cheeks. This guy sounded normal."

"Which doesn't tell us anything," Diamond said.

"Right."

"Did the guy who got away say anything?" Diamond asked.

"Something about being inventive in how he was going to produce maximum pain."

Diamond gestured toward Flyboy Bosstro. "And this guy?"

"He said, 'McKenna, you are so dead.'"

Diamond paused and looked at me in the dark. "Could be true." He shined his flashlight around at the dark parking lot. "A crime scene like this could use the full treatment. Would we find anything of note?"

"I don't think so. We know what the crime was. We know the perpetrators. We know the pickup's description but we don't have the pickup's license. I don't think it's worth it to get a team and a bunch of lights out here tonight. Maybe swing by at dawn before the park opens and see what you find."

"Sounds like a plan." Diamond and his deputy cuffed Jeff Bosstro, read him his rights, squeezed him into the back of their patrol unit, and headed off toward the Stateline jail.

Spot and I drove home. This time we both had a beer. Then we went to bed.

THIRTY-THREE

Sunday morning dawned bright and cloudless, with little wind. Perfect for looking down into the water as the Tahoe Steamer Festival got underway.

Street drove her VW bug with Blondie, and Spot and I drove the Jeep. We arrived at Daniel and Mae's houses at 8:30 a.m.

When Daniel let me into his house, I said, "Are you still okay with this? Going out on the water? Being near dogs?"

Daniel nodded. "The guy beat me up. I don't let anybody bully me like that." Daniel breathed out with a touch of sibilant sound escaping his lips. Almost like a hiss. "He probably left me for dead. Then he shot out my window. I want to get that bastard." Daniel said it with the bravado of a teenager looking for revenge.

I didn't want to have to worry about him out on the water. But I couldn't say either of those things. It would have made him feel like a burden.

"I've never been on this particular boat. I don't know if it would be comfortable for you," I said.

"Does it have a shady place to sit?"

"There is a lounge, yes."

"Does it have a railing or something to hang onto when it pitches in the waves?"

"I believe all tourist boats have that," I said.

"Then I'll be fine."

Next I called Airwaves Andy.

"Just checking to see that everything is on for our event," I said.

"You got it, McKenna. I haven't been this excited for on-location reporting in years. I'm not too proud to admit that the radio business has felt stale these last few years. But this whole create-and-stage-a-play thing has made me feel twenty years younger."

"Glad to hear it. Good luck, and I'll look for you on Glenbrook Bay.

For comfort, we put both Blondie and Spot in Street's VW bug, and I drove Daniel and Mae in my Jeep. We pulled into the Blue Sky Marina parking lot on the South Shore at 9 a.m. The marina was the home base mooring for the Mountain Belle. Street and the dogs waited with Daniel and Mae while I trotted toward the water and introduced myself to a long-haired young man wearing a name tag that said, 'Noah Davis, Blue Sky Marina Dockmaster.'

"Hi, Noah," I said. "My name is Owen McKenna. I have a party booked on the Mountain Belle for their Tahoe Steamer Festival ride. Matt Bronsky reserved us space in the lounge."

"Oh, this trip is going to be so cool. I wish I didn't have to work the dock. I hear they're bringing up sunken treasure!"

"Maybe. It certainly is exciting."

Noah scanned his clipboard, running his fingertip down the paper. "Here we are. Come with me. I'll introduce you to the first mate."

He led me out the pier along rough, worn dock boards. Near the end of the pier was our boat. The Mountain Belle was a sleek cruising yacht design. She was moored to a dock that attached to the main pier at a right angle. Noah took a hard right onto the intersecting dock. As we turned, something back by the shore caught my eye. I turned to look down the pier. In the doorway of a small dock building we'd walked past stood a man wearing jeans and snug T-shirt. His face was in the shadow of the roof overhang. From the fit of his clothes over wide shoulders and narrow waist, he appeared to be a fitness buff. I could see no details from my distance. But it seemed he was looking at me. As I looked toward him, he moved farther back into the shadow of the overhang. His arms moved as if he was holding a phone and tapping out a number.

For a moment I thought about running toward him to see what he would do. But Noah was walking fast toward the Mountain Belle.

As we got closer, I could see through the side windows of the bridge. A woman was at the controls, leaning forward, checking instruments. The woman was wearing a white suit with black-and-gold-barred epaulets, and a white captain's hat with a black bill and gold insignia above. The woman's hair beneath her hat was blonde, cut very short. She moved with a kind of crispness. Even from a distance, she telegraphed competence. It was reassuring to see professionalism. Captaining a tour boat full of people might be less complicated than flying a commercial jet, but the responsibility was similar. If a boat were to go down in Tahoe's cold water, the result would be no different than a plane crashing.

Beneath the bridge was the lounge, an indoor cabin with large windows that would provide good viewing.

In front of the lounge, below and in front of the bridge, was the foredeck. Because of the converging rails leading to the cruiser's narrow bow, it was a small space that would provide a great view but would only hold a few passengers who'd have to stand on a sloping deck.

Behind the lounge was the Mountain Belle's largest space, the aft deck. In addition to standing space, there was a diving corner with enough equipment to be a complete onboard diving rental store. Next to the boat's gunnel were several scuba tanks and a compressor for refilling them. There was a rack of buoyancy compensators as well as the older-style flotation vests that have a gas cartridge to inflate them, and a shelf/bin arrangement that held diving masks, several sets of swim fins, weight belts, and regulators.

Up on the second level, behind the bridge and above the aft deck was an upper deck. It was covered by a fabric canopy. The upper deck would provide the best view. But the access was a spiral staircase on the starboard side. The staircase had a generous diameter and would be easier to negotiate than most spiral staircases. But it was not a good fit for an old blind man.

Above the bridge and the upper deck was a small flybridge. It was accessed by a ladder stairs. Because the flybridge was small enough that it probably couldn't hold more than two people, it looked to be more about design than function. The flybridge made the Mountain Belle look sleek and fast and even a little exotic, like a rock star's yacht in the Mediterranean.

We came to the gangway and walked up the sloped, non-skid surface to an open gate in the Mountain Belle's port railing.

Noah called out. "Eileen, I've brought Owen McKenna." A woman appeared. "Owen, this is Mountain Belle's first mate Eileen Hughes."

"Good to meet you," I said.

The woman reaching out her hand to me was a bit like Mae O'Sullivan, with an athletic build, thick with muscles. By her grip, I could tell she was strong enough to lift anchors. Instead of Mae's long dark blonde locks, Eileen had short black hair that was neatly trimmed at her jaw. The hair contrasted with very white skin and blue-gray eyes. Unlike the captain's uniform, the first mate wore navy pants and blazer with brass buttons and epaulets with gold bars like on those of the captain. Around her neck was a light blue kerchief knotted at the throat. On her head was a navy cap with a gold anchor pin and a thin, light blue sash wrapping the cap just above the hard navy bill. Completing Eileen's look was a strong frown and no makeup. The effect communicated that she took her job very seriously, was proud of her accomplishments, and perhaps hoped to one day don the captain's white uniform.

"I'll show you your quarters," Eileen said.

Noah made a little nod toward me, turned, and went down the gangway.

I followed Eileen across the aft deck and into the lounge. When I booked our reservation, I'd been told the lounge would comfortably hold twelve passengers. Now, it seemed that the space was not as spacious as I'd envisioned. But it was comfortably appointed with wood paneling and wall sconces between the large windows. There were four tables with upholstered chairs around each. At the forward end of the lounge were two doors.

One led to a galley, and the other led out to the foredeck. Inside the lounge next to the galley door was another spiral staircase, no doubt leading to the bridge.

Eileen gestured at a grouping of four chairs around a rear, port-side table. The chairs were old, but they looked comfortable. On the table was a folded card with a picture of the Mountain Belle. It was printed, 'Reserved for...' Below that was a little box in which had been written 'the McKenna party.'

"I saw on the manifest that you have a party of four," Eileen said.

"Yes," I said. "Our party is actually four adults and two dogs."

Eileen flared her nostrils and looked concerned. "They didn't tell me that. We have rules regarding dogs."

"I would expect so."

"First, they must have recently done their business."

"Indeed," I said.

She looked at me through narrowed eyes, no doubt wondering - because of past experience - if what I said would be true.

"Also," she said, "dogs are not allowed to bark. They must remain in their kennels or on a very short leash at all times."

"Of course," I said.

"Good," Eileen said, her no-nonsense demeanor on full display. "One more thing, they can't be more than fifty pounds."

"I wasn't told that."

"Yes, we tell everyone verbally."

"Sorry, I don't remember that. I'm quite sure I wasn't told that when I spoke to Matt Bronsky."

Now Eileen's eyes were scrunched even more. "How much do your dogs weigh?"

"One of them is forty or forty-five pounds. But the other is over fifty. How much more, I'm not sure."

She looked around. "Where is your dog? I can judge by looking whether or not he'll be acceptable."

"My girlfriend is bringing him."

"You can guess his weight. Is he sixty pounds? Sixty-five?"

I hesitated.

"Seventy?" she said.

"The number seventy rings a bell," I said.

"Seventy is way over fifty."

"I'm sorry. Tell you what. If my dog causes a problem of any kind, I'll submit to whatever accommodation you demand."

Eileen was exasperated. "Mr. McKenna, this isn't elementary school. We don't catalogue infractions and then make you sit in a corner for punishment."

"Okay, how about a simple bribe?" I gave her my best smile. "If my dog makes you the least bit uncomfortable, I'll buy you a cheeseburger and fries at your favorite restaurant."

Her frown became more severe.

"Oh, sorry," I said. "You're not a cheeseburger-and-fries type of woman. How about a bottle of Irish Whiskey?"

That made her crack the tiniest of smiles. "You guessed I'm Irish."

"Black Irish," I said. "The name is a giveaway. The light skin. The black hair. The serious, no-nonsense, don't-mess-with-me, non-joking attitude."

"That last isn't Irish, and you know it." Another hint of grin. "But what I said about your dog still applies."

"Tell you what. If he's an ounce over seventy, you can name your price."

At that, Street and Mae came walking along the dock. Mae was between Daniel and the dogs. Daniel had one hand on Mae's arm and held his white cane in the other. His head was turned toward the lake. Despite the aviators, he could sense the bright light coming off the water. Street held Blondie's leash in one hand and Spot's collar in the other.

"Here's the rest of my party," I said. Eileen and I went back out to the aft deck and down the gangway to the dock.

"Hi Owen, sorry it took a bit for us to get organized," Mae said. "Wow, what a cool boat."

Eileen saw Spot. Her eyes went huge. She turned and glared at me. "Seventy pounds?! That's a Great Dane. He's probably more like one hundred and seventy!"

"Like I said, the word seventy sounded familiar."

THIRTY-FOUR

At the mention of dogs, Daniel spoke up, turning his head in Eileen's direction. "You shouldn't let dogs on the boat," he said.

"I may not," Eileen said. "As first mate, my word is the law."

"Mr. Callahan is unnaturally afraid of dogs," I said. "I promise these dogs are fine." I stepped next to Spot.

"Spot, sit," I said.

Spot looked at me, turned back to look at Eileen. She was more interesting than me.

I pushed down on his rear. "Spot," I said again, "sit."

He sat with reluctance.

"Now meet Eileen Hughes. Shake her hand."

It was one of the few commands he usually followed, probably because he always got a good reaction. Spot lifted his paw high and pawed at the air.

Eileen seemed frozen, staring, transfixed.

Spot's paw slapped back down on the deck boards.

"Shake again," I said.

This time, Eileen caught his heavy paw with both hands and shook it up and down. Spot started panting.

"Oh, my God," Eileen said. Her frown had been replaced by a huge grin.

Street stepped forward. "Hi, I'm Street, and this is Mae and Daniel, and this relatively-little pooch is Blondie."

"Eileen Hughes," the first mate said. They all shook. Eileen glanced again at Spot and suddenly seemed less serious. "Pleased to have you come aboard."

Eileen turned toward me. "Will he obey me, walk with me?"

"Obey is kind of a fancy word for Spot's behavior. But walk, yes. Take him by the collar. He loves going for boat rides."

Eileen took Spot's collar and started walking up the gangway. Halfway up the incline, she turned back toward me and said, "I get to pick the brand of whiskey." Then she and Spot headed onto the boat, went across the aft deck, and disappeared into the lounge.

I escorted the others onto the boat. When we got to the lounge, Eileen and Spot were not in sight. Maybe she'd taken him out to the foredeck. Then I saw movement up at the top of the forward spiral staircase. Eileen wisely had him on the outside of the spiral. I would have thought it might be awkward for him. But I remembered when we stayed at Diamond's house, and Spot climbed up the narrow little ladder stairs to the attic bedroom like it was a fun game. So maybe the captain's staircase was no big deal. And it meant he got to meet the captain. Spot was always curious about meeting people. And except for a few female cops, he hadn't met that many women in uniform.

I showed the others our seats. Daniel took one of the chairs. Mae and Street oohed and aahed and started exploring, heading up the rear staircase to the upper deck.

Over the next 45 minutes, the boat took on many passengers. Most looked like tourists, with cameras and phones out, snapping selfies of themselves on the boat with the lake in the background. As I've noticed before, there were people who, staring at their phones, seemed more interested in looking at the pictures they took than in looking out at the scene itself.

There were several people who did not appear to be tourists. One group of six carried diving gear, tanks and wetsuits and swim fins. They stowed their gear in the racks near the boat's own diving gear. Four were men and two were women. Another group of four men seemed like divers although they carried less gear. To a person, the divers wore sunglasses. Many had on baseball caps, brims pulled low against the brilliant sun off the water. Several wore hats like Daniel's, with neck flaps to keep the sun off their ears and necks and upper backs.

When the boat had taken on thirty-some people, the crew disengaged the gangway and shut the railing gate. Eileen's voice came over the loudspeaker announcing that the boat would be departing in five minutes.

"The seas are calm," she said. "And the weather is perfect. Our ride should be very smooth. However, we recommend you take your seat or hold onto one of the rails or hanging straps to ensure you don't lose your balance."

The engines rumbled to life. The deck hands released the big lines that went to the dock posts.

Another voice came over the loudspeaker. "Good morning. This is Captain Lisa Glass speaking. Welcome to the Mountain Belle, Tahoe's premier cruise boat. Today, we're going to witness history. The Tahoe Steamer Festival organizers believe there may be a secret treasure that has remained hidden four hundred feet below the surface. The Steamer was scuttled eighty years ago in Glenbrook Bay, so this is very exciting. You will all have a ringside seat for this exciting event. There will be video from underwater submarine drones and a radio simulcast. On the big screen in the lounge and also on the upper deck under the canopy will be the live broadcast video footage of the ROVs, which is short for remote operated vehicles. The commentary will be by Tahoe's very own Airwaves Andy from KXcellence radio. So sit back and enjoy as we depart for Glenbrook Bay."

The engines revved a deep rumble, and the boat began to move away from the dock.

The ship's horn gave a single prolonged warning blast, and we headed out toward the center of the lake.

I saw in the near distance the buoys marking our channel. As I looked behind us, I noticed a speedboat just beginning to leave the dock. I guessed it at 28 or 30 feet long. In it was a bunch of what looked like scuba gear. There were three men in the boat, two at the front seats and one at the rear seat. Then a fourth man stepped from the dock to the boat as the gap widened. Although I couldn't see detail from our distance, the man making the leap seemed like the man who'd been in the shadows, watching me, dialing his phone.

THIRTY-FIVE

When the Mountain Belle cleared the channel buoys, she sped up to a comfortable cruise speed.

In the shade of the lounge, the air rushing in the large open windows was quite cool, chilled by Tahoe's cold water. Mae had rejoined Daniel, staying nearby like a protective mother. Street and Blondie joined me on the upper deck. Through the windows into the bridge, I glimpsed Spot with Eileen and the captain.

Eileen opened the door and gestured to us. We walked over.

The captain was squatting down, hugging Spot.

"Mr. McKenna, this is Captain Glass. I was just telling her how you are a rule breaker. She agreed that your dog has no right to be on this boat and that we need to escort the two of you off the ship the moment we make landfall. Fortunately, landfall won't be for several hours." She grinned.

The captain stood up and reached to shake my hand. Her left hand was still on Spot's head. His eyes were half closed and his tail was on slow wag. Dog bliss.

"He seems so at home on a ship," the captain said.

"He is at home wherever there is attention and affection and dog treats."

"What kind of treat does he like?"

"Oh, the usual. Steak and potatoes and beer followed by cupcakes and ice cream."

The captain turned and looked at Eileen. They seemed to exchange some kind of knowing look. Probably a trade secret known only to those in the tourist boat business.

Eileen took Spot's collar. "We're still making my rounds. The passengers are getting the message that they have to behave themselves lest we call out our enforcer."

Eileen took Spot out the forward passage and headed back

down the stairs. Her hand was on his collar, apparently friends for life.

While Captain Glass focused on the bridge controls, I walked out onto the upper deck and looked down at the divers below us. They clustered to one side of the aft deck, checking their regulators, tanks, pressure gauges, buoyancy compensators, and wristwatch computers. As we got closer to Glenbrook, they started pulling on their wetsuits, thick neoprene insulation with colorful stretch-nylon coating. The last time I'd been diving, most wetsuits were black, with the occasional color stretch panel at the shoulders or waist. Suits had obviously evolved since then.

Two of the divers had suits that were royal blue with orange chevron shapes across the upper back. One had a suit that was printed front and back like a playing-card joker, a fun and dramatic persona to carry down into the depths. A fourth had a suit that looked very much like Batman but without the pointy ears. Just one had a plain black suit. Although next to him was a green tank and dayglo green fins and face mask.

Forty minutes later, the Mountain Belle slowed as it approached what was already a flotilla of boats in Glenbrook Bay. The wind was calm and the water was placid. Except for the waves from boat wakes, one could see far down into the water. I stared down toward the dark depths imagining the large hulk of the Steamer lurking in the night shadows 400 feet below, too far down for sunlight to penetrate.

The slight breeze was out of the north. So the captain headed toward the north shore of the bay where the water was shallow enough to anchor. After a minute, she cut the power. The crew started dropping the anchor. The anchor bit into the bottom. The captain reversed the props for a moment, and the boat coasted back at a very slow pace until the anchor dug in and stopped it. If the breeze remained constant, we'd stay in position.

In the distance, a dark-colored boat approached. As it got close, I saw that its hull was black over white, and it had a white cloth canopy. It slowed as it reached the middle of Glenbrook Bay. Two men were under the canopy, one piloting the boat, the other talking on his phone. A third man was sitting in front of black cabinets that held what looked like a rack of electronic gear.

They turned as they came near the Mountain Belle. I saw the boat's name emblazoned in red script on the stern.

THE BLACK JACK POT

The boat with Airwaves Andy.

I called his cell as we had arranged.

"Everything okay?" I said after I identified myself.

"We're locked and loaded, dude." His radio voice projected so well that I could have heard him across the water without the phone. "The remote operated vehicle company is actually running its submarines from a townhouse on shore. They'll be working two robot crafts, one filming the other. They control it all from shore. The ROV control group will patch their video feed to me. Then my tech guy here on the Black Jack Pot will be editing for maximum entertainment, if you get my drift. And I'll overdub my patter and sound effects and music."

"Sounds great."

"I haven't got to the coolest part. I put together a whole song list with a water motif. From Brad Paisley's Water, going all the way back to The Doobie Brothers' Black Water. It'll be great fun. Of course, I've also got Deep Purple's Smoke On The Water. And get this. One of my tunes is Jethro Tull's Aqualung. Is that perfect or what?!"

"That's perfect," I agreed. "How can I help?"

"The Mountain Belle is supposed to send the feed to their big screen monitors. You could check to make sure they've got that covered."

"Will do. What time will you start your broadcast?"

"I've already been hammering it on a.m. radio, with a lead-up enticement every ten minutes. The idea is that you tune in at noon and listen to the three-hour broadcast and try to find the clues. Tomorrow, I'll have a call-in mystery show. I'll pose ten questions that any alert listener can answer. The first person to get all ten answers right wins the Airwaves Andy prize of an on-air interview and award program."

He paused.

Maybe he expected praise. "Sounds really great," I said.

"Oh, here we go. The ROV video feed just came up. Oh, wow, that's beautiful blue water down there. I better get ready. We go full channels at noon. And that's... seven minutes away! Later, dude." He hung up.

I went back to the lounge. Eileen had returned Spot, and he was lying on the indoor carpeting next to Blondie. Blondie looked alert. Spot looked drowsy. "A lot of work being a public figure, eh, Largeness?"

"Anything happening, yet?" Street asked.

"Getting close. The ROVs are in the water. The internet channel goes live in a few minutes. Perhaps you could sweet-talk one of the crew into turning on the video screen. I'll find Eileen and inquire about the wifi."

Street stood and pointed out the rear door of the lounge. "After she dropped off Spot, she went up to the upper deck."

"Thanks." I trotted up the stairs. Eileen was not on the deck. I tapped on the door to the bridge. Eileen opened the door.

"I'm just inquiring about the simulcast and video screen."

"We've got the wifi on and..." Eileen looked past me. She frowned.

The sound of running footsteps came from behind me. I turned.

Street was running across the upper deck.

"Owen, come quick!" Despite running, her face was pale. "Something serious has happened." She about-faced and ran back. I ran after her. We charged down the circular steps. Street was already inside the lounge.

Daniel was standing up, one arm hanging onto the nearby table, the other pointing with his white cane. Despite his aviators, I could see the stress on his face.

"What's wrong?" I put my hand on his skinny shoulder.

"That's him," he said.

"What do you mean?"

"The man who broke into my house and beat me up."

"How can you tell?"

"His gait. I recognize his walk."

I turned to look where Daniel was pointing. There were several divers. "How can you tell? They're all wearing swim fins. Everyone walks funny when they put on fins."

"It's him. I can tell. The flex of his knees. The roll of his shoulders."

"There," Daniel said. He pushed forward, away from Mae. Before I could stop him, he was out of the lounge door, onto the back deck. He pointed with his cane. "That man. In the middle of that group."

Several people looked at Daniel, then turned to stare. The divers seemed oblivious. They had on their scuba tanks, the harness straps pulled tight. They had neoprene hoods pulled down over their heads, and they were adjusting their face masks. They probably couldn't even hear Daniel.

"I can't even see the divers," I said. "They're all wearing face masks."

Daniel raised his voice. "It's him! I guarantee it. Movement is like a fingerprint. Unmistakable."

One of the divers turned and saw Daniel pointing at them. He touched two others on their shoulders. They turned. There was movement to my side. Close to Daniel. It was another diver I hadn't noticed. Several divers came forward. I turned back toward Daniel. He was still pointing. Two of the divers pushed past me. Both were wearing their full gear including face masks. In a sudden movement, one of the men reached out and shoved Daniel hard.

Daniel stumbled back, the beginnings of a backward fall. I lunged to catch him. A fall onto hard boat surfaces could be deadly for any man, regardless of age. I reached out with my arms, trying to grab him. Luckily, Daniel hit the rail at the edge of the deck. I stopped lunging, relieved.

Except that, when Daniel hit the rail, he flipped over it and plummeted down to the water far below.

THIRTY-SIX

The old man who couldn't swim and was terrified of water plunged down ten feet to the ice-cold lake.

I ran to the rail. The water seemed far below. Daniel's body and head were underwater. His arms thrashed, making feeble little splashes on the surface. My immediate instinct was to leap in after him. But the lake was cold enough to make anyone hypothermic in a short period of time. I might need help.

I turned, looking for Spot. He was with Street. I took two running steps. Grabbed Spot's collar. Ran to the railing gate where the gangway had connected. Jerked the gate open. Pulled Spot with me as I leaped off the boat.

Like all Tahoe locals, I know that the water temperature is shockingly cold. But still it surprised. The cold made me gasp as I rose to the surface to breathe.

"Come, Spot! Come with me!"

I swam over to where Daniel had been struggling. There was no sign of him. I dove beneath the surface. There was nothing but blue water. I turned around. Looked up. Looked down.

There. Below me to my left. The old man sinking.

His arms barely moved. But it was enough movement to mean he was alive.

I made three quick kicks, swam down after him. Grabbed his clothing. Pulled him up with one arm. Stroked with the other. Kicked hard. Over and over.

We popped up on the surface. People were shouting. I turned him around and held him up.

He coughed out water, gasped for air, and flailed his arms.

"You're okay, Daniel. I've got you."

Daniel didn't speak. Didn't cry out. It was impressive control.

He was on the verge of drowning, but he stayed silent.

I held him as I looked up at the boat. There was a lot of commotion. But no one dropped a ladder. Maybe the boat had an access ladder at the stern. That was a good swim just to find out.

Daniel was choking and coughing.

I turned around, looking toward shore. There was a small beach about thirty yards away.

I saw Spot swimming nearby.

There was a splash next to me. It was Street.

"Thank God he's still alive," Street said as she swam up to us. "I told Mae to watch the man who pushed Daniel."

"Good." I turned. "Spot. Come here. Swim over here. Daniel, the boat is high above us. It will be hard to get back into the boat. But there's a beach not far away. Spot will take you there."

Daniel sputtered. He was incapable of speech.

"How can I help?" Street said, her teeth already chattering.

I knew that Street was too thin and small to carry Daniel any distance. She was going to lose her body heat too fast. "Spot will carry Daniel to the shore," I said. "You can swim along. Help Daniel out onto the warm sand."

"Okay."

I turned to Daniel and spoke near his ear. "Daniel, here's what you need to do. I'm going to put your arms around Spot's neck. Like this. Just hold onto him. Just let him swim. You'll float along his back. The water is cold and you want to get out of it. But don't push him down into the water. Street will be right at your side. But don't grab her. Just let Spot carry you to the beach."

I got Daniel into position, his arms reaching forward, his hands at the base of Spot's neck. He hadn't uttered a word. He was probably already hypothermic, losing control of all of his muscles.

"Okay, Spot. Let's go." I started swimming next to him. "Atta boy. Just like when we've played in the water. But Daniel's half my size. An easy swim. Over to that beach." I bent my elbow, then dropped my hand next to Spot's head just like when we do search training. "Find the beach, boy. Find."

As always, a dog doesn't need to understand every word. If they've done the move before, they recognize it.

I swam some more. "That's it, Spot. Get to the beach, and you get to leave the ice water and run around in the hot sun. Daniel, you're doing great. Spot will have you on the beach in no time. Just hang on and don't push Spot down. Let the water flow at your neck level. Street is right here next to you. She'll guide you."

I squeezed Street's shoulder. She was speechless with cold. I kissed her shoulder.

"You'll all be on the beach in no time."

I turned back to the Mountain Belle.

I swam around to its stern. There was an access ladder.

I climbed up it, clambered over the edge of the boat.

Mae rushed up. "Street said to stay here and watch the man who pushed Daniel. Was that right? Is he okay?" She looked past me toward the lake.

I turned to see. Daniel was still on Spot's back. Street was holding one of Daniel's arms. Probably helping him to keep his grip on Spot's neck.

"Yes, Daniel's okay." I didn't know if it was true. Daniel would be seriously hypothermic by now. But it seemed appropriate to reassure Mae. And I believed that Street would see to it he was able to warm up in the sun, in a sheltered place, perhaps next to Spot for warmth.

"Did you see the man who pushed Daniel?"

"Yeah. He waved at that other boat over there and then jumped into the water with another diver from this boat. Two divers from that other boat also jumped into the water." The boat she was pointing at held the man who watched me back at the dock and stepped onto the boat as it pulled away from the pier.

"Did you see where the divers went?"

"Most of them, no. Especially the divers off that other boat. That boat is too far away to see into the water beneath it. But the guy who pushed Daniel off this boat seemed to dive straight down. His companion went more that way." She pointed. She looked around and said, "North."

I glanced over at the lounge. Looking through the windows, I could see a bit of the video screen. I asked, "Do you know what was on the video before Daniel recognized the diver?"

Mae frowned. "I think they had been showing a picture of an ROV coming up from the depths with some kind of package in its robot arm."

"And now the divers are going down to try to intercept the robot."

"And get its cargo," Mae said.

I nodded.

"But I could intercept them," Mae said. "Or at least the guy who pushed Daniel. I could kill that guy for doing that."

"What do you mean?" I asked.

"I could do a freedive." She looked over at the rack of scuba gear. "There are a bunch of weight belts and flotation vests. I could use the weight belts to pull me down fast. I would aim for the guy who pushed Daniel. He probably wouldn't see me coming from above. I could rip his face mask off. He pushed Daniel to his potential death." Mae sounded outraged. "Daniel never hurt a soul. I want to hurt the guy who beat on him. I want to hurt him bad."

"Mae, I appreciate your thoughts. I know how you feel. But this could get you killed. That diver is probably far below us. You could run out of air. He could grab you and hold you down. You could drown. Daniel would be much worse off if he didn't have you."

Mae didn't even pause to think about it. "I'm going."

"How would you find the man who pushed Daniel?"

"He's got a wetsuit with an orange chevron shape across the shoulders. It's easy to see."

"I saw two men with that wetsuit."

"Right. But this guy has a tear across the chevron. So it's more like a right-handed chevron. Like a big checkmark."

"What if you didn't go down in the right place?" I asked.

"The water is very clear. As I get close, I'll be able to see which guy I'm after and steer toward him on my descent."

"But you don't even have swim fins."

"I don't need them." She grabbed three weight belts off the rack and put them around her waist, one by one, the quick-release buckles in front. "I'll descend head first. With my arms in front of me, I can angle them and hold out my hands like fins. I've learned I can glide where I want as long as I don't try to go too far sideways." She ran to the lounge, grabbed the bag she'd brought, reached in and pulled out a face mask, one of the ones she always carried. Then she ran over to the equipment rack, lifted a flotation vest off the rack, and put it on.

"I don't think it's smart," I said. "We can find the guy when he comes up."

Mae shook her head. "Maybe not. I don't want to wait. I want to surprise him."

"Let's say you succeed in surprising him. You knock off his facemask. Then what?"

"Maybe I can pull his air hose out of his mouth, too. Either way, without a face mask, he'll probably return to the surface. Of course, I'll need to come back up right away. I'll pull my flotation cord, the cartridge will fill my air vest, and I'll be back on the surface in two minutes or less."

"All on one breath of air," I said.

She nodded. "That's what freediving is."

"What about a wetsuit? The water is very cold."

"It's more than very cold," Mae said. "When you get down to seventy feet, you go through the thermocline. The water temp drops to thirty-nine degrees. Even if I had more air to breathe, that temperature will freeze my muscles. So one breath is enough."

"One of these wetsuits might fit you."

"No, I can see that they're all for men. A wetsuit that's too big is worthless. Anyway, I don't have time."

"The scuba divers could already be far away."

"Freedivers with weights descend much faster than scuba divers. I'll have over a minute to find and strike Daniel's attacker," Mae said. "I'll go down, hit him, inflate my flotation vest, and come back up. If I make it back up before I run out of breath, I'll survive. If I don't, I'll be too numb to feel the pain of death.

Eileen walked up and faced me. "What's going on? I saw you jump overboard with Spot." Her calm demeanor suggested she hadn't seen Daniel get pushed overboard.

"Someone bumped our older companion, and he fell over."

Eileen inhaled.

"We jumped in to make sure he was okay. I thought he might have trouble climbing back aboard. So Spot and Street swam with him to shore." I turned to point. I could see them on the beach. "They're already there. But I do have a favor to ask." I pointed over toward Blondie, who was sitting watching us, her brow furrowed with concern now that Street had jumped overboard and swam away. "If you could please watch Blondie, our other dog, while we deal with the festival activities."

Eileen was staring off toward Spot on the distant beach. Then she reached for her phone and looked at it. "The captain texted me. I have to go to the bridge."

"Can you take Blondie with you?"

Eileen frowned, then nodded. "No problem," she said. She took Blondie's leash, and they walked toward the spiral staircase.

I turned to Mae. "Are you certain you want to do this?"

"Yes." Mae pulled on her face mask. She took a deep breath, closed her eyes, exhaled slowly.

She spoke in a low voice with a hint of venom. "May the devil drown!"

She took another, deeper breath, and jumped off the back of the boat.

I found a face mask that seemed to fit and put it on. I pulled on a flotation vest and grabbed three weight belts. I carried them down the rear ladder to the small platform at the stern of the boat. I kneeled down on the platform. Water splashed over me. Even though I'd just been in the water with Daniel and Street, it still felt very cold. I hung onto the platform supports so I could bend over and put my face in the water. With the face mask underwater, I could see. I scanned back and forth, looking for Mae. She was nowhere to be seen. There were multiple dull, dark shapes moving this way and that, divers whose images were hard to perceive from the surface. The only clear indications were the streams of bubbles from their exhalations. The expanse of white bubbles against the deep blue backdrop of water seemed to go down forever. Against the distraction of those bubbles, it was impossible to see a lone freediver, leaving no trail of bubbles.

The sunlight streaming through the shallower depths was easy to see, brilliant rays of light interrupted by bubbles, masses of bubbles rising up from unseen scuba divers, bubbles that obscured everything beneath them. And when there were pauses in the bubble plumes, I still couldn't see because farther down, 60 or 70 or 80 feet, even Tahoe's water was not clear enough to let divers be seen from the surface.

I looked in all directions. From the Mountain Belle, even if I plotted a very steep descent, moving only a small bit to the side in any direction, it still made for a huge area. A descent without knowing where to aim would be pointless.

I kept my face underwater, searching, watching. I had to repeatedly lift my head out of the water to breathe. At one point, I didn't rise up enough, and I choked on inhaled water.

I coughed long and hard, then lowered my face down once again.

Mae was down there somewhere. I didn't know how long it had been. But it seemed like over two minutes since she'd jumped in. If she hadn't already inflated her flotation vest and begun her ascent, she'd be in danger from lack of air. She'd told me that two minutes and thirty seconds was her longest time ever. And that was with proper relaxation beforehand. With the tension of Daniel being pushed into the water, her metabolism would race, and she wouldn't be able to last nearly as long. She had to stop descending and start back up before she reached the halfway point of her time limit or she'd die.

And then I saw Mae below me. Still descending. Maybe 50 or 60 feet down. She was maintaining a dancer's form, head down, her body straight, her toes pointed and trailing behind. She used her arms like wings, angling them to glide this way or that. I could see that she also angled her feet, controlling the angle of her descent.

As I stared through the icy water, I began to make out the man she was chasing. He was ten feet below Mae. The torn checkmark chevron on his suit was an unmistakable identification.

The mass of bubbles rising from the depths increased. Mae and the scuba diver disappeared into the rising curtain of air bubbles. I was about to jump in when I realized that without a visual fix on Mae, I had little chance of finding her.

But as I stared, it seemed there was some movement to one side, movement without accompanying bubbles.

A freediver?

The movement gained some clarity. I waited. Held still. Stared.

The moving object was a diver. Barely visible. I thought it was Mae. Maybe 65 or 70 feet down. Her vest seemed full as if it had been inflated. As she rose, there was a tiny stream of bubbles coming from her mouth. She wasn't making swimming motions because the flotation vest was bringing her to the surface at a good pace. Her arms were at her side. And her bare feet were pointed, the most streamlined posture for rising to the surface at maximum speed. I wanted to yell encouragement. All looked good. She would be on the surface in less than a minute.

Except that as she rose into the penetrating sun rays, the light illuminated something else just six or eight feet below her pointed feet.

A scuba diver without a mask was swimming after Mae, kicking furiously with his fins. He was gaining on her. It was clear that he would grab her ankles in a moment. And even if he didn't kill her with a weapon, once her path to the surface was interrupted, it would be less than a minute before she'd run out of air and die.

THIRTY-SEVEN

As I realized that Mae was being attacked, I did like she did before she jumped in. I took three quick breaths to blow off some of the CO2 in my system. Then I took a deep breath, exhaled completely, took an even larger breath and, holding three weight belts, jumped in after her.

As the weights pulled me head first down into the depths, the water temp became much colder than the surface water.

Very quickly, the pressure in my ears became painful. I pinched my nose and blew lightly to force air into my eustachian tubes and equalize the pressure.

A face mask also needs to be pressurized when you go deep or it will squeeze into your face, and your eyes and flesh will bulge out. So I breathed small amounts of air out of my nose and into the mask.

I realized I hadn't put the weights around my waist. As I held the weights with my arms stretched out at the sides of my head, I was only able to steer my descent just a little. They pulled me down very fast, face first, into the depths. The water quickly turned deep, dark blue. I scanned the scene below me, looking for Mae and the man chasing her. But all I saw was bubbles spilling up from the divers below. There were a few vague dark shapes visible through the bubbles, but nothing clear. I angled my arms so that I rotated as I descended. I tried to see 360 degrees. There was nothing. Where there had once been a diver swimming up fast, overtaking Mae, I now only saw waves of bubbles billowing up from below.

My body ached in the freezing temperatures. The water was so cold that I doubted my perception. I had no wetsuit, no hood. Without any protection, even my brain was being frozen.

Same as Mae.

Mae had gone in without a wetsuit, wearing her street clothes. She knew that a freedive was short enough that if she returned to the surface before succumbing to lack of air, she'd survive the cold.

Her determination gave me focus. I would do whatever I could to help her.

But first I had to find her.

I'd been in the water for at least a half minute, maybe 45 seconds, racing down into the dark. I didn't know how deep I was, but I assumed I was 60 or more feet down. I should have already come to Mae.

I scanned in all directions as I plunged down, trying to see where Mae was.

Then it felt as though I'd been dropped into ice.

Mae said the thermocline was 70 feet down, the point where the water below didn't mix with the water above. I'd never been in 39-degree-water. It was brutal. It seemed to burn my skin. Even if I had an air supply, without a wetsuit my life expectancy would be a few minutes at the maximum. I could feel my muscles going numb from cold. I was losing control of them.

The wicked cold ache in my body was overtaken by the need to breathe. The need was desperate. Overwhelming. I tried to resist the sharp panic of drowning.

Mae had explained that, in the beginning, the need for air was more perception than physical need. A freediver needed to resist that terrifying perception. Mind over matter. But I couldn't resist. My lungs wanted to expand. As much as anything I'd ever experienced, I wanted to suck in lungfuls of air.

But there was only water. I was far below the surface.

I was distracted by movement. To my side. Down below. I moved my arms to let the weights pull me in that direction.

I saw two figures. The scuba diver without the mask was swimming down into the depths. He was holding Mae. Dragging her deeper despite her flotation vest. Forcing her to drown.

Mae struggled. She writhed and jerked. Air bubbles escaped her mouth as she fought. Her vest no longer appeared inflated. Had it not worked? No, it was carrying her to the surface when I first saw her. Something had happened that caused it to deflate.

The man had her from behind, one arm locked around her. She was helpless against his size and strength.

I adjusted my downward glide to come from directly above and behind the man. The bubbles from his exhalation rose up around me, obscuring my vision. I had no choice but to make my best guess as to his position.

For a brief moment, the bubbles stopped and I could see.

I was almost on him. I transferred my weight belts to my left hand and used them to strike his head from behind. He was wearing a thick neoprene hood, so the blow was cushioned. But it startled him. He let go of Mae and twisted trying to see what happened, trying to grab me.

With my right hand I grabbed for his air hose and jerked it hard. It came out of his mouth. I held the mouthpiece toward Mae. She understood, grabbed it, put it in her mouth and inhaled.

The man was reaching down toward his leg.

His hand came up with a knife, a long blade, shiny despite the darkness of our depth. Because I had a face mask, I could see better than he could. I grabbed at the free end of the weight belts so that I had them at each end. By rotating my body, I got the belts around his forearm. He stabbed up with the knife. I leaned to the side, dodging the blow, and twisted the belts on his arm. My need to breathe was causing black spots in my vision. I was close to losing consciousness. And the cold was taking all the strength out of my muscles. But I managed to jerk the weight belts hard as I kneed the man in his stomach.

The thickness of water reduces any attempt at a blow to a fraction of what it would be in air. Nevertheless, the blow made the man bend at the waist. His knife struck again but hit one of the weights on the belts. I turned and swung my elbow across his mouth. My skin was numb from the cold, but I could tell my elbow hit something hard. I hoped it was his teeth. Then I dropped the weight belts and grabbed his wrist with both of my hands. I tried to break his wrist, hoping the pain would cause him to loosen his grip on the knife.

It worked. He dropped it, the shiny blade shooting down into the deep blue. He reached up and jerked off my face mask.

Now I couldn't see. Where once I could clearly see Mae and the scuba diver, now I saw vague shapes that seemed like more divers. But all was obscured by the never-ending curtains of bubbles.

The cold was paralyzing. I could barely move. And my need to breathe seemed greater than any desire I'd ever experienced. In my wavering consciousness, I realized that I was down to a few seconds before I passed out.

I also realized that Mae was still there, somewhere in the bubbles. If the scuba diver still had a hold on her, maybe my last act could be to break that hold. I twisted one last time. The diver was just a dark shape. It seemed there was another dark shape. But I knew I might be hallucinating as I went unconscious. I got my hands on the diver's neck. He made a guttural scream as if in agony beyond any pain I could cause in my weakened state. As if with a herculean effort, he got away from me and, in a huge cloud of bubbles, started swimming up.

Something hit me in the face. The scuba regulator. Mae was handing it to me. I grabbed it, felt it being pulled away because it was still attached to the diver.

I hung on and put it in my mouth and breathed hard and fast. Over and over.

I held onto the regulator hose as the diver swam up. He was obviously desperate to get to the surface to breathe.

Mae hung onto my arm. All three of us were rising in a cloud of bubbles.

Mae grabbed my hand. She felt my fingers. She was obviously so cold that her muscles had mostly stopped working. But I sensed that she tried to pry the regulator hose from my grip.

She obviously needed another breath. I took the mouthpiece from my mouth and handed it to her. But as she reached for it, it slipped out of her grasp. I didn't understand.

The diver rose up above us, faster and faster. He didn't reach for the regulator. It trailed behind him.

I finally understood. He was already dead, rushing toward the surface like a human beach ball, his insides filled with air from an attack that none of us saw because of the cloud of bubbles.

Mae was hanging onto me. With her flotation vest deflated, we were sinking. I pulled the cord to inflate my flotation vest. It filled fast and started pulling us toward the surface.

We rose slowly. My lungs were back to agony. I didn't know if I'd make it. But if Mae could tough it out, maybe I could as well.

She breathed out bubbles as we rose.

Then I remembered one of the major rules of scuba diving.

If you inhale compressed air at depth and then rise toward the surface, you have to continuously breathe out. Otherwise, as the surrounding water pressure diminishes, the compressed air you inhaled will expand and rupture your lungs.

I focused on that, slowly breathing out, telling myself that the roar and scream of needing to breathe was something one could fight. Mind over matter.

An eternity later, Mae and I broke the surface. We were nearly paralyzed with hypothermia. But we gasped for air, choking and coughing, barely able to keep our heads above water in spite of my flotation vest.

"There they are!" a voice called out. It sounded like Eileen's. "Behind you, Barry! Hurry!"

A moment later, someone grabbed us. An arm. Gripping me. Then letting go to grab Mae. I floated, held up by my vest, frozen motionless. The man swam with Mae toward the Mountain Belle. Multiple men were at the rear platform. They lifted her up and out of the water.

My head lolled, face dipping into the water. I'd lost all control over my muscles. I couldn't even hold my head up. I choked. The man was back. He grabbed me and dragged me to the boat. The other men repeated their motions, yanking me out.

They carried me into the lounge where they put me on a chaise near Mae. They brought in some kind of propane heaters, turned the fans onto us, and sent a warm drying wind over us. They held blankets behind us and partially over us, creating a tent shape to trap the warm air.

After warming for ten minutes, my shiver reflex, deadened by hypothermia, was revived, and I began to shake violently. I sensed that Mae's body was locked in equally fierce shivers.

A very long time later, I was somewhat able to think. Later still, I could talk and ask brilliant and perceptive questions like, "Mae, are you okay?"

"Yeah," came her tense reply. Her teeth chattered loud enough that I wondered if they would chip as they banged on each other.

As my thoughts gained focus, I thought of Street and Daniel and Spot. "Eileen?" I called out. "Eileen?"

"I'll get her," a crewmember said.

Eileen appeared. She looked stressed.

"My girlfriend... The blind man." I could barely make my lips move. "They swam to shore."

"Not to worry," Eileen said. "Your girlfriend borrowed someone's phone and called the Mountain Belle. She wanted me to tell you that the man is doing fine. She said he'd been shivering, but that he was warming up well. In fact, I could tell that he was feisty."

"Feisty?" I repeated.

"Yes. I could hear him in the background yelling."

"I don't understand. I would think something's wrong if he was yelling."

"Okay, maybe yelling was the wrong word. I believe he said - and I quote - 'Tell McKenna and Mae to kill the bastard.'"

"Ah," I said. "Feisty, indeed."

I thanked her, and she went back to her duties.

After another eternity, Mae and I were both sitting upright, wrapped in blankets, no longer shivering. If we eventually cooked to death, it would be a good way to meet our end.

"There was a diver who came to the surface before us," I said to the nearby crewmember who'd been assigned to watch over us. "He was swollen with air."

"No kidding," a young man said. "One of the passengers is a nurse. She said he's dead. His body is over by the scuba tanks. Is that what they mean when they talk about the bends?"

"No. The bends happen when dissolved gas bubbles inside of your blood vessels. It's very painful. But this is something different. He got stabbed by a pressure wand. It shot air into him."

"Who would do that?"

"Good question."

I'd stopped shivering. And the constant flow of hot air from the heaters had taken enough moisture out of my clothes that I didn't have to find a way to change.

I stood up and walked out of the lounge. The other passengers had cleared the aft deck, no doubt wanting to keep their distance from the dead body. There was one crewmember sitting on a nearby chair as if guarding the body, but she faced away.

"I just need to take a look at the victim," I said.

"Help yourself," she said, still staring off at the beautiful view of blue water and sunny, sandy beaches, no doubt trying hard to focus on the beauty that had probably motivated her to take the job.

I walked next to the body.

Unlike with Colin Callahan, whose chest was expanded to an inhuman point, this man was swollen through the abdomen. Despite his wetsuit, he looked like a surreal cartoon of a Michelin tire man, absurdly round through his midsection.

His limbs and chest were normal. His head was closest to me, so that I was looking at him upside down. I walked around to see him from the normal orientation.

Death takes away beauty and vitality. But the man's eyes were a brilliant - if foggy - watery blue.

At the base of his hood and above the neck opening of his wet suit, was a patch of skin. Just visible was a bit of orange cord that came around his neck like a necklace.

"Do you know him?" a voice said.

I turned to see Eileen just behind me.

"No," I said. "I've never seen him before."

"What do you think he was doing down there?"

"This is the man who pushed our older companion overboard. Mae watched him jump into the water. She's a freediver. So she was able to track him by the torn orange chevron on the upper back of his suit. She raced down and pulled off his face mask, so that he would have to come back up. Unfortunately, he caught her. I was able to help her get away. There was a lot of commotion and bubbles obscuring everything. During the process, someone stabbed him with an air wand and injected high pressure air into him."

"Which killed him," Eileen said. "Not pretty," she added.

"If you have a latex glove or a handkerchief, I could unzip his wetsuit a bit and see what's on this orange cord around his neck."

Eileen brought me a clean, smooth cloth.

I used it to grasp the thin edges of the zipper tab and pulled the zipper down six inches. On the orange cord at his chest was a clear plastic pouch. I used the cloth to flip it over. There was a driver's license that said Jack Wormack with an address in Merced, California.

The name was familiar. Jacky Wormack. I said it to myself two or three times, trying to jog my memory.

Then I remembered.

When I went to the place where the first murder victim, Colin Callahan, had lived, it was in Citrus Heights. The man in charge of renting out the bedrooms of two condos owned by his mother was Brand. Jay Brandon Morse. A very handsome man who seemed to possess the intelligence of an oil filter. Brand mentioned having raised the rent of a previous roommate by $25, and that caused the roommate to move out and go live with his father in Merced. The roommate's name was Jacky Wormack.

This meant that two of Brandon Morse's roommates were now dead by lethal compressed air injection.

THIRTY-EIGHT

Mountain Belle Captain Lisa Glass recognized one of the boats in Glenbrook Bay. It was a small pleasure craft, no radios. So she hailed the boat by megaphone. The boat came near, and the captain came down from the bridge to request ferry service for three of her passengers who had to swim to the nearest beach, a woman, a man, and a large dog.

Twenty minutes later, Street and Daniel and Spot were aboard the Belle and reunited with Blondie, Mae, and me. There were hugs and some tears and warm-up huddles, and a studious avoidance of the dead body at the stern of the Mountain Belle.

An hour later, we were back at the Blue Sky Marina on the South Shore. In keeping with the excessive 911 dispatch rules, an SLTPD patrol unit, a firetruck, and a rescue vehicle were waiting to take away the murder victim.

Mae and Street had convinced Daniel to visit the hospital for a checkup, and he'd only agreed because he was having trouble breathing and with the qualification that he would not ride in an ambulance and he would walk in on his own two feet.

After Daniel was checked in for an overnight hospital stay, Street and I accompanied Mae back to her house. Mae insisted that she'd be fine, and we said we would call her in the morning.

I stopped at my cabin for a change of clothes and quick thank-you calls to Glennie and Airwaves Andy.

They both wondered if the mission had been successful, and I assured them that we'd caught at least one bad guy. I left out the stress and turmoil.

That evening, Street and I had a quiet dinner at her place and then sat with the dogs in front of her gas stove fireplace insert, soaking up the warmth. Blondie eventually moved away to a cooler part of the condo. But Spot and Street and I happily baked, unable to get too warm.

Street wanted me to sleep over, and I obliged.

The next morning, I headed off to learn about the man who rose, dead, from the depths of Glenbrook Bay, his insides filled with air.

All I knew about Jack Wormack was that Daniel identified him as the man who kicked in his door and, with a mouth full of dental cotton, tried to torment Daniel into telling what went down with the ship when they scuttled the Tahoe Steamer. For a time, Wormack was a roommate of Colin Callahan, both of them living in a condo managed by Brand Morse.

That both Callahan and Wormack ended up dead by compressed air injection suggested lots, but I wasn't sure what it meant.

I guessed that it was simple. Jack learned from Colin about the treasure, so he tried to find it by terrorizing Daniel. He likely killed Colin so he could keep the treasure for himself. Because Jack probably had some connection to Lemon Hills, he left a citrus mite in Daniel's door when he kicked it in. How the Bosstro brothers got involved, I had no idea. Jack moved out of Brand's house because of a $25 rent increase. That made it unlikely he could afford to hire Carlos and Jeff Bosstro. But the Bosstro brothers were from Lemon Hills, so there were possibilities for a connection.

Jack had likely used a pre-charged pneumatic gun to shoot out Daniel Callahan's window. Then Jack had probably called on the phone and terrorized Daniel into telling about his sister murdering a man named Frank while they were on the Tahoe Steamer. Frank, who had a plan to steal something worth a fortune. Frank, who may have stolen that treasure and had it on him when Callahan's sister killed him and sent him to his death at the bottom of Lake Tahoe.

In Lemon Hills, I'd found the Bosstros' PCP gun and air compressor equipment at the farm where they worked. It was possible that the Bosstro's PCP gun was the one Jack used. Maybe Jack had been the silent foster brother decades ago.

Why Jack was killed, I had no idea. Maybe I'd find out in

Merced.

Jack Wormack's license showed his address as 1249 Fecher Lane, Apt 21, in Merced, the Central Valley city that is the gateway to Yosemite. I took Spot with me. It took a little over three hours to get there. I found the address number on the front of an old brick apartment building. I would have driven around looking for shade to park in, but on this day the Central Valley heat was too extreme for a dog in a vehicle even in full shade. All the parking on the street was taken, so I put the Jeep in 4-wheel-drive, drove up the curb, across the sidewalk, and sideways up onto the slope next to the building, so that the Jeep leaned to the left at a substantial angle. The slope had a sparse coating of dried, brown grass. In years past, the building would have looked woefully neglected. Now it looked eco-sensitive, the unwatered lawn helping to conserve California's increasingly worrisome water supply.

I didn't think the grass was long enough to catch fire from the heat of the Jeep's exhaust system, so I left the Jeep running, windows half-open, and the air conditioning on high. Because of the incline, Spot slid across the seat until he hit the left rear door.

He swung his head around to stare at me as I got out and shut the door. His brow was furrowed, not with worry but with confusion.

"Sorry, Largeness. You might not sleep well on such an incline, but life is full of compromises. At least you have cool air." I gave the roof a light pat and left.

Apartment 21 was the front left apartment on the second floor. I knocked.

After a short wait, the door was opened by a small man in his 80s, with pale skin and wispy white hair that stuck out to the left as if he were in a permanent windstorm. He said nothing and just stared at me with watery blue eyes that were very much like Jack Wormack's eyes when they pulled his body out of Lake Tahoe. He was probably a dozen or more years younger than Daniel Callahan, but he seemed more frail and less present.

"Hello, my name is Owen McKenna. Are you Mr.

Wormack?"

He nodded.

"I'm a private investigator from Lake Tahoe, and I've come to talk to you about your son Jack. Is there someplace we can sit?" One never knows how a father is going to react to the news of his son's death. If he fainted or got very upset, it would be best if he was sitting.

Mr. Wormack seemed to think about my request, then turned and walked into the apartment. We went through a small entry into the living room. The apartment was furnished with comfortable old furniture, upholstered in floral patterns. The floors were oak stained the color of walnut. Each of several end tables had lamps with shades that looked opaque so that the light could only escape up to the ceiling or down to the tables. The most modern item in the apartment appeared to be a '70's-vintage console TV, with the curved screen set inside a large wooden case. On it was a flickering, black-and-white soap opera, probably a rerun from the '50s. The sound was turned off.

Mr. Wormack sat on a chair that had yellow daisies against a purple background. Draped across the back of the chair was a decorative lace doily about 12 by 20 inches. The doily looked hand-stitched. At the bottom of the chair was ruffled fabric with the same daisies-on-purple fabric. The ruffles circled the base so that one could hide magazines or a small dog or a gun under the chair. I sat on a loveseat with white orchids against a green background. The couch had a doily similar to what was on the chair, only it was three times as long.

Both the chair, the couch, and another chair were all angled toward the soap opera. I turned toward Mr. Wormack.

He finally spoke. "What has he done now?"

"I'm very sorry to tell you that Jack died yesterday."

The man made a hint of a nod. His skin paled more and his eyes got a touch more watery.

"Someone killed him," he said. It was more statement than question.

"We won't know for certain until the pathologist makes a report. But his death looks suspicious, yes."

He made another, single, nod. He looked very sad but resigned as if he'd known for years that this would happen. He said, "Jacky said the game was very realistic. So I guess that includes killing."

I didn't understand what he meant, but maybe it would become clear as I talked to him.

"The address of this apartment is listed on his driver's license," I said. "Did he live here with you?"

Another nod. "Now that Mabel died, I've got extra space. I don't have friends, so I'm glad to have Jacky around." Mr. Wormack was staring vacantly at the wall, perhaps thinking of his son when he was a child and was filled with exuberance and possibility. Most parents I've met who've lost sons to violence hold on desperately to the memories from when their sons were very young, before their boys made friends with older boys who started prodding them in the wrong direction.

"How did Jacky die?" he asked. "I suppose it would be shipwrecking. He said that was the main point of the game."

I still didn't understand the reference to a game. "He was scuba diving in Lake Tahoe," I said.

He looked down at his lap. "Looking for sunken treasure?" he said.

"It would seem so, yes," I said. "Can you tell me about his treasure hunting?"

Wormack lifted his head up from his lap and looked at the TV. "Years ago, on one of Mabel's soaps, there was a good man in Seattle. The man's brother was no good. There was a woman who knew she should go with the good man. But she fell for the bad brother. She knew he was bad. But he was handsome. And he talked a line. He wore fancy shoes. The bad man was exciting, and he was a treasure hunter. He went out on Puget Sound where a ship had sunk. His whole life was a dream about some treasure on that ship. The good man got left behind because he wasn't exciting enough."

I waited some time, then said, "And your boy Jack saw that show."

He nodded.

"And he was captivated by that character and wanted to have

that life."

"Yes. I knew what Jacky was doing was bad, just like on the show. But nothing I said made any difference. Anyway, it was just a game."

"When you say it was just a game, what exactly do you mean?" I asked.

Mr. Wormack looked puzzled. "I don't know what else to call it. Jacky didn't tell me much. They get together and play the game on the computer. But sometimes they go to certain places in the game. There's different versions. The game Jacky played was called Shipwreck Treasure. He said it was virtually like real life, whatever that means."

"When Jacky played, where did he go to use the computer?"

"I think it varied. But mostly it was where he used to lived in Sacramento. He rented a room in a house. But then the landlord raised the rent, so Jacky moved back home with me. We're very close."

"What are the rules of the game?"

"Well, pretty much anything goes, even death. But it has to make logical sense. So you can't just kill anyone. You have to have a good reason. Jacky said it has to fit Mars Logic."

"What's that mean?"

"If a person from Mars came and watched, would they understand what the players do? They would if it made sense. So you can't do things just 'cause you want. It has to fit Mars Logic."

"Do lots of people die in the Shipwreck Treasure game?"

"I don't know. But Jacky said there was a rule about shrinking. They had to shrink the gang as the game went on."

"How many players are there?"

"I don't know."

"What determines when someone wins the game?"

"When someone finds the treasure, that person wins. Or if there are two people, they are co-winners."

"Did Jacky say if any other players had died?"

"Just Colin. Jacky had to kill him. Now Jacky's dead. I think the game rules are strange."

"Do you know the names of anyone else in this game?"

"Not the human names, no."

"Do you know where any of them live?"

"No. But Jacky sometimes goes to Lemon Hills to pick up a load. He's a produce trucker. He sometimes sleeps overnight in Lemon Hills. So maybe some of the players lived there. Maybe he sleeps at their house."

"Can you think of any other details about the game? Anything Jacky said?"

He shook his head. "No." He paused, stared at the old black-and-white soap opera, and frowned.

"You said you don't know the players' human names. Do they have other names?"

"They have titles. Jacky talked about them a lot. There's the diver, the enforcer, the scientist, and the foster brother."

"Which one is Jacky?" I asked.

"Oh, I forgot to say his game name. He's the cleaner."

"But you don't know the names of any of the people who go with the other titles?"

"No." He frowned. "I kind of remember who plays the enforcer. The name was like Boss."

"Bosstro? The Bosstro brothers?"

"Yeah."

As the man talked, it seemed that a possible explanation for his strange tale was that Jacky wanted to have someone to talk to about his treasure-hunting activities. Perhaps Jacky knew his father was a bit on the far side of common sense. Jacky might have presented what he did as if it was part of a fantastical, grand game.

"How did Jacky become part of this game?"

Mr. Wormack suddenly seemed more engaged. "That's what I wanted to know. So Jacky told me all about it. He told his roommate about the soap opera treasure hunter from TV when he was kid. Then his roommate said his great grandfather was a man who once owned a great treasure, but it was stolen from him."

"Did Jacky's roommate tell him the name of the man?"

"Yes. I remember the man's first name was Jack because it was the same as my Jack. But I don't remember the last name. Jacky said the man was rich."

I thought about what Daniel Callahan had said. When he was a boy and he overheard his sister Nora and her friend Frank, Frank had mentioned a robber and murderer named Jack Questman. "Could his last name be Questman?"

Mr. Wormack's eyes widened. "Yes, that sounds familiar. Jack Questman. Now I remember that Jacky said he was on a Questman quest."

"And Jack Questman's treasure was stolen?"

"Yes."

"What was the treasure?"

Wormack shook his head. "I don't know. I don't think my son knows, either."

"How did Jacky's roommate learn about it? He probably hadn't been born yet when his great grandfather was still alive."

Wormack nodded. "Sometimes fathers tell their children things. And the kids tell their kids. People remember a story about a great treasure."

"Did Jacky ever learn who they thought stole Questman's loot?"

"No."

"Do you know the name of Jack's roommate? The man who told him about the treasure?"

"No."

"Could it be the man he had to kill? Colin Callahan?"

"I don't think so."

"Why do you think Jack went to Tahoe to search for treasure?"

"Jack met a man who knew about a ship that sunk. The man said there was treasure on that ship. Jack was smitten."

"Could that man have been Colin?"

Mr. Wormack frowned. "Maybe," he said.

"Where else did the players live?"

Wormack shrugged. "Just Lemon Hills, I think."

"You said that Jacky maybe stayed there when he was driving

his truck. Do you have any idea of where in Lemon Hills?"

"No."

"Was there any other place Jacky talked about besides Lemon Hills?"

"Just Tahoe. He just said he was going to Tahoe to get rich."

"When they release Jacky's body, do you want to take possession of it?"

Mr. Wormack was silent for a long moment. "No. I don't care what you do. I want to be left alone. It's just a game."

When I opened the apartment door to leave, I turned and faced Mr. Wormack.   In the dim light of the entry, his blue eyes looked foggy. He was confused to some degree, of that I was certain. But the confusion didn't seem to trouble him as it did some old people. What did seem to trouble him was his sadness. His wife Mabel had died. Jacky had taken up some of that emotional space. Now Jacky died. Mr. Wormack said he had no friends. He was all alone. His confusion would multiply. He wasn't fortunate like Daniel Callahan, who had Mae.

"Thank you for your time, sir," I said.

Mr. Wormack made a little nod and shut the door behind me.

The Jeep was still running, but the driver's door was open. Spot was still in back. It had happened before. Probably, a kid saw the running vehicle and thought he could take it for a ride. So he jumped in and was about to drive off, when he realized there was a giant dog in the back seat. Maybe the dog growled. Or maybe the dog just lifted his head - a head the size of a basketball - and sniffed the kid on his neck. The kid jumped out and ran for his life.

As I drove back to Tahoe, I went over the likely sequence.

Colin Callahan, whose parents died young, inherited letters written by his aunt's aunt. From those letters, he deduced a treasure that the first aunt created when she killed her boyfriend on the Tahoe Steamer, which was scuttled shortly afterward.

Then Callahan met Brand Morse. It was probably Brand who had the great grandfather named Jack Questman, who'd gained and then lost a fortune through theft and possibly murder. Colin's aunt's aunt, Nora Callahan, wrote letters that revealed she'd come to have a fortune because her boyfriend had stolen Questman's stolen property.

Brand Morse and Colin Callahan had decided to find the intersection of these two people, learn where the treasure might be all these decades later, and take it for themselves.

But it was likely that they made the mistake of talking to others. Jacky Wormack, who had business in Lemon Hills, probably told the Bosstro brothers. They may have developed an agreement. The Bosstro brothers would provide intimidation and enforcement as needed.

At least one of the men figured out that Daniel Callahan was that intersection point, and they went to put the squeeze on him for information regarding what his older sister did with the treasure. Then, they realized that Colin Callahan was expendable. So they killed him to reduce the number of ways the treasure would be split and also because his death would intimidate the old blind man and motivate him to talk.

Complicating the plan was a foster brother in the Bosstro household 30 years ago. At one extreme, the foster brother could be the leader and, at the other extreme, a mere apparition dancing in the ether.

If the foster brother existed, I had no idea who he was or even if I'd met or heard of him.

I drove through the enveloping night, heading toward the foothills on the east side of the Central Valley and then up the mountains toward Tahoe.

I went through everyone I'd met from the beginning. There was Ivan Manfred, the Ink Maestro, tattoo artist who seemed all fluff and self-importance and who, despite being a painter, didn't even notice that Colin Callahan's tattoo was based on a famous German painting. There was Officer Holden, the tatted-up SLTPD policeman who sang Manfred's praises and probably put Mallory onto Manfred as a consultant. There were all of Daniel Callahan's neighbors, some of whom I'd met, and some of whom seemed to have grievances against Callahan. Everyone agreed that he was not the most pleasant fellow much of the time. The neighbors I had met were Ed Filusch, the silent handyman and his roommate Carter Sampson, the boisterous blowhard who didn't like Callahan for reasons that were unclear.

My Tahoe Steamer Festival had been a great success if measured by the underwater murder of Daniel Callahan's assailant and a victim who came complete with ID. But unless I could find a connection between Jacky Wormack and one of the other people, I still didn't have a murderer.

The air rushing in our open windows cooled Spot and probably calmed him as well. But it did nothing to quell my confusion.

Spot eventually pulled his head in from the window and lay down on the back seat. I eventually closed the windows as I climbed up to cooler elevations. But I found no calm.

I found myself thinking about all the divers who'd been at Glenbrook Bay, some serious about seeing what the remote operated vehicle might bring up from the depths. Some might have wanted to steal the goods, even though the decoy package that the company had put in the ROV's robot arm was never taken. Yet other divers may have just wanted to be part of the excitement, a high-altitude diving adventure that they would, one day, talk about with their grandchildren.

THIRTY-NINE

The next morning, my phone rang. I answered it.

"Hey, Owen, this is Ivan Manfred, the Ink Maestro calling. Heard something you will want to know."

"Can you tell me over the phone, or do I need to stop by?"

"Phone works for me. I had a man stop by today. He asked if I ink tattoos to look like a painting. I said not really. He said he knew an artist in Sacramento who did tattoos of paintings. Said his work was great but he was a jerk. So when this guy heard that I was a nice guy, he wondered if I could do what he wanted."

"Which was what?"

"He wanted the Mona Lisa inked on his butt."

"And you declined?"

"Yeah. I'm a painter. I could do a fabulous painting of Mona baby. But like every other inker, I can't make a painting look good as a tattoo. Unlike every other inker, I have standards and ethics. So I'm forced to turn down jobs. Even if the man has a hot butt. But still... Then I remembered that you would want to know. Unfortunately, I didn't get the customer's name. But I asked who this other inker was who does painting tats. He told me his name is Wilbur Neally Lopez. Strange name, so I had him write it down. The business name is Sick Tats and Craft Brews."

"Sick? Oh, sick like the bomb? Like awesome?"

"Right! I guess you're not as square as you look."

"Wilbur Neally Lopez," I said. "Thanks a bunch."

"A bunch?" The Ink Maestro said. "I take it back. You're as square as all those other cops."

"Guilty as charged," I said.

"While I've got you on the line," he said. "Have you thought any more about your hound sitting for a painting? He is the cutest boy."

"I haven't had a chance. But I'll let you know as soon as I do."

We said goodbye and hung up. I looked up Sick Tats and dialed.

"Sick Tats, Jasmine speaking." She spoke American vernacular but with an Hispanic accent. Like her parents might be first-generation immigrants, but she was born here.

"Hey, Jasmine. Will around?"

"I'm sorry, he's recently left our employ."

"Really? And he didn't even tell me? What's that about? Do you have his contact info?"

"Sorry, Mr..."

"Alejandro. Just the one word. Like Prince."

"Sorry Alejandro. Is Will a personal friend?" She sounded doubtful.

I decided to make a guess, which would have enough specificity to encourage her cooperation. "I've known Will since he was in the third grade and I was assigned to be his mentor for our Freshman project. I got an A, and Will got a mentor for life. We haven't had much contact recently. Frankly, I'm calling because I want one of those tats that looks like a painting. I have the painting already picked out, a Diego Rivera. I want it across my back. Price is no object."

"Then Will is certainly not your man. You are Yankee, and Will went to third grade in Costa Rica." She hung up on me.

FORTY

Daniel Callahan spent two days in the hospital. For general observation, they said. Nothing specific. When you take a man in his mid-nineties - a man who can't swim - and throw him into water cold enough to stop his heart and then keep him there until he's hypothermic and past the point of shivering, it might be a good idea to watch him closely for a time.

Mae and Street and I visited Daniel the third morning. He was propped up in bed, wearing the aviator mirrors. His hair was wild and going in all directions. He looked like an aging rock star.

"Is your hound in your car?" Daniel asked when we walked into his room.

"Yes."

"I haven't properly thanked him for saving my life. Bring him in. Please."

"I thought you were afraid of dogs," I said.

"I am. I'm bracing myself. And with you nearby, I'll probably be safe."

"One can't just bring dogs into the hospital," I said. Spot had been up to see Diamond when he was recovering from multiple gunshots a couple of years before. But Diamond's cop status had created a sense of authority, and the staff did not want to object.

"I'm certain you can bring dogs," Daniel said. "They're allowed everywhere these days." Daniel pressed his signal button.

A nurse came in the door. "You need assistance?"

Daniel nodded, then waved her over. He spoke softly.

"I'm sorry, I can't hear you," the nurse said.

"Bend closer," Daniel said.

She put her ear near his mouth. He spoke for ten seconds.

The nurse straightened up and said to me, "Sir, a therapy

dog is welcome in our hospital. The last therapy dog was so cute. Yvette, the Yorkie. Her handler carried her in a little doggie basket." She turned to me. "So bring your dog. Bring him in your doggie basket, if you like."

I nodded, smiled briefly at Street, and left, muttering that my doggie basket is barely big enough to carry the doggie biscuits.

"Excuse me?" the nurse said.

"Never mind."

I went out, fetched His Largeness, and brought him into the hospital. They were wheeling two people and their wheelchairs into the elevator, so Spot and I took the stairs. Three different times, people gasped, one with alarm, two with delight.

When we walked into Daniel's room, he immediately realized we were there.

"Come, Spot, come," he bravely said, patting the bed. He took off his sunglasses. I wasn't sure why. Maybe he thought he'd be safer if my dog could see him without his cover, as if Spot would recognize him sooner. His flying saucer eyes looked toward Spot. I sensed Daniel's worry. His jaw muscles bulged.

Spot looked up at me. I let go of his collar. "You've been summoned, boy. Best you obey."

Spot took two steps toward Daniel's bed. His tail was on medium speed.

Daniel held out his hand. Spot sniffed it. At the touch of the cold wet nose, Daniel jerked his hand back. Then he reached out again. Soon, Daniel was caressing the side of Spot's jaw and then rubbing his ears. Spot twisted his head and leaned into it. He glanced at me as if I should take note of Daniel's technique.

A nurse came, saw Spot and gasped, then gathered her wits and said that the doctor had okayed Daniel for immediate discharge.

Daniel said, "I've steeled myself to doctors and nurses and beast. I'm ready to face the world."

A half hour later, we accompanied Daniel as a nurse wheeled him out of the hospital in a chair. He was fully dressed. His aviators were back on.

We helped him stand up, me on one side and Mae on the

other, while Street held the chair. Daniel tried to shake us off. "You two treat me like I'm an old geezer."

"No," I said. "We're treating you like you're an old curmudgeon. According to the manual, geezers are befuddled. You've never demonstrated befuddlement. But curmudgeons are cranky. They rant. And complain. And they harass and dismiss their caregivers. All your forte. You're clearly a curmudgeon. A curmudgeon, I might add, whose hair is all mussed up."

"What? I've lost my comb." He reached up the hand that held his navigation cane. He used that hand to smooth his hair. Which made the cane stab me in the side.

"That hurt," I said. "A curmudgeon who uses his cane to physically abuse others. Let's get you locked inside a vehicle so you can't hurt anyone else."

Soon, we had Daniel home and ensconced in his rocker. Mae made a pot of tea and poured cups for each of us. Daniel had taken off his glasses. He seemed in good spirits although weary. Spot lay on the floor next to him. Spot was on his side, stretched out, taking up as much space as possible. Daniel let his arm hang off the side of the chair so he could pet him.

"I guess not all dogs are dangerous," he said. "Will he mind if I measure his neck for a triquetra necklace?"

"No. He'll think you're fashioning a collar, which he likes because they make him think he's going on a W-A-L-K."

At the sound of the letters, Spot lifted his head and looked at me. I stared the opposite direction, toward the kitchen, staying as unresponsive as possible. Eventually, Spot put his head back down.

Daniel reached over to his leather spool, found the end of the strap and pulled it out, unspooling a long piece. As Daniel reached down to thread it under Spot's neck, Spot rolled up onto his chest and elbows, his head up. He started panting.

"Neck like a horse," Daniel said as he wrapped the leather around Spot's neck, gauging the length he needed. Then he removed it, added substantial extra length, and cut it off with his wire cutter. Daniel took one end of the strip and made a loop.

With deft movements that showed years of practice, he worked the leather into a complex shape, pulling and tugging just so to create something that initially looked like a large knot with multiple loops and intersections. He used his index finger as a measuring stick, working the intersections gradually tighter as he adjusted the loops into a careful shape that would eventually be an uncanny shamrock.

"Daniel, I've been thinking…" I said as he worked.

"I'm glad someone is. You listen to the news and find out it's just about celebrities, you get the idea that most people regard thinking as an affliction best to be dispensed with."

I nodded. "When you showed us the framed picture of Nora and sang the lines that were printed in Braille on the frame's backing paper, I watched you use your fingertips on the dots."

"Of course. That's how you read Braille," he said with a bit of an edge to his voice. He looked up toward the mantle where the picture sat. I noticed that he was looking at the wrong angle. But that was as good as his foggy vision provided. He knew the picture was up there.

"It seemed like you didn't sing all the words on the back of the picture," I said.

"What do you mean?"

Daniel had doubled up the leather loops to make them stiffer. Even though I'd seen his finished triquetras and was watching him create a new one, I still couldn't understand how it worked.

"Your fingers went along," I said, "and you sang the words. Then you stopped singing at the end of the chorus. But your fingertips seemed to be feeling more Braille."

"Hand me the picture."

I lifted it off the mantle and handed it to him. He set the knot of leather cord in his lap. He took the picture, turned it over, and ran his fingers over the dots. His mouth made little silent movements. At the bottom of the backing paper, he stopped moving his lips as his index fingertip came to the last dots.

"I understand the confusion," he said. "The words are 'Oh Danny Boy, Oh Danny Boy, I love you so.' Then come more dots as if more words are to come."

"At the bottom of the backing paper," I said.

"Yes. This was done with the Hall Braille Writer. It was a cumbersome process back then, punching keys to make the corresponding dots. After Nora ran the paper through the Braille writer, she must have torn off the end of the paper so it would fit the back of the frame."

"What if whatever words came next were put inside the frame behind the photo?"

Daniel held the frame without moving. Then he pushed in on the backing paper as if to judge what might be behind it.

"Mae," he said. "Would you please get me my scissors?"

Mae stood up, went into the galley kitchen and opened a drawer. She came back and reached out with a small scissors, holding the handle end toward him.

Daniel took the scissors and, feeling very carefully, inserted the pointed end through the backing paper next to the edge of the frame. He slowly snipped with the scissors, cutting with precision around the frame's perimeter.

Daniel set the scissors aside. He caught the edge of the paper with his fingernails and lifted out a group of several papers. Gripping them as a group, he carefully set the original backing paper on his lap. The paper below it also had Braille dots. Daniel felt carefully. He made a strong frown.

"Yes, you are right, Owen. There is more here to read. Much more. It seems Nora wrote me a letter about eighty years ago."

FORTY-ONE

Daniel began to read with halting words.

"March twenty-six, nineteen forty-two.

Danny darling,

I've been working on this note for some time, typing it on the Braille writer. I'm not good at typing Braille like you, so you will see typos. But of course you already know that. I'm actually not good at anything the way you are. The only thing I can do better than you is see, I suppose. But even vision is something where you eventually developed superior skills to mine and those of most people. You may not see well, but your powers of observation are amazing.

You know that I've always wanted to write. Virginia Woolf said that if a woman wants to write, she needs some money and a room of her own. I've started many different writing projects. But they never came to anything. I thought it was because I was broke and didn't have the physical space or mental space. So I worked hard arranging for both. But once I had a little space and money, it didn't help me.

Writing is for loners. But I'm a social creature. I belong in an office with all the commotion.

Now that I realize I don't have the right temperament to pursue my dream, I'm giving you what I've got. It's not cash money, but it's almost the same. The main thing I want you to know is that I only hurt two people. One was to protect you. And the other was you.

It's time to tell you a story. Two stories.

First, when I met Frank, I learned that he had tried his hand at barnstorming during the depression around Fresno, where he grew up. Despite Frank's interest in me, his first and main love was a girl named Jenny.

He flew a Jenny, a type of plane first used in The Great War. After the war, all the leftover Jenny planes were sold cheap. Frank said you could land that plane on any field. And of course, there's nothing but fields near Fresno. When I got to know him better, he said he'd let me in on a secret. He'd met a man who also flew Jenny planes. A rich man named Jack Questman who had a mansion at Lake Tahoe. Jack Questman didn't get rich from hard work but from crime. He made a business of stealing valuable things, items that didn't have something called chain of ownership. Frank said the word for it was provenance. The way he explained it was that with some things there is a way to identify the item, like an identification number. And many things come with a bill of sale that names the seller and the buyer and the date of the transaction. That is what makes provenance an ongoing record of ownership. So if you find an item with provenance, then you can know if it is held by its rightful owner or not. But if you have something that doesn't come with provenance, then simple possession of it is the main qualification for ownership. Whoever has it can sell it. And if the person who has it stole it from someone else who previously stole it, then the former owner would have no claim on it.

Frank said that the rich man had stolen treasure from others far across the country. According to Frank, Questman had even committed murder. Frank said one of the rich man's greatest treasures was a stamp with a picture of a Jenny airplane, only the plane was mistakenly printed upside down. Which made the stamp extremely valuable. Frank said the rich man stole the stamp from a New York collector who was in trouble with the Mafia, and that's why the collector kept his possession of the stamp secret.

Frank realized that if he stole the stamp from the rich man and wasn't caught in the process, the rich man couldn't prove he'd ever owned it. Frank often talked about his plan to steal the stamp. But his statements were sometimes contradictory. I came to think that it was a charade, that he'd already broken into the man's Tahoe mansion and stolen it. Then one time, I went to visit Frank at the campground where he was staying. I could see

Frank in his tent. He didn't know I was there. He was holding a sheet of paper folded in half. And it was taped on all the edges for protection. Frank put it in a pocket on the inside of his jacket. Several times, when we were close, I sensed that folded paper in his inner pocket.

Because he pretended he hadn't yet stolen it, I knew his lies were expanding.

Frank also thought that you would figure out his plan and betray him to the authorities. He said you'd been nearby when we'd discussed things, and that you could have overheard us. Of course, we never explicitly stated what we were doing. But Frank said you were smarter than anyone he knew and that we couldn't trust you.

He made frequent references to you being a threat. I was so afraid that he'd hurt you or worse. Maybe I was suffering from paranoia. But I think my concerns were realistic. After some scary things Frank said, I came to believe that Frank was going to do something terrible to you so you couldn't ever tell anyone about the stamp. And there were other things about Frank, certain things he did, that were very troubling, things I can't even bring myself to mention. All I'll say was that I discovered the hard way that he was a very bad man.

So I figured out how to get him out to the Tahoe Steamer before they scuttled it. I did it under the guise of explaining how we could kill and hide the rich man's body. I was showing him the ship's lockers and said we could hide the rich man's body there. When Frank leaned into the locker, I hit him on the head. He fell inside. I reached into his inner pocket and pulled out the folded paper with the inverted Jenny stamp taped inside. Then I shut the door and locked it with his body inside. They scuttled the Steamer the next day.

Anyway, now that I have something worth lots of money, I realize that you're the only one who really needs money. So I'm putting the stamp in the safest place I can think of, behind a picture of me to give to you, my sweet kid brother who I love more than life. I'm going to put something in Braille on the back of the frame, so you'll know to look inside. I know they say that surgery for your eyes isn't very helpful or reliable, either. But they keep developing new techniques. When the time is right, you'll have money to pay for it."

Daniel paused and set the Braille letter down in his lap. He was breathing hard.

"So I was wrong all these years," he said. "Frank wasn't two-timing Nora for a girl named Jenny. How could I have made such a misjudgment? Things always seem crystal clear to us until we find out we are wrong."

After a minute he resumed reading.

"Now there is just one more story to tell you. This is harder to admit than telling you what I did to Frank. But I've decided to tell you so you will understand what I'm about to do.

When you were burned, mom and dad swore me to secrecy. They said that if I ever told you the truth, it would take a situation that was already unbelievably bad and make it much worse.

They are no doubt right. But if I don't tell you, you will think that I'm just a flighty, ditzy girl, incapable of controlling my moods. I would be one of those silly people who, despite having most things people need, think life is so unfair that they'll just end it.

Well, I may be vain and self-indulgent. I may overreact. I may be unrealistic.

But I have my reasons. I hurt you badly. It was a terrible wrong.

You of course remember that I've read a lot about both the Japanese Samurai warriors and Virginia Woolf. The Samurai have multiple ways of finding an honorable end to a very shameful experience. The way they die depends on their circumstances, such as if they've committed a serious crime. Or maybe they're about to lose a battle in a war. There are even death traditions for expressing ultimate indignation over something their leaders have done wrong.

The tradition that applies to me is called Sokotsu-shi. It is for when a Samurai has committed a serious transgression that brings endless shame on him even if it's not a crime. You will probably find it a very flawed concept, but it's a Samurai way to make up for reckless behavior, something terrible that one did wrong. For some, it's about making amends to their gods. For me, it's about a personal honor. It's called expiation. Although, you're so smart, maybe you already know that. One of the ways that Samurai performed Sokotsu-shi was to weigh themselves down by putting on their heaviest armor and jumping into the sea. In a sense, that's what Virginia Woolf did. Sokotsu-shi. It will work for me, too.

As you know, I've struggled mightily over the years, always charging one way or the other to find some kind of balance in my moods.

The reason is this. What you never knew is that you didn't cause the accident that ruined your eyes. You didn't pull the boiling water down on yourself. That was something mom and dad wanted you to think. They were trying to protect me.

It happened one night when mom and dad were out on one of their rare summer dates. They had asked me to be your babysitter.

I remember the scene like it was burned into my brain. I was cooking us dinner. I had chicken thighs in the fry pan and potatoes and green beans boiling in the sauce pan. I had the radio on loud so I could hear it in the kitchen. They were playing big band swing. While I cooked, I danced around, stepping and jumping and turning, practicing the steps to the Lindy Hop. I was imagining that someday I'd meet a dream boy who would sweep me out onto the dance floor.

You were standing there, looking up at me, reaching up to the edge of the counter. You were a tiny kid, asking me if you could have a drink of water.

I was very stupid. While I reached for a glass in the cupboard above the sink, I kept dancing. I pulled the glass out, held it above my head, and spun around, singing to the music.

My dress caught the handle of the pan with the potatoes, and it tipped off. The boiling water fell onto your upturned face.

Danny, I could never say how sorry I am. I'm the one who destroyed your vision and so much of your life.

They say that an accident is just that, an accident. The person who was hurt didn't deserve it. The person who caused it didn't mean to do harm. If we accept that accidents happen - that it isn't fate - we have to accept that we could be on the receiving end or on the causing end of any accident, no matter how bad. Even the most cautious people still have accidents, right?

The problem is that it wasn't just an innocent accident. I caused it through gross negligence, dancing while I was cooking, ignoring the fact that my baby brother was near the stove. I was conjuring up my dream boy, while my real dream boy was right there in the kitchen with me.

What I'm about to do after writing this will also cause you pain, too. But I can't take this next step without you knowing that it is about taking an honorable action in the Samurai tradition. To have honor, a terrible wrong needs to be balanced with some kind of response, even if it brings pain to those we love. The response is aimed at myself, no one else. Is that selfish? Yes, certainly. But this is what I must do.

Please try to accept my feelings even though you won't agree. You are my light, Danny. When I spiral down, it's real dark. When the cold winds suck the fire out of me, I look to you for warmth and sustenance. And I always will. Oh, Danny Boy, I love you so.'"

Daniel stopped reading. He held the papers in one hand and wiped his eyes with the other. He seemed to have trouble getting enough air into his lungs.

None of us dared interrupt the moment. It was some time before he spoke.

"Now I learn the truth," he said. "Eighty years later. What a terrible, terrible mistake she made. Nora was always the most important person in my life. Now, because of her decision, I've lived my entire life without her."

Eventually, Mae said, "I'm so sorry, Daniel."

"Her hero Virginia Woolf died on March twenty-eighth, nineteen forty-one. Woolf struggled with mental illness just as Nora struggled. When Woolf couldn't bear it any longer, she filled her coat pockets with rocks and walked into the River Ouse near where she lived in Sussex, England. Exactly one year later, Nora did the same thing in Monterey Bay. She was twenty-three."

Mae raised her fist to her mouth.

Street was sitting next to me. She reached for my hand and squeezed it hard.

After a long silence, Daniel set the Braille letter to the side. Underneath it was another paper, folded once. It had decorative tape around the perimeter. He ran his fingertips around the edges, then handed the folded paper to Mae. "Maybe you better do it so I don't tear anything."

Mae used the scissors to slit one of the edges, then flexed it open an inch. She looked inside and inhaled. "Daniel, the stamp Nora mentioned? The Jenny airplane that was printed upside down? This is a whole bunch of them in a sheet." She pulled out a rectangle of stamps, unfolded it twice, and counted. "There's twenty of them."

Daniel breathed hard. After a long moment, he said, "I remember hearing about the inverted Jenny stamp when I was a boy. I think there are only a few in existence. Or at least until this group joins the stamp world. Years ago, they were a million dollars each or something. Of course, the price of a collector's item is supported by the item's rarity. So this quantity would lessen the value. But twenty of them would add up. Oh, Nora, Nora, Nora…" he trailed off, shaking his head. "All these years on my mantle. But I'd rather have you."

Daniel had Mae put the stamps back into the frame. Daniel said he needed time to adjust to what suddenly seemed like a new world. He said he thought he would like to take a nap, a comment that seemed true but also seemed like a polite way to ask us all to give him some solitude.

Mae helped Daniel to bed.

When she came out, Street and I walked with Mae to her house, and we three spent some time sitting together, talking, thinking about the stamp development. We all agreed that we should give Daniel time to sort out his mind. I said that Daniel would be able to finally relax knowing that the man who assaulted him was dead. But another killer was still alive. I also told Mae once again how brave she was to jump into the lake and pursue the killer.

Mae smiled shyly, said doing a freedive was no big deal, and told us she'd be in touch in the near future.

Street and I said goodbye and left.

FORTY-TWO

I called Diamond. "Your new inmate, a guy named Jeff Bosstro, the one with the attractive tattoo on his nose…"

"Fly baby?"

"He's a whiner, huh?"

"I'm filling in at the jail, and I can hear him from this desk. It never stops," Diamond said. "The temperature is too warm. It's too noisy. The food sucks. He's threatening to go on a hunger strike. I'm threatening to plug that mug with a gag."

"How about I come over and spend some time distracting the man?"

"Would this include re-education and attitude adjustment?"

"Something like that."

"Good. We've removed his blankets so he can't hurt himself. But the lack of easy, self-exit mechanisms hasn't dampened his tendency to emote. Maybe you will be the missing ingredient."

"At your service," I said. "I'm also wondering if you took a phone off of him."

"Sí. It's a nice iPhone, locked with passcode instead of fingerprint or face recognition."

"And he ain't telling."

"No," Diamond said. "Ironic that we can get into the ones with the fancy security, but can't get into the simpler ones."

"Any chance you're in possession of any burner phones that you may have taken during suspect arrests? It wouldn't need much battery charge. Just enough for a few minutes worth of calling."

"You want to borrow one."

"Actually, I think Flyboy would love to borrow one. Although he doesn't know that, yet."

"Lemme look," Diamond said. I heard what sounded like desk drawers opening and closing. "Here we are. Come take your pick."

A half hour later, I was at the Stateline jail. Diamond was at one of the desks, talking on the phone. He gave me a little wave, then covered the phone and called out. "Deputy Mortand."

A deputy appeared from around the corner.

"Mortand, this is Owen McKenna, ex-SFPD, currently private, one of the good guys in case you can't tell by looking at that wholesome face. He wants some quality time with Inmate Bosstro."

"Got it," Mortand said.

"Here's your burner," Diamond handed me a primitive-looking phone. "No stored numbers, no recents. I'd guess it's never been used." He turned to Mortand. "Let McKenna take that with him into Fly baby's cell. And you can leave McKenna alone in the cell."

"Will do."

Deputy Mortand took me to sign the login register. Then to the visitor lockers.

"Sidearm and pocket stuff," he said.

"No sidearm," I said as I put my keys, pocket knife, and nail clipper into the box.

Mortand said, "No sidearm? Unusual, isn't it, for an ex-cop?"

"Yeah. Long story."

He nodded.

I held up the burner phone. He held it while I walked through the metal detector. Then he handed me the phone and took me to Flyboy's cell.

"He's alone in there," Mortand said, "and he's pretty mean. I'd be concerned, if I were you. But the sergeant says to leave you in there alone with the perp. I guess that means you can handle yourself."

"Let's hope," I said.

Mortand wanted to say something else. He hesitated. "Maybe you know this, but the guy in this cell is huge and strong and beyond mean. So if you want, I can cuff him. Or I can come in with you. Or both. He's pretty beat up, broken ankle and smashed knee. Even so, I can imagine bad things could happen."

"I think I'll be fine," I said. "I'm the one who caught and held him while your colleagues came to pick him up."

"You're the guy who busted him up?! I'd think that would take a few men," he said.

"Or a big dog," I said.

"I was told this perp had a baseball bat. Bats can hurt dogs same as people, right?"

"Yeah, I had to take away the bat before the dog did his thing."

"Does that mean biting? I read an article on police dogs and bite force. It said that big dogs have a bite so strong they can break your biggest bones."

"Yeah, maybe. Best not to get bitten by any animal, including people."

"Holler when you want out." The deputy let me in and shut the door behind me.

Jeff Bosstro was lying on the hard bench. He didn't lift his head to look at me, but he could no doubt see me in his peripheral vision.

"Good to see you again, Flyboy. That was fun at Cave Rock, wasn't it? It's a good feeling to put in some mano-a-mano time, keep the reflexes sharp. Although, I guess yours weren't quite sharp enough, eh?"

Jeff Bosstro stared at the ceiling. The tattooed fly looked squished and covered with blood. Flyboy's neck was in a brace similar to an inflatable white life ring beach toy. His left arm was swaddled in bandages. One of his legs was in a cast that extended down over his foot only letting three toes show.

"I'm here for a tattoo referral," I said.

Flyboy didn't move a muscle.

"I can't stop thinking about how cool your face tattoo is. Other people just have ordinary stuff on their faces. But you... Your tattoo is really inspired. It got me thinking that I'd like something like that. So I'm wondering who the artist was?"

He didn't respond.

"Maybe you hit your head so hard you can't think anymore?"

No answer.

"Or maybe you never could think. I was told that you are world-champion stupid. And it kind of makes sense considering the way you charged me at the park. You didn't talk. You didn't try to reason with me. You didn't try to strike a deal. You just acted like an idiot bull who doesn't know the matador has a sword behind the cape."

Bosstro didn't react. Impressive. But a vein throbbed in his forehead. And his right arm was very tense. His right hand was pulled into a fist so tight, his knuckles were white.

"Just a referral," I said again. "Easy to tell me the artist and make me happy. But then, that would offend your sense of stubbornness. You won't tell a friend of the cops anything on principle, right? Or wait… Maybe now I have it figured out. You won't tell me the artist's name because you think I just want to find the artist and shake him down for information on the sunken treasure! Cuz, he probably has that info, doesn't he?"

I turned and paced toward the door, rotated again, paced back toward Jeff Bosstro. I didn't talk for a bit because I wanted my last comment to sink in.

"Here's a better idea," I said. "You're afraid I'll get the same tattoo as you. A big horsefly right on the end of my nose. Then your only claim to fame will be my claim to fame too. Am I right?" As I talked, I kept watching his right fist. I decided it was his tell. He'd keep his face unmoving. But his fist would indicate when he was about to explode.

"It makes sense," I continued. "Your horsefly tat is the coolest thing about you. But then, that's to be expected with world-champion stupid. Even your bro doesn't have a tattoo that dumb."

I leaned over closer to Flyboy. "Do you want to know what a Central Valley cop told me? That Chinless said you couldn't have any weapon other than a baseball bat, because if you had a gun, you'd probably shoot yourself as you tried to pull it out of your pants. Is that true? Would you be that stupid? For that matter, you could hit yourself with a baseball bat. It wouldn't take much of a blow to make you even more stupid."

His fist had raised off the bench an inch. In a flash, it slammed down, and Flyboy seemed to explode toward me as if out of a slingshot. I never would have thought a guy that big could move so fast, especially one with a severely damaged leg. But because of the tell, I was ready. I took a fast step back as his big right fist arced toward my head. With my right hand, I grabbed his wrist. I rotated clockwise and dropped my left arm over his right, so that his arm was trapped in my left armpit. At the same time, I let myself drop, pulling him down until my butt hit the floor. The motion jerked down hard on Flyboy's arm. He was already lunging forward with his entire body. My move seemed to accelerate him forward, head first into the wall.

It might have caused deadly blunt force trauma if he'd taken the full blow with the top of his head. But he turned his head at the last moment and struck the wall with his cheek. I heard the crunch of breaking facial bones. Breaking bones can absorb force just like a crash-absorbing bumper on a car.

Jeff Bosstro collapsed to the floor.

I expected him to remain motionless.

But like a bull that won't stop until the matador's sword pierces his heart, Flyboy moaned and grunted and got his arms beneath him. He pushed back from the wall. His face was a mess of blood and mashed flesh. But he was alive and conscious.

Mortand called through the closed door. "Everything okay in there?"

"Yeah, we're cool," I called back. I looked at Flyboy.

"Jeanie Pritchard," he said.

"What about Jeanie Pritchard?"

"My tattoo. She did it."

"Where does she work?"

"Merced."

"Does she have a business name? Or does she just work under her own name?"

"I dunno. I jus' went 'cuz Carlos tol' me about her."

"Your brother Carlos. Chinless," I said.

"You call him that, he gonna hurt you bad before he kill you."

I nodded.

I helped Flyboy turn around so that he was leaning back against the cell wall.

Then it was my turn to sit on his bench. I sat all the way back against the wall.

It was time for me to do what I came for.

I made a show of feeling my pocket as if my phone were vibrating.

"I didn't think I could get a cell signal in here," I said as I pulled out the burner phone. I held it up, looked at it as if to see the readout.

I made a fake motion with my thumb, pretending to answer it. Then I held it to my ear and began my phony conversation.

"Hello?" I said.

Pause.

"Yeah," I said. "This is McKenna."

I tried to make my pauses seem an appropriate length and somewhat varied.

"You got it?" I said. "Really? Is it like we thought?"

Pause. This time I made it a longer silence.

"Okay, I'll be there at quarter to midnight."

Pause. I covered my mouth with my other hand and turned away from Flyboy as if to keep him from overhearing, when in fact I wanted him to listen extra carefully. "Yeah, I got the money. One hundred K. I'll pick it up and bring it over."

Pause.

"If I can't turn it for at least a mil, I'm coming after you."

Pause.

"Right, I meant what I said. A mil is the minimum. I'm shooting for two mil. I took you at your word."

Pause.

"Okay, see you then."

I looked at the phone display and pretended to press the button to hang up. I also looked to see if it had a memory that would record calls and numbers. It appeared to be a dumb phone.

Just buttons and a simple one-line display.

Still sitting on the bench, I made as if to slip the phone back into my pocket, which was next to the wall. But I fumbled the move on purpose and slid the phone next to me on the bench. I tapped the fabric of my pocket, pretending that I'd gotten the phone in place. Then I stood up, knowing the phone was not in my pocket but visible on the bench, next to the wall.

I walked over to the cell door and called out. "Deputy Mortand. I'm done in here."

I looked down at Flyboy. It was obvious that he was staring at the phone I'd left on the bench. And, despite all contrary reports and indications, it appeared he was smart enough to keep his mouth shut until after I'd left.

The cell door opened.

"All okay?" Mortand asked.

I nodded and raised my forefinger to my lips to communicate silence. At nearly the same time, he looked down at Flyboy sitting on the floor, leaning his bloody head back against the wall. His eyes followed Flyboy's gaze to the phone sitting on the bed. I bounced my finger against my lips.

"Mr. Bosstro tripped and fell against the wall," I said. "He may need some medical attention."

"Hurt himself, did he?" Deputy Mortand said. "I'll see what we can do."

We walked out of the cell, and Mortand shut the door. We were back to the metal detector before he spoke.

"You pretended to misplace the phone and then left it in there on purpose," he said.

"Yep."

"Because you want him to make a call."

"Yep."

"He will call somebody because of something you said."

I nodded.

"Do you know who he's going to call?" Mortand asked.

"Nope. But I think it'll help me catch a killer."

"They didn't teach us that trick at the academy," he said.

"Right."

FORTY-THREE

Mortand opened the locker, and I collected my pocket stuff. I walked out to the desk area. Diamond had a filing cabinet open and was digging for papers.

"Flyboy accidentally lost his footing and bumped the side of his head against the wall," I said. "I heard something break. Maybe more than one bone. It should be looked at."

"He was trying to smash you to death?"

"Yeah. But he telegraphs, so I was able to step aside. Maybe don't go into his cell just yet. I pretended to accidentally leave that burner you gave me on the bench in his cell. I'm guessing he's using it to catch up on his business."

Diamond nodded. "We wouldn't want to interrupt that. You get what you came for?"

"Ask me tomorrow."

I thanked Diamond and left.

Out in the parking lot, I used my own cell phone to track down Jeannie Pritchard's number. The listing said Pritchard Tattoo Art, and it gave a Merced address and phone number. I dialed.

"This is Jeannie," a woman said in a raspy smoker's voice.

"Jeannie Pritchard of tattoo fame?"

"Well, honey, that fame part might be a little overstated."

"Not according to Jeff Bosstro, who says you did his horsefly-on-the-nose tattoo and his life hasn't been dull ever since."

"Now I know you're making this up. Flyboy Bosstro couldn't string that many words together if the reward was having his brother leave him alone for a year."

"Okay, maybe he didn't say all those words. But he's got reverence for your work."

"Reverence? In this business, we don't have reverence. That

sounds like a new model of Cadillac. I can tell you're a tattoo virgin. So here's a lesson for you. Tattoo people like certain kinds of tats and styles. Some, we like a lot. But we don't - what would be the word - we don't revere them. Some words are in the tattoo vocabulary. Some aren't. Do you understand what I'm saying?"

"Got it," I said.

"Whew. Now that we got that straightened out, you want a tattoo? I should tell you up front, I don't do repeats. Every client gets an original. I could do a fly on your nipple or any other part of your anatomy but not on your nose."

"No fly. I'm actually an investigator. Owen McKenna. I'm trying to find the killer of a man named Colin Callahan. I thought the killer might be Jeff Bosstro. Now I think he probably isn't the killer. Do you know the name Colin Callahan?"

"Never heard of him."

"Okay, try this. Callahan had a full back tattoo based on a painting called The Wreck of Hope. It's an early nineteenth century painting by Caspar David Friedrich. Any bells now?"

"Sorry. Most of us, we don't do tattoos of paintings. That would be like stealing a pic, right? Even if it's nineteenth century stuff, that doesn't mean I would steal it."

"Can you think of any tattoo artists who have done things like paintings even if they didn't base it on a real painting?"

"No. Tattoos are more what you might call illustration. A vibrating needle can do great lines and a few great colors and such. But paintings have mixed color and a thousand shades. They can communicate without any lines at all. That quality doesn't translate to skin. Do you hear what I'm saying?"

"Yeah. Tattooing needs a good match between image and medium."

"Hey, that's good. Can I use those words, image and medium? I teach a class Tuesday nights at our church's soup kitchen. I'd like to write those words down and use them in my class."

"Be my guest. Another question or two?"

"Sure."

"Are you familiar with an artist named Wilbur Neally Lopez?"

"No, why?"

"He's apparently done tattoos of paintings. Any idea of how I might find him?"

"Well, we've got the guild and the alliance and the national association. But I don't know a single tattoo artist who belongs to any of them. From what I can see, they are money-making businesses that charge a hundred bucks or more just to say you're a member. Like that's gonna help your business? Not a chance. People pick an inker for just one reason. They see one of the artist's tattoos and really like it, so they ask who did it. Simple as that. When someone contacts me for a tattoo, they never say they got my name from an association, and they never ask if I'm a member in good standing of some trade group. So if I were you, I'd go to one of the festivals. Just Google them. You can meet a hundred tattoo artists and look at their work."

"Good information, thanks. Do you know who did Carlos Bosstro's tattoos?"

"Chinless? Yours truly. Most of them, anyway."

"In your dealings with Bosstro brothers, did you ever get the idea that they were interested in shipwrecks? Or sunken treasure?"

She was silent for a moment. "I try not to talk about my client's interests, if you understand my meaning. But just because I want to help you, I don't think I would be out of line to say that shipwrecks and sunken treasure don't seem like Chinless's style. And Flyboy, he doesn't really have any style beyond doing whatever Chinless says."

"Thanks, Jeannie. You've been very helpful."

"When you want a tattoo, you know where to come."

"To the woman who drives a reverence."

"Yeah."

FORTY-FOUR

It was well into evening. So I drove home and called Street at her condo.

"I couldn't remember if we had dinner plans," I said when she answered. "I have an appointment tonight with flexible timing."

"No plans. But sometimes the best experience comes by accident and experiment."

"Are you talking about science or amore?" I asked.

"This time I'm talking about food. I might have some leftover wild rice soup in the fridge."

"Now that will get a steak eater's heart pumping."

"Perfect," she said, in spite of my lack of enthusiasm. "You got a time?"

"That's the tricky part. It could be after dark. This appointment doesn't have a time. I'm expecting a guy to follow me. After he approaches me, we're going to have a talk."

"That sounds worrisome. Like you're going to poke an animal you shouldn't."

"I'll be careful."

"Will you have backup? Maybe you should call Diamond."

"Actually, Mallory will be there. He might bring other officers as well. I'll call you when I'm finished, and we'll pretend we're having dinner in Italy."

"You mean, eating at midnight," Street said.

"It'll be romantic."

"Okay, Blondie and I will be waiting," Street said. "Although we might be napping."

"I love you."

I made a peanut butter sandwich, ate it with milk and chips, and then looked in my closet for appropriate nighttime clothes.

Something about my motions must have been unusual, for Spot appeared next to me.

"Up from bed, Your Largeness? What motivates that?"

His head was at my hip. He leaned forward and stuck his head into the closet, sniffing.

"The same clothes as always," I said. I reached all the way to the left, which isn't saying much in a closet sized for a 500-square-foot log cabin. Against the rough log wall was a vest on a hanger. It was heavy, made of Kevlar.

I pulled it on over a T-shirt and zipped it up. I put on a navy blue flannel shirt over the vest. The combo was relatively slim. If I stood up straight, most people would just think I was a slightly beefy guy.

The vest had been in the closet since I quit the SFPD and moved to Tahoe. The vest had never been exposed to gunfire. But it had Level III protection and was designed to slow down and tangle up any bullets that weren't hardened or high-powered. Which of course meant that a wide range of bullets could penetrate it. Another weapon it wouldn't stop was a good knife or ice pick. I never understood why the physics of a knife getting through tough fabric are different than a bullet. But life is full of mysteries. And stopping a bullet doesn't always save your life, anyway. Some vests can even stop a .50 caliber round from penetrating. But the impact on your chest, like that of a well-swung baseball bat, will still kill you, breaking your ribs, rupturing your aorta, and stopping your heart.

So as I headed out, I knew I was taking a risk.

To make a convincing pack of money, I wrapped an old Tahoe phone book inside a paper grocery bag, taped it up, and put it into an old gym bag. The book gave the bag some heft and volume, not unlike a thousand pieces of paper the size of a $100 bill. I also needed to bring something that would look like valuable treasure that had spent 80 years on a sunken boat, 400 feet down in Lake Tahoe.

It didn't have to be a container for stamps. No one but Daniel, Mae, Street, and me knew that was the treasure. Although a savvy killer might surmise that stamps made sense. The main requirement of my "treasure" was that if, as I expected, the killer relieved me of the treasure, he would want to take a look at what the treasure was to verify that I hadn't set him up in some way. It would need to be convincing.

So I poked around in my cupboards and drawers looking for an idea that would work with the 1940 timing of the scuttling of the SS Tahoe Steamship. I went through my kitchen nook, some old boxes at the back of my bedroom closet. I opened the bathroom vanity. Nothing.

I went back to my little living room and looked at the few knick knacks on the top of the bookcase.

Nothing was both old enough and also waterproof enough to look like it had been on a sunken ship for eight decades.

Outside, I looked under the deck, the only place in a garage-less cabin to tuck stuff out of sight. There was the snow shovel, a rake, the garbage can I use for recycling, and the one I use for trash. There was the wooden bin with the flip-up, roof-shingle lid in which I store stuff I don't want to get wet: a couple of paint cans, a spare gas can, my tool box, and miscellaneous hardware that I couldn't fit inside the cabin. Nothing looked valuable or old enough for my purpose.

I went back inside and sat at the fold-down linoleum table in the kitchen nook. The table was one of the only things in the place that looked ancient. But what could I do with a table? I ate at that table, paid my bills at that table, kept my calendar and the landline phone on that table.

Maybe I could make a list of priorities. I reached a pen out of the jar where I kept them. An ancient jar.

I picked it up and looked closer. It was an old, Atlas, aqua blue canning jar with the wire bail lid. Probably made around the turn of the 20th century, which was roughly when the SS Tahoe Steamer was launched. Not only was it old, it looked old and had accumulated 100-plus years of stains and grime.

When the steamer was scuttled in 1940, plastics as we know them had not yet been invented. There were very few ways anyone could waterproof something. One of those few ways was inside a canning jar.

It made sense that a treasure that was physically small could be put into a canning jar. With the top sealed tightly, it was possible it could remain dry inside the jar for decades. Even 400 feet down in Lake Tahoe.

More importantly, it seemed plausible. The person after the Tahoe Steamer treasure might well believe that an old canning jar could protect a treasure.

Now the question was what kind of treasure could fit into it. If they didn't know it was stamps, something like gold and diamonds and jewelry of all sorts would be more believable. But I had nothing like that. No old watch. No antique keepsakes.

I took another tour of my little cabin, looking at odds and ends, trying to find some old item that could possibly seem valuable, even if it was worthless. Spot was puzzled by my unusual actions. He followed me, watching me, maybe wondering if I had lost something extremely important. Like a package of dog treats.

I focused on anything that was old or looked old. In my utensils drawer was an ancient fork. Could I convince someone that it was a collector's item, a fork that Ben Franklin ate with and was, thus, extremely valuable? Probably not. But that was my task.

After a second circuit of my cabin and its possessions, I looked at my bookcase.

On the second shelf, left side, I had a few books with poetry, a couple of anthologies, a collection of Yeats, Shakespeare's sonnets, Maya Angelou. Tucked in was a tiny leather-bound volume of Robert Service. It was chapbook size, about four inches wide and six inches tall and contained the collection called The Songs Of A Sourdough including the famous poems The Shooting Of Dan McGrew and The Cremation Of Sam McGee. The leather cover was originally dyed red but was now crinkled and missing most of its color. I didn't remember when the famous poems were published, but it was probably around the same time that the Atlas canning jar was made. I flipped the pages. Other than some notes and asterisks penciled in the margins, there was nothing.

It reminded me very much of the chapbook of Nora Callahan's

poems that I'd stolen from Brand Morse when I looked into Colin Callahan's footlocker.

I took the Robert Service chapbook and gave it a substantial curl. I was able to slip it in through the mouth of the canning jar. I closed the lid and flipped the wire bail up to lock it.

It looked like an ancient treasure, an old leather book inside an old jar. It didn't sparkle like jewelry. But if someone believed it was treasure, they might logically assume that somewhere in the words or penciled notes in the margin was a key to something of substantial value. If the people after treasure were looking for an Inverted Jenny stamp, an old chapbook might be the perfect place to hide it.

I put the jar with chapbook into a paper grocery bag and put that into the gym bag as well.

I went outside with Spot and we got into the Jeep.

My first stop was Street's condo, where I left Spot with her and Blondie.

I thanked her, kissed her, and left.

FORTY-FIVE

It was 10 p.m. when I turned left onto the highway and headed toward the tunnel and the South Shore beyond, looking for a possible location for my phony meeting place. I drove at a medium pace, easy to follow for the killer, who, I assumed, was somewhere behind me, or would be shortly.

Even though my fake appointment wasn't until 11:45, I expected to pick up a tail soon after I left. I would give that tail a nice long job following me. Because my tail wouldn't expect me to be on guard until I anticipated the meeting, I might get a chance to catch that tail and do some interrogation.

Shortly after I turned onto the highway heading south, I saw a vehicle appear behind me. It stayed farther back than is common in our rush-rush world that seems to turn everyone into a tailgater. The vehicle's headlights were on, obscuring the make of the car. I kept looking in my rearview mirror. I'd gone less than a mile when the vehicle turned off onto a side road and then pulled back onto the highway going north, back toward where we'd come from.

In the short moment that it was sideways to me, I got a glimpse of it in the rearview mirror.

Not a car. A pickup. Maroon.

To avoid making my brake lights flash, I hit my parking brake fast but soft, pulled a quick U-turn, and raced after it. I fumbled my cell phone out and hit the one other number I have in speed dial besides Diamond's.

"Hello?"

"Sweetheart, we have a change of plans. There is a man driving your way. I don't know his intentions. But it's possible he is coming to intimidate you and use you to get at me. I'm following him and will be at your door in a few minutes." I was already up to 70 miles an hour, but still couldn't see the maroon pickup.

"What should I do?!"

"Take hold of Spot's collar and hold him in front of you. No one can get to you through him. Once you have Spot with you, dial nine, one, one and report a home invasion. I'll be there as fast as I can."

I hung up and concentrated on my driving. When I got to Street's condo development, I pulled into the lot. There was no maroon pickup in sight. But all that meant was that the driver had left the pickup out of sight, around back or in the forest.

I jerked to a stop and ran to Street's front door. It was shut and showed no damage. Nevertheless, I put my key into her lock. It wouldn't fit. Wrong key. I pulled it out and was trying to grab the correct key when I heard a crash and a scream. Spot started barking ferociously.

I got the key in the lock, turned it, and pushed inside.

Just past the living room, was Blondie. She was in the kitchen, barking in fast, high-pitched yips. To the right side of the kitchen, stood Street in the bathroom doorway. Spot was in front of her, barking and growling. On the floor near his paws was Street's phone. The floor sparkled with pieces of broken glass. Behind Street, holding her arms from behind, was Carlos Chinless Bosstro, a huge man with a grimy face. I immediately understood that Street had taken Spot and backed up to the bathroom, expecting that any home invasion would be through the front door or one of the large windows in the living room. Instead, Bosstro had dived through the bathroom window, an opening I didn't think was large enough for him to fit through.

The man held Street in front of him in the small space of the bathroom doorway. He used Street as a shield to protect himself from Spot. Street was immobilized in his grip.

The man saw me come in. "Call off your dog or I break her neck!"

"Spot. Come here," I said, knowing he would not obey. He was still growling, lips lifted, fangs exposed. I walked forward slowly, reached out and took hold of Spot's collar. "Easy boy, let's back up."

"Take the other dog, too."

I reached my other hand down and grabbed Blondie's collar. I pulled both dogs back until we were in the living room.

The man marched Street forward into the kitchen, putting the counter between himself and me. He held her near the counter, again using her as a shield in case I started firing bullets.

Street eyes were huge, and she shook with terror. The man had his head right over her shoulder, his mouth near her ear. When he spoke, it would be so loud that she wouldn't be able to think clearly.

The big man practically barked. "Where's the shipwreck stuff?"

Street jerked from the volume.

Spot was still growling.

"I'm meeting a man tonight," I said. "He has the treasure. I have a hundred thousand dollars. We trade." Chinless had heard as much from his brother. I wanted my story to match what I'd told Flyboy.

"Let Street go, and I'll give you the money," I said. "It's in my Jeep."

"What is the treasure?"

"I don't know. It was brought up by an underwater drone from the Tahoe Steamer."

"You must have an idea."

"I have several ideas. But they might all be wrong."

"What are they?"

I hesitated.

"WHAT ARE THEY?" he shouted.

Street quivered in terror.

"I'm thinking!" I tried to make a focused look directly at Street. "This is not the easiest situation to put me through a memory test." As I said the words 'memory test,' I made an almost-imperceptible nod toward Street, a motion she'd notice, but not one a stranger would recognize. I hoped she'd remember when I broke her pepper shaker and used those same words.

In a sudden movement that caught the big man off guard,

Street bent forward hard, yanked one arm free, and reached out for the pepper shaker I'd broken and on which I'd delicately perched the broken top. As she grabbed it, the top flew off. Street jerked the shaker up and back, over her shoulder. I saw pepper fly, some of it striking the man in his face.

He made a gargled choking sound, let go of Street, and reached for his eyes as he began coughing.

I let go of Spot and leaped forward, grabbing the fire extinguisher that Street had mounted nearby. I pulled the quick release catch. Chinless had recovered and was reaching for Street once again.

I leaped across the counter, sliding on my stomach, and struck the side of his face with the base of the extinguisher. It staggered him. He took two steps back to catch his balance. The back of his head hit the exhaust hood above Street's stovetop. I was back on my feet in the small confines of Street's kitchen. I was about to strike another blow, when he got his hands up and grabbed the body of the extinguisher. He was stunned, but he was still very strong. I couldn't jerk the extinguisher away from him.

I took the chance of releasing my grip with one of my hands. I knew that would give him complete control of the extinguisher. But very quickly, I pulled the safety tab and squeezed the trigger.

White foam shot toward the side of his head, mostly missing him. But some overspray went into his eyes and nose.

The man let go of the extinguisher and put his hands to his face.

I jammed the nozzle into the man's mouth and shot a full force spray.

Chinless choked and went down, dropping to his knees. He grabbed blindly, trying to get a grip on anything but air. Unable to see, his hands found the cupboard door beneath the kitchen sink. He jerked it open and felt inside, trying to find a weapon. But there was nothing but a trash can and plumbing.

I swung the extinguisher at him again. He was jerking so hard that I only succeeded in a glancing blow. But he dropped to the floor, flat on his back. I kneeled on his abdomen.

He gagged and writhed, trying to breathe.

I heard growling and realized that Spot had grabbed his ankle.

In an incredible show of strength and self-control, Chinless grabbed once again for the extinguisher. But his hands, covered in foam, slipped off the cylinder. I raised the cylinder and slammed it down on his head, hard enough to break bones, but not hard enough to kill. I sprayed more foam in his eyes, in his ears, up his nose, and in his mouth.

He stopped flailing with his arms.

I set the extinguisher to the side. There was a choke collar clipped onto his belt. I undid the catch, and put the collar around his neck. I stood up. On Street's counter was an electric hand-held mixer. I unplugged it, kneeled down, and threaded the plug through the ring on the end of the choke collar. I pulled it tight so that the mixer slid up to the collar ring and pulled the collar tight around his neck, the mixer next to his ear. Then I reached under the sink with the power cord and tied it to the plumbing. The man would be able to rip it out, but it would slow him down.

Spot still held the man's ankle. The fact that he'd stopped thrashing despite what must be significant pain from inhaled foam and broken ankle flesh, and maybe broken ankle bones, indicated his weak condition. Maybe he was unconscious.

I stood up, turned to Street, and held her.

"Are you okay?"

She nodded. Her face was wet with the tears of terror.

"I'm so sorry. It was my fault. I underestimated the man."

Street gripped me hard as sirens grew in the distance.

Diamond must have seen the dispatch with Street's address. He was the first to her door. I let him in.

"Is Street safe?" he asked.

"Physically, yes."

Diamond nodded at me. He walked in, reached out and took Street's hand in both of his. It was a silent moment, an important and reassuring gesture.

Diamond looked at the glass on the floor and the broken bathroom window, taking it all in.

I knew I didn't need to make any explanation. I took hold of Spot, pulled him off Bosstro, and brought him to where Street was standing.

Then Diamond stepped around us and went to the kitchen. He bent down and looked at Bosstro. "He's still breathing despite an interesting restraint system." Diamond leaned forward and peered under the kitchen sink to see where the electric cord was tied.

"A deputy in the Central Valley told me that this man is known for putting choke collars on the people he kills," I said. "I found the choke collar on his belt. So I borrowed it to use on him."

Two other deputies had come in the front door. Behind them was an EMT standing in the open doorway. Moths were buzzing about the outdoor light. Two of them flew into Street's condo as I watched.

"Help me pull this beef out from under the sink," Diamond said to them.

I opened Street's tool drawer and pulled out a wire cutter. I handed it to one of the deputies.

The two men cut the cord and dragged Carlos Bosstro out onto the living room floor.

"Roll him over," Diamond said.

"He's barely breathing," one deputy said. "The EMTs should get him on a stretcher and take him to the hospital."

"First, roll him over."

They did as told. Diamond pulled Bosstro's wrists together behind his back and cuffed him.

"Now you can roll him back."

They got him onto his back, his arms beneath him.

"Shackle his feet," Diamond said.

A female EMT came through the door. "Sir, the man is unconscious, and it looks like he might not even survive."

Diamond looked at Street as he spoke. "Then he'll die with shackles on his feet."

One of the deputies went out to the patrol unit, came back with shackles, and put them on Bosstro's feet.

The EMTs brought in a stretcher and used it to carry Bosstro out to the ambulance. Diamond had one of the deputies ride along as they took Bosstro to the hospital.

After everyone else had left, Diamond stayed and talked to Street and me. Street sat on her couch, her hands on Blondie, who had her head on Street's lap. I was on Street's other side, rubbing Street's knee. Diamond sat opposite her, on the fireplace hearth, his back against the gas stove. His ability to say a few perfect words here and there was masterful. Street calmed almost to normalcy.

In time, Diamond looked at his watch and said to me, "You have an appointment tonight, right?"

"How did you know? I've told no one but Street."

"I see that you are bulky under your shirt. That implies an appointment."

"It's not critical," I said.

"That kind of bulk suggests it is."

Street frowned, not understanding Diamond's meaning.

"I should stay here with Street," I said.

"I'll stay," Diamond said.

She looked at me. "You said you were going to provoke someone..."

"Yes. I thought it would turn out to be Chinless. But he came here instead, to get you as leverage. So maybe I no longer have an appointment. Or maybe there is another man, a ring leader."

Street frowned. "I'll be fine with Diamond here. But maybe you could leave Spot with me and figure out how to board up my broken bathroom window."

"Are you sure?"

"Yes. I don't know if it would help, but there are some scraps of plywood in the woods out back. Some kids were using them to cobble together a fort."

So Diamond and I collected some of Street's tools and some screws that were in her drawer. We took our flashlights out back. We didn't have a saw, but we found a narrow piece of plywood that was wide enough to span the width of the window. The extra length just made it so the wood went from close to the ground to well above the window. When we were done, it would require some time and effort for anyone to remove it.

"How long can you stay here?" I asked Diamond.

He looked at the time. "Thirty minutes."

"That will be fine," Street said. "The window's boarded up and I've got both dogs."

I said goodbye and left Street with Diamond, Spot, and Blondie.

FORTY-SIX

I watched the sides of the highway as I drove south. I watched my rearview mirrors as well. Unlike when Carlos Bosstro followed me, nothing stood out. If a vehicle was following, it was far enough back that I couldn't track it. Or, if a vehicle was old or had a way to turn off the automatic running lights, it could be closer, running dark.

After my adrenaline surge from having Bosstro break into Street's and taking her hostage, I was so tense I felt my fingertips digging into the steering wheel.

I tried to focus on places suitable for trading 100K in cash for sunken treasure worth much more, according to the fiction I'd been weaving. I'd be safe until that meeting supposedly happened. After that, I'd be dead or not quite dead or gloriously alive, depending on the skills of the person hunting me and my own reaction and luck.

I was still trying to think of a good meeting spot as I approached the Stateline hotels. An idea occurred to me.

I pulled over at one of the casino hotels and dialed Commander Mallory of the South Lake Tahoe PD. I left a voicemail saying that I thought Colin Callahan's killer was following me and that I was up against a time deadline.

After ten minutes of waiting, I gave up and had just started the engine when my phone rang.

"Mallory, here." His voice sounded extra rough.

"Getting a cold?" I said as I pulled out onto Lake Tahoe Blvd.

"Just getting old," he said, and cleared his throat. "I turned fifty yesterday. Do you know what I did last night to celebrate? I stayed in by myself, drank an extra beer, and was in bed and asleep by nine-thirty. You guys with girlfriends don't know how good you've got it. Or maybe I don't know how good I've got it."

"Either way, extra beer and early to bed sounds like a good birthday to me," I said. "Maybe we'll have additional reasons to celebrate tonight, if you agree to help. I'm leaving the hotel casinos at Stateline, heading toward your fair city. I assume - but don't know for certain - that someone is following me. I believe that person killed Colin Callahan."

"And this person got word to follow you because of your phone trick at the Douglas County jail."

"Word gets around?" I said.

"I had to call Sergeant Martinez on another matter. He was amused by your techniques. But he's hoping there won't be fallout from the injuries the inmate suffered at your hands."

"The guy lunged for me. I admit that my evasive maneuver may have helped steer him toward the wall. But if he hadn't hit it, he would have had more energy to beat me to a pulp."

"So, regarding the guy following you now," he said, ignoring my comment, "how did that come about?"

"The man in the Stateline jail cell is large and violent and of limited intelligence. His name is Jeff Bosstro and he's called Flyboy because of a fly tattoo on his face. I let myself be overheard talking on a burner phone. I arranged a meeting to pay one hundred thousand in cash for a much more valuable treasure. Then I accidentally-on-purpose left that burner phone in Flyboy's cell because I wanted him to call his brother or the ring leader of this sunken treasure game and explain what I was doing. But before I could stage my bogus meeting, that brother, Carlos Bosstro, broke into Street's condo in an effort to control me. Fortunately, Diamond and I apprehended him an hour ago. If Carlos is the leader who was planning on intercepting my phony meeting tonight, then my job is done. If not, I believe the man in charge will be following me. I think he killed Colin Callahan and Jacky Wormack, the diver at Glenbrook Bay who was killed the same way."

"You mean, compressed air shot into the body."

"Right."

"And why would this man be following you?"

"Because what is motivating these guys is treasure brought up from the Tahoe Steamer during the Tahoe Steamer Festival. That's what they think I'm purchasing."

"And what is this sunken treasure?"

I paused for a moment, thinking about how to answer now that I knew that the real treasure was in the back of a picture frame on Daniel's mantle.

"That's the question everyone wants to know. So I mocked up a treasure using an antique-looking, leather-bound book rolled up inside an old Atlas canning jar."

There was a long silence before Mallory spoke. "This whole thing is a charade? The Steamer Festival, the treasure, phone calls… I feel like I'm in Hitchcock's Gaslight movie. A setup to make people crazy."

"Kind of, yeah." I said. "Anyway, after overhearing me have a fake telephone conversation in the jail, Flyboy thinks I'm paying one hundred K for the treasure because I have the contacts to resell it for a million or two."

"Is that reasonable?" Mallory asked.

"Reasonable enough for the Bosstro brothers to believe it. Hopefully, the man in charge too."

"What's your next move?"

"I pick a place for my meeting and go there."

"Why are you contacting me?"

"Because a big-kahuna cop like you might want to be there, too. After the man shows up and tries to take the treasure I've bought, you can reveal yourself, corral the bad guy, and ride off into the sunset a hero."

"Big kahuna?"

"It sounds snarky, but it actually means wise shaman," I said.

"This sounds complicated. Where is this meeting being held?"

"Wherever you want. You could choose a place that suits your purposes, and I'll lead the man to you."

"What will you do at this meeting?"

"I'll walk into the shadows, pretend to meet my fictional contact, pull out my fictional bag of money, and apparently exchange it for the fictional sunken treasure. Then my contact will seem to melt into the shadows with the money I'm paying him, which should be easy for him considering he doesn't exist. And I'll make as if to head back to my vehicle with the fictional treasure."

"The old jar," Mallory said, disbelief in his voice.

"Right."

"This hundred big ones you're supposedly paying the guy who doesn't actually exist. What are you using to mock that up?"

"I wrapped up an old phone book in a brown paper bag. It's about the right size and weight."

Mallory seemed to be taking heavy breaths over the phone. "What would you have me do, now?"

"Pick a meeting spot."

"Where you will lead the man who maybe wants to kill you."

"Right."

Mallory paused. "Okay, let's go to El Dorado Beach. Where we first found Colin Callahan's body. But I worry that someone else could get hurt."

"I don't think you need to worry. This killer has never used any weapon that would likely miss and hit someone else. The only murders I know of have been the two compressed-air deaths. The only attempted murder that failed was when Flyboy Jeff Bosstro tried to kill me with a baseball bat at the Cave Rock park. And when he tried to smash me in the Stateline jail. In the compressed-air deaths, there is very little risk of collateral damage. In the attempted beatings, the more people there are around, the more likely it is that the attacker will hold off and try to accomplish his mission with threats alone."

Mallory didn't immediately dispute me. After a long pause, I realized he wasn't even going to respond, which I took to be tentative agreement.

"And there are lots of shadows on that beach," I said. "Especially near the boat launch. If I can find the best place for someone to kill me, I'm more likely to draw an attack, and you're more likely to get your killer."

"You got any sense of how I might identify him?"

"No. I don't know who he is. The only way to identify him is when he approaches me to steal my treasure or shoots me with compressed air and then tries to run off with the goods."

"Got it. When will you get there?"

"I just went by Heavenly Village. I'm just five minutes out."

"Stretch it to ten before you go in," Mallory said. He hung up.

I took it slow and made some extra turns. Someone tailing me might think I was trying to lose a tail. Ten minutes later, I parked in the lot nearest to El Dorado Beach. Because it was the peak of the tourist season, there weren't many empty spots. The lake was almost as beautiful to experience at night as during the day.

I took my gym bag with the fake money and treasure jar inside of it and started walking.

As I crossed Lakeview Avenue and walked into the little park, there were several people, some in groups, some alone. They sat at the top of the grand steps, watching the distant boats and the more distant lights across the lake. Other groups were in the park area above the beach, huddled around charcoal fires in the barbecues, cooking late-night dinners and S'Mores, drinking verboten alcoholic beverages, and smoking joints.

Maybe the relative crowds would scare off an attacker. But an advantage was also apparent. The killer might be more inclined to attack because he would think that he could escape detection by blending in with the other people, especially after I was dead or wounded on the ground.

I paused at the top of the steps and gazed at the stretch of beach below.

The beach was dark and, beyond it, the lake was darker, a pool of black that stretched 22 miles to the North Shore. Lights twinkled in the distance, bright to the east, dimmer to the far north, and almost nonexistent toward the sparsely-populated West Shore.

There were multiple lights moving across the blackness, boats wandering, most on slow cruise. It was the high-altitude version of a water paradise. Take a popular seaside town, remove 90% of the residents and tourists and casinos alike, raise it 6200 feet in the air and nestle it into mountains, lower the temperature accordingly, purify the sea to something close to distilled water, throw in some yachts and Jetskis, trade in the exotic cars for four-wheel-drive SUVs, and you'd have a loose approximation of South Lake Tahoe. What people remain are largely there for the beauty and recreation. They come from all over the world, and you hear four or five languages in the supermarket produce section. This late at night, those same languages were in the air at this beach park.

I didn't turn around because I didn't want to inhibit my potential attacker. The lights from the vehicles on Lake Tahoe Blvd provided some illumination to the groups in the park. But the beach below was shrouded in darkness. Two couples and a threesome, walked along the black water. Over to the left was the boat launch. Beyond it, a private pier extended into the water.

As soon as I looked at it, it seemed obvious that the boat launch would provide the most tempting place to attack me and take my loot. So I headed that way. I watched for any man on or near the beach.

The boat launch was a steep ramp that came down from the street. It went through a short tunnel under a utility building and then emerged back into the open air near the water.

At the bottom of the boat launch was a pickup with a boat trailer that had driven down the ramp. It was on the wide apron of pavement just above the water, jockeying back and forth so that it faced back up the launch. From there, the pickup could back the trailer down into the water. About fifty feet out from shore floated a small boat on the dark water. Its running lights were on. The red port light, green starboard light, and white stern light showed that it was pointing toward shore. All I could see of the boat was a short canopy over the cockpit and an outboard motor at the stern. I couldn't see any passengers. But I knew that at least one person was onboard, waiting to motor in when the boat trailer was positioned in the water.

The pickup and boat would provide good cover for my "meeting." Anyone pursuing me would feel comfortable knowing that his and my presence wouldn't be notable when there were others nearby, pulling a boat out of the water.

I headed down the steps. When I got to the sand, I angled toward the boat launch.

Now that I was below the highway, the beach was even darker, the only light from distant buildings and vehicles. Despite the darkness, I could see many vague shapes of people. Some, I'd have to pass by as I walked across the beach toward the boat launch. A couple strolled at the water's edge, moving toward the pier. They wore long summer coats, like what San Francisco people sometimes wear when they're walking through cool, foggy air to a bar after the theater. The couple were more focused on each other than their surroundings. Although they were both large people, one was clearly a woman. I thought that made them less likely to be my attackers. Although the man could be with the woman for the cover she provided, he still didn't strike me as someone who might be after me. Too focused on the woman, too soft in his movements.

Except that he seemed to be stealing glances at me. After the fourth glance, he pulled out a phone and called someone.

Hobbling from the direction of the boat launch was a man dressed in a loose patterned jacket. He had a matching cap. I realized the pattern was camo coloring like what hunters wear. But there is no hunting in Tahoe. Maybe he was homeless and picked up the jacket at a thrift store. Tahoe doesn't have many year-round homeless people because of our brutal winters. But some homeless come in the summer, by bus or by hitchhiking. This man was hunched, and he leaned on a cane, perhaps lost in his thoughts. The man had an old Army-green duffle with a long strap slung over his head and across one shoulder. The homeless guy walked by the couple as if he didn't even notice they were there. I'd seen his demeanor in depressed people. An inward focus, difficult plodding movements that suggested pain, no visceral appreciation for beauty of any kind. He struggled along past me, noticing nothing, wavering, his cane sinking into the sand.

The couple had stopped and were still standing in one place, the man still on the phone. He glanced at me again and then looked down the beach as if he could see the person he talked to on the phone.

I continued walking and angled down toward the boat launch so that I would stay some distance from the homeless man and come in behind the couple.

I had to walk by a threesome. They were three men, arms over each other's shoulders, singing an old raunchy song about Barnacle Bill The Sailor. Either they were drunk or doing a good job acting the part. Two of the three were really big guys. After they went past me, I turned around to check. One of them quickly turned his head, indicating that he'd been looking at me.

I slowed as I got closer to the boat launch. When I reached the paved apron, the pickup had gotten into position and was starting to back the trailer down into the water. The paved area was raised a couple of feet up above the sand, the pavement held in place by a short retaining wall. I pulled up my sleeve a bit as if checking a watch. Then I stepped up onto the pavement and walked into the boat launch underpass.

Just before I went into the shadows of the underpass, I reached into my gym bag and pulled out the wrapped phone book so that any onlooker could see that I had a package.

I walked into the underpass and set it down next to the tunnel wall. I pulled out my keys and clicked on my tiny keychain LED flashlight. I had nothing to see, but I thought it would make my actions clear to anyone pursuing me. They'd see a flash of light coming from the underpass, and they'd interpret it as part of my "meeting."

Then I walked back out of the underpass, across the apron, and stepped down to the sandy beach. I was still holding my bag as if I'd put in the treasure I'd purchased.

"Owen, it's me!" a woman said.

Street Casey.

Her voice shook with terror.

FORTY-SEVEN

I turned toward the voice.

A different threesome approached. A man and two women, one petit, one medium-sized.

My vision narrowed to a tunnel, as if blackness was squeezing my brain. Street looked as afraid as a person can be. They must have been waiting and grabbed her right after Diamond left.

"I'm so sorry, Owen!" the other woman said. "He knocked on the door, and I opened it. I was so stupid!"

I realized it was Mae.

"Street had to open her door because he already had me," she said, nodding toward the man.

"Shut up!" The man held two leashes, barely visible in the darkness. The leashes went to a choke collars around the women's necks. "You should know how this works, McKenna," he said.

The voice seemed familiar, but I couldn't recollect it. And the man's face was in shadow. What was clear was that the man was using the Bosstro brothers' choke collar trick.

"Each collar has a rachet that is almost bomb proof. If I jerk on a leash, the collar rachets tighter, and it can't be released without a bolt cutter. If I jerk hard, the collar tightens hard, and the woman can't breathe, and no blood flows to her brain, and she dies in two or three minutes."

In addition to the collars, the women were zip-tied to each other, right hand to right hand and left hand to left hand. The result looked like they were affectionate friends standing close, side-by-side, arms interlocked in front of them.

From a distance it would look like I was just talking to three beach strollers.

"We can make this real simple, McKenna. You give me the goods, I give you the women." His face was still in shadows.

His voice, though familiar, had a distinct style of diction and enunciation that I didn't recognize.

"Set your gym bag on the retaining wall of the boat launch. If you make any unusual moves, the women die."

I took a step forward and did as he said.

He turned to watch. As the distant lights played across his face, I realized it was Brand, the handsome actor wannabe.

"Bad choice of acting jobs, Brand," I said. "You coulda been a contender with that dumb landlord act you laid on me. Instead, you're playing the stupid thug. What a waste."

"Shut up, McKenna. Back up. Four steps."

As I did as I was told, I wondered how Brand could kidnap the women and also know where I was. He must have been communicating with an accomplice.

The man made a little shake on the leash that went to Street's neck. "You're going to pick up the bag, girl. You mess with me, I do my bullwhip maneuver and you die."

Street walked forward several steps, pulling the leash and choke collar slightly taut.

I desperately hoped she wouldn't make the rachet move a notch.

Street bent over and picked up the bag.

"Open it," the man said.

I realized he was smarter than I'd thought. Grabbing Mae and Street and bringing them with him as he followed me was shrewd. Simply holding the leash was enough of a threat. He didn't even need a weapon, although I imagined he had one in his jacket pocket. Having her open the bag kept him from sticking his face into a potential booby-trap. I also realized that his prep showed that he was thorough. He might also have someone else looking to follow the fictional man I pretended to buy the treasure from. An extra $100,000 would be a nice bonus from their perspective.

The problem was, if they couldn't find the man with the money, they might start to wonder about the whole operation.

Street opened the bag.

"What is it?" Brand asked.

"There's a jar in here," she said. "And there's a little book inside the jar."

"If you screw with me, man, your girl dies."

"I'm not screwing with you," I said. "I just paid a hundred thousand dollars for that. I haven't even looked at it yet. But it's supposed to be a first edition chapbook of Robert Service poems. Supposedly, there are pencil codes written in the margins. They tell the location of a stash of gold coins from the Klondike gold rush. Robert Service wrote those poems when he was in the Klondike. Even the chapbook itself is worth a fortune."

"What's that mean, chapbook?" Brand asked. "Wait, don't answer." He turned to Mae. "You're the book lady. What's that mean? Your answer better make sense with what he said. Tell it quick. I don't want you making stuff up."

"A chapbook is a small booklet with just a few pages of poems," Mae said. Her voice wavered and cracked, her fear making it impossible to speak clearly. "Sometimes they're for short stories. Chapbooks are often handmade. Robert Service was a poet and Scotsman who moved to northwest Canada after the Klondike Gold Rush in the early nineteen hundreds. Nineteen Oh Seven, I think. He wrote lyrical, rhyming ballads including The Cremation Of Sam McGee and The Shooting Of Dan McGrew. He got rich off of his poems. Any first edition Robert Service chapbook would be extremely valuable."

"A million?" the man said, no doubt thinking of what I'd said in front of Flyboy Bosstro in the jail cell.

"No, I don't think it would be that much," Mae said. "But maybe. I'm not an expert."

"Then what's this about pencil notes?"

I said, "I don't really know. But the seller said it's a code. It involves some letter substitution, and there's something you have to read backward. The seller said any good puzzle expert could figure it out. You don't have to find one of those code experts. I forget the word."

"Cryptographer?" Mae said with perfect timing. It added to the reassurance that we weren't colluding on the story.

"Yeah, that's it," I said. "Anyway, anything hidden on the

Tahoe Steamer when it was scuttled must be very valuable."

"Okay, you carry the bag," the man said to Mae.

She picked it up.

Brand pulled on the leashes and steered her and Street. His movement turned him sideways to me, and I saw his silhouette against the lights of the pickup with the boat trailer. He looked mean and dangerous.

He spoke to me.

"You go first. Down the boat-launch ramp."

I did as he said, sensing from my peripheral vision that he and Street and Mae followed.

The two men from the pickup had a line clipped onto the bow cleat on the boat and were pulling it toward the trailer.

"You can stop there," Brand said to them.

"What d'ya mean?" one man said.

"We're taking your boat."

"You can't take our boat."

"Yeah, I can. If you make any noise or do anything other than help us, I shoot you dead. And I kill these women."

Brand's voice was so intense and frightening that the two men stood still with wide eyes and skin so pale I could see it in the twilight.

"Pull the boat in from the water."

They angled the boat next to the side of the trailer and forward until the bow touched the pavement of the ramp.

Brand took the line from the men. "Now you boys get in your truck and drive up the launch ramp with your trailer and disappear. You call the cops or anyone, I kill these people and then I track you down and kill your families. I have your license number."

One of the men looked about to cry. The other made a solemn nod. They did as told, and the pickup and trailer moved away slowly, up the ramp, through the underpass, and up toward the city streets above.

The entire sequence had no raised voices, no physical altercation, no brandished weapons. Because the leashes were dark, anyone watching from the beach or up at the park area would notice nothing.

Brand grabbed the bow line, lifted up on it, and walked the boat several feet up the ramp before he set it back down. The bow of the boat now rested on the ramp pavement.

"You women first," Brand said to Mae. "Into the boat. You're going to have to stay close and coordinate. McKenna will boost you up."

I tried to think fast. I knew that if he got all of us in the boat, it was a death sentence. We'd be dropped overboard with weights tied to our ankles, never to be seen again. But if I turned and ran for help or resisted, it was still a likely death sentence for us all. He'd kill me with whatever weapon I hadn't yet seen and be able to take his time with Street and Mae.

I walked up to the boat and kneeled down on one knee. My other leg was bent so that my thigh made a level step. If Street and Mae moved carefully, they could both step up at the same time.

Mae looked at me with a wild look in her eyes as if she knew we were going to be killed. Street looked deathly afraid but calculating. Both of their leashes arced down and then back up to Brand's hand.

I made a tiny nod of understanding. "Go slow," I whispered to Street.

Street set her left foot on my thigh and then looked at Mae. Mae did the same thing, and then both of them stood. They reached out their bound hands in unison and gripped the gunnel of the boat.

"Hurry up!" Brand said.

"I'm trying," Mae said.

Street spoke up. "We have to turn together. Otherwise, we'll fall off. You don't want us to fall off, do you?"

As both Street and Mae dawdled, I had one of those moments where a great number of thoughts seemed to rush through my consciousness. Maybe it's the panic of one who realizes he's about to die. Or maybe it's an evolutionary adaptation that allows a brain to think very quickly in an effort to avoid being killed by the saber-toothed tiger.

The bow of the boat was sitting on the boat launch pavement. But the rear was floating in the water. It started bobbing and shimmying with the incoming flow of waves from distant vessels. I was thinking of how I came to this beach and these murders. Mallory had asked me to look at a tattoo. He didn't realize it was a shipwreck. Not even the tattoo expert, Ivan Manfred, the Ink Maestro realized what it was.

Then I remembered that Manfred had said he got an MFA in painting from CalArts. A premier degree from a premier school.

I realized that everyone who got an MFA from a good American school would know virtually every famous and important Western painting, including The Wreck Of Hope by Caspar David Friedrich, the painting the tattoo was based on.

Which meant that the Ink Maestro lied, either about his MFA, or the painting.

Why would he lie?

The only logical reason was that he was Colin Callahan's tattoo artist. And lying about it could only be because Ivan Manfred was somehow involved in Colin's death.

Maybe Ivan was the missing foster brother. Or maybe, working for hours and hours during multiple sittings on Colin's tattoo, he had ample opportunity to learn about the sunken treasure and figure out how to involve himself in finding it and putting that fortune in his own pocket.

How he got involved with Brand, I didn't know.

Street and Mae were now in the stolen boat, standing near the stern. Mae was holding the gym bag. Their heads were closer than required by the attachment between the choke collars.

Whispering to each other.

I was aware that from Mallory's point of view - if Mallory was near - their movements still looked like innocent people who'd climbed into a boat to go for a ride.

"Your turn, McKenna," Brand said. I turned to look at Brand.

For a moment, he glanced from me to the women and then at something out of my line of sight. Something behind me.

At the same moment, I saw Brand make an almost

imperceptible movement. Possibly a nod.

I spun to the side. A blow struck my back at an angle. Something seemed to catch on my back, something that snagged in the fabric of my kevlar vest. I kept spinning as a roar of escaping air ripped at our ears like the exhaust from a jet engine.

FORTY-EIGHT

I swept the dark with both hands. My right fingers caught a pipe that was the diameter of a cane. I grabbed it and kept rotating, spinning fast. I jerked the pipe hard, and it came free from the grip of my assailant. But it was still tethered at one end.

I couldn't see it well in the dark. But it seemed like a pipe that had been outfitted with a T-section. And at the ends of the T were two points, eight inches apart. I couldn't see what the points were made of. But I assumed they were inflation needles. Perfect for piercing both sides of a victim's chest. There was a long, thick, black cord that went from the handle end of the pipe into the duffel bag.

No, not cord, a thin, high-pressure air hose. In the duffel bag would be a small air tank, 3000 or 4000 pounds of pressure, enough air to kill an elephant if it were all expelled in the wrong place.

I swung the compressed air weapon around as I turned yet again, trying to see my attacker in the dark. But he turned with me, deft as a dancer.

An engine revved. Brand taking the motorboat out on the lake. Taking the women to their deaths.

I stabbed out with the pipe weapon. The man jumped back like a fencer, then jumped forward. I stabbed again. The figure came into view. This time I saw Ivan Manfred, the Ink Maestro, blond hair at the fringes of the camo cap, shimmering in the dim beach light. He had another pipe, shorter, smaller. I realized he had carried two weapons, like a swordsman who also has a dagger on his belt. Ivan thrust the shorter pipe toward me, and I thrust forward with the longer pipe. I struck something, but I couldn't see in the dark.

Ivan's short pipe caught me in the middle of my chest. I knew that a sharp instrument can stab through bullet-proof kevlar, so I dodged to the side as his weapon struck. He didn't know if it had penetrated my chest. But his other hand must have squeezed his hidden air trigger, and the rush of high-pressure air escaping was a shriek in our ears.

The shriek stopped and was replaced with the strong roar of the motorboat.

Over that roar, barely audible, came the sound of shouted voices. Women's voices.

"May the devil drown!"

Ivan had moved behind me. I tried to spin, but lost my footing in the beach sand.

Something glinted. A shadow went over me, and Ivan hit me from behind. I took a step to catch myself, but I tripped and went down.

Ivan grabbed the long pipe and jerked it back out of my hands.

I pushed up fast and got to my feet, but I was too slow. I felt a blow to the upper right side of my back, and I felt a wasp sting on my right tricep. There was a piercing shriek of compressed air. My tricep seemed to explode into fire.

I turned, swinging my leg without much focus or energy. The hot poker jerked out of my tricep. But the muscle still screamed. My arm was immobilized with pain. Almost immediately, my right hand went numb.

My leg hit the man on his shin. He was braced and ready, and the blow had no apparent effect. He had pulled his weapon back as if preparing to throw a spear.

When someone is trying to spear you, you can only hope to deflect the spear and get out of the way.

I had my vest on, but he'd already seen that his spear needle wouldn't easily go through it. Maybe the needle that hit the vest had broken off. But the one that stabbed my arm was still good. And if he aimed away from the vest, he could put that needle into my neck or head. If it went into my skull through the natural openings - eye, ear, nose - the air pressure would blow my head apart. For all I knew, a needle could be stabbed through the skull bone. I had to keep him from stabbing me with the good needle, and I only had one good arm.

For a moment, we stood facing each other, feinting and bobbing like boxers. "Despite the MFA and the top art school, you're still just a thug looking for a score," I said. "But hiring your old foster brothers to beat up people is so crude and cheap. I would have thought you were above that."

Manfred was dodging, making short stabbing motions with his air dagger. "Carlos and Jeff saved my life. Those women tried to beat me to death. I owe my brothers everything. When I sell the treasure, they'll get half the money."

"What treasure?" I said. I parried and thrust and jumped forward and back. "It's a fiction, maestro. Brand has that fiction. A little book in a jar. Call him. He'll tell you."

Ivan Manfred jerked as if he'd been slapped.

His distraction was my best chance. With as much speed as possible, I shot my left hand up into the air to his right side. I turned my head that direction at the same time to make him look that way.

Then I dropped to the ground, rolling hard toward him. I hit his legs, locked my good left arm around them, and he went down backward. He didn't flail much, which showed impressive control. He knew how to land with a rolling motion.

But I hung on to his legs so that he couldn't do much to cushion the blow to his butt and back. More important, for the moment, he was unable to stab me.

I shifted my grip on his legs so that I could get my arm around his ankle as I rolled onto his knee. I rolled him just enough, then jerked on the ankle, putting sideways pressure on the knee. Knees only bend one way well. I put serious effort into bending his a different way.

He screamed.

In spite of his pain, he stabbed again with his spear. It hit my hip, the needle missing my flesh. A jet-plane hiss of compressed air rushed out.

As fast as I could possibly move, I let go of his knee and reached my functioning left arm out and over the spear, the way

I had with Flyboy's arm in the jail cell. I clamped my arm down hard and rolled. As I went over my inflated right tricep, it felt like I had an explosion of fire in my arm.

But Ivan's spear came with me.

Ivan kicked out with his good leg. He hit me square in the center of my back, knocking the wind out of me.

I kept rolling, trying to suck air into my lungs. The spear came to a stop as its air hose drew tight. I jerked on it, trying to rip it free. The hose wouldn't come loose. But the air tank, a metal container about the size of a liter bottle of soda, flew out of Ivan's duffel bag onto the sand.

Ivan kicked at my head and my inflated arm with his good leg. My head throbbed with pain. I rolled farther. Jumped to my feet. I held the compressed-air spear. I couldn't breathe. I couldn't see straight. But I had the weapon in my left hand. The pipe had a grip on it, some kind of handle. Attached to the grip was a lever. I couldn't see it in the dark. If felt like the lever on a fire extinguisher. But with my right arm going numb, I couldn't hold the weapon and also pull the lever with one hand.

Ivan struggled to get to his feet. He held his bad knee with both hands. He moaned with pain.

In the distance beyond him, I saw Mallory hustling across the sand.

"Don't move," I said. "Don't move an inch, and you'll be okay. The cops are here."

Ivan pushed off from his good leg, and lunged toward me. I was still holding the spear. But it was dark. The blow knocked me down onto the sand. Ivan fell on me with rage. He grabbed for my neck. His hand hit the air lever. Maybe he thought the inflation needle had stabbed me. Instead, he apparently pierced himself with the needle. He gave the air lever a long squeeze, not realizing until it was too late, that he'd just filled himself with air.

Ivan screamed again, this time a strangled gargle. He fell over onto his side, his belly swollen like a beach ball.

I fell upon him, put my knee against his back, and used my good hand to jerk one of his arms behind him, hard enough to dislocate the shoulder socket. But he wasn't screaming with arm pain. It was his insides being crushed by the beach ball of air in his gut.

"McKenna!" Mallory's voice cut through the air. "You okay?"

I felt his hands on me.

"Yeah, I'm fine." I was trying to see out onto the black water. The sound of the motorboat was receding.

I grabbed Ivan's other hand and held it while Mallory put on cuffs.

Ivan continued to howl like a baby. I didn't know how much air had gone into his gut. But it was certainly enough to cause severe pain, and it would probably kill him fast.

Mallory toed the inflated, writhing body on the sand.

"Ivan Manfred, the Ink Maestro. You're the killer? You lying piece of scum."

I turned toward the water, trying to see the lights of the motorboat. "Ivan lunged onto me," I said absently. "He thought he was stabbing me with his compressed air weapon. Then he pulled the trigger. But he actually stuck himself with his own weapon and then filled himself with air."

"Fell on his sword and killed himself," Mallory continued.

"How dead he gets depends on how fast we get him to the hospital."

Mallory spoke into his radio, requesting an ambulance.

When he clicked off the radio, I pointed out at the black lake. "That motor boat sound is Ivan's fellow thug on a stolen boat. Brand Morse. He's got Street and Mae O'Sullivan with him." My eyes stung as I said it.

"No, he doesn't," came a voice from the water. I turned fast.

Street and Mae were walking out of the black water. In the dim illumination from distant lights, I could see that they were still zip-tied arm-in-arm. The leashes Brand had held now draped down behind them, down into the water. They shivered violently.

I ran into the water. Held them both with my one good arm.

"He slipped in the boat and dropped the leashes so he could catch himself," Street said. "Then Mae shouted, 'May the devil drown!' I realized immediately what she meant. So we grabbed each other and jumped off the speeding boat."

The women leaned against each other, crying.

"Mallory," I said, "their collars have ratchets. We need a bolt cutter immediately."

I carefully lifted up the leashes and handed them to Street and Mae. "Make certain no one pulls on it."

Mallory got on his radio and shouted more orders.

In a minute, an officer ran up with a bolt cutter. He cut the collars and the zip ties that bound their hands.

Mallory had his shoe on Ivan as if to prevent him from slithering away. "So Ivan the Scum, here, had help from another guy who stole the motorboat."

"Yeah. He's carrying what he thinks is the treasure. Possibly he was planning to come back and pick up Ivan. But I doubt it."

Another officer ran up with blankets. I used my one arm to help wrap Street and Mae. I could feel them shake.

"We need to get Street and Mae into a warm car as soon as possible."

"We've got several up on the road by the park."

I spoke to Street and Mae. "Can you two walk with me?"

"To heat?" Street said, her teeth chattering. "I'd walk into the fire of the sun if I could."

I walked Street and Mae up the sand, holding onto them, moving carefully.

Mallory came along. "Was Brand part of this plan all along?"

"I think so. The first victim, Colin Callahan rented a room from him down in Citrus Heights. Colin was living there when he got some old letters that hinted of treasure. I think Brand - AKA Jay Brandon Morse - set the whole scheme in motion, putting Colin in touch with Ivan, who gave Colin his tattoo and, during the process, learned all he could about the treasure and where it might be. Brand had another renter, Jacky Wormack, who was also part of the operation. When Brand and Ivan had gotten whatever information Colin and Jacky had, they killed them both to increase their share of the take."

"What about the guys who tried to beat you up at Cave Rock and Street's place?"

"I'm guessing that the Bosstro brothers were just as advertised, dumb enforcers, eager to beat on people for money. And happy to work for Ivan, their foster brother."

EPILOGUE

Two days later, Ivan Manfred died from his self-inflicted air wound. Brand had been intercepted by Placer County deputies in Tahoe City. He and the Bosstro brothers were all charged and held without bail. My arm, which had been relieved of its air by Doc Lee, was no longer on fire, and I was getting the feeling back in my hand.

Most important, Street and Mae were okay physically. Their mental state was dicier. When you believe you are going to die by being dropped with a weight into the blackness of Lake Tahoe at night and then aren't, it leaves you with lots of issues that psychologists have names for. But Street and Mae had spent most of those two days together, Blondie at their side, talking, processing, eating, trying to get their sense of humor back. Street had even stayed overnight on Mae's couch.

Much of that time, they'd spent at Daniel's house. They found that his perspective on life was as valuable as one might think. After 90-plus years' experience, he had a lot of wisdom to share.

Meanwhile, Spot and I had spent two long evenings with Diamond, eating chips and salsa and drinking beer. During the intervening day, we'd gone over to Daniel's and had a little party with him and Street and Mae. Daniel invited Spot and Blondie in as well.

We filled Daniel's house wall-to-wall, five adults and two dogs. Daniel turned his jazz standards up high, and we even did a little dancing. Mae coaxed Daniel up out of his rocker, and we moved the furniture aside. Then Daniel wowed us all doing the Lindy Hop, the dance he'd learned as a child from his precious sister Nora.

As we left, Daniel said it was the best time he could remember since Nora was alive. He removed his aviators and wiped his eyes, then gave each of us a hug.

At 6:30 a.m. the next morning, my phone rang. I picked it up and said, "Hello?"

"Owen, this is Mae."

I was groggy, still on my first cup of coffee, barely awake enough to perceive that she was upset.

"What's wrong?" I asked.

"Daniel died in his sleep last night."

I called Street, picked her up fifteen minutes later, and we went to Daniel's house, where Mae filled us in.

The evening before, after we'd all left the party, Mae had made dinner for Daniel. He hadn't eaten much. Then he said he didn't feel very well, and he went to bed, where he did a little leather work.

In the morning, she'd checked before dawn because she knew he was an early riser. His body was long cold.

Following Daniel's instructions, she called his doctor. Daniel had told her that should she ever find him dead, she shouldn't call 911. He wanted her to be spared the stress of dealing with paramedics and their flashing emergency lights.

Following Daniel's instructions, Mae had also called Daniel's lawyer and left a voicemail.

Street and Diamond and I were with Mae when Daniel's doctor arrived. He went into Daniel's bedroom and came back out in a couple of minutes. In a soft and comforting voice, he explained to us that he'd been monitoring a femoral aneurysm that he had fully expected would be Daniel's cause of death. He said Daniel knew about it and refused to consider the surgery that would possibly give him another year, a difficult surgery that also might kill him on the operating table. The doctor said that Daniel's end was peaceful and from natural causes. The doctor said he would take the necessary steps to expedite the paperwork, and he notified the funeral home to pick up the body. After he answered Mae's questions, he left. We sat with Daniel until the funeral home vehicle arrived. Mae stood up and combed Daniel's hair. Two workers wearing white coats with embroidered funeral home patches came in and took Daniel's body away.

We three were still in Daniel's living room, sitting in front of the new window that Ed Filusch had installed, when a silver Mercedes pulled up and a man got out.

"This must be the lawyer," Mae said. She made a little shake of her head. "I know this shouldn't be a surprise, but I never visualized that this would actually happen." As she shook her head, I noticed that the red abrasion marks on her neck had darkened toward purple.

Mae answered the door.

"Good morning. I'm Percy Rodriguez, Daniel Callahan's lawyer. I understand he has passed. I'm very sorry." He turned toward Mae and Street. "Would either of you be Mae O'Sullivan?"

Mae nodded. Then she introduced us, her voice soft. "These are Daniel's friends. Street Casey and Owen McKenna and Diamond Martinez."

We shook hands all around.

"I've handled Mr. Callahan's legal affairs, so I know that you agreed to be his executor."

Mae nodded.

"Based on my recommendation, Mr. Callahan kept the will here at his house. Did he tell you the location?"

"No," Mae said. Her voice seemed weaker still.

"Ah." Rodriguez nodded. "When I asked him to let me know the location, he said it was in his desk, in a folder labeled 'Landscaping Quotes.' Because you are a party to the will, it might be useful to have me go over it with you."

Mae nodded again.

The lawyer looked at the rest of us. He turned back to Mae. "This is a personal affair. Perhaps you'd like privacy."

Mae seemed to find some internal strength. "I'd like my friends to stay."

Percy Rodriguez made a small nod. "As you wish. Shall we see if you can find the folder labeled Landscaping Quotes?"

Mae turned and walked into Daniel's bedroom. Percy Rodriguez followed close behind. The rest of us waited in the living room. Diamond stood at the window, staring out toward the vacant lot from which we believed Jacky Wormack had fired the shot that broke the window.

Soon, Mae and Rodriguez came back. They sat next to each other on the living room couch that we'd earlier taken apart to find the burner phone when Jacky Wormack was tormenting Daniel.

Rodriguez opened Daniel's file folder and removed a black paper binder and flipped through a number of pages.

"I'm just checking to see that this is as I remember. It is. I can report from memory. Mae, this will be a relatively easy job for you as executor because Mr. Callahan left everything to you."

I saw Mae bite her lower lip.

Rodriguez continued. "He mentioned the real estate, this house and the house next door, which I understand you rent from him. He also mentioned two bank accounts with small dollar amounts and a brokerage account that handles about twenty thousand in mutual funds."

Rodriguez paused.

I said, "I think Mae will also be wondering about personal effects. Furniture, collectibles, things like that."

"The will explicitly states that everything that Daniel owned goes to you, Mae, from accounts to personal mementos. Because the real estate is old, you will likely spend substantial amounts of money bringing things up to modern code if you want to sell at market prices. But if you plan carefully, you should be able to more than recoup expenses. Two houses, however small, add up."

During the lawyer's comments, Street sat at Mae's side, close, as if to hold her up should Mae falter.

After the lawyer left, I turned to Mae.

"You have a lot to adjust to," I said. "If there is anything we can do to help, let us know."

She nodded. We all stood and moved to the door.

Mae reached over to the coat rack and lifted off a large braided loop of Daniel's forest-green leather. "This triquetra is for Spot.

When Daniel went to bed last night, he finished it as he lay in bed. It was the last thing he did. He handed it to me and said, 'Spot saved my life. The least I can do is make him a good-luck triquetra.'"

When I got home, I spent a little time doing some research on Inverted Jenny stamps and the art of stamp investing. I learned that the sudden appearance of multiple Inverted Jennys would probably do exactly as Daniel predicted and drop the price they would fetch by 75% or more. Which meant that twenty inverted Jennys might only fetch 2 or 3 million dollars. A very nice parting gift from an old man to his neighbor and best friend.

The next day, I called Mae and gave her the information I'd learned.

Three days later, we gathered at Daniel's favorite place, Emerald Bay. We arrived at the Vikingsholm castle parking lot an hour before dawn, the only way to beat the summer tourist crush. Mae had explained that from the first time Daniel had visited Emerald Bay as a young boy, he loved the calm of the bay's waters, the roar of Eagle Falls, and the softness of the beach sand. Many times after that first boyhood visit, he'd asked to be taken there on his birthday, to witness dawn among the rocks and trees and water.

We gathered at the top of the trail, Diamond included. Even Ed Filusch, the silent carpenter, had asked Mae if he could attend, and she agreed.

Mae had asked me if Spot had some kind of a dog backpack. So I strapped on Spot's hiking pack that we used for his dog food.

Mae had me put the box with Daniel's ashes in Spot's pack. Mae planned to bury them in Daniel's flower garden later in the day. But she wanted some part of Daniel to take the trip down to Emerald Bay once more.

"Daniel has ridden on Spot's back before," she said. "Now he can do it once again."

I took Spot's triquetra necklace from my pocket and lowered

it toward Spot. He tried to take it in his teeth.

"A necklace, Largeness. Not a chew toy." I looped it over Spot's head. It fit like a perfect collar, the shamrock decoration hanging down at Spot's throat.

As far as I could tell, everyone wore the triquetra necklaces that Daniel had made.

Spot trotted down the trail.

Diamond spoke up. "Hound's looking stylish. Got his triquetra collar and his diamond ear stud. No wonder he prances."

As we started down the dark trail to the water, I heard someone trot up behind me. I turned to see Mallory. I hadn't expected him to come and had only told him about our plan to keep him apprised of the ebb and flow of life in his town.

Perhaps something about Daniel's life had made Mallory become more aware that life passes quickly and that significant connections with others are rare.

I saw in the dim twilight that he too had a triquetra necklace like the rest of us. It hung outside of his collar.

"I didn't realize Daniel had made you a shamrock necklace," I said.

Mallory spoke in a low voice, much quieter than his norm. "Several days ago, I stopped by to check on him. I just… I don't know. I suppose it made an impression on me that he was such a fighter."

I nodded in the dark.

"Callahan was real gruff when I visited," Mallory said. "Kind of reminded me of my old man that way. But Callahan was tougher than my dad ever was. Refusing to give info to the guy who assaulted him. Trying to swim when he was terrified of the water. Hanging onto a dog that scared him half to death. All at his age. Amazing."

The trail entered a section of forest that was so dense, no pre-dawn glow could penetrate it. Some of us had flashlights, but no one turned them on. Everyone apparently preferred to navigate through the darkness without aid, seeing the world a little bit as Daniel had seen it, a vague, blurred place where perception comes as much from hearing and smelling and feeling as it does from seeing.

Mallory continued. "The next day, I got a call from Callahan. He said he'd made me a good luck necklace. So I stopped by again, and he gave me this triquetra. Imagine that. The cranky old guy made a gift for me. We sat and talked a long time. After I left, I felt like he was my old best friend from way back. Maybe that seems strange."

"No," I said. "It seems exactly right."

Our group made the mile hike down to the water in time to be on the beach in front of the Vikingsholm Castle fifteen minutes before the sun rose.

Street pulled mugs out of the pack she carried and poured Daniel's favorite Irish tea from a large thermos. We handed them around.

Mae opened an insulated cooler. She'd gotten up very early to make Irish soda bread, and she handed out fresh-baked slices, still hot. Everyone took a piece, including Spot.

We stood in a circle, raised our mugs, and said, "Sláinte." We sipped tea and ate hot bread. Spot was already drinking lake water, his toes getting bravely and thoroughly wet and cold, an irony considering that he recently swam to shore through ice water with an old man clinging to his back.

After our toast, we all turned and faced east. The Vikingsholm castle was behind us. The soft roar of Eagle Falls behind that. In front of us, less than a half mile out, was Fannette Island. The tea house was silhouetted against the growing skylight to the east. Two miles beyond the island was the narrow opening from Emerald Bay out to the main lake. Ten miles past that was the East Shore on the far side of Lake Tahoe, not far from my cabin and the Carson Range rising above. The dawn light began to increase at a faster pace. We all went silent as a tiny orange diamond of light popped out on the top ridgeline of the mountains, and the sun began to rise to its full brilliance.

Mae held her tea up, toasting toward the sky. She said. "The song Danny Boy is about being called away on a journey. Daniel, this is for you."

Mae led us in song, her voice strong. Even Mallory and Ed

sang.

At first, our tones seemed somber. Some were out of tune. But our voices grew in strength and found their unity on our last lines.

"Oh Danny Boy, the pipes, the pipes are calling
From glen to glen and down the mountainside
The summer's gone and all the roses falling
Oh Danny Boy, oh Danny Boy, I love you so."

About The Author

Todd Borg and his wife live in Lake Tahoe, where they write and paint. To contact Todd or learn more about the Owen McKenna mysteries, please visit toddborg.com.

A message from the author:

Dear Reader,

. If you enjoyed this novel, please consider posting a short review on any book website you like to use. Reviews help authors a great deal, and that in turn allows us to write more stories for you.

Thank you very much for your interest and support!

Todd

PRAISE FOR TAHOE SKYDROP

"ANOTHER IMPRESSIVE CASE FEATURING A DETECTIVE WHO REMAINS NOT ONLY DOGGED, BUT ALSO REFLECTIVE."
- Kirkus Reviews

"A SURPRISE TWIST WILL GIVE YOU AN EXTRA JOLT...a great addition to the Owen McKenna series." *- Gloria Sinibaldi, Tahoe Mountain News*

PRAISE FOR TAHOE PAYBACK

"AN ENGROSSING WHODUNIT" *- Kirkus Reviews*

"ANOTHER GREAT TODD BORG THRILLER *- Book Dilettante*

"FAST PACED, ABSORBING, MEMORABLE" *- Kittling: Books*
Borg's Tahoe Mystery series chosen by Kittling: Books as ONE OF THE TEN BEST MYSTERY SERIES

PRAISE FOR TAHOE DARK

"ONCE AGAIN, BORG HITS ALL THE RIGHT NOTES FOR FANS OF CLASSIC DETECTIVE FICTION in the mold of Dashiell Hammett, Raymond Chandler, Ross Macdonald, and Robert B. Parker."
- Kirkus Reviews

"TAHOE DARK IS PACKED WITH ACTION AND TWISTS. THE SURPRISES JUST KEEP ON COMING...THE FINAL SCENE IS ANOTHER TODD BORG MASTERPIECE." *- Silver's Reviews*

PRAISE FOR TAHOE BLUE FIRE

"A GRIPPING NARRATIVE...A HERO WHO WALKS CONFIDENTLY IN THE FOOTSTEPS OF SAM SPADE, PHILIP MARLOWE, AND LEW ARCHER" *- Kirkus Reviews*

"A THRILLING MYSTERY THAT IS DIFFICULT TO PUT DOWN ...EDGE OF YOUR SEAT ACTION" *– Silver's Reviews*

PRAISE FOR TAHOE GHOST BOAT

"THE OLD PULP SAVVY OF (ROSS) MACDONALD...REAL SURPRISE AT THE END" *– Kirkus Reviews*

"NAIL-BITING THRILLER...BOILING POT OF DRAMA"
- *Gloria Sinibaldi, Tahoe Daily Tribune*

"BORG'S WRITING IS THE STUFF OF A HOLLYWOOD ACTION
BLOCKBUSTER"   – *Taylor Flynn, Tahoe Mountain News*

"ACTION-PACKED IS PUTTING IT MILDLY. PREPARE FOR FIRE-
WORKS"   – *Sunny Solomon, Bookin' With Sunny*

"I LOVED EVERY ROLLER COASTER RIDE IN THIS THRILLER
5+ OUT OF 5"   – *Harvee Lau, Book Dilettante*

PRAISE FOR TAHOE CHASE

"EXCITING, EXPLOSIVE, THOUGHTFUL, SOMETIMES FUNNY"
      – *Ann Ronald, Bookin' With Sunny*

"BE WARNED. IT MIGHT BE ADDICTING"
- *Gloria Sinibaldi, Tahoe Daily Tribune*

"OWEN McKENNA HAS HIS HANDS FULL IN ANOTHER THRILL-
ING ADVENTURE"   - *Harvee Lau, Book Dilettante*

PRAISE FOR TAHOE TRAP

"AN OPEN-THROTTLE RIDE"
- *Wendy Schultz, Placerville Mountain Democrat*

"A CONSTANTLY SURPRISING SERIES OF EVENTS INVOLVING
MURDER...and the final motivation of the killer comes as a major surprise.
(I love when that happens.)"   – *Yvette, In So Many Words*

"I LOVE TODD BORG'S BOOKS...There is the usual great twist ending
in Tahoe Trap that I never would have guessed"   – *JBronder Reviews*

"THE PLOTS ARE HIGH OCTANE AND THE ACTION IS FASTER
THAN A CHEETAH ON SPEED"   – *Cathy Cole, Kittling: Books*

"AN EXCITING MURDER MYSTERY... I watch for the ongoing develop-
ments of Jack Reacher, Joanna Brady, Dismas Hardy, Peter and Rina Decker,
and Alex Cross to name a few. But these days I look forward most to the
next installment of Owen McKenna."   - *China Gorman blog*